shy girls
can't date
frenemies

First Published by Halo & Claws Publishing 2023

Shy Girls Can't Date Frenemies

SHY GIRLS SWEET ROMANCES – BOOK 3

2nd Edition Published by Halo & Claws Publishing 2025

For information contact: https://hcpbooks.com

Illustrated character art by Jasmine Little

Cover Design by Emily Bourne

Paperback ISBN: 978-1-925990-46-1

Ebook ISBN: 978-1-925990-32-4

shy girls can't date frenemies

MILLY ROSE

One

"I'm so bummed I have to work," I grumble from behind the counter at the cafe. "What fun stuff have I been missing out on?"

"We haven't headed to the skatepark yet, if that's what you're asking," Tyler says with a smirk as he takes the cardboard box of bakery treats. "Kai was adamant we can't go there without you."

I groan. "I wish my aunt could cut me some slack and let me skip one Sunday shift."

Tyler laughs. "You act like you've got the strictest parent out of all of us. Do you realize we'd all do anything to live with your Aunt Maddy."

I roll my eyes. Everyone thinks I get away with murder because my aunt is in her twenties. Plus, my friends are guys who think she's hot.

"Hey Tyler," Aunt Maddy says, walking out of the kitchen with two plates of food. "Are you picking up Mrs. Nelson's order?"

Tyler pats the cardboard box. "Yeah, I'd better get back before she flips her lid."

Aunt Maddy smiles and moves over to a table, saying, "See you soon."

Tyler looks back at me, gesturing to the box. "Thanks again for these."

"No problem," I say as Kylie makes her way behind the counter. "Kylie made the cookies and muffins this morning."

Kylie glimpses Tyler, and then puts her head down as she moves past me. Tyler waves and leaves, and anxiety floods through my body. It happens around most women, but especially girls from my school. Whenever I'm around other girls, I get the same feeling. Slight dizziness, dreaded clamminess, a sloshing stomach, knocking knees, and horrible stammering.

I flex my trembling fingers, trying to get it together. Perhaps if I envision Tyler still standing at the other side of the counter, my body will calm down. Kylie turns from washing her hands at the sink, and there's a calmness about her. With Tyler gone, so is the redness blotting her face.

She eyes me warily, frowning. My shoulders lock and I recoil.

"How do you do that?" she asks in a timid voice.

"Huh?" My heart pounds as my imagination fires up the worst possible things she could ask me.

She huffs and grabs a wet cloth, running it along the counter. "You talk to them like it's nothing."

I scratch my head, digging my nails into my scalp. My mind whirrs, creating a more horrible situation than what's currently happening.

Kylie scowls, muttering under her breath, "I don't get why boys like you."

I turn away, letting my eyes roll. Yeah, freaking, right. Boys don't *like* like me. I am the most friend-zoned girl ever. Not that I'm romantically interested in any of my friends, but besides them, there are no other boys in my life. Plus, they keep me around because I'm a tomboy. If they knew I secretly wanted a boyfriend and fantasized about kissing my perfect guy, it'd be friendship over.

I don't know if life would be easier if I had other girls to talk about this stuff. I mean, I have Aunt Maddy, but she's not another sixteen-year-old girl. Kylie is, and in a year of working together, we've barely shared a five-minute conversation. Part of me wants a friend that is a girl, but the other part remembers how my mother warned me about other women.

"Hi Jamie," an enthusiastic yet grating voice says from the other side of the counter.

My jaw clenches and I push all my effort into a smile as my head pivots toward him. "Hi David. Maddy's taking orders at a booth."

David glances over his shoulder and turns back to me with a cheesy grin. "I know. I gave her a wave as I came in. If I hadn't seen her on the way in, I would've thought you were her. You both have such similar side profiles."

"Mhmm." It comes out through tight lips. Everyone asks if Maddy and I are sisters because there's only twelve years between us. It trips most people out when they learn that the reality is Aunt Maddy is my sole caregiver.

"Oh, but you're so young," customers always say to Maddy. Regardless of her age, she didn't have a choice. Mom was gone when Maddy was eighteen, and it was only us and Grams left.

Kylie leaves the counter to clean an empty section, and David asks, "Has it been a busy day?"

"Sundays always are," I reply, looking at his linen charcoal suit, crisp white shirt, and red with white pinstripe tie. Who dresses like this on a Sunday? Unfortunately, he's like most people in Victoria Falls. Mr. Stuffy wants everyone to know he has a high-paying job.

"Yeah. The pancake stacks are legendary," David says, cheesy smile maxing out.

I wish he'd stop trying so hard with me. Does he not realize I find him so annoying?

I tap the register screen and open a new order. "Do you want to order a stack?"

A phony laugh rumbles out of David as he pats his flat belly. "Not today. Instead, I'll take a double shot caramel latte."

As I tap the screen, Aunt Maddy jogs toward the counter. "Don't key that in," she tells me in a rush. "I'll just make it for him."

I huff and delete the order as Maddy pecks David on the cheek. She blushes and murmurs, "Hello," and then slips behind the counter. The two exchange moony-eyed glances and I need to turn away.

Aunt Maddy never lets David pay. I get it, she wants her new boyfriend to like her, but he has money. His repeat business would be good for daily takings. Granted, my best friend Kai never pays, but he's been in our lives for years and he helps out while here. David has never rolled up his sleeves or even offered to help. He just stares at Aunt Maddy with that cheese ball grin and gives her flirty compliments.

Okay, yes, I might be jealous. More importantly, however, I don't get what Maddy sees in him besides the flirty banter and dope suits.

Aunt Maddy hums as she works at the coffee machine. Her lips quirk like she can't wait to finish and cuddle up to Mr. Stuffy.

"Aunt Maddy, don't forget we gotta go soon."

She looks away from pouring the frothed milk. "Huh?"

"Kai's birthday," I say like it's obvious, because it is. "You gotta drive me over soon. I've already missed out on most of the day because I had to work."

Aunt Maddy finishes up David's latte while simultaneously mocking me. "Oh, poor baby, she had to help pay the bills."

I groan with a whopper of an eye roll. "Ugh. I don't care about the work. I just don't want to be late because you've got your flirt on."

"Chill out," Maddy replies, turning from the coffee machine with the latte. She slides it across the counter with a pearly smile. "Here, David."

"Thanks, honey," David says, lifting the tall paper cup.

Honey? Really? That's where they're at?

Aunt Maddy moves to the back corner of the work station near her office. She picks up the wad of unopened mail and says, "I'll just finish up and we can go."

David sips from his cup and purrs an "Mmm."

Maddy grins like she's won a trophy. "Good, hon?"

"Perfection, as always," David replies. He then motions the cup at me and says, "You know, I can give Jamie a ride to wherever she has to go. That way, I'll be out of your hair until you've finished up."

"No," I blurt before Maddy has a chance to speak.

Aunt Maddy splutters a cough, her eyes wide like she's both shocked and disappointed in my blunt tone.

I clear my throat and backtrack. "Didn't you want to say happy birthday?"

Aunt Maddy purses her lips, and it's a sweet relief when she nods. *Phew.*

"Thanks for the offer, David," Aunt Maddy says, "but I do want to say hi to the boys on their birthday."

"Boys?" David asks with intrigue that seems at least half fake.

"Twins," Maddy elaborates. "They're Jamie's friends."

"Well, Kai's my friend," I clarify.

"Jamie," Aunt Maddy grizzles as she tears open an envelope. "You be nice to Milo today. It's just as much his birthday as it is, Kai."

"Oh my gosh, of course I'll be nice to him."

Aunt Maddy gives me a dubious look. "You got him a gift?"

"Well, no."

Maddy frowns, tossing the open bill on the workstation counter.

"Why would I? Milo's a snitch."

"Be nice," Maddy says, moving onto the next envelope.

"It's true," I persist. "Anytime Milo hears about something Kai and I are planning, he rats us out to his parents."

Aunt Maddy chuckles. "It's a good thing too, or I wouldn't have a clue what you guys get up to."

I groan. "Ugh. You are being so uncool right now."

"Do I have to remind you that Milo got you a gift for your birthday?"

"He just chipped in for the rollerblades."

"His name was on the card," Aunt Maddy doubles down.

"His parents made him do that."

"And now your aunt is making you get him a gift."

"It's Sunday afternoon," I argue. "We'll never find something and get to the house on time."

"And whose fault is that?" Maddy says matter-of-factly as she slides the next bill on the counter. She lifts the next sealed envelope closest to her eyeline and takes in a sharp breath. "Why is your school sending me a letter?"

"Huh?" My posture slumps as I step closer to her.

Aunt Maddy tears open the envelope and yanks out the letter. She unfolds it, reading each line carefully.

"What is it?" I ask with trepidation.

Maddy lowers the letter and shakes her head, keeping her rigid expression steady. "You're in so much trouble."

I suck in a breath and hold it for two beats. "What?"

Maddy grabs my wrist and calls out to Kylie, "Kylie, can you watch the counter, please? Jamie and I will be in the office."

"Sure thing," Kylie calls back.

Maddy tells David, "We'll be right back," and then yanks me into the office, closing the door behind us.

"Aunt Maddy, you're freaking me out. What did the letter say?"

Maddy swishes the letter beside her with an angry grip. "Ashworth Academy is threatening to take away your scholarship."

"What?" I yelp. "They can't do that."

"Yes, they can," Maddy replies. "When you slack off and let your grade average tank, they have every right to take it away. You knew the scholarship was contingent on your grades. How could you do this?"

"I didn't mean to," I say with a pathetic pout.

"Don't give me that," Maddy says with disappointment levels spiking. "You know I can't pay the tuition. How could you risk your place at this school when you know how important it was to your mother?"

Bringing up my mother is like a blow to the heart. "I'm sorry."

"I know you and Kai act like you don't care about school," Maddy says, gripping my shoulder, "but he's in a different boat. His parents can pay for his schooling. We've had to be scrappy to make this happen. If you get kicked out, that's it."

"I don't want to go to a different school. I want to stay with Kai."

Aunt Maddy squeezes my shoulder tighter. "And you care Lily wanted you to go to Ashworth Academy?"

I roll my eyes. "Yes, I know it was Mom's dream."

Maddy's eyes water. "Don't roll your eyes. You don't know how hard Lily worked to make sure we didn't struggle."

I lower my guard and wrap my arms around Aunt Maddy. "I do know. She worked too many jobs to take care of us and Grams. I promise I won't let her down."

Maddy holds me close, whispering, "I just don't want it to be all for nothing. She can't come back and fix it for us."

"Maybe she can. They never found..." Why did I let that slip out?

Maddy pulls out of the hug and presses her hands against the sides of my face. Her eyes bore into mine as they shine with unbroken tears. "Baby," she whispers. "You know she's gone. She'd never disappear. She'd never leave *you*."

I gulp and nod. For the past ten years, Maddy has always felt this way. Mom's file is still marked as a missing person with the Sheriff's department, despite Maddy's protests. Maddy is adamant something deadly happened to Mom. She told law enforcement countless times Mom is dead because, with every fiber of her being, she knew Mom would move heaven and earth to get back to me.

To be honest, I don't think about Mom often. Aunt Maddy does a good job of keeping her memory alive. Lily West was an empowered woman. At sixteen, she took herself, her twelve-year-old sister, and her baby girl out of an abusive home in Logan's Point.

We moved to Victoria Falls with nothing to our names. We were so lucky Grams took us in. Not only was she the owner of Morton's Cafe and gave Mom and Maddy jobs, but she also gave us room in her two-bedroom house. Grams was a widower and didn't have any kids of her own. Mom said there was an instant connection the first day they met. I miss Grams just as much as Mom. She died a few years after Mom was gone. It was a lung disease, and in the end she needed machines to help her breathe. She left the house and the cafe to Aunt Maddy and me in her will.

"I promise to study more," I say as Aunt Maddy's hands tremble against my cheeks. I have no idea how I'll magically learn how to study, but I can't let down these women who helped raise me.

Maddy releases my face and wipes under her eyes. "I know you will, baby."

"Kylie and I have cleaned most of the workstation," I say in a weak tone. "Any chance we can take off soon?"

Aunt Maddy nods, opening the office door. "We'd better get going. You've got a last-minute gift to buy."

I groan as I walk out of the office. "What am I supposed to get him?"

"He's your best friend's twin brother," Maddy says, following me out. "You have to know something he's into."

My mind shutters through memories of Milo. I barely acknowledge his existence. As I think about each of our encounters, he's always a background character in my story with Kai. Lightbulb. In most of those instances, he's in the background reading a book.

"Let's just play it safe and go to the bookstore."

Maddy claps. "Well done. You figured it out on your own."

"Okay, genius," I tease. "What book should we get him?"

Maddy's face droops with puzzlement. "I dunno. He's such a whiz kid. Just get a gift card."

I wink. "My thoughts exactly."

"Everything okay with you two?" David asks, approaching the counter.

"It will be once Jamie improves her grades," Maddy says.

Kylie gives me subtle side-eye. Any classes we share, she always seems to coast through.

Maddy leans into the kitchen, calling out to Jake and Laura. "We're heading off. Are you okay with cleaning and locking up?"

"No problem," Jake calls back.

Aunt Maddy turns around and Laura emerges from the kitchen. She'll give Kylie a hand, keeping an eye on the cafe floor.

"I'm driving Jamie to the bookstore, and then to the boys' house," Maddy says, grabbing her coat and rounding the counter. "I'll meet up with you after?"

David meets her with a quick kiss on the lips. "Sounds perfect."

After changing out of my work uniform and into my trademark ripped jeans, t-shirt, and tartan shirt, I pry Aunt Maddy away from David. We make a pit stop at the bookstore with the slowest store clerk in the world, and finally arrive at the Nelson household.

"Thanks, Aunt Maddy," I say, racing toward the two-story, white house with four pillars decorating the front exterior.

"Wait up," Aunt Maddy calls, jogging behind me. "I'm coming with, remember?"

Whatever. I leave her in my dust. I have FOMO about missing out on whatever the guys got up today. Mostly, I just want to see Kai. I feel incomplete when I don't see him. His parents always make a big deal out of birthdays, so he didn't hang out at the cafe, despite Maddy offering free breakfast to the whole family. I was so peeved when Mrs. Nelson declined the offer, saying she wanted to do something special at home.

Kai is so lucky to have parents who can afford to spend time at home with him and his brother. They have time and money to make a whole day special. Most of my birthdays were spent behind the counter or in a booth at the cafe. Not that Grams, Maddy, and Mom didn't try to make them special.

I knock on the front door and twist on the handle before anyone has a remote chance of answering. Maddy trails behind as I enter the brightly lit foyer with shiny, gray-marbled tiles.

"Is that James?" Kai's voice calls out from the top of the stairs.

"Hi King Kai," I call back, moving into the house with his gift.

"Hi Jamie, how was work?" Mrs. Nelson says, moving out of the kitchen and meeting me in the heavily furnished living room.

"It was fine."

She looks beyond me with a happy smile. "Hi there, Maddy. Nice to see you."

"Thank you, Mrs. Nelson. You too," Maddy replies.

Mrs. Nelson's cheeks plump as she giggles. "Maddy, dear. I told you; you don't need to be so formal with me. You can call me Grace."

"I don't think I'm gonna break the habit anytime soon," Maddy replies.

Mrs. Nelson grins, watching me cradle the awkwardly bulky gift. "I suppose you want to give that away."

"It's a little tough to carry," I say, turning towards the staircase. "I'll see you later, Maddy."

"Don't you want to say hello to Milo first?" Aunt Maddy asks.

I turn back and view Milo and his dad walking in from the rear of the house where the ground floor bedrooms are located. Milo's long-haired ginger cat, Alfred, purrs and walks alongside Milo's legs.

"Hi Jamie and Maddy," Mr. Nelson says in his usual jovial tone. "Have a busy time at the cafe?"

"Sundays are always hectic," Maddy replies. She moves in toward Milo and lifts her arms wide for a hug. "Happy birthday, Milo."

"Thanks," Milo says, leaning down to meet her in a hug.

Aunt Maddy giggles as Alfred rubs against her leg. "Wow, Alfie seems in a good mood today."

"He's happy now because I gave him some extra treats," Milo says. "He was anxious because he couldn't escape into my bedroom before Kai's friends went upstairs." He gives me an awkward wave. "Hi Jamie."

I wave back. Ugh. Why did Maddy hug him? Now I have to hug him, or I'll look like a massive jerk.

I move toward a side table, slide on Kai's gift, and grab Milo's card from on top. Okay, let's just get this over with.

"Happy birthday, Milo," I say, lifting the craft paper envelope housing the bookstore gift card. "It's just a little something. We weren't sure what to get you."

"Thanks," he says, taking the envelope with one hand as he pushes his glasses up his nose with the other. "But you didn't have to get me anything."

See, Maddy. "No, it's fine. It is your birthday." Here goes nothing. I lean in for a brief hug. "Hope you've had a good day."

When Milo leans in, he trips over his own foot, lurching further forward than expected. I wince, bracing myself for his fall. When he awkwardly pulls himself up, we embrace.

"Sorry," he mumbles. "And, yeah, it's been good."

Yuck. I hate this. Milo taps my back, which feels horribly awkward, and then pulls out of the hug.

I fake a smile. "That's good. I'm glad."

Milo scratches behind his head, looking down. "I was just on the phone with my grandparents. They usually come for our birthdays, but they've had to delay their trip."

"Oh, that's a shame," I say with a pout. "I always like when they visit."

"You'll see them soon enough," Mr. Nelson replies as he pats Milo's shoulder.

"James!" Kai calls from the second-floor landing. "What's taking so long?"

"Kai, you'd better stop yelling in this house!" Mrs. Nelson yells in the direction of the staircase. "I don't care if it is your birthday or not."

Mr. Nelson cups his hands around his mouth. "Why don't you boys come down? We'll do cake."

"We're in the middle of a mission," Kai calls back. "Give us ten minutes."

"No, fifteen!" Parker shouts.

Mrs. Nelson sighs, shaking her head. "Those boys."

"I better head up," I say, retrieving Kai's gift from the side table. "Once I get the controller, I'll finish the mission in under ten minutes."

"Are you heading upstairs too?" Aunt Maddy asks Milo.

I focus hard so my eyes don't roll.

"Uh, no," Milo says, looking off to the side.

"You'll stick around for cake?" Mrs. Nelson asks Aunt Maddy.

"I'd love to," Aunt Maddy replies. "I actually have something I want to run by you."

Before I get sucked into whatever Maddy's conversation is about, I bound up the stairs two at a time. A grin stretches at my cheeks as I hear the boys yell and cheer against the sounds of video game lasers and blast explosions. Time to see the man of the hour.

Two

I race upstairs, toward the roaring cheers. Parker and Lewis's eyes are glued to the flatscreen hung on the wall, but Tyler and Kai's eyes have found me. I place his gift on the ground, jittering to wish him a happy birthday.

Kai gets up from the three-seater couch in the second-floor living room and bounds my way. Behind the living area are Kai and Milo's bedrooms, separated by a bathroom. Kai's door is open, funneling the sounds of a metal band playing from his stereo.

"Hi Jamie," Kai says, giving me a one-arm hug.

"Hi, happy birthday," I say, patting his back. "I hear you guys can't finish a mission without me."

"Oh, get real," Parker bites defensively, controller in hand. "We're doing just fine, missy."

Kai crooks an arm around my neck and guides me to the couch. "We've totally needed you. Ty, move it so Jamie can sit down."

Tyler slides across and I watch Parker and Lewis on the edge of their armchairs, failing hard at the game.

Kai beckons Parker. "Hand it over."

Parker releases the controller. "Excuse me, I've gotten us this far. I doubt you can ace the rest."

Kai signals Lewis to give his controller to me. "She will when we team up."

"Good luck, bro," Lewis says, seemingly happy to give up the controller.

Kai taps his controller against mine. "We got this, James."

I move my character along the rock formations above the molten lava river. Kai pushes his character ahead, just as in life, he has to lead. Not that I mind. Kai's viewpoint gives me the advantage of seeing what's ahead before my character gets there.

Our characters race across a rope bridge as axes swing from above. Next is a series of landings we have to jump across while avoiding booby-traps. I watch Kai's character and memorize the traps and pitfalls. When his character plummets to his death, I jump the first few landings while he respawns.

As I jump higher than Kai managed, Lewis gasps and throws a pointed hand towards the screen. "There it is!" he cheers. "The emerald danger is at the top. You guys gotta get it."

"Dang it," Parker blurts. "You guys are gonna finish the mission."

Kai smirks. "Why'd you ever doubt me?"

"Well, you seemed useless without Jamie by your side," Parker jokes.

"It's his birthday," I pipe up. "Don't call him useless."

"Thanks, James," Kai says, leaning forward and lifting his controller as if it'll help his character gain more air. "Come on, little Kai, you can do it!"

Tyler laughs at the screen. "It always weirds me out when you call your character that."

Nevertheless, little Kai leaves little Jamie in his dust and collects the emerald danger.

Kai launches off the couch, lifting his arms in the air as he cheers. The guys jump up, cheering with Kai. I cup a hand around my mouth, muffling my laugh. My goodness. Have they been trying to achieve this all day?

Kai turns from the screen and bows in front of me. "Thank you for your service."

I clap and stand with the boys. "Cake now?"

Parker jogs to the staircase. "Heck yes. Sugar is a must."

As the boys head downstairs, I signal for Kai to hang back. "They can't start without you, and I want you to open your gift."

"Aww, Jamesy, is this from you?" Kai asks in a cutesy tone as I lift the gift from the carpet.

"Happy birthday, King Kai."

"Thanks," he says, taking the foot tall, wrapped gift. He gives it a slight shake. "It's such an odd shape."

I giggle. "Come on, open it already."

Kai grins and perches on the arm of the couch. He rips the paper from the taped seams, revealing parts of the gift.

I clasp my hands together and squeak. "I hope you like it."

The last of the gift paper falls to the carpet and Kai's mouth falls open. He stares at the open-boxed drone covered in hard plastic and takes two goes to get a word to come out.

"Jamie, this is insane." He looks up at me with worry. "Is it okay that you got me this?"

"What do you mean? Of course, it is. I know how devastated you were when your last one crashed. I saved up to buy you the latest model."

"But..." he pauses after the word, gritting his teeth. "It's a lot of money."

I smile. "Okay, when I say I saved up, Maddy did help out. She's downstairs, so you can thank her too."

"I don't think you're getting what I'm saying. It's fine for my parents or grandparents to buy something like this for me, but you and Maddy..."

I stare into his eyes, knowing the word *"poor"* is rolling around inside his head.

"We wouldn't have gotten it for you if it was a problem." I squeeze his shoulder. "Just say thanks, Jamie."

Kai exhales, tension easing out of him. A goofball grin lights up his face as he says, "Thanks, Jamie. We gotta head to the skatepark and test this out."

"My thoughts exactly."

"Cake first."

"*Malakai*," his mother shouts from below the stairs.

Kai rolls his eyes. "Good lord, she must be pissed if she's using my full name."

"Will you hurry up?" she continues to shout.

"We're coming," Kai calls out, tucking the drone under his arm as he dashes downstairs.

I follow and watch Kai veer toward Aunt Maddy and give her a hug and a kiss on the cheek. Mrs. Nelson corrals everyone into the dining room to gather around the table. Mr. Nelson finishes lighting the sixteenth candle on the heavily frosted cake and waves his hands like an orchestra conductor as we sing "Happy Birthday" to the twins.

After the twins—mostly Kai—blow out the candles, Mrs. Nelson encourages them to bunch up for a photo. It's the annual tradition, even though it's obvious both boys would rather not celebrate together.

"Mom," Milo grizzles, flinching as his mother smooths his hair with her hand.

"Okay, okay," Mrs. Nelson says, moving around the table and readying the camera on her phone. "Say cheese."

Kai slings an arm around Milo and smirks at the camera lens. "Cheese."

Milo's smile is much more subdued, and he doesn't say a word. Despite being identical, it's easy to tell the boys apart when standing close together. Kai has short, cropped hair, whereas Milo's has grown out to a longer length, making his hair appear fuller. They're both tall with slim builds, however, Kai stands an inch taller and has some muscle definition. Then there are the glasses Milo wears, yet Kai has perfect vision. However, Kai has a scar below his left eye. How he got the scar is still a mystery. Kai refuses to tell anyone the story because he swears we won't be able to handle it.

People at school randomly get them mixed up, but I just don't get how it's possible. Not only do their physical differences make them stand out as individuals, but their personalities couldn't be more opposite. As Kai puts it, *"Milo's commitment to the man makes him the enemy."*

After some small-talk and too much chocolate layer cake, standing around indoors gets too much for us.

"Okay, let's get going," Kai says with a thunderous clap.

"Are my blades still in your garage?" I ask.

Kai points toward the garage, nodding. "Yep. Let's go."

As the boys and I move out of the kitchen, Aunt Maddy calls out to me, "Wear your pads. I don't want to deal with any broken bones right now."

I huff, calling back. "Fine."

"Have fun guys," Mrs. Nelson says, clearing the plates from the table.

I turn and wave as Milo leaves the dining room in the direction of the staircase. His cat races upstairs, taking full advantage of the guys leaving. Milo gives a small smile and then I turn back to follow the guys out.

The boys ride skateboards, but I find rollerblading way more fun. I love bending low, widening my stance, getting as much speed as possible, and feeling the air whip around me. In my opinion, it makes taking the turns, jumps, and rails at the skatepark much more daring.

With my knees and elbows padded up, and head protected by a helmet, I'm ready to tackle the open road. Well, the neighborhood streets toward the skatepark, that is. Two months ago, I wrecked it on the way to the skatepark. I hadn't even made it to any ramps or rails. I tumbled against the asphalt, gained some scrapes and bruises, a sprained wrist, and swollen ankle. Now, if I fall, I can aim for a padded area.

I didn't break anything last time, but I don't want to risk it. We live in the mountains, meaning it can be icy on the roads. Plus, it's the middle of the soccer season. I want nothing jeopardizing my place on the team. It doesn't help when Kai brags about his string of broken bones. First, he dislocated his shoulder at five-years-old, and lastly, he broke his collarbone before his fifteenth birthday. His history makes Aunt Maddy nervous, and I don't need her stressing about me.

"Hey, what's up with you?" Kai asks, latching onto my elbow. "Why do you seem so down?"

"No, it's nothing," I say, trying to keep my tone light. "I'm good. It's your birthday. I don't want to get into it."

"Jamie," Kai says in a supportive tone. "You're my best bud. If something's wrong with you, it's wrong with me too."

I grit my teeth, staring into his eyes. "Are you sure?"

"Tell me," he insists. "What's happened?"

I swipe a hand over my face and avert my eyes when I spit it out. "The school sent Aunt Maddy a letter. My grades are too low and they're threatening to take away my scholarship."

Kai's mouth drops open. "What? They can't do that."

I frown, nodding. "They can. My grade average is a condition of my scholarship."

Kai's shoulders broaden and his expression grows serious. "But the school sets the grades. They're forcing you to fail."

I chew a fingernail, digging my toes into the sole of my blades. "You think?"

"You have to follow their rules and what they make you learn," Kai says, his eyes darting like they always do when he's unearthing a conspiracy. "They want to kick you out because you won't follow their rules. Since when do we all need to be robots?"

"But if I don't follow the rules at Ashworth Academy, I have to go to another school."

"So they have set an arbitrary number for you to hit?" Kai says, unimpressed. "School is already filled with facts they want us to swallow without question. Now they're forcing you to memorize the curriculum to the point they find satisfactory? And if you don't, they'll punish you by forcing you out. This is bull, James."

"I knew you'd see it my way," I say, forlorn. "But what can I do? Aunt Maddy can't pay the tuition, and I don't want to change schools."

"Yeah, not an option," Kai says, shaking his head. "You can't leave school."

I roll alongside a guardrail, looking up at the clouds patch-working the blue sky. "Maybe dropping out will be the easiest option."

"And then what?" Kai asks, dragging his foot alongside his board to follow me. "You want to work now and be a slave to the man? Nope, you gotta figure out a way to stay at Ashworth Academy."

"It's impossible. I'm so used to tuning out everything our teacher's drone on about."

"You're not dumb. If you do listen, you'll get it. It just sucks you have to feed on their version of facts and history."

I sling my arm around Kai's back and rest my head against his arm. "Why can't I be like you and have parents who can pay for my education?"

"Because if that were the case, you'd be boring like everyone else. Don't let anyone turn you into the version they want you to be."

"I'm not interesting, I'm poor."

Kai laughs. "You're not poor anymore. Maddy's cafe is one of the most popular places in town."

"We still don't fit in. Most people in Victoria Falls have ten times the money we do."

Kai pats my shoulder. "Don't compare yourself to the masses. You're better than that."

I nudge him off and shake sense into myself. "Ugh. What am I doing? I'm being such a downer. Your birthday needs to be more fun than listening to me whine."

Kai grins. "Don't worry. My birthday will be super fun."

I smile with surprise. "You look sure about that."

An excited grin grows wider on his face as he rolls his skateboard away. He gains speed and moves toward a ramp. My heart thumps with glee. I'm so glad my school news hasn't brought him down. He's right. I can't let the teachers and administration bring me down. I'm an individual, and I'm awesome.

The good vibes bubble inside me. I lower into a squat position and force one leg forward, and then the other. With each movement, I gain more speed.

I dip down a ramp and fly up the next. I gain air and grab my ankle and let out a *whoop*. As I hit the ground and circle around Tyler, he cheers me on. Lewis calls out, challenging me to race him around the obstacles.

Like it's even a challenge. I run rings around these boys.

Lewis barely waits, flying on his board toward a ramp. I gain in pursuit, with Tyler on my tail. As I take the ramp and head for the row of small jumps, Parker moves in from my left. I leap up, taking advantage of my blades over their boards. I fly over two jumps at once, and then glide around the next two. I'm on Lewis's tail as he takes air, aiming for a rail. I skid, aiming for the rail as I lower to the ground. As Lewis shreds the wheels of his board against the rail, I slide underneath, zooming out from under before Lewis leaps off the rail.

I swirl in circles, throwing my arms in the air. "*Woo*! You guys got nothing on me."

Lewis kicks his board up and grabs it. "Yeah, yeah, Jamie. Whatever."

I slow down and look around me. There's someone important missing.

"Where's Kai?" I ask and get shrugs in response.

I look around the surrounding green parklands. My eyes follow the winding cement path and find Kai walking with his board tucked under his arm. I cup my hands around my mouth, ready to ask where he's going, but soon lower my hands.

Ahead, Kai waves to someone. Under a shady tree stands Tabitha Jones. Olive skin, full lips, tight chocolate curls, and a figure that highlights the curve of her hips. The ultimate Miss Perfect.

I almost tumble off balance. I roll towards a rail and hold myself upright. Kai runs a hand over his head and leans in to talk with her. Tabitha twirls a curl between her fingers, pops a knee, and sways her hips as she listens and giggles.

Wait... What?

What is happening? Are they flirting? I didn't even know they talked.

Why is she here? Why is he talking with her on his birthday? Why isn't he over here hanging with us?

With me.

"What are you staring at?" Parker asks, stopping by me on his board.

"Ahh, I'm not sure."

Parker follows my gaze and then laughs. "Whoa. Is Kai with Tabitha?"

"Yeah. What's up with that?"

Parker nudges me. "Hello? She's hot."

I roll my eyes, hanging onto the rail as I slide away from Parker.

My gaze steadies on Kai and Tabitha. He can't be talking to her because she's hot. Kai has never talked about dating. If any of the guys bring it up, he always changes the subject to something more important. If he did talk about crushes, he'd know I want a boyfriend. But I keep all that stuff a secret, because I know it weirds him out.

At least I thought it did.

Should I go over there? If they're just talking, then as his best friend, it should be normal for me to join them. But what if Tabitha asks me a question? I really don't want to be made the fool when I mumble gibberish at her.

I swipe the sweat droplets off my nose. I try to pull it together, but before I can compose myself, they've both leaned in. Their lips press together. The boys around the skatepark cheer and wolf-whistle, but I'm mute. I feel like I'm sucked out of my body. I need life support right now. What am I witnessing? Kai and Tabitha. Locking lips. Kai's first kiss. He's kissing her. Why is he kissing her?

Am I taking crazy pills right now? Am I hallucinating? This is why my best friend thought his birthday would be awesome?

Kai and Tabitha's shoulders jiggle as they pull out of the kiss. Tabitha covers her mouth as she giggles, and Kai turns in our direction, laughing.

"Would you guys quit it?" he calls out. "Get a life."

Get a life? That's the response we get. That I get? I need more than this. I need a proper explanation about what the heck I just saw. Since when has he wanted to kiss Tabitha?

I roll on my blades, shaking my head. I take a few laps around the obstacles, and then Kai and Tabitha approach. She sits on a bench, watching us, and Kai gets back on his board.

My stomach flips, and I swallow hard. Oh my gosh. I think I'm gonna hurl.

"I gotta go," I say, moving down a ramp.

"Hey, where are you going?" Kai says, reaching out for me.

I hang a thumb over my shoulder as I back away from him. "There's a bus leaving in five minutes. I'm gonna catch it because Maddy is with Mr. Stuffy."

"Don't go," Kai replies. "Hang out with us. One of my parents can drive you home if Maddy is still out by the time we get back to my place."

"No, it's okay." I move toward him and throw my arms around him. "Have a great rest of your birthday."

"You're really leaving?" his tone is wounded.

I shrug, trying to act like it's not a big deal. "It's getting late, and it was a long shift at the cafe."

"Aw, lil Jamie is tired," Kai mocks, pinching my cheek. "Okay, you go. But tomorrow you won't need the bus. I'll be able to drive us."

I dig my toes into my rollerblades, feeling more upbeat. "What time is your test?"

"I get to skip the third period. Then I can drive us around after school."

I cheer. "*Yes.* I'm so excited."

"I'm not gonna flunk out like you," Kai teases.

I punch his arm. "Hey!"

"I'm just playing." Kai pats my shoulder and half-turns away from me. "Okay. You'd better get your bus."

My jaw rocks as I look past him, where he'll inevitably turn.

Her.

Tabitha Jones sits in wait.

Maybe I should stay, just to keep them apart. But to what end? What does it matter if he hangs with her?

I give him a dubious look. Why didn't I know she'd be here?

He double-takes at me. "What?"

I shake my head and backtrack. "No, nothing." I wave as I turn away. "See you tomorrow. Happy birthday, bro."

He grins, waves, and turns away. "Thanks, James."

My stomach tenses as I glide away from the skatepark and into the town square. Kai's hanging out with Tabitha. He gave her that look. The look every guy in a romantic comedy gives to the main character. That she's the one.

I tried to blank out as much as I could during the bus ride to the outskirts of Victoria Falls. Once I get into our small two-bedroom home, I race to the kitchen and plonk a packet of popcorn into the microwave. The popped bag fills a large bowl, which I take to my bedroom. I sit cross-legged on the end of the bed with the bowl placed on my lap as I stream a new release rom-com. I'm twenty minutes in when Aunt Maddy's keys jingle at the front door.

"Mmm," Maddy hums as she strolls toward my bedroom. "I smell popcorn. Is it rom-com time?"

I scrunch a handful of popcorn and lift it toward my mouth. "It's dire."

"*Oof.*" Maddy plonks down beside me and grabs a handful of popcorn. "What happened?"

"Kai." I murmur his name, shaking my head as I stare blankly at the screen. "He…"

Maddy slides in close, tucking her free arm behind my back. "What'd he do?"

I drop the popcorn and turn to Maddy, letting the incomprehension filter through my expression. "He had his first kiss."

"Oh, baby," Maddy coos, stifling a laugh. "You got jealous?"

"How could I not?" I whine. "He's always acted like he didn't care about dating, and then he gets someone so easily. That'll never happen for me."

"Don't say that. You guys are only sixteen. You've got plenty of time for dating. Plus, it's normal for feelings to change as you grow older."

I turn back to the screen and drag my hand through the bowl. "I just can't believe who he was kissing."

"Who?"

"Tabitha Jones."

"Should I know who that is?"

My nose crinkles as I think about how Tabitha and her friends strut through the halls at school. "She's one of the Miss Perfects."

Aunt Maddy stifles another laugh, this time less effectively. "Miss Perfect?"

"You know. Those girls who think their crap doesn't stink. Shiny hair, makeup, and loads of attitude."

"Well, you've got attitude to boot."

I grumble, hunching over the popcorn bowl. "Not like other girls."

"Why would you want to be like other girls? You should feel proud that you stand out."

"Aunt Maddy, I don't want to stand out." I huff, plonking the bowl on the bed beside me. "I wanna fit in."

"Well, maybe if Kai and Tabitha became an item, you can get to know her, too?"

I chew my lip, thinking about the comments the Miss Perfects have made about me. "Yeah. Maybe."

"Don't feel so down, baby," Maddy says, rubbing the space between my shoulder blades. "I've got your studying problem figured out."

I crook an eyebrow as I wait for more. "How so?"

"Milo has agreed to tutor you."

"*Eww.*" I groan. "No way."

Maddy nudges me. "Be grateful. You're the one who got yourself into this mess."

"Why would he agree to tutor me?"

"Maybe because he's a nice person."

I smirk. "Maybe because he's such a big nerd, and can't get enough of his own homework, he needs to take on mine as well."

"Stop being such a brat. Don't go thinking Milo will do your homework for you. He's helping teach you how to do it."

"I don't need him to teach me."

"Obviously you do. Now, hand me the popcorn. I could do with a rom-com fix, too."

I pass the bowl. "Everything not perfect with Mr. Stuffy?"

"Stop calling him that. David and I are doing great. It's just been a long week and I need to chill out."

"I can't believe you asked Milo to tutor me. That's low."

"He's smart and you need help." Maddy digs into the popcorn bowl. "So, was there much lead up to Kai and Tabitha's kiss?"

"No." I gasp as if reliving the shock. "I've never seen them interact before. It's like he's been texting her without ever saying anything."

Aunt Maddy gestures to the screen. "Kinda like he doesn't know you watch rom-coms every night."

"Hardly the same thing. My secret taste in movies is nothing compared to a secret crush."

"I'm sure he was just nervous. You two will talk all about it at school tomorrow."

I sigh out, resting my chin in my hands as I watch the hunk on the screen. "We'll see."

Three

"You need to focus today," Aunt Maddy says as we near Ashworth Academy. "Listen to your teachers and ask for help when you don't understand something."

I slink down in the front passenger seat. "Yes, Aunt Maddy."

"This is serious, Jamie," Maddy says, turning the car into the west parking lot. "You don't want to get kicked out of school, do you?"

I grumble as she parks the car. "Of course not."

"Then take your classes as seriously as you do soccer."

I open the car door and pull my backpack from between my calves. "It's a tall order, but I'll try."

Aunt Maddy pats my shoulder. "You can do this. It's time to turn things around."

I step out of the car, hoisting the bag over my shoulder. "Or I could just do what you did and drop out at sixteen."

Maddy deadpans me. "Hardly the same situation."

"You can't tell me you enjoyed school."

"I had bigger problems to deal with than you do. We're doing much better now. You don't have to worry about the lights staying on or how to get food in the fridge while writing an essay."

I look down at the asphalt below and frown. I hate that Mom and Maddy spent their teens struggling so hard. Plus, they had a whiny baby to deal with. Oh, dang. I'm still that whiny baby.

I look up at Maddy and smile. "I'll try harder."

Aunt Maddy grins and waves me off. "That's my girl."

I shut the door and wave as she backs out the car. As I make my way toward the girls' locker room, I hear Maddy's car slow. Over my shoulder, I spy Coach Anders's truck pulling into the parking lot. He halts beside her, and the two talk between rolled down windows.

I hug my arms around my middle, creating more warmth under my sweatshirt, and keep walking. The good thing about having soccer practice before school is I don't have to arrive in my school skirt, blouse, and blazer. If I have to change schools, at least I wouldn't be going to another private school with a uniform. But, geez, I don't want to give up the uniform if it means giving up going to school with Kai.

A few of my teammates are ahead, walking into the locker room. The grass is dewy and wets my cleats as I walk down the slope from the parking lot. I keep my head down as I enter the locker room. I pass Hayley and Leah as they chat about the rom-com I watched last night. They're arguing about whether Jeremy, the main love interest, was in fact a dream boat or not.

I grip my backpack straps as I move across to a vacant bench. My internal monologue can't help running into overdrive. *No, Jeremy isn't a dream boat. He's fundamentally flawed, and Katarina could do way better than him. He disrespected her parents, showed up at her workplace unannounced, and spied on her when he didn't know the guy she was with was her cousin.*

I want to scream it at them, but the thought of going over there makes me sweat and we haven't even warmed up yet. Talk about fundamentally flawed. It's not like I'm one of those tomboys who *"just doesn't get other girls."* I'm into girly stuff. I could hold a conversation, if only my tongue would release the words! After spending an entire season with these girls, I doubt I'll ever hold an entire conversation with them. I wish I could play on the boys' team. It'd make life so much easier.

After I pull out my shin pads and mouth guard from my bag, I make my way to the field. Coach Anders drags a netted bag with soccer balls and cones toward the field with our keeper, Sally. Coach calls us to get moving with a mile run and then get onto stretches. When I run during practice, I always imagine Kai ahead of me. It's more motivating than competing with my teammates. Whenever I train with him, he always beats me. One day I'll be faster than him.

After stretches, Coach gets us to pair off for passes as he sets up for drills. Even though I don't have any friends on the team, I never worry about partnering up. Someone always kicks a ball toward me and asks me to kick it back. At least I can hold my own on the team and others respect me for it.

Hayley passes me a ball and we start on a jog, passing square and then on the diagonal. Her comments about Jeremy replay in my head. Maybe I could just blurt out that I watched the movie too. That wouldn't be so bad. Maybe if I just say the title, she'll go on a rant and I can just nod along.

I watch Hayley's face as I pass back. She's concentrating hard on her footwork. She doesn't look back at me before she passes and kicks the ball too far ahead. I pick up the pace, collecting the ball before it goes too far.

Hayley groans, punching her thigh. I slow my pace, seeing her stop in place.

"Are you okay?" I manage.

Hayley cracks her neck and breaks back into a jog. "Yeah. Let's keep going."

I nod and pass the ball back. It was a sentence. I call that a win.

Hayley and I make it back to Coach first. After we place the soccer balls back in the netted bag, he gets us to follow him to mid-field.

"Everyone, line up for drills," Coach calls beckoning us toward the line of cones.

At the opposite end of the cones are the goal posts where our keeper waits.

"Dominica, head down the other end of the cones and be the defender," Coach says and Dominica jogs toward the top of the goal circle. "Everyone else, line up here. Dribble around the cones, beat the defender, and then shoot. When you're done, become the defender for the next person."

As I wait for my turn, I jump on the spot, shaking out my hands to keep my circulation pumping. The line moves quickly, and Coach rolls the ball my way.

My cleats grip to the ground as I jog, nudging the ball with care. Weaving in tight circles, I head straight for the defender, ready to fake her out. Her stance is wide and I take the opportunity to pass the ball between her legs. I smirk, holding back my laugh as I swing around her and tap the ball ahead. With open space, I wind my leg back and shoot. The keeper deflects the ball off her gloves, but I keep flying forward and connect the ball with my knee. The ball lifts into the air and I steady myself under it. When it falls back to earth, I direct my head to hit and send it darting into the net.

"*Woo!*" I cheer, punching the air above my head.

"Good work, Jamie!" Coach calls from mid-field.

The previous defender has already jogged toward mid-field when I turn around. The keeper kicks the ball to Coach, and my next victim gets herself ready at the other end of the cones.

Leah navigates the cones with downcast eyes. She's one of the weaker players on the team. It almost feels mean. My lips curve. *Almost.*

I run up to her at an angle that forces her to the left. It's important to learn your teammates' weak points. Leah tries to pass around me, but I connect my foot with the ball, sending it out of bounds. I shoot her an apologetic look before she runs to chase it.

"Okay, get up here, Jamie," Coach calls. "Hayley, you're up."

"Hey, what did you do with your feet back there?" Dominica asks when I get back to mid-field.

"Huh?"

"You did a little flick before shooting the ball away from her," Dominica says. "Could you teach me how to do that?"

"Oh, umm, no it's..." Oh, geez. Here comes the nonsensical sounds right on cue. "It's easy. You don't... I can't... Teach? Umm, no."

Dominica's face screws up. She looks away, clearly mumbling, "*Loser.*"

My stomach somersaults inside me. A perfect opening to make a better connection with a teammate and I screw it up. Why must I do this every training session and game? There's an entire team of girls who could be potential friends, and I have to alienate myself with my brash awkwardness.

We run through a few more drills until it's time to pack up.

"Good job today, team," Coach says. "Hit the lockers."

The team helps pack up cones and gather soccer balls before leaving for the lockers.

"Jamie." Coach beckons me closer. "We need to talk."

"Yeah, Coach?"

He eyes the team disappearing toward the lockers and I hope this isn't another speech about being a better sport or being more encouraging to other team members.

Coach turns back to me when everyone is sufficiently out of earshot. "You're off the team."

I splutter a cough, leaving my mouth hanging open. "Excuse me?"

"Not permanently," he continues, and my normal breathing function becomes operational. "I'm benching you until you improve your grades."

"You're what?" I shake my head, dumbfounded. "Did Maddy put you up to this?"

Coach folds his arms. "I make the decisions for this team and its players."

I gulp. "Yes, Coach."

"Maddy told me her concerns. I don't want soccer to get in the way of your studies."

"It's not a big deal. I can improve my grades while still playing. Please don't bench me."

"I don't want you at games until your scholarship is out of jeopardy."

"This isn't fair," I complain. "You know you don't have any other forwards that can do what I do. Do you really want to lose your best striker?"

"It's moot, Jamie," Coach says, unmoved by my sass. "You won't be on the team if you're kicked out of school. Improve your grades so I can keep my best striker."

"So, what now? Am I still allowed at practice?"

"Will you let it distract you from your more important goal?"

I frown, crossing my arms. "You know I want to stay in school. I'll try harder, I promise. Just don't exclude me from practice. Please?"

"I believe in you, Jamie," Coach says, holding my gaze. "You'll be back on the team in no time. But I don't want you rusty, so yes, you can train with the team. Under one condition."

My eyes widen. "What is it?"

"You can only practice with the team. I don't want you messing about with a soccer ball on your own time."

I screw up my face. "What kind of rule is that?"

"Any time you think about kicking a ball around, I want you to study instead."

"That's crazy. I'll be studying around the clock."

Coach points a finger gun at me and winks. "Bingo."

I click my tongue. "Ugh. Lame."

"Go on, now. Get yourself to the locker room. I want you to improve your attitude toward schoolwork."

I kick the grass as I turn away from him. "Fine."

I scuff away from Coach. This is a living nightmare. Studying is a challenge, but also having no soccer? Unbearable.

Once I've changed into my restrictive school uniform including a blazer, blouse with irritating neckerchief, tartan skirt, knee-high socks, and shiny black shoes, I move into the main school building. I have zero energy to get to my locker. I just want to be done with the day already and it's not even 9 a.m.

My backpack slings over one shoulder and it's wearing me down. I fling it behind me, aiming for the other arm stretched behind my back.

Someone yelps behind me. "Ugh. Watch it!"

I look over my shoulder and see the hard edges of Camila Garcia's reddening face as she grits her teeth and scrunches her fists. "Oh, ahh, sorry."

Camila smooths down her blazer and fixes her sleek black hair. "Sorry? You'd better be. You just whacked me in the head."

Before I can yammer a feeble response, Camila looks up and into my eyes. Her lips crook into a sinister smile, realizing it's me who has wronged her.

"Well, well," she says in a throaty voice. "If it isn't the little harlot's daughter."

I jerk backwards, running into a student behind me. "Excuse me?"

"You almost sound as sickened as I was when I found that dirty, dirty picture," Camila says in a menacingly mocking tone.

"What," I stammer. "What picture?"

Camila pulls out her phone and taps on a photo. "Here's dearest Mommy, looking her absolute finest."

Air constricts in my chest as I look at the under-lit and awkwardly framed photo. But it doesn't matter how bad Camila is at photography. What matters is why she found a deteriorating flyer of my mother in a silver bikini, posing against a metal pole.

"How?" the word trembles out of me. "How did you...?"

"How did I find this?" she asks teasingly as she locks her phone. "Everyone knows my father is a property developer. Imagine my shock when I found out he'd taken me to such a seedy location."

"My mom," I stutter, "umm, she hasn't... It, umm... Not for ten years."

Camila huffs, brushing me off. "Oh my gosh, I've no idea what you're talking about. But it's your mother. I found old ledgers in the building. Oh, and don't worry, I have the original for safekeeping."

Sweat builds on my forehead. "Why? What are you...?"

Camila flicks her sleek chestnut hair, looking off to the side as she says, "Like, I didn't even want to post it to my story last night, because it'd be admitting I was in such a seedy location."

My heart pounds rapidly as hope burns inside me. "You didn't?"

She eyes her glittery manicure and grins. "Only five-hundred people saw."

I gulp hard, feeling all the blood drain to my feet. "Why... Why?" It's all I can manage as she struts away from me.

I blink hard, watching the student body merge Camila into the crowd.

Why would she do this? Even though I hate when she personally attacks me, it's better me than my mother. It's not like she did that work because she thought it was fun. She got that job to make the most money she could to get us out of Logan's Point. Grams gave her a job at the cafe, but Mom still wanted to provide more for Maddy and me. She spent the next few years completing her cafe shifts and then would drive back to Logan's Point to work nights at the club. Of course, if I had understood what was happening when I was an infant, I would've told her not to do it. But Mom did what she thought was right. Even if it meant going back to the place she fled and avoiding any contact with my dad.

"Hey, James, how was practice?" Kai asks, walking toward me. He stops dead when I'm still paralyzed with shock. "Whoa. What's happened?"

I shake my head, keeping my mouth clenched tight. The whole interaction makes me sick to my stomach.

"Jamie?" he asks softly, pulling me off to the side. "You look completely rattled."

I swallow hard, wincing at the sour taste. "Camila."

Kai rolls his eyes. "What'd she do now?"

"Have you seen her latest story?"

He pulls out his phone. "I don't follow her junk."

I wipe my brow and hunch over. "She posted a picture of my mom."

Kai makes a strange face. "Why?"

I hug my middle, my eyes darting around the students passing us in the hall. "She found it. My mom's wearing very little, advertising a club."

Kai quickly searches on his phone, and I smack my hand over it. "No, don't. I don't want to see it again."

"Let me see it," Kai says. "Then I know what I'm up against when I tell her to take it down."

I drop my hand and exhale a shaky breath.

Kai clicks on Camila's page and shakes his head. "It's not here."

I peer over at his phone. "What do you mean?"

"It's just pictures of her breakfast and her dogs."

"Maybe it's already expired?"

Kai slips his phone back into his pocket. "What have I told you about her? She's all talk, no action. I don't know why you let her get to you."

I give him a sharp look. "It was a picture of my mom."

"I get this time, but I mean the other times. So, she says some things about you being one of the boys. So, what? If you didn't let her see it hurt you, she'd look for a new target."

I push away from him. "I'm sorry. I can't just switch off like you."

Kai grabs hold of my arm, tugging me back. "Where are you going?"

I turn around and blurt, "How can you date someone who's friends with her?"

Kai smirks. "Dating? I'm not exactly dating Tabitha. We kissed, that's all."

"And apparently you've been texting heaps without ever telling me." I look him up and down with concern. "Since when did you get flirty?"

Kai folds his arms across his middle, leaning against a locker. "I dunno. We partnered up in chem lab and started vibing. Tabby's gorgeous."

"Tabby? You're on a nickname basis with her?"

Kai laughs and I swear his cheeks are growing pink. "Give me a break. Everyone calls me Kai. It's not a big deal that I shortened her name."

"It's cutesy. It's just weird because you never mentioned liking her, and then I see you two kiss. It was a shock, that's all."

Kai peels off the locker and pats my shoulder. "Don't worry, I'll keep you in the loop from now on."

"Oh, I wasn't saying..."

"I like her, Jamie," he says softly. "I don't want to mess it up. Maybe we will start dating for real. You know, like, official."

A jitteriness runs through my veins. Kai. Dating. Weird.

"Look, I'm sorry if I was harsh before," he says. "I knew something was off with you when I saw you. Makes sense now."

My chin dimples as my bottom lip balloons out. "Camila wasn't the only thing ruining my day." Kai leans in, waiting. I blow out a breath and blurt it out. "I'm off the team."

Kai's mouth hangs open. With the way his eyes grow circular, it's like he wants to gasp, but he's on mute.

I rake my hands into my hair, shaking my head. "I know. I can't understand it."

Kai clears his throat, life coming back into his face. "What? I mean, what? Has Coach Anders had a total breakdown or something? He'd have to go insane to kick you off the team."

I slump against a locker, my legs officially turning to jelly. "To be fair, I'm not kicked off the team. I'm benched until my grades improve."

Kai scoffs, throwing his head back. "What a load of crap. As if what you do in the classroom matters on the field."

"Coach said he doesn't want soccer to be a distraction."

"But you love soccer. It'll be a distraction thinking about not playing. James, did you protest? How could you walk away without fighting this?"

I pull myself off the locker to stand taller. "Because it's useless, Kai. If my grades stay low, I lose my scholarship and I'm off the team, anyway. I can't stay on the team if I no longer attend Ashworth Academy."

Kai settles an arm across my shoulders and leans his head against mine. "I get it. This sucks. Then Camila puts the cherry on top before you even get to your first class."

"I..." I don't know what I'm supposed to say. Never mind, the bell rings overhead, giving me an easy out. "I gotta get to my locker. See ya later."

Kai smiles, squeezes my shoulder, and then turns in the opposite direction. "See ya."

Why does this bother me so much? As I watch Kai walk away, I want to be happy for him. He genuinely seems to want to know Tabitha better. I just thought we were non-daters together. He acts like I'm supposed to be neutral and not into guys or anything girly. Since when was it okay for him to show some vulnerability?

I swallow uncomfortably and move toward my locker. I know why this is so uncomfortable. Because I doubt this will be a two-way street. He's never given me any indication he'd be okay with another guy hanging around who happens to be my boyfriend.

"Okay, students, get moving," Vice Principal Franklin calls as he strides down the hall. "Classes won't teach themselves."

I grab what I need for class and shove the rest of my bag into my locker. Oh, man. I'm jealous of my bag. I just want to hide away for the rest of the day, too.

I get it together and meander my way to my math class. Ahead, Camila and Yvette giggle and chat behind cupped hands. My mood plummets further as I walk into the classroom behind them. Not only did I have a run-in with ragey Camila, but now she has her partner in crime to back her up. The only thing worse is when Tabitha joins and the trio is united.

Ugh. I can't stand the Miss Perfects.

I sit at my desk in the back row, slumped down, and tune out their girlish giggles. Aunt Maddy has accused me in the past of being jealous of them. In what universe would I want to be friends with these girls? My friends are absolutely gaga about Yvette, calling her, *every man's fantasy.* And now I live in a world where Kai is into Tabitha. In the past, Kai always said he liked me because I'm not a girly-girl. Is that, so he's not attracted to me? Am I a complete turn off?

Oh my gosh. Will I never find a boyfriend because I'm not like these girls? Will no boy ever want to date a tomboy?

I search the classroom for couples. The playing field is lowered at school because we all dress in this stupid uniform, but there are some girls who strive to make this look cute. And there are guys who eat it up. My eyes land on Tim Field, one of the Mr. Handsome types all the girls fawn over. He makes the uniform have that effortless, dapper look. Something Kai could never pull off. So, why is Tabitha into him?

This is so confusing.

To make matters worse, my teacher, Mr. Pritchard, has started the lesson and I have no idea what he's talking about. There's a long equation on the board with lots of letters, minus signs, and parentheses. He walks to his desk, asking us to solve the equation. I can tell by the way other students lower their heads and begin working on the solution that Mr. Pritchard gave us a starting point.

Oh, geez. I got nothing.

I copy the equation into my notebook and then glimpse the kids on either side. Even though I see some of their work, it doesn't help me understand what I've written or what I'm meant to do with it.

Oh, crap. What's he doing?

I gulp.

Mr. Pritchard is making his way toward my desk.

"Miss West," he says, landing in front of me.

He's holding a wad of paper and pulling my classmates' attention my way. From the corner of my eye, I spy Camila and Yvette looking over. As they whisper behind cupped hands, heat prickles my neck, and I know I'm turning a brighter shade.

Mr. Pritchard puts the papers on my desk. "This is a study guide and some extra problems for you to work on. I'm also available during office hours for extra help."

Murmurings rustle around the classroom and shoulders nudge in my direction.

Mortifying.

He taps the papers. "I don't want you falling behind any further."

Oh my gosh, just go away! "Okay," I mutter.

He walks away, and the murmurings have a hint of laughter to them. I slink further down in my seat. Seriously, won't this day just end?

I don't want to, but I can't help it. I turn Yvette and Camila's way. They're both intently staring at me, shaking their heads.

"Does she need to go to a remedial school?" Camila says loudly enough for everyone to hear.

An eruption of laughter follows.

"She can't help it," Yvette replies. I shift in my seat, cringing. "It's hereditary."

It's hard to take a breath, like she's just whacked me in the chest with a bat.

Camila giggles, nodding. "We know who her mother was."

As rumbling laughter swells around the room, Mr. Pritchard clears his throat and sits at his desk. "Okay, okay. Settle down and get back to work."

Well done, sir. Let them get their jabs in first.

The classroom quiets except for the sounds of scribbles against paper. I try my best to get the girls out of my head. Even though that was pretty mild compared to other insults I've heard, it still takes a minute. I look down at the formula on my page. I then look at the papers Mr. Pritchard left. How are more of these problems going to help me figure this stuff out? It won't suddenly make sense.

I flinch for the rest of the class, ready for another slanderous attack. A few boys mutter about a tiny silver bikini, and my skin crawls. The girls don't say anything else. However, it's Mr. Pritchard who gets on my nerves. He remarks three more times about my extra homework and to see him between classes or after school for more tutoring.

Hard pass.

Four

The only good thing about my last class of the day is that Kai is by my side. We sit at the back of our English classroom, scribbling in our notebooks, tuning out Ms. Jenkins's lecture. Who knew school could make the English language so complicated? We're reading a Shakespeare play, but it may as well be in French. Whenever Ms. Jenkins has someone read a passage aloud, I have zero comprehension of what they're saying. Can't they modernize the play? Why must we read it like they did hundreds of years ago? It makes no sense to me.

Another saving grace is there's no ragey Camila in this class. Although, there is Tabitha Jones. I barely held any of Kai's attention at lunch. He kept making eyes at Tabitha who sat a few tables away. I managed to cut off enough of his sentences, so he didn't suggest we go over there. He was verging on lovesick puppy territory. It's only a matter of lunch periods before they're sitting together. I'll die if I have to spend lunch with the Miss Perfects. Or, I'll be a stuttering mess, more like it. Ugh. I don't even wanna think about it.

Tabitha keeps an eye on the board; however, she seems totally disinterested. Her body has shifted in our direction, and every other minute she glances at Kai.

I turn to Kai, and he continues to doodle in his notebook. *Ha.* I knew it. He's not really that keen on her. Hopefully, he'll dump her after class.

My head turns back in Tabitha's direction, and we accidentally lock eyes. I shift my head, dodging any impending insults. My gaze pans across the row and lands on Kai's brother, Milo. I don't have a lot of classes with him, but whenever I do, he acts the same way. Head down writing, or eyes up and laser-focused on the teacher. I have no idea how he concentrates so hard during every class.

When the bell rings, I slap my notebook closed and drown out the homework assignment Ms. Jenkins calls over the bell. She's already given me her extra homework and study guides, just like every other teacher. Boy, I think I'm set. I scoop up all the papers and move away from my desk.

"You wanna go for a drive?" Kai asks as we walk toward the classroom door.

"Yeah, sure. Can we stop by my house so I can get my blades?" I look down at my skirt. "And change. I gotta get out of these stupid clothes."

Someone taps my shoulder from behind. "Umm, Jamie?"

I turn around and find Milo with an element of fear behind his clear-framed glasses.

Kai turns around and smirks at his brother. "What are you doing?"

"Umm, I just heard you two making plans." Milo's eyes dart between us. "But, umm, Jamie, aren't you going to your aunt's cafe?"

"What, why?"

He shows me his phone screen. "Aren't we having a tutoring session?"

I read the text. *"Hey Milo. Come to the cafe after school so you can tutor Jamie."*

Ugh, Maddy, I'm going to kill you.

I pull out my phone and find an unread text. *"No going out with Kai after school. You need to be at the cafe to study with Milo."*

Does anyone have a lamer aunt than me?

I look back at Milo, who's waiting for a response. Frustration twists my lips into a scowl. "Why are you texting with my aunt?"

Milo's head jerks back. "Huh? I'm not. My mom gave her my number when I agreed to tutor you."

My scowl intensifies. "And why did you agree to this? What could you possibly get out of it?"

Milo's eyes seem to grow behind his glasses as his stare turns to his brother and then back to me. "I dunno. I thought you'd want to stay at this school."

Kai smirks, patting my back. "He's got you there."

I retch and turn back to the door. "Whatever."

"Be careful, James," Kai says teasingly. "Now that Milo has your aunt's number, he might go straight to her with his snitching."

Milo huffs behind us. "I wouldn't do that."

"Yeah, right," Kai says dryly. "There must be another reason why I never tell you anything."

We walk out of the classroom and Kai hurries ahead to throw an arm around Tabitha. My whole body shudders. He kisses her cheek and says, "I'll text you later, okay?"

Tabitha nods, replying, "Sure thing," and pecks his lips.

Eww. Why is he kissing her? I thought this relationship was supposed to be over by now.

I stomp toward my locker and dump my gear into my backpack. I meet Kai by the foyer, and we walk out onto the front steps where Milo hangs by the side.

"That was quick," I say to Milo as he moves closer to me and Kai.

Milo fidgets with the strap of his backpack as he catches up to our pace. "My locker's close to the foyer."

"Lucky," I mutter as we make our way to the parking lot.

"I could go for a burger," Kai says, throwing and catching his car keys. "My coach is being way strict about what I eat and my mom's on his side. I need Maddy to make me something on the down-low." He stares down Milo. "Don't nark on me."

I turn to Milo in time to see his eyes roll behind his glasses. "As if I care."

I rub my lips together, burying my urge to laugh at the dryness in Milo's tone.

On our way to the car, Milo adjusts his backpack and haphazardly dodges loose gravel below. His feet twist, and he almost goes down. Scuttling his way forward, he picks himself back up.

Kai and I burst with laughter.

"Oh man," Kai wheezes, wiping under his eyes. "You are a wealth of entertainment, Milo."

"I've never known someone to be such a klutz just walking," I tease.

Milo scuffs behind us, keeping his head down without comment. My gut cramps, feeling bad for him. He wants us to move on. But, heck, it was funny.

We make it to Kai's car and I ride shotgun. Milo slides into the backseat, and Kai proudly sits behind the wheel.

"Are you excited, James?" Kai asks, grinning. "It's my first time driving you without parental supervision."

"Say a prayer," Milo mutters.

Again, I swallow the need to laugh at Milo's sarcasm.

"Shut it," Kai snaps, pulling his seatbelt across his body.

"You have to let me take the car for a spin," I say, buckling my seatbelt.

Kai laughs, turning on the ignition. "What?"

"Come on," I say, patting the dashboard. "I'll never afford my own car and Maddy never has time to supervise me."

"I'm not letting the girl who failed driver's ed twice wreck my car."

I blow out a breath. "I'm not a bad driver. It's that darn written test that held me back."

Kai smirks, motioning to the back seat. "You did better than Milo. He gave up after day one."

"I don't need to drive to get around," Milo replies flatly.

Kai pulls out of the parking space. "Don't think I'll turn into your chauffeur."

"Believe me, that's the last thing I want."

I look over my shoulder at Milo. "How can you not want to drive? I don't get you. You never even rode a bike."

Milo shrugs a response.

Kai laughs as he drives the car through the exit and onto the road toward the center of town. "It's because he can't."

I face the front, sliding down the seat. Whatever. I don't care about these bickering brothers right now. I'm headed toward an afternoon of studying, after a day of struggling through my classes. The migraine is already building.

After the drive into Main Street and finding a parking spot at the back of the cafe, the three of us walk inside and find Maddy clearing a booth.

"Aunt Maddy, do I really have to study right now?" My protest comes out in a lethargic tone as I sit my backpack on the front counter. "It's been a really crappy day."

Maddy carries a stack of dirty plates behind the counter and into the kitchen. She walks back out and scrutinizes my face. "What's got you in such a crabby mood?"

I shrug. "Coach benched me."

Maddy almost trips as she nears the counter. "Come again? I don't think I heard you right."

"You heard. But as if you didn't know. You talked to Coach Anders on your way out of the parking lot this morning."

Aunt Maddy shakes her head, dumbfounded. "I told him about the letter we got from the school and how serious it was, but I never mentioned you not playing soccer. Baby, I'd never do that to you."

I lean against the counter, crossing my arms. "Well, it happened."

"Her coach is crazy," Kai interjects. "He can't afford to lose Jamie."

I click my tongue, looking up at the ceiling. "He thinks I can't focus on classes and play in games at the same time."

"Okay," Maddy says with a solid hand clap, gaining my attention. "This is just more incentive. Studying makes you want to rip your hair out, but I know you love soccer. You gotta earn your place."

"I already earned it at try-outs and being the best on the team. I shouldn't have to quit soccer just to focus on schoolwork."

Aunt Maddy gives me a knowing look. "If you could focus on classes as much as you do soccer, you wouldn't be in this mess."

I roll my eyes as Kai coughs, "*Burn.*"

"Kai, you've gotta go," Maddy tells him.

"Excuse me?" Kai asks, placing a hand on his chest. "You're kicking me out?"

"Yes," Maddy replies. "You're a major distraction and Jamie needs her focus."

Kai scoffs, turning on his heels.

I look at Milo and then back at Kai, mumbling, "She's got a point."

Maddy hands me my bag and pushes me toward Milo. She signals for him to move to a vacant booth.

"Remember, Milo," Aunt Maddy warns, "don't let her talk you into doing the work for her."

Milo slides into the booth. "She's not the first person I've tutored. I can handle this."

I plonk myself down on the opposite side of the booth before Maddy shoves me there.

"Okay, play nice," Aunt Maddy says, tapping my shoulder and giving me an unconvinced look.

"Whatever," I mutter, shimming my backpack closer. "We'll be fine."

"Okay, Maddy, I'm heading out," Laura says, tugging at her apron ties.

Maddy gives her a grateful smile. "Okay, see you tomorrow. And thanks again for opening up this morning. Seriously, you and Jake are lifesavers."

Laura pats Maddy's shoulder and gives me a wave. "It's no problem. We've got your back."

Aunt Maddy leaves the table to walk Laura out, and I tug at the zipper on my bag.

Milo clears his throat. "So, what do you want to work on?"

I shrug. "Beats me."

"See ya, suckers," Kai says, moving past our booth while texting on his phone. "How long are you guys gonna be?"

Milo looks at me and then back at his brother. "An hour, maybe?"

"I'll be cruising around so I'll be back to drive you home."

Jealousy writhes inside me. "Where are you going?"

"I dunno," Kai says, backing away with a happy glint in his eyes. "Parker and I were talking about meeting up. Maybe we'll go for a spin around Mountain Drive and see who can take the curves the fastest."

I pout, hugging my bag against my front. "Aw, I wanna go."

"Well, when I pick up Milo, we can..."

"Nope," Aunt Maddy cuts him off. "Get going Kai. Jamie, you're not going anywhere tonight. Hello? Your homework has never been more important."

I groan. "Whatever."

Kai pushes open the front door, smirking as he waves goodbye.

I frown, feeling every good vibe falling to the pit of my stomach.

As Maddy walks back to the counter, Milo fidgets against the vinyl seat, asking, "Anything in particular you want to work on?"

"According to all my teachers, I'm failing. They all gave me extra study guides, but I don't see how they'll help."

"That's why you're getting my help too," Milo replies. "Can I look at the study guides?"

I open my bag and pull out a wad of paper and toss it onto the table. "Here you go."

Milo's nose crinkles as he looks at the scrunched papers, some balled and some torn. He flattens them out best he can. "Umm, okay."

"Hey, at least I didn't throw them out."

Milo fixes his glasses as he looks up at me. "Yeah, I guess."

I lean forward. "Hey, do you actually understand that Shakespeare stuff?"

"What Shakespeare stuff?"

"You know, how they talk and all that stuff."

"Yeah." He nods. "I mean, sometimes I have to read it again or go backwards once I have more context of the scene, but yeah, I get it. Did you understand the scene we went over today in class?"

"I never understand any of the scenes we talk about."

"But you get what the story is about, don't you? King Lear and his daughters. Love, jealousy, and hatred."

I deadpan him. "I guess I know the names of the characters. Kinda... If I look at the page."

Milo stares at me blankly. "They're capitalized before the character speaks."

I slump against the back of the seat. "You don't have to be condescending. I know you think I'm dumb and all, but..."

"I don't think you're dumb," he blurts. He chews his lip, his eyes moving from the pages on the table, and then back up to me. "I can help you with this stuff. I promise."

"Why do you want to help me? Maybe I'd get it if it were one class," I sweep my hand across the mess of papers, "but I need help with all of my classes. Why would you put this much effort in?"

"Well, I'm not struggling that much in class. Plus, I tutor people anyway." He shakes his head, looking down at the papers. "It's not a big deal."

I avert my eyes and mutter, "It's not like I'm struggling with every single thing."

"Is there anything you want help with first? We can work on our King Lear homework."

I wince. "Nope. Thinking about Thy and Thou gives me a headache, and my head already hurts enough."

"But you need to hand in the homework. If you don't turn things around now, your grades won't improve."

I rub my temples, frowning. "I can't do this."

Milo sits taller, and a perkiness bounces in his tone. "Don't give up before we get started. Why don't we start with something easier? Like a warm-up."

"A warm-up?" My head tilts as I look at him. "I don't think of any kind of homework like a warm-up."

"You have those at soccer practice, right?" Milo replies. "You do easier things to warm-up to harder things? I don't know, stretches or something?"

"Well, you need to do stretches or you seize up." I look down my nose at him, the beginnings of a smirk curling the corner of my lip. "You did know that, right?"

Milo shrugs, straightening the papers on the table. "I dunno. It doesn't matter."

"It does if you want to be good at the sport," I counter. "Is Milo struggling with phys-ed?"

"Let me guess," he says, resting his chin in his palm, "phys-ed is the only subject you're *not* struggling with."

"I could do without the health class portion, but yes, I do all right."

"To be honest, I could do without it."

"No way. Not uncoordinated Milo," I joke. "I can't believe that."

He flicks at the papers. "*Ha ha.*"

"If I was a skeptical person, I'd guess you're tutoring me so I'll help you with phys-ed."

Milo looks away, fixing his glasses as his raised eyebrows poke over the top. I laugh. "Am I right?"

"Would that be possible?" Milo asks cautiously. "Hypothetically speaking."

"So, you're not asking for my help?"

"Would you agree if I asked you?"

This is too much fun. How much can I make him squirm? "Ask me what?"

Milo exhales hard, looking up at the ceiling. When his eyes connect with mine, he asks, "Will you help me pass my phys-ed assignment? I need to show three skills in a sport. I have nothing."

"Three skills?" I ask doubtfully. "In what sport?"

He shrugs. "You could teach me soccer."

"Soccer? I couldn't get you to my level."

"I don't need to be at your level. I just need to kick a ball and have it go where I want to."

"You want me to teach you coordination? That's a tall order. Have you asked Kai?"

Milo snorts. "Umm, no. This is way less humiliating. Kai would never let up about this."

"So, why ask me? Kai and I are basically the same person."

"No, you're not," he says softly. "Plus, you need my help. There has to be some payoff. I'll tell your teachers, or whoever else, that you're improving faster than you really are, and you can keep our soccer practice a secret from Kai."

"You don't want me to tell Kai? That's impossible."

Milo's eyes flick to Aunt Maddy at the counter. "I can tell Maddy things that will help get her off your case. You can have more time to skate, or maybe get off the bench quicker and get back into soccer games."

I sit up. "How will this work?"

Milo taps the papers. "You have to put the work in. No matter what, I'll keep it positive. I just need your help and get Kai off my back. I don't want to flunk a class. I just need some pointers."

Wow. He's worried about one class. He really takes school seriously. Dang. If I get anyone's help, it should be from Milo. He cares so much about this stuff.

"Okay. How hard can it be?"

Milo grins. "So, it's a deal?"

I reach my hand across the table. "Deal."

Milo shakes my hand. "Okay. We should get some homework done then."

Ugh. It's going to be *very* hard.

Five

"The King Lear homework is fresh in my mind," Milo says from across the table. "We should tackle it first and get it out of the way."

"I thought we were gonna start with something easy."

"English is an easy subject. It's easier than math or chemistry."

"*Geez.* Just the mention of math turns off my brain."

"We'll get there. I promise to teach you in a way that you'll get it."

I frown. "We'll see."

Milo goes over the scene we discussed in class that wasn't more interesting than figuring out Kai's thing with Tabitha. He explains that King Lear being trapped in a storm symbolizes his realization that his cruel daughters are capable of victimizing him.

It's weird how it starts sinking in. I click my pen, take a deep breath, and promise to try my best with the discussion questions Ms. Jenkins gave us at the end of class. I take a long time on each question. Milo finished his answers by the time I finished question two out of eight.

"It's not a race," he says. "I'm just going to work on my chemistry homework. Tell me if you need help and I'll take a look at it."

"I'm too slow," I counter. "I have math homework too."

"Just make a start and then I'll take a look," Milo replies. "We'll have time to look over your math homework too."

I wiggle my eyebrows and smirk. "Or you could just do it for me."

"It's all right for your teachers to know you're getting help, but they don't want to see you straight-up cheating."

"What's the difference?"

"Don't play dumb," Milo deadpans. "Do you want to stay at Ashworth Academy, or not?"

I raise a palm in surrender. "Fine."

I go back to my question set and work on my third answer. As it nears closing time and patrons clear out of the cafe, I'm close to finishing question seven and moving onto my final discussion question.

"Guys, I'm going to clean the kitchen," Aunt Maddy says, stopping by our table. I huff and shift off the seat. Maddy presses onto my shoulder, making me sit back down. "No, I'm just letting you know you have at least thirty more minutes to work. Make the most of it."

I double-take at her. "You don't want me to help?"

"I want you to finish your homework," Aunt Maddy says, backing away. "Keep at it."

I smile and nod. *Ha.* I could get used to this studying thing if it keeps me out of work.

Milo leans over to view my work. "Do you need help with anything before we go over your math homework?"

I slide my paper over to him. "I'm done with this. Will you let me know if I'm even close?"

Milo takes the paper. "The good thing about English lit is the answers are subjective. Generally, if you can back up your statement, you have a right answer."

I rock my jaw, not entirely understanding what Milo means. "So, does that mean I have right answers?"

Milo lowers the paper and chews on his lip. He winces as he meets my gaze. "Not really. You haven't given full explanations."

I slouch in my seat. "Dang it."

"But you're close," Milo adds quickly. "All you have to do is expand on these."

"Expand?"

Milo pulls a red pen from the front pocket of his bag and begins writing below my answers. "I'll fill in what you need to add, then you can rewrite your answers when you get home tonight."

I huff. "I have to redo my homework?"

He smirks. "Only if you want your grades to improve."

I rub the side of my head. "Fine."

"You've got this, Jamie."

"Thanks."

He smiles at me, and I can't help smiling back. Wow. I never knew finishing homework could swell such a feeling of accomplishment inside.

The front door opens, and I look up ready to tell the person we're closed. I grizzle and hunch my shoulders when I realize it's David walking through the doors.

"Oh, hi, honey," Maddy calls from the front counter. "We're just closing up. I'll be done soon."

David throws his arms wide and wears his cheesy grin. "What can I do to help?"

"You don't have to," Maddy says, walking toward him with an awkwardly flirtatiously strut.

"Come on, I'm here. Put me to work," David says, with googly eyes all over Maddy.

Maddy giggles and scoops up a spray bottle and a cloth from a table. She hands them to David, leaving her hands lingering by his. "You could wipe down the tables along that wall."

David leans down and pecks Maddy's lips. "I'd love to."

Aunt Maddy giggles in the kiss. When they pull apart, she gestures to our booth. "David, have you met Milo Nelson? He's Jamie's tutor."

David turns toward us. "Oh, hey, kids. Nice to meet you, Milo. Jamie, looks like you're busy at work. Good to see."

I give him my phoniest smile and return to my paper.

"Nice to meet you," Milo says to David.

"This is David," Maddy tells Milo. "He's my..." She pauses, stammering over an embarrassed giggle. "My boyfriend."

"Oh," Milo says, and I look up to see the surprise and enthusiasm running over him. "I didn't know you were dating someone. That's awesome."

Aunt Maddy tucks loose hair behind her ears and fixes her ponytail. "Yeah, it just sort of happened."

"Maddy catered a function at my office," David explains. "I couldn't let our story end there. I had to get to know her more."

Milo nods, watching the couple smile and laugh together.

Aunt Maddy takes David's hand and moves him toward the tables on the opposite wall. "We should let you guys finish up," she says.

"Okay," Milo says. He clears his throat and says to me, "He seems nice."

I retch. "He makes me want to barf."

Milo rears back. "Oh. You're not into lovey-dovey stuff?"

"I..." My mouth hangs open after the syllable. Is that what he got from that? Do I really want to project that I'm not into romance? I just don't like David, that's all. I don't care if he brings Maddy flowers. The fact that no one will ever do it for me isn't why he irritates me. It's that... Well, that... Oh gosh, it's been ages since I spoke. "Ahh, it's fine, I guess."

Milo watches the counter and smiles. "Well, Maddy looks happy."

I look over my shoulder and witness Maddy smiling at David. I turn back to Milo and reply, "Yeah, she does."

Milo goes back to his notes, and I think about his comment. Did Kai not tell me about Tabitha because he assumed I wouldn't care? That if he admitted he liked her, I'd puke in response?

"Did Kai tell you about Tabitha?" I ask.

Milo looks up from the page. "What about Tabitha?"

"That he's into her."

Milo furrows his brow and pushes his glasses back. "No, he... Oh."

He pauses, thinking over something, and I need him to speak, not think. "Oh, what?"

Milo shakes his head. "Nothing. It just makes sense."

My fists curl. "What makes sense?"

"Kai was yammering about a girl," Milo says nonchalantly. "I guess, Tabitha was the girl."

"He was talking about a girl? What did he say?"

"I dunno. I wasn't really listening."

"Come on, think. Use that big noggin' of yours."

Milo shrugs. "I don't butt in when he thinks out loud. Last time I did, he punched my arm. I just ignore him these days."

"Hmm." In the past, I've seen Kai get irate when Milo tried to talk to him. "But you heard something?"

"He got my attention because he had this whiny tone to him. It actually seemed like he wanted advice."

"From you?"

"Anyone, maybe. He was thinking about asking someone out but didn't know if it was the right call. He couldn't tell if she really liked him back. Anyway, he kept muttering about it while walking into his bedroom and shutting the door behind him."

I frown, picking up my pen. If he needed someone to talk to, why didn't he text me?

"He probably didn't ask you about it because he figured you'd make fun of him," Milo suggests.

I wince. "You think?"

Milo grins. "Yeah. He was off brand, being pretty pathetic."

I smile back. "It is weird to see him with puppy-dog eyes."

Milo nods. "Very weird. Besides, if he couldn't talk to you about it, I doubt there'd be anyone else he would tell."

"Yeah? I just thought maybe he'd open the twin vault."

Milo smiles and looks down at his homework. "Nope. We haven't been like that in a long time."

Oh my gosh. He looks kinda sad about that. Yikes. I need a subject change. "Umm, can we look at my math homework now? Aunt Maddy still needs to finish in the kitchen, but can't seem to pry herself away from Mr. Stuffy over there."

Milo sends out a hand. "Let's take a look."

I pull out my homework and give it to Milo to decode. He flips the textbook so it's upright for me and uses a pen to tap against the numbers and letters. When Milo explains how to solve the equation, his voice turns into white noise. It's the same magic trick my teacher does. Why do they think these explanations will work?

Milo snaps his fingers, breaking me from my trance. I jolt forward. "Huh?"

"You were glazed over."

"What? No, I wasn't."

"Then why did you jump and say, 'huh'?"

I fidget in the seat and lean an elbow on the table. "Okay, fine. I drifted off. Do you have to make this so boring?"

Milo stares at the textbook page. "What's boring about it?"

I snort. "Are you kidding?"

Milo taps the page, looking up at me. "Okay, I like a challenge. I'll figure out how to explain this so even cool girl Jamie West is interested."

I smirk. "Cool girl Jamie West? I don't think so."

"What? You are cool."

The honesty in his expression makes me pause. No one from a school outside of Kai, Parker, Lewis, and Tyler has ever talked about me positively. There's a tingle under my skin that makes me want to smile, but I ignore it.

"If you can make math non-boring, I'll make you the most coordinated soccer player that ever lived."

Milo laughs, slipping a hand under his glasses to rub his eye. "Oh man. I love your optimism."

"It's probably the most optimistic thing I've said all day."

Milo smiles at me, and the tingles come back.

I clear my throat and pick up my pen. "Okay, try explaining the solution to this problem again."

Milo cracks his knuckles and repositions on the seat. He leans over the page, dragging his finger over the numbers and letters in the equation. Wow, his nails are really neat. Kai's are always dirty and chipped, and his hands are calloused. Milo's appear smooth and probably feel really nice.

"Oh, man. You're drifting again."

I blink hard, averting my eyes from Milo's hands. "What, no. Sorry, I got distracted. Try again. Please?"

Milo huffs and goes back to his explanation. I plant both elbows on the table, positioning my hands on the sides of my head. *Come on, Jamie, focus on his words, not his hands. Why are you even fantasizing about Milo's hands? It's Milo, for goodness' sake! Ah, stop talking to yourself, and just listen.*

"Got it?" Milo asks, bracing himself with wariness.

I'm so blank I may as well be drooling. "One more time?"

A quirk of annoyance changes his face for a split second. His finger underlines the equation.

$$-4X + 7 = 15$$

"We need to find the variable. In this case, X. So we need to move the constants, as in the actual numbers, to one side. In this case, that's seven. Seven is behind a plus sign, so we need to subtract it from this side and move it to the other side." Milo draws it out before my brain cracks in two.

$$-4X + 7 - 7 = 15 - 7$$

"See how they're now balanced because minus seven is on both sides? We subtract seven on both sides to move onto the next step."

-4X = 8

I stare at the now smaller equation. "Is that it? I was moving around so many numbers and was making it so complicated."

A whisper of a laugh slips out of Milo. "We're not done."

My shoulders slump. "Oh."

"We need to find X, remember?" He taps the page. "There's still a minus four in front of it."

"Yeah. It does look messed up. You know, this explanation is still not exciting."

Milo smirks. "At least you're actually listening now instead of becoming a glazed donut. I think it's an improvement."

"Okay, I'll give you that."

"So, what would you do now if you got down to this step?"

I stare at the equation, and it distorts into three different layers. "Umm?"

He taps the line above. "What did we do before?"

"Umm. Subtract seven?"

"From?"

My palms lift upwards. "From both sides."

"Yes!" Milo cheers.

He sits back with a laugh as I peer around us, noting David turning our way and smiling.

"Sorry," Milo says, stifling his laugh. "I'm just so happy you're following along. Okay, so what does that tell you to do now?"

I stare at the -4X and my heartbeat thumps loudly in my ears.

He taps the space I'm focused on. "You need to get that number away from the X."

I look up at him. "I minus four from each side?"

He winces, giving a slight head shake.

I look back down at the messed-up number. Why not? We minused the seven. Why the heck is there a minus near the four? It always confuses me when they stick minus in front of numbers. What does that mean?

I tap the -4X. "Add four to each side?"

Milo chews his lip, waiting for me to try again.

I scrunch a hand into my hair. "Help me."

He circles the -4X. "When a number is attached to the variable, it means..."

"Oh," I draw out the word as it dawns on me. "They're multiplied."

An elated grin expands on Milo's face. "Yeah, Jamie, you're right."

I take my pen and fill out the next line before Milo does. I need to divide. "Therefore, X equals minus two."

"*Woo*. You got it," Milo cheers, lifting his hand across the table.

A flutter of happiness bursts into my chest. I feel totally lame for feeling so giddy over a stupid math problem, but look at how happy it made him. I give in and connect with his hand in a high five.

"Sounds like things are going well," Aunt Maddy says, approaching the booth with nervous enthusiasm.

"She solved the equation on her own," Milo replies.

"No way, Milo did most of the work," I say.

"But you got there in the end," Milo says, still grinning.

I smile back and turn to Aunt Maddy. "It does feel really good to actually understand what I did."

Aunt Maddy smooths my ponytail. "I'm so proud of you, baby."

"Usually, I just copy what Mr. Pritchard wrote on the board and call it a day. But maybe I can actually get this stuff."

"Of course you can," Maddy cheers. "It'll just take some time. I just need to mop and then we'll go. Maybe you guys will have time to work on more problems?"

Milo nods. "Kai's not here yet, so I'm in no hurry."

"Excellent," Aunt Maddy says and walks away from the table.

Milo leans forward. "You should feel proud of yourself. You're gonna get this stuff."

I nod. "Thanks, Milo."

Even though I struggled a lot with the next two problems, at least I didn't have to help clean up the cafe with Aunt Maddy.

"When did you want to work on your coordination?" I ask while Maddy mops away from our area.

Milo turns a slight shade of green as he packs his bag. "Any time there aren't other people around the fields."

"I also need to make sure Coach Anders isn't around. I promised him I wouldn't touch a soccer ball outside of team practices."

Milo frowns. "I'm not getting you into trouble, am I?"

I slide out of the booth. "Chill. When I'm helping out my tutor, I'm sure he'll be cool with it. I just don't want to chance it."

Milo slides out of the booth and pulls on his backpack. "Ask for forgiveness, not permission. Right?"

"Yeah. That's what Kai always says."

Milo nods. "I know. I hear him say it all the time." Milo turns toward the door. "He's wrong, you know."

I frown and shake my head.

Milo waves to Aunt Maddy. "See you next time. And nice to meet you, David."

"Bye, Milo," Maddy says as she and David wave back. "Thanks so much for helping Jamie today. Are you alright to get home?"

Milo nods. "Kai will be driving past soon. Bye, Jamie."

I give a mediocre wave. "See ya."

His words tumble around my head.

Is Kai wrong? No. Kai is never wrong.

I shake out of the ludicrous thoughts and pack up my stuff so Maddy can finish mopping my station.

"So, what do you ladies want for dinner?" David asks as I help Aunt Maddy pack away the last of the supplies. "Pizza? Chinese food?"

"We had pizza on Friday night," Aunt Maddy says, patting her stomach. "Even though I love it, my body won't love me afterwards."

"Oh, hush," David says, leaning over the counter as his eyes turn to goo. "You look fantastic every day."

Barf.

Aunt Maddy giggles. "Thanks, honey. But it's not just how I look. It's the feeling an hour later that doesn't leave until the next day."

"Okay, no problem," David says, backing off. "We can have something else."

I grit my teeth. I don't like to go for something he suggests, but I can already taste the beef and broccoli in plum sauce mixed with thick rice noodles. "Umm, I'd love Chinese food."

"Done," David cheers. "I'll pick it up and bring it to your place. Give you ladies some time to decompress from work and school."

I keep my face flat even though it sounds like the ideal situation.

Maddy walks over to David and plants a kiss on his lips while flexing her fingers into his hair. "Thanks, honey," she whispers, staying close to his mouth. "You're a prince."

David grins, pulling away. "Anything for you." He flicks his eyes to me and then back to Maddy, falling deeper into lovesick puppy mode. "And your niece, of course."

I head out the door first, followed by Maddy, who waits for David to exit before locking the front doors. I look around our area as the sky grows darker and then I double-take at a nearby bench. "Milo?"

Milo sits on the bench with his phone to his ear. He talks in a low tone to the person on the phone and then ends the call. He stands, lifting his bag from the bench. "Hi, I'm just on my way home."

"Where's Kai?" I ask. "I thought he'd be here by now."

"Me too," Milo replies. "But he's not answering his phone. I'm heading to the bus stop."

"The bus?" Maddy chimes in. "Your parents aren't around?"

"Mom's still on her way back from the city, and dad works late on Monday nights," Milo says, hiking his bag on his shoulder. "It's cool. There'll be a bus coming by soon."

"Don't be silly," Maddy says, beckoning him over. "Your Mom will drive past our neighborhood on her way back into town. Why don't you come with us for Chinese food and text your mom to pick you up from our place?"

Milo's eyes dart from Maddy, to me, and back. "Are you sure? I'm really fine to go home alone."

Maddy tilts her head as she replies, "And what? Eat a frozen meal? Come with us. It'll give you an opportunity to help Jamie with the last of her math homework."

I huff, rolling my eyes. "Oh, yay."

Milo's Adam's apple bobs as he looks at me. "Is that okay?"

I look away and wave him over. "Yes, because we all know I won't finish it without you looking over my shoulder."

Aunt Maddy links an arm with me and asks Milo, "Are you okay with helping her out more? I know it's over the hour we discussed, but she's behind in everything."

"It's fine," Milo replies. "I need to finish my homework anyway, and I won't say no to Chinese food."

"What will you have?" David pipes in. "I'm ordering while Maddy and Jamie head home."

"Kung Pao chicken," Milo replies. "Thanks."

David mumbles a laugh. "Same as Maddy's usual."

"I can't get enough of it," Maddy gushes.

"Aunt Maddy, can we go home?" I whine. "I need to get out of this uniform."

Maddy giggles and holds my arm tighter. "Okay, let's go. Milo, hop in the car with us. David, we'll see you soon."

The three of us move toward Aunt Maddy's car. I take the front passenger seat as Milo moves to the back without comment.

"I can't believe Kai didn't show up," Maddy says, pulling out of her parking space. "That kid is such a scatterbrain."

"Maybe he'd show up if he were picking up Jamie," Milo says, leaning forward in the backseat. "But I'm not surprised he forgot about me."

Maddy nudges me as she waits at the parking lot exit for a safe moment to pull out. "Have you heard from him? I want to know what his excuse is."

I lift my phone and check if there are any texts from Kai.

"Maybe he's out with his girlfriend," Milo jokes.

I lower the phone, turn between mine and Maddy's seats, and glare at him. Milo's eyes widen behind his frames, and he sits back in his seat. As Milo fidgets and stares out the window, I face the front and check my phone. There's nothing. Clamminess builds between my palms and the phone. He said he was meeting up with Parker, but what if Tabitha was there? Is he only with her, or has Tabitha taken my place and hanging with all the boys? Could they replace me like that? Would they all prefer a hot girl who doesn't stammer her words around anyone?

I drop my phone to my lap and rest my elbow against the car door with a groan.

Maddy laughs to herself. "*Duh.* He's sixteen with a brand-new license and your parents aren't home yet. He's out on a joyride."

"Without me," I grumble.

"Don't pout about it," Maddy says as we drive through Main Street. "You need to focus and concentrate on schoolwork, not your social life."

"So I can be as interesting as Milo?" I jab.

"*Jamie,*" Aunt Maddy scolds. "You should count yourself lucky to be anything like Milo. He'll do great things with his life."

My ears prick to Milo's uncomfortable shifting behind us.

"And, what? I'm going to be a lifelong waitress who barely passed high school?"

"If you finish high school, you'd already have a better education than I got," Aunt Maddy replies. "And I don't want you aiming to be a waitress. You should be thinking about co-owning our expanding catering business."

I sigh. "We don't need catering. The town likes our cafe just fine."

"We made bank on those catering jobs. This town has a lot of stuffed shirts who throw big functions. There's so much money up for grabs if we take this opportunity and run with it."

"Yeah, yeah, okay. Whatever."

Maddy huffs, shaking her head as she makes the turn toward our neighborhood. "You need to care more about the things that matter."

"Aunt Maddy, you're the one with the brain to make the business better. It's not me."

She looks at me for a beat. "But it can be."

I'm not appreciating the pep talks everyone's throwing my way.

I quickly unlock my phone and text Kai. *"Where the heck are you? Your dorky brother is on the way to my house!"*

Six

People always say Victoria Falls is a small town, but it's sprawling. Nothing proves its size more than our journey home. It's still surprising our neighborhood is considered part of Victoria Falls. From here, we may as well keep traveling until we reach Logan's Point. This weird wave of embarrassment fizzes inside me. I never enjoy the reminder of where Mom, Maddy, and I come from.

Now the feeling of not being good enough comes from Milo being in the car. Kai visits our house plenty, and he's such a part of our family, I never question what's in his head. But the other boys never visit. Even Kai's parents always give excuses not to stop by. *"Oh, it'll be easier if we gather at our house. We have more room."* I wonder what they say about our home when we're not around. Will Milo judge us because of what his parents have been saying? Getting those looks at school is one thing, but to have it in our home...

That's how I know Mr. Stuffy came by our house before I met him. He was way too cool about our tiny, non-flashy home.

When we finally arrive home, I move inside quickly. Not only do I still want out of this ridiculous uniform, but I'll also avoid the look in Milo's eyes when he steps inside.

After I get changed into sweats, I move to the kitchen, where Maddy flicks through papers at the kitchen counter and Milo sits at the table.

"Milo, here's Jamie's grade report," Aunt Maddy says, holding out the paper as she approaches Milo.

"*Maddy*," I scold.

She hushes me, standing by Milo. "There's a few classes where she's at a C plus," she tells Milo. "They're her good classes. I think her first step will be to get her other classes up to a C plus. At least her grade average will be better. If she then can work her way into the Bs, she'll be doing a lot better."

Milo nods, looking over my grades. "We can do that. So, we'll work on math, history, and English first."

"Great," I mutter, sitting opposite Milo.

"Are you in any of those classes with her?" Aunt Maddy asks.

"History and English."

"He's in the genius-level math class," I remark dryly.

Aunt Maddy pats Milo on the shoulder and moves back to the counter. "That's why we're so lucky he's here. Thanks again for helping, Milo."

Milo's lips press together, and he nods. His face flashes with a pinkish hue. "It's no problem," he mumbles.

I tilt my head, watching Milo sit his backpack on his lap and rummage inside. "Do you feel cramped here?" I ask.

He looks up at me. "Huh?"

"It's not a big house like yours." I can't help myself. I need to know if he's looking down at me. "Our dining table is in the kitchen and our couch is six feet away. Do you think that's weird?"

His arms rest on his bag and his expression draws blank. "No. Should it?"

My elbows rest on the table as I lean forward. "I was just wondering what was your first impression?"

"I dunno. I don't remember."

"What do you mean? You just walked in."

His eyes narrow in confusion. "But it's not my first time here."

I jerk backward. "It isn't?"

He deadpans me. "No."

Aunt Maddy laughs. "Oh my gosh, Jamie. You can be such an airhead sometimes. No wonder your schoolwork isn't sticking in your brain."

I throw my hands up at Maddy. "When was he ever here?"

"Plenty of times," she answers.

"Not in ages," Milo says, brushing it off. "We were a lot younger."

"Oh," is all I can manage to say. When Kai and I became friends, all I remember is hanging out with him. Everyone else around us became a blur.

"If anything," Milo says, looking around, "it seems bigger than I remember. Maybe it's newer furniture?"

"Yep," Aunt Maddy says, nodding. "Grams had really bulky old-fashioned furniture. I upgraded them two years ago."

Milo smiles at her. "It looks nice."

She smiles back. "Thanks." She then nods at me. "Where are your books? You have time to study before David gets here with the food."

"I can't do homework when I'm thinking about food," I protest.

Maddy wags her finger at me. "Nuh-uh. No more excuses. You can't skip your homework anymore. Don't you want to get off the bench and play in soccer games?"

I slide my chair back and stand with a huff. "Fine."

I drag myself to my bedroom, pull out my homework from my backpack, and trudge back to the kitchen.

"Did you want to continue on with your math homework?" Milo asks.

I put my extra homework from Mr. Pritchard on the table. "This is my extra math stuff. Do you mind taking a look at it?"

Milo smiles. "Sure thing."

The extra sets are more complicated than the algebra we worked on before, but Milo has a way of breaking it down where it feels less daunting. His finger runs under each number or symbol as he talks it out. There are those perfect fingernails again. Man, he really doesn't play sports, or rock climb, or do anything fun with those hands. But maybe it'd be fun if those uncallused hands ran along my skin. Perhaps my arms, or my thigh.

"Earth to Jamie," Aunt Maddy's voice brings me out of my thoughts.

I jolt, the heat of embarrassment sizzling against my skin. "What?"

"Milo asked you a question," she says.

"Oh... Sorry, what was it?"

Milo gives me a disappointed look, and then re-explains what he'd just said. This time I'll use all my willpower to listen to him. You know, he does have a really nice cadence to his voice. It's calm and reassuring. Oh my gosh, he really does care if I get this stuff. Kai just motormouths his way through conversations, and it never bothers him if everyone else checks out. Alternatively, the way Milo glances up and pauses, he leaves room for me to voice my concerns.

I use a gap in between two of his sentences to suggest what he might say next.

A happy grin sweeps across his face as he taps against a number. "Yes. That's exactly it, Jamie."

"Oh my gosh, baby," Aunt Maddy cheers, landing behind me and rubbing my shoulders. "Well done. To be honest, I was having trouble following along."

"Thanks," I say softly. "It's the way Milo explains it. Umm, thanks, Milo."

He chews his lip, nervously holding onto his smile. "No problem."

Aunt Maddy cheers, moving back to the counter. "*Woo.* Props to me for setting this up."

I laugh. "Yes, congratulations for setting up a study date with one of the smartest guys in my grade."

We keep going with the math sets until the front door swings open. Aunt Maddy left it unlocked so David could walk in. I'll absolutely die if she ever gives him a key. It'll literally be over my dead body.

"Ah, more math, I see," David comments, walking into the kitchen and plonking the takeout food on the table.

"They've been hard at it," Maddy says, opening the bag to hand out the containers.

Thank goodness. With the food out, Maddy is happy for us to press pause on the studying. Beef and broccoli have never tasted sweeter. It even drowns out Mr. Stuffy as he drones on about filing paperwork for a corporate merger his boss is working on. Even Milo seems bored by the story, so that's saying something.

After David helps Maddy clear the emptied takeout containers from the table, he leans against the kitchen counter, eyeing her as she runs a damp cloth against the countertops.

"What is it, hon?" Aunt Maddy asks him. "You seem nervous."

"There was something I wanted to talk to you about," David says. He steals a glance at the table and then returns his attention to Maddy. "But maybe I should ask you privately."

"Is it serious?" Aunt Maddy asks, tensing.

Aunt Maddy has never spent time with David in her bedroom. She always makes a point of being with him in the open, even when I escape their barf-inducing antics by going into my bedroom. The only other place they could talk would be on the living room couch, but we'd still hear every word of their conversation.

David grins. "No, it's fun. Believe me. I just wanted to gauge how into it you would be before..." he trails off, turning his head in my direction.

"Is it something I'll have to discuss with Jamie? Then you may as well just say it in front of her. Unless it's because Milo's here? Is it something only family should hear? No offense, Milo."

Before the new wave of embarrassment colors Milo's face, David grabs a hold of Maddy's shoulders. "Honey, you're spiraling." He smiles, rubbing his hands down her arms and clasping her hands. "Relax. I wanted to know how you'd feel about jet-setting to Hawaii?"

Aunt Maddy's mouth falls open, but before a word comes out, it puffs out of me. "*What?*"

"Hawaii?" Maddy questions, her eyebrows slanting as her forehead creases. "What are you talking about?"

"My company is sending me to a conference there," David explains. "I have a few hours daily in meeting rooms, but the rest of the time is a glorified vacation."

Aunt Maddy's hands escape David's and hover over her lips. "And you want me to go with you? That's amazing, but there's no way I can go."

"Why not? You'd love Hawaii."

"I can't shut my business down."

"You were just telling me about how happy you are that you have reliable staff you can trust to run the place while you're gone."

"That was when you and I went out for lunch," Maddy replies. "Sure, I've had a sick day or two where I couldn't come in. But I haven't left them for days."

"Come on," David coaxes. "I'm sure they can handle it."

"Maddy," I splutter. "You're not seriously considering this?"

Aunt Maddy turns to me and then quickly pans back to David. "You're inviting me and Jamie?"

David sucks in a breath, his teeth gritting. "Ah no. I kinda thought this could be a good getaway for the two of us."

Aunt Maddy shakes her head as if sense is falling into place. "Even if the cafe could run on its own, I can't leave Jamie alone. I mean, it's not just overnight in Hawaii, is it?"

David tries to subdue his smile. "I was thinking a week."

"*A week?*" Maddy and I shout in unison.

Milo swivels on his seat. "Maybe I should let you guys talk alone."

Maddy lifts a hand, which halts Milo from getting off his seat. "When is this? A month away or later? I'd need time to organize everything."

David hesitates. "This weekend."

"*What?*" Maddy and I yelp.

David takes Maddy's hands. "I didn't bring it up before because our relationship was still so fresh. But now that it's here, I don't want to be apart from you. Plus, I think it'll bring us closer and make us stronger."

"Of course, I want that," Aunt Maddy replies. "But..."

I skid my chair back, making an ear-piercing screech that grabs everyone's attention. "You want to take away my aunt for a week?" I angrily cross my arms as I frown. "What kind of conference goes for a week?"

"The conference is five days long, which is standard," David admits. He gives Maddy puppy-dog eyes. "I was hoping we could go the weekend before to soak up some true alone time."

"Should I just come for the weekend instead?" Aunt Maddy says, her eyes darting like she's looking for a loophole. "Oh no, it's still so far away. What if something happens while I'm away?"

David brushes back her hair. "Honey, I didn't bring this up to panic you."

"Seven days is too long for Jamie to be alone," Aunt Maddy says, glancing down with saddened eyes. "There's no way."

"This is why I wanted to gauge your feelings on this," David says. "I don't need an answer today. One thing I didn't know was if Jamie had someone else to look after her. A neighbor, a friend, a co-worker?"

"Why doesn't Jamie stay with us?" Milo pipes up.

Aunt Maddy and David fall into silence, looking at him with consideration. My arms cross over my body as I seethe. Why does he have to open his yap right now? Can't he see I want to win this argument?

Milo shrugs. "I'm sure my parents wouldn't mind. She's stayed with us plenty of times before."

Aunt Maddy nods. "That's true."

David lifts a hand, a smug smile curling his lips. "See? Problems solve themselves."

Did he really just call me a problem?

David wraps his arms around my aunt. "There's plenty of time to figure out the logistics. You don't have to say yes today, just don't say no either."

Aunt Maddy blows out a long breath and ends it with a perky smile. "Okay, I'll keep an open mind."

"What?" I gasp, knocking a fist on the tabletop.

Aunt Maddy holds the sides of David's face and pecks his lips. "Thank you, honey. It's a crazy, exciting idea."

Crazy is right.

David rubs Maddy's back. "Let's take a breather."

I narrow my eyes and grit my teeth as I stare down Mr. Stuffy.

Aunt Maddy smiles at him. "Sure. I'll meet you on the couch."

When David walks away, Maddy closes her eyes and exhales.

"Are you okay?" Milo asks softly.

Aunt Maddy opens her eyes and smiles at him. "Don't mention this trip to your parents," Maddy says quietly to Milo. "I need time to think things over first before involving more people."

"That's cool," Milo replies. "I should've left the room. Sorry."

Maddy giggles, pointing out the couch within earshot. "There's not really any other place to go. Don't worry, Milo, I didn't want you to feel like you had to flee."

Milo nods. "I won't say anything."

She squeezes his shoulder. "Thanks. I'd have no hope if your loudmouth brother was here."

Milo smirks, looking down at his book.

"Kai's just passionate," I butt in.

"He spreads other people's news much too quickly and easily," Maddy says, moving over to the counter.

"Whatever," I mumble.

Maddy walks away, joining Mr. Stuffy on the couch.

I look down at my math homework and huff. "This'll be so much easier when it's me teaching you soccer."

"You know, I don't want to put you in a bad position with your coach," Milo says. "You don't have to help me with soccer. I don't want you to get caught and risk your chance to get back on the team."

"But it gives me an excuse to kick around the ball during this mess," I reply. "There're plenty of pockets of time to get in a little training."

"Yeah, but you said..."

"Don't worry about it," I blurt. "I've used free periods before to train for upcoming games. Like tomorrow, third period is usually when I'm on the field, and I've never seen Coach Anders around. It's my favorite time of the day because it's so peaceful out on the field."

Milo sits back in his chair. "You have third period free? I've never seen you in study hall."

"Wait. You have third period free?"

He nods.

"Well, I think we've got our time and place. Meet on the soccer fields?"

He chews his lip with apprehension. "Yeah, sure."

I stare at him. "What is it?"

"It's like you know how to study but refuse to use your skill with books and in classrooms."

I frown. "What are you talking about?"

"You use a free period to get ready for a game," he replies. "You could use that time to study for an upcoming exam. You need to refocus and use your time to work on your classes."

"I will," I say bluntly. "We will. We'll meet up after school again and work on homework. Please, let's just use third period to work on soccer. I'll go crazy without it."

Milo nods. "Okay. But if we call it close with your coach, I'll work something else out."

"You worry too much."

"Maybe you shouldn't change into your gym gear, just in case. We could pretend you were just walking by."

"Milo, stop. I already told you I never see anyone."

"That doesn't mean they don't see you," he counters. "You could just be laser-focused and not notice that your coach or anyone else is watching you."

I raise my palms in surrender. "Okay, whatever."

"I have phys-ed during fourth period, so I usually change early, anyway. After this, you need to learn to use study periods actually for study."

I smirk. "Stop nagging me. Can we go to your house tomorrow to study?"

His eyebrow quirks. "Why? So you can hang with Kai?"

Yes, but let's not admit that. "For a change of scenery."

"It doesn't bother me. Ask your aunt."

I grimace, sending my attention to the couch where Aunt Maddy and David cuddle together. I click my pen and send my eyes back to homework. "I'd rather work on solving equations than approach the jet-setting lovebirds."

Milo fidgets in his seat, ready to say something. Although he settles, obviously thinking better of it.

We work in silence for ten minutes. I'm shocked I'm actually working on this stuff. I usually get halfway through working out the solutions and give up with little protest. I'm broken out of my concentration when a car honks out front.

"That'll be your mom, Milo," Maddy calls, standing from the couch.

David stands with her. "I should go too."

I look over their way in time to see their quick peck of the lips. Maddy walks David to the front door and then moves back our way.

Milo packs his stuff into his bag. "Thanks for dinner, Maddy."

"Anytime," she replies.

Milo slings his bag onto his back and stares at me for a beat. "Do you need any more help before I go?"

I pat my paper. "I'm good. Seriously, I think it's good. Thanks."

Milo smiles and moves toward the front door. "See you tomorrow."

Aunt Maddy walks Milo out. I move from the table and peer out the window. Milo gets into the front passenger seat and Maddy talks with Mrs.

Nelson through her open window. Soon, she waves them off, and the car pulls down the street.

Aunt Maddy comes back into the house, and I give her a dubious look. "Did she make an excuse about not coming into the house?"

Maddy locks the front door and turns to me, hugging her waist. "She said she didn't want to make things crowded."

I roll my eyes. "She's one person, and we don't live in a sardine can."

"She does it so we won't feel self-conscious," Maddy replies. "She's so welcoming and open at her house. I'm sure she doesn't want us making the comparison."

"She's the one making it weird by not coming in. Just because it's a small house doesn't mean it's an abnormal house."

Aunt Maddy drops her arms and moves closer to me. "I know that, and you know that." She squeezes my shoulder and turns me toward the couch. "But it's not Mrs. Nelson we need to discuss. Take a seat and tell me how you really feel about Hawaii."

"He made a point of excluding me," I say, sitting cross-legged on the couch.

Aunt Maddy winces. "Well, taking a sixteen-year-old with us doesn't exactly scream romance."

"It's a business conference," I deadpan. "Does that really turn you on?"

Maddy bites her lip, and her eyes shine with excitement. "Jamie, it's Hawaii."

My shoulders slump. "You really want to go?"

"Who wouldn't?" she replies. "But I have to think things through both work-wise and you-wise. Like David says, I'm not saying no or yes yet."

I frown. "So David tells you how to think now?"

"Stop being so harsh on him. Can't you be happy for me?"

"I just don't see what you see in him."

"It's not up to you to understand why I'm in love with him."

I double-take. "Love? You're in love with him?"

Maddy huffs and rubs her hand over her face and into her hair. "Yes, Jamie. We've said it to each other."

I grimace. "*Eww.* Why?"

"Jamie," Aunt Maddy scolds. "Stop it. After all the swooning you do at rom-coms, I thought you'd be happy for me. I was hoping so hard that you wouldn't be petty and jealous."

I leap off the couch. "Did you really just call me that?"

"Why else would you be pulling faces and being rude to David?"

"Because he's a pompous snob!"

"Only in the fantasy in your head," Maddy argues. "There isn't a snobby bone in David's body. Yes, he comes from money, but he has never once made me feel inferior. I thought you'd be glad I brought someone like this into our lives."

"I should be glad he wants to take you away from me?"

As I stare hard at Aunt Maddy, tears build behind my eyes. I stomp my foot and take off toward my bedroom. I slam the door behind me and take three deep breaths. The threat of tears dissipates as quickly as they emerged. I'm not a crier, and I'm certainly not letting Mr. Stuffy make me start.

Seven

I pace my bedroom floor, clamping my hands into fists. How dare she call me names like that? *Gah*! She makes me so mad! On impulse, I draw my foot back and swing it at the wall. Something smacks to the floor, but all I see is white.

Ouch!

I hop around the floor, holding my foot. As a soccer player, I should know better than to kick something by leading with my toe. Pain pulses through my big toe and ricochets up the rest of my foot.

I perch on my bed with my ankle crossed over my thigh. I take a few steady breaths and squeeze my foot until the pain dissipates. My eyes refocus and I blink until they clear. With a heavy exhale, I release my foot and let it slip onto the floorboards.

I pan across to where I kicked the wall and see a baseboard flipped on its side a foot away from the wall. I guess I kicked fairly low, but how crappy are they to just fall off? Maybe it's normal for old homes? I move off the bed and pick up the painted piece of wood. The piece is only two feet long and is the middle section of the baseboard. So weird. I always figured this piece was one long strip running the entire length of this wall.

As I bend down to put the piece back in place, something catches my eye. Diagonally edged inside is a thin, oblong-shaped item. Surely it doesn't belong. With little thought, I yank it out. It gives some resistance and shakes off some dust, but I budge it all the way out.

After some coughs and splutters from the dust, I take the object in my hand. It's a diary. Carefully, I open the front cover. Chills spread the length of my arms and numb my hands, causing me to drop it where I kneel.

Holy crap.

It's my mom's.

A sudden noise behind me sends me into a jolt. I breathe out when I realize it's my ringtone. I leave the diary on the floor and scoot over to my bed. I smile happily at the screen. *Kai Calling.*

I answer, putting the phone to my ear. "Hey."

Kai huffs into the phone. "Man, I'm in so much trouble."

I frown. "What did you do?"

"Forgot Milo."

"Oh yeah. Thanks for that. He had dinner with us because Maddy thought it was the perfect opportunity for more studying."

Kai's laughter plays through the phone. "My bad. Did any of it sink in?"

"Yeah, kinda. Despite Aunt Maddy and Mr. Stuffy trying to sabotage me."

"Whoa. What happened?"

"David wants Maddy to go to Hawaii with him for seven days. Right when everything in my life is on fire. It's so selfish!"

"*What?*" Kai shouts. A smile tingles at my lips. "She can't abandon you when you've just been kicked off the soccer team."

"Not to mention this whole getting kicked out of school thing."

A frustrated grunt flies out of Kai. "Isn't Maddy supposed to be your guardian? The parental figure? And she just wants to fly off for a vacation when your world has done a one-eighty? Nope. You have to fight her on this."

"I tried," I whine, falling back on the bed. "But then your brother opened his big yap, helping Maddy find excuses to leave me."

"Wait, Milo did what?"

"Aunt Maddy was figuring out how she could leave when I'd be home alone, so Milo blurts, 'Why doesn't she stay with us?'"

Kai sighs. "Well, that's a no-brainer. Of course, you'd stay with us."

"But I didn't want Maddy to realize it. She could've squashed the whole idea right then. But no. Milo was here."

"He barely adds to conversations," Kai replies. "Why would he start then?"

"Exactly!" I whine, sitting up. "You are in trouble. If you hadn't forgotten him, he'd never have been here."

Kai laughs. "Sorry. It's not like I truly forgot him. I was just doing something better."

"Something better?" Better than having another excuse to see your best friend?

"Tabby texted me that she and her friends were shopping. Parker made us turn the cars around because, you know, he has a thing for Yvette." A nervous laugh puffs out of him. "And an excuse to see Tabby again took little convincing."

"Oh." My hand squeezes the phone and the other cramps into a fist. "So, you were on Main Street the whole time?"

"Mmm. Part of the time. Wait, are you mad? You sound a little mad."

"No." I blow out a breath, hoping to relax and change my tune. "Like I said, it's your fault Milo was still with us. If you'd just answered your phone or returned a text saying you were on Main street, it would've been cool to leave Milo waiting."

"What can I say? When I'm around Tabby, my phone is the last thing on my mind."

"Oh."

"Chill out. I'm not ignoring you. Hello, we're on the phone right now."

I smile and an awkward laugh fumbles out. "Yeah, I know. Guess I'm just on edge after fighting with Aunt Maddy."

Kai blows out a breath. "How can she not think about your needs? No wonder you're pissed."

I rub the side of my head. "It's all giving me a headache." I peer around the bed and spy the diary on the floor. "And then I found something super weird."

"Huh? What is it?"

"My mom hid a diary in the baseboard."

"Whoa. How'd you find that?"

"I slammed my bedroom door and then kicked the wall. In all the room shaking, the baseboard fell off the wall. My mom must've jammed it inside."

"Did you know she kept a diary?"

"Nope. I'm guessing no one did, or she wouldn't have hidden it."

"Are you going to show it to Maddy?"

"With the way I'm feeling right now, I'd rather keep it from her."

"Have you read any of it?"

"No. I found it and then you called."

"Well, crack it open," Kai says with excitement. "I wanna know what it says."

I slide off the bed and creep toward the dusty old book. I crouch, reaching for it, and then pull back. "I can't."

"What do you mean, you can't?"

"I haven't seen my mom in ten years. I can't just crack open her diary."

"I can read it for you and tell you what it says." I can tell by his tone he'd have already snatched it if he were here.

"I just need some time to psych myself up."

There's a knock at my door. "Jamie?"

"Ugh. Aunt Maddy's at the door," I say to Kai. "I gotta go."

"Don't give in," Kai blurts.

"I won't. See ya tomorrow."

"Yep. See ya."

I hang up from Kai and march toward my door. I swing it open and then cross my arms and pout. "Yes?"

Aunt Maddy sighs, hunching. "Can we talk? I hate how we left things."

I give her my brattiest look as I pop a hip. "You mean when you called me petty and jealous?"

"Can we please just rewind and talk about this? I hate fighting with you."

I trudge back to my bed and plonk down. "It was just a shock that someone could whisk you away from me."

"It was a shock for me too," Aunt Maddy says, sitting beside me. "I had no idea David would ask me to go away with him. I've been in Logan's Point and Victoria Falls my whole life. Sure, I'd love a vacation, but Hawaii was never on my radar. Come on, you have to admit, it's a bit of a fairytale moment."

I give in, nodding. "Yeah, it is. Feels like you're being sucked into your own rom-com."

Aunt Maddy nudges me. "Admit it, you are jealous."

I give her an indignant look.

"Not of David or anything," Maddy clarifies, "but the whole rom-com thing. You want your own romance, don't you?"

I slouch and rest my head on her shoulder. "You know I do."

"Don't take it out on David. He's a nice man. A good man. He cares about me and also cares about you."

I take my head off her shoulder. "He tolerates me to keep in your good books."

"Can you blame him? You're not exactly the nicest to him. I have to commend him for his patience with you. He'll make a good father."

I recoil. "*Eww.* You're thinking about having kids with this guy?"

"Of course. I wouldn't date someone who'll waste my time. I want an endgame."

"I'm never calling him Uncle David."

Maddy splutters a laugh. "I don't care. You'll probably be out of school by the time we get married."

"Probably?" I question. "I can't believe you're already thinking about marriage."

"Most rom-coms end with a marriage," she says, pinching my cheek. "You've conditioned me with the constant movie streaming."

I retch, smacking her hand away. "Don't put me off the movies."

"Do you want to watch one now?"

I give a sly smile. "Yes."

"Have you finished all your homework?"

I roll my eyes and look up at the ceiling. "*Dang.* Do you really have to turn into an uber-nag?"

Aunt Maddy laughs, latching her arms around me. "Yes, because I care about you, Jamie. Hey, what happened to your baseboard?"

Aunt Maddy unravels her arms from around me and I scoot off the bed. I move over to the wall and pick up the dusty old book.

I show it to Maddy. "Did you know about this?"

She shakes her head, confused. "What is that?"

"I found it stuffed inside the wall." I pause before dropping the bomb. "It was Mom's."

"Whoa," Maddy murmurs as I gently set the book in her hands. Tears bud in her eyes as she stares at it. "I wondered where this went."

I eagerly sit beside her. "So, you knew she kept a diary?"

Aunt Maddy sets in on her lap and turns to me with a smile. Her eyes have a watery shine. "She started writing in it while we lived in Logan's Point. The last time I saw it was around the time you were two-years-old."

"Whoa," I mutter. I take the book and hold it carefully at the edges, like it's an invaluable treasure. "So, there's stuff in here from before I was born?"

"Should be." Maddy then lays a hand on the book and her tone turns stern. "Be careful when reading this. There could be stuff about your dad in it."

I instantly drop the book and it bounces off my knees, smacking onto the floor. My mouth stays open, and Aunt Maddy and I share a hesitant look.

"She didn't tell us who he was for a reason," Maddy says, alarm bells replacing the tears in her eyes.

I suck in a breath and swallow hard. "I know. He was dangerous."

Aunt Maddy scoops the book up from the floor and holds it out to me. "You can read this if you really want to. But there are things in here that Lily didn't want us to know."

I take the book and feel the weight of my heart growing heavy in my chest. I hug the diary close and eye the floor. "I'll think about it."

Aunt Maddy smooths my hair and kisses the side of my head. "She loved you so much."

I purse my lips, forcing the threat of tears to disappear. I clear my throat and say, "I miss her."

Aunt Maddy exhales and stands. "Me too. Shall I get the popcorn ready?"

"And chocolate," I reply.

Maddy snaps her fingers at the TV. "Find us something good to watch."

Maddy leaves the room and I switch on the TV. I scroll through the movies, but I'm not paying attention. The diary lies beside me and consumes my thoughts. I have a piece of my mom back. She wrote in it when she was my age. I can't believe she was pregnant this young. How did she ever have the courage to be a parent? I can't even look after myself. I guess she and Maddy took care of everything, so I don't have to. They sacrificed their childhoods so I could have mine.

I lean back on the bed with a sigh. Aunt Maddy has to go to Hawaii. I owe her that much.

I get up and move out of my bedroom and toward the kitchen. Maddy stands in front of the microwave with her back to me.

"Aunt Maddy," her name comes out in a wounded tone.

She turns around with concern etched on her face.

Before she can ask what's wrong, I blurt, "You should go to Hawaii."

"What?" she gasps, stepping forward to clutch my hands. "Baby, I'm gonna think this through. It was just a silly idea of David's. It doesn't mean I have to go."

"No, you don't understand," I say with more strength behind my words. "I think you should go. No, I *want* you to go."

Aunt Maddy's eyes fill with bewilderment as a smile creeps across her lips. "Where's this coming from?"

I wrap my arms around her and hug her tightly. "You deserve to go, Aunty. You've looked after me since you were a kid. Someone should take care of you for a change."

She rubs my back and her voice breaks. "Are you serious?"

"Yes. Truly."

"Oh my gosh," she whispers. "Thank you."

"I want you to be happy, Aunt Maddy."

"But what will I do about the cafe? And you? I can't leave you."

I pull out of the hug to look her in the eyes. "I'll stay with Kai, and I'll still work my shifts at the cafe. Jake and Laura can run things while I'm at school. Plus, we have Kylie on the weekends."

"But you can't work every afternoon," Maddy replies, sadness drooping her expression. "You need to focus on school."

"We'll handle it, Aunty. Maybe they can shut earlier in the afternoon. Just talk with Jake and Laura about what hours they can cover."

Maddy blows out a long breath. She nods. "Okay. We'll talk it out. Oh, crap." Her eyes grow wide. "I'm going to Hawaii."

"*Eep!*" I squeak, squeezing her upper arms. "This is your fairytale."

"What on earth will I pack?"

"Is this part in the rom-com where we montage a shopping spree?"

Maddy giggles as the microwave dings. She pulls out the popcorn and gestures toward my bedroom. "No. This is the part where the two girls curl up on the bed and watch a fictional girl's fairytale."

We walk back to my bedroom, and I hit play on a classic romantic comedy we both know by heart. After the opening credits roll and the main character starts her inner monologue, I ask Maddy, "Is David the one?"

Maddy sucks in a breath, massaging the pieces of popcorn that lay in her palm. "I have no idea."

"But he's good to you?"

"He's the best." She nudges me. "You've seen him."

"I don't buy him. I was just wondering if I'm missing something."

"Just because I'm into him doesn't mean you have to be. We are different people, you know."

"I guess. I'm just worried you'll travel so far away and see a different side of him. You know, like a bad side."

Maddy winces. "Nice. Thanks for casting a dark shadow over the trip."

"Sorry." I huff. "I just don't want him to break your heart."

Aunt Maddy kisses the side of my head. "Don't you worry about that, baby. I'm the one protecting my heart. If David and I don't work out, I'll be okay. Even though I really, really want it to work out."

"Do you think Kai and Tabitha will work out?"

Maddy shrugs. "I don't know Tabitha. Do they seem into each other?"

"Kai does."

"Then you'd better hope Tabitha reciprocates, or your best friend's heart might get crushed."

"He will be crushed," I murmur. "She's not a nice person."

"Just support Kai while he's with her. He's not blind. If she's bad news, he'll see it."

"But she's always been bad news," I counter. "Her friends were picking on me before they got together."

Maddy stiffens. "Which friends?"

I frown, tasting something sour. "She's friends with Camila Garcia. Ugh. You wouldn't believe what she did today."

"Tell me."

I wipe my eyes, frustrated. "She found an old picture of Mom when she was posing in that club. She wanted to show everyone at school."

"What!" Maddy screeches. "Why on earth would she do that? And why did she have it?"

I groan, shaking it off. "I don't know. She's just a tormentor. And, for some reason, Kai thinks it's fine to date someone who hangs out with her."

"Did Tabitha help spread the picture?"

I shake my head. "No. I only heard Camila and Yvette talking about it."

"Okay, so maybe give Tabitha the benefit of the doubt."

I give her a skeptical look.

Aunt Maddy sighs. "Just ask Kai why he's into her. She might not be as bad as the others. There has to be a reason he's into her. Maybe you'll find out you also have things in common with her."

"*Ick.*" I grimace. "I sure hope not."

"Me too. No one can turn what Lily did into something heinous. She went to that club to provide for us."

I nod, eyeing the diary. "She was amazing."

Maddy smiles, sitting back against the pillows and chucking popcorn into her mouth.

I sigh, scooping a handful of popcorn from the bowl. There's no way Tabitha is magically better than her friends. Why must all the people in my life pick such horrible people to date?

Eight

The next day, during second period math, Mr. Pritchard goes through our homework by showing the solutions on the blackboard. He has us swap with a student beside us and mark their work in a red pen. John Hughes always gets the right answer. However, this time I can tell he messed up some of his working out. I remember how to solve these equations because Milo went over them several times, breaking down each step until it finally clicked in my brain. John Hughes's work isn't correct, but his answer is.

I suck in a breath, and my shoulders are tense. He's cheating.

I've never paid attention to Mr. Pritchard's explanations before, and I've spent all semester just checking or check-minusing John's work, depending on the final answer. I tap the red pen against my lips, figuring out if I should go along as per normal, or if I should alert Mr. Pritchard to John's lackluster effort. I make check marks against John's work. I don't want to ruffle feathers, and I also don't know if my work is up to scratch yet. I can't one-eighty my life in a day and suddenly become a tattletale.

When John and I switch papers, I smile at the check marks. The first three sets I knew would be correct because Milo walked me through them. The final three he left me to do on my own without his help. Two were incorrect.

Nothing shocking there. But one was correct! Whoa. How in the world did I pull that off? Wow. I've learned something.

Mr. Pritchard sets out our work for class. I half pay attention. I can't help the fact he still drones on. At least Milo changes the lilt in his voice when he's explaining stuff. When he leaves the blackboard after explaining today's lesson, Mr. Pritchard strolls around the classroom desks. I glance at the extra work he gave me yesterday. Milo said, I'm on the right track, but I guess I should get my teacher's opinion, too. Maybe he'll be so impressed that he'll say I don't need to do the rest of the extra study.

The enthusiasm instantly dwindles from my body. It's more likely he'll be underwhelmed and pile on more equations to solve.

Oh well. Let's bite the bullet.

"Mr. Pritchard," I say softly, raising my hand as he passes by my desk. He turns to me, and I slide my notebook to the top of the desk. "Can you look over this? I worked on it last night and I think I'm starting to get it."

A happy smile graces Mr. Pritchard's face. "Certainly," he says, lifting the book. He nods along as his eyes run along the work I did to get my answers. He lowers the book with a smile. "This is a vast improvement, Jamie. There are still ways you can improve, but this is a step in the right direction. Did someone else help you with this?"

I nod. "I'm getting tutoring."

He places the notebook on my desk. "Excellent. Keep up the good work."

As he walks away, I slink down in my seat with a sigh of relief. Thank goodness. I didn't want the hours of homework with Milo to be for nothing. Hopefully, he can give me enough pointers over the next week or so, and we can end the tutoring as quickly as it began. As long as my grade average improves, the school administration will get off my back.

When the bell rings, I notice how relaxed my shoulders are. Another bonus of manning up and showing Mr. Pritchard my work caused him not to call out to me in front of the entire class. Without being singled out, Camila and Yvette didn't make horrid comments about me.

I file out of the classroom with everyone else. I just need to dump my gear in my locker and then meet up with Milo for soccer drills. At least I'll feel more in control out on the field and giving the instructions instead of struggling to understand him.

I bypass the Miss Perfects, but unfortunately, not in time.

"Tabby," Yvette calls, waving at her friend.

Tabitha smiles and waves at her friends. While she struts toward them, she locks eyes with me.

Dang it. These girls are always so much stronger as a trio.

"I see that look, Tabby," Camila says with a wicked grin. "The tomboy looks absolutely bizarre in a skirt." Camila sizes me up. "They should just let you dress like the boys. You'd fit in better."

I keep my stare on Camila as all three girls look me up and down. Their faces twitch like they're about to burst into laughter.

"I don't know how you can stand it," Yvette says, twirling her platinum blonde hair around her fingers. "Look at your long hair. You just let it become a knotty, gross mess."

I swallow hard, touching my hair out of instinct. I didn't think it was that bad. It's gross?

I hug my books and pen case close, bunching my shoulders high as other students pass by, easily able to hear the girls hurl verbal abuse at me.

"She can't help it," Tabitha mutters, turning away like it's a conflict of interest to tease her boyfriend's best friend. "She *is* one of the boys."

At this point, she should just admit she's trying to get me out of the picture so she can have Kai all to herself.

"Well, she certainly has the figure for it," Camila sneers. "Or, should I say, lack of a figure."

Yvette laughs, elbowing Camila's ribs. "What did you say earlier about her mother?"

I almost drop my books, sickened to my core.

"Oh, what?" Camila asks with feigned forgetfulness. "That she'd never be able to pull off the tricks her mother did?"

A soft gasp pours out of Tabitha as her mouth falls open, staring at me.

Yvette cackles alongside Camila. "Come on, Tabby," Camila says, linking arms with her. "Let's get going."

The laughter continues as they sashay along the hall.

I stand still for a few moments, taking in their barbed words. Again, throwing in my mother just for kicks. All she did was dance in a bikini, nothing worse. At this point, I've heard worse about myself. It's ridiculous that they're picking on me for being a tomboy while I'm wearing the same feminine uniform as them. It's like they already had the insults locked and loaded.

Oh my gosh. What if they were firing off the same insults around Kai last night?

Gah! How can he be with someone like that? Seriously. I need to shake sense into that boy.

I turn away and stop in place, stunned. Milo stands ahead, his face shocked. He obviously heard the whole thing.

"It's nothing," I mutter, averting my eyes. "Don't worry."

"They're wrong, you know," Milo says softly.

It causes me to look up at him.

His eyes are comforting, framed by his rounded glasses. "You're beautiful."

The word causes me to jolt backward. My insides contort, rejecting the word. I grit my teeth, disconnecting any association the compliment could possibly have with me. I shake my head and tell him, "Don't brown-nose me. I already agreed to help you today."

Milo is taken aback and utters a few sounds before spitting out, "Umm, I wasn't. I didn't mean..." His shoulders slump. "Sorry."

I huff and wave it off. "Whatever. Are we doing this or what?"

A weak smile twitches on his face. "Yeah, let's go."

Milo has already changed into his gym uniform, but I stay in my normal uniform as a cover. If my coach or any other gym teacher catches us, perhaps I could play dumb enough and convince them I didn't touch the soccer ball at all.

When I dump my books, I hand Milo the soccer ball from inside my locker. He cradles it under his arm as we leave the school building and head outside toward the soccer field.

It feels super weird to be stepping onto the field in my shiny black shoes. If the girls thought I looked ridiculous before, they'd have a field day seeing me in a blazer and tartan skirt by the goal posts.

Milo drops the ball to the ground, letting me take the lead.

"Okay, just kick it back to me," I say, nudging the ball toward Milo.

Milo takes a deep breath as apprehension sweeps across his face. As the ball rolls closer, his leg winds back. His body isn't in position to aim the ball at me. He hasn't looked up to check where the ball is headed. Instead, his framed eyes fixate on the ball. His tongue juts out as he rushes his foot forward, connecting with the soccer ball. He went toes first, and the ball propels a foot off the ground. There was little strength in the kick, so the ball bounces back down, and does little hops in a thirty-degree angle to my left.

"Ugh. *See*," Milo complains. "I need help."

"You weren't even close to aiming," I say, jogging after the ball and dribbling it back to my position. "How have you not learned how to do that?"

He shrugs. "How do you not understand act one scene two of King Lear when we've discussed it in three classes?"

I rock my shiny leather shoe over the ball. "Because it's boring."

Milo gestures at the ball. "Well, this is useless."

"It's not useless." His words feel like a personal attack. "It keeps you fit. It teaches you to use your peripheral vision, so you stay alert. It teaches you hand-eye coordination. It teaches you balance and agility. I could go on and on."

"You need to start listing off the good things about classes like that."

I turn to the side and aim at Milo. "Not gonna happen. Now, when I kick it over, just stop the ball, don't try to kick it back."

When the ball rushes toward Milo, he sets his foot forward, letting the ball ricochet off his foot.

I groan. "Dude, you've gotta stop going toe first."

"What does that mean?" he asks, throwing his hands up. "I told you I don't have any skills, and you haven't taught me how to do anything."

"You can't stop a ball?"

"I'm obviously doing it wrong. I don't just tell you to equal out the sides for an algebraic problem. I'll show you how to do it."

I throw my head back and drag myself over to him. "Fine."

"Don't you remember being taught the basics?"

"No. You know, I never said I was a teacher. This was all your idea."

"Just think of me as someone who has never seen a soccer ball before, and that I don't know how to use my feet."

I smirk. "That seems accurate."

Milo gives me an uneasy look. "Can you teach me?"

I collect the ball and stand square with Milo. I plant my right foot edge-wise against the soccer ball. "This is how your foot should look when you're stopping the ball."

Milo turns to view my foot's position. I step my left leg in front. "Your other leg should be in front." I tap the ball ahead to demonstrate. I jog up as the ball rolls to a stop. As I do the actions, I say them aloud. "I hop on my left, bringing it to the side of the ball, and behind, my right foot anchors, sliding to the side and cradling the ball against the inside of my foot."

"Huh."

I look over my shoulder to view Milo with his hands on his hips and a curious look on his face.

I step to the side of the ball. "Do you want to try?"

"Show me one more time?"

I force myself to slow down and go through each movement slowly, trying my best to describe my actions to Milo. I plant the ball in front of him, telling him to approach it like it's moving and do the actions like he were to stop it.

When he steps his left leg beside the ball, his toe digs into the earth, causing him to stumble. He overcompensates with his right foot, tripping over the ball. After three more awkward steps, he stops himself from face-planting the field.

I press my palm hard against my mouth and wrap my other arm around my midsection, pressuring myself not to laugh out loud.

Milo straightens up, and as he turns, I spy the frustration in his expression. As he glimpses at me, it morphs into embarrassment.

Hurriedly, I drop my hands and smile. "It's okay. Try again."

He walks toward me to reposition himself and start again. "You already know I'm an uncoordinated mess, so I guess you're not seeing anything new."

"It's still amusing," I tease.

His eyebrows lift. "*Ha ha.*"

Milo tries the drill a few more times. One time he stops short, fumbling forward to connect with the ball. Another time, his right foot connects with the ball before his left foot gets into position. This causes him to push the ball forward and stumble over his feet, falling forward while over-correcting. The last time he gives up while on the pathetic jog toward the ball.

"This is dumb," he complains.

"You're the one who wanted to practice."

"Yeah, so I could pass the class. Still doesn't change the fact that this having any bearing on my academic record is a joke."

"I have to admit, I never thought stopping in place could be so hard," I tease.

"I did," Milo mutters. "That's why I gave up on soccer the week I started."

"What do you mean?"

"Kai and I were supposed to play soccer together," Milo explains. He shakes his head with frustration, narrowing his eyes. "Why my parents thought that was a good idea is beyond me. They already knew about my issues."

I chew my lip, busting to ask. "What issues?"

Milo rubs his index finger against his ear. "I have an inner ear thing. It throws me off-balance sometimes."

I puff a soft laugh of surprise. "So, there's a medical reason for your awkward lack of coordination?"

Milo shrugs. "It's Kai's fault. He wrapped his umbilical cord around my neck and deprived me of oxygen before we were born."

The smirk washes off my face. "Oh. I didn't know."

He taps the side of his glasses. "Why do you think I need glasses when my identical twin doesn't? Or the fact I'm two inches shorter?"

I throw a palm up. "It's just a couple of inches."

"I took a lot longer to walk and talk than him, too. I can't help how off-balance I am sometimes, but my brain works fine. That's why I enjoy studying. I'm always good at it, plus, I'm way better than Kai."

"If Kai knows all this, he should lay off," I say. "There's kidding around, and there's being mean about something that's not your fault."

Milo folds his arms and his jaw strains like he's wondering if he should say something. "Like you and those girls earlier?"

I shrug it off. "That's nothing. They're always like that."

Milo's eyes narrow as he tries to work it out. "Is it just because you're from Logan's Point? That's no big deal. Everyone goes to Logan's Point to hike, or jump off cliffs into the lake, or whatever else adventurous people do."

I frown. "It's fine to go to Logan's Point for fun, but it's not okay to be born there. My mom moved us here when I was a baby, but it doesn't matter. I guess because she still worked in Logan's Point, they consider my ties to be stronger. But she did that because she got better money doing that stuff than when she worked at the cafe."

"I wasn't sure if you knew about the picture that was going around."

I wince. "You've seen it?"

"It was a really bad photo, but I glimpsed it when some guys were passing it around in class." Sadness creeps over Milo's face. "She's been gone a long time. You'd think they'd lay off."

His sadness leaches into my body. "That's not what bullies do. I'm sorry if I've laughed at you or been mean about your tripping. I thought you were just goofy. I didn't know you couldn't help it."

A cute smile brightens Milo's face. "Thank you, but you don't need to apologize. I don't think you're mean to me. I think you can be snappy and a bit harsh, but I don't take it personally. I know you just argue or act out to get your own way."

"I could say I'll back off, but when it comes to studying, I'm gonna resist harder than any protester has before."

He laughs. "I'd expect nothing less from Jamie West."

The fact that almost rhymes and comes out like a sing-song catchphrase is off-putting. My expression dulls and I cross my arms. "Are you gonna try the drill again, or are we done for the day?"

Milo takes a step back with a slight wobble to his knees. "I haven't got it yet, so I guess I should practice a few times. You don't have to stay. I'll figure it out."

I view the school building over my shoulder and shrug. "The alternative is going back in there. I'd prefer to stay out here and kick the ball around."

Milo twists his lips and eyes the ball with doubt. "We haven't even gotten to how to kick a ball."

I sigh. "I'll show you, but first keep going with how to stop. I'll just watch and pull you up if your positioning is wrong. Cool?"

He nods, angling himself behind the ball. "Cool."

I crouch to the ground, watching Milo perfect his skill. He's moving at a snail's pace, but at least he's not stumbling. I want to tell him to move faster, but perhaps getting the muscle memory right is more important at the minute.

"Did Maddy decide anything on Hawaii?" Milo asks when I stand up to view him from another angle.

My chest puffs out as I sigh, and then I force a smile. "I told her to go."

Milo almost loses balance because of the surprising news. "Whoa. Really?"

"I know, it's shocking to me too," I reply. "But she deserves it. She's worked so hard since she was a kid with no breaks. She deserves to be whisked off her feet."

"That's so cool of you," Milo says. "And, you know, my parents will be happy to take you in."

I cross my fingers. "That's what I'm hoping for."

Milo swats a hand. "You're over all the time, anyway. We can ask Mom when you come over to study this afternoon."

I roll my eyes. "Yay. More studying."

"Just remember, I'm suffering through this, so you can get through this afternoon."

"I'll have countless days of studying ahead for multiple classes. All you have to do is perfect three skills for one class. It'll take five minutes during your phys-ed class to demonstrate, and then you're done."

"But it'll be catastrophic if I'm in front of the whole class and all I can accomplish is tripping and landing on my butt."

I giggle. "It'd be entertaining, though."

"*Ha ha*. Now, help me out before the bell rings."

I steal the ball, dribble in a tight circle, and then pass it to Milo. My fingers stay crossed as he positions himself to stop the ball. I can't help beaming with pride when he effortlessly connects with the ball, stopping it dead and skidding to a stop.

He grins at me, and something weird happens inside my chest. Like a flutter in my heart.

<h1 style="text-align:center">Nine</h1>

We called it a day after Milo finally stopped behind the ball without falling over or accidentally nudging it forward. It was a relief to have it over and done with. Unfortunately, this means training him will take forever. If the time this one skill took is any indication, we will need to dedicate entire days to kicking, passing, and dribbling.

The rest of the day played out much like yesterday. My teachers kept pestering me about my study habits and the importance of concentrating on my work. Maybe if they'd cared during the prior months of school, I wouldn't be in this mess. Now, I'm overloaded.

And if it wasn't annoying teachers I had to deal with, it was my lovesick best friend. Kai was constantly staring at Tabitha. Either from the lunch table, the school halls, or from his desk in class. His fingers would hover over his phone, as if he were agonizing over the perfect words to text her.

Give me a break, man.

At least it's the end of school now. Who knew a tutoring session would feel like a relief?

"I don't see why Mom and Dad would have a problem with you staying," Kai says as we walk into his home after he drives us from school. "But a week is a lot more than just a weekend, so we might have to put the pressure on."

"Pressuring Mom and Dad isn't how you get your way," Milo grumbles behind us.

Kai groans as we traipse toward the dining room. "Have you been living under a rock, Milo? It never fails."

"Only because you keep arguing until they give up," Milo bites back.

When we enter the dining room, Kai chucks his school bag in the corner and lifts his arms out wide. "Case closed."

Milo rolls his eyes, rounding the table. He pulls out a chair, sets his bag on top, and sits on the adjacent chair.

I dump my bag and immediately pull off my blazer and necktie. How is this not the first thing Milo does? Is he so lame that he actually enjoys wearing this stupid school uniform? I mean, he does fill it out well. Wait, what was that? I guess I mean, because he's so lanky. Yep, that has to be it.

Kai snaps his fingers. "You with us, James?"

I shake out of my thoughts. "Huh? Yeah. Just thinking."

Kai pats my shoulder. "All you gotta do is show those sad puppy eyes."

I pull out a chair opposite Milo. "It's easy because I am the poor girl, living on the outskirts of town, who can't afford her education."

"That's the spirit," Kai says, sitting beside me.

Milo lifts a pen, pointing it at Kai. "What are you doing?"

He shrugs. "What?"

"I'm tutoring Jamie. You shouldn't stick around."

"I'm waiting for Mom to get home. Relax."

"You'll distract her."

Before it gets heated, I butt in. "He'll just stay until your mom agrees to let me stay here. I need him."

Milo chews his lip, and then nods.

I pull out my books to impress Mrs. Nelson. If she thinks I'm eager to study, it'll give me brownie-points to win her over. But, let's face it, I'm not learning anything while I have an opportunity to chat with Kai.

"Hi everyone," Mrs. Nelson says, walking through the dining room with a bag of groceries. "Oh my gosh, Kai, are you sitting down to study? Has the world flipped upside-down?"

"Chill out," Kai says as his mom continues on toward the kitchen. "I'm just hanging with Jamie while Milo bores her to death."

That remark brings Mrs. Nelson back into the dining room, which in turn sends Kai grinning.

"It would do you some good to learn from your brother." She then turns her attention to me. "How's everything going, Jamie? Is it all sinking in?"

I nod. "Yeah, kinda. I'm just getting distracted because of Aunt Maddy's trip."

Intrigue pulls Mrs. Nelson in. "Maddy's going on a trip?"

"Her first ever," I reply. "She's going to Hawaii and leaving me alone for seven days."

"Wow," Mrs. Nelson says, stunned. "Hawaii. That's amazing. But wait, you're not going with her?"

I shake my head. "Her boyfriend is whisking her away. I have no idea where I'm gonna go."

"Come on, Mom," Kai pipes up. "Give her a break. Just tell her she'll stay with us next week."

"She can't stay next week," Mrs. Nelson replies, and it's like a gut-punch. "Do you have a sieve for a memory? Your grandparents get here tomorrow night and are taking the guest bedroom."

"So?" Kai argues. "She can stay in my bedroom. It's not like she hasn't before."

Mrs. Nelson sighs, exasperated. "That was when you were little kids. I told you, once you became teenagers, no girls in your rooms."

"*Please,*" Kai splutters, gesturing at me. "I don't even think of Jamie as a girl."

I scoff, folding my arms. "*Geez.* Thanks."

Kai huffs. "You know what I mean."

Mrs. Nelson focuses on Milo. "How do you feel about Jamie staying with us?"

Milo shrugs. "I don't care. It's fine."

Kai leans forward, pointing at Milo. "Mom, he's the one who suggested to Maddy that Jamie stays with us."

Milo leans back in his chair, eyes wide. "It was just a suggestion if they were in a bind. I didn't think it'd be a big deal."

"I can sleep on the couch," I say to Mrs. Nelson while clasping my hands together.

She shakes her head. "No way. You can't sleep on a couch for seven days."

Kai groans. "Then where else is she supposed to go, Mom? You want her to live alone when she doesn't have a car and lives on the outskirts of town?"

"No, of course, I don't want her to be alone. Okay, if Jamie's staying here," Mrs. Nelson says in a steady tone, "then you boys will share a room."

"Huh?" the twins respond at once.

Mrs. Nelson pat's Milo's shoulder. "Milo, honey, you'll move into Kai's bedroom."

Milo throws his hands up. "Why am I getting punished?"

"Your room is neat and tidy, sweetie," Mrs. Nelson says, grinning. "That's much nicer for a girl to stay in."

"I'm not that neat," I say, feeling awkward at the thought of stepping into Milo's bedroom.

"You'll never find anything in Kai's bedroom," Mrs. Nelson says to me. "Plus, you need an organized environment to study. Milo's room will be perfect."

Milo gives his mother an incredulous look. "But it's like that because I use it to study. Where am I gonna go?"

His mother pats the table. "The dining room will be fine for you. Besides, I'm sure you and Jamie will continue your tutoring down here, anyway. Don't worry, honey. It'll all work out."

Milo looks away from his mother, shaking his head. I squirm in my seat, feeling like a true invader. Milo glances my way, and I sink further down in my seat. I want to be the one bunking with Kai. Where in the world did Mrs. Nelson get the idea something would happen between me and Kai? *Eww.* He's basically my brother.

I don't dare speak up. I just need a yes to me moving in. Once I'm in, and Aunt Maddy has landed in Hawaii, I'm sure Kai and I can protest our way into the same bedroom. Milo can then happily disappear into his "neat and tidy" room.

Kai takes a deep breath in, the sign he's about to launch into a tirade. I draw his attention, slicing my hand across my neck. He shuts his yap, tilting his head at my signal. He relaxes on his seat and gives me a nod. I smile, happy our non-verbal communication is as on point as ever.

"Now, Kai, get going," his mother says, shooing him.

"Huh?" Kai says, screwing up his face.

"You need to leave Jamie and Milo alone," Mrs. Nelson says. "It's a tutoring session, not an excuse for you two to hang out."

"Jamie can talk while studying," Kai protests.

"No, she can't," Mrs. Nelson persists. "Her aunt asked me to keep you two separated."

"She did what?" I blurt.

Mrs. Nelson nods. "Last night when I picked up Milo, she asked me to keep Kai away while Milo tutored you. I'm happy to oblige and ensure you keep focused."

I huff. "Ugh. She's the worst."

"No, she loves you," Mrs. Nelson replies and sends me a sweet smile. "And so do I. Meaning, I'll do what's best and keep my scoundrel son away from you."

Kai leaps from his seat. "Scoundrel?"

She smirks at her son. "You are a pain in the butt."

Kai shrugs, turning away. "Fine. I'll go upstairs and play a video game instead. Tyler is probably online."

"Uh, man," I whine.

"Sorry, James," Kai says with a smirk as he backs out of the dining room.

Every thud of him jogging up the stairs is like the hammering of nails into my coffin.

"You'll have plenty of time for games once you pass your exams," Mrs. Nelson says, patting my shoulder and then leaving the room.

"Yay," I grumble.

"What do you want to work on?" Milo asks.

I wince. "I don't want to, but we should probably start with King Lear again. My brain just doesn't compute the way they speak."

Milo nods. "That's fair. And it probably doesn't help you have Kai yapping in your ear all class."

"Well, he's a little distracted these days, texting with his girlfriend."

"Oh."

"Whatever." I pull my books from my bag. "If Kai were talking to me or not, I still wouldn't comprehend this stuff."

"Did Ms. Jenkins like your answers today?"

I slide my notes over to him. "See the big red smiley face she drew at the bottom?"

Milo laughs. "That's her trademark happy face. Good job."

"Thanks, but credit goes to you. I still don't think I understand what I wrote."

"Do you think you can memorize it, though? We could work on you memorizing quotes for the essay assignment."

I blow out a wary breath. "Hmm. Maybe."

"If you can memorize the quotes, then you can memorize why they're symbolic."

"Won't that take forever?"

Milo gives me a hopeful smile. "Only until you get the hang of it. Think of it like learning how to stop a stationary soccer ball."

I laugh heartily. "I can't believe how hard you made that look."

"Now you know how it feels to be a tutor."

I hiss, feeling the heat of embarrassment coating my skin. "*Geez.* I didn't realize I was so painful to watch."

"You just haven't tried. I really think that once you get ahead of this stuff, you'll nail it."

I smile and nod. "Same with you and soccer."

"We can only hope," he jokes.

Milo marks up three sections of my copy of King Lear, asking me to rewrite them until I no longer need to look at the source material. Like that'll happen.

When my page is half-full of scribbled quotes, the sound of Kai barreling down the stairs pulls my focus. There's a thud and then a screeched *meow*.

Milo lifts off his seat as Kai calls out, "Good lord! Milo, can't you cage this stupid cat?"

"Did you hurt him?" Milo calls back.

Kai grunts. "Nice. You care more about that ginger furball than your own brother."

"Are you all right, Kai?" his mother asks, seemingly out of obligation.

"Yes, I'm fine. Almost face-planted the stairs, but I kept my balance. Stupid thing cowered on a step and tripped me up."

"Because he's scared of you," Milo says, rounding the table to find his cat.

"He went upstairs," Kai says, passing the dining room. "The thing is fine. Relax." As his mother enters the room, Kai waves and says, "I'm heading out."

"Where are you off to?" she asks as the two continue into the living area.

"Tabby needs a ride home after dance practice," Kai replies, pulling on his sneakers.

My chest constricts. He's leaving the house to be with her?

"Drive safe," Mrs. Nelson warns. "I don't want you showing off to impress some girl."

Kai groans. "*Mom.* She's not *some* girl."

How the heck did Kai become a doting boyfriend when I was certain he thought dating was lame? Seriously, has Tabitha brainwashed my best friend to be obsessed with her?

Mrs. Nelson's footsteps sound up the hall. "If she's your girlfriend, I want to meet her."

"I don't want you scaring her off," Kai argues.

His mother laughs. "Me scare her? You just worry about yourself."

"Look, it hasn't even been a week yet," Kai replies. "Let us work each other out first before you invite her over to dinner."

"Okay, okay. But I don't want you to keep secrets. I want to know what's going on with you two."

"*Eww*, Mom. I'm not gossiping with you about my girlfriend."

"I just want to know you two are being respectful and taking things slow."

"Relax, Mom. I'm in no rush."

My eyes nearly burn holes through my note pages. I've never stared harder at one space. Every word that was spoken kept me frozen. If I didn't keep my cool, I would've blurted out something that'd surely annoy Kai.

"I'll catch ya tomorrow, Jamie," Kai calls, and I hear the jingling of his car keys.

"We're not gonna meet at the skatepark later?" I call back, leaning over the table to peer into the living area.

He doesn't come into view, instead opening the door to the garage. "Naw. I promised Tabby I'd take her to the mall."

It's an effort to keep the hurt out of my tone. "Oh, okay."

The garage door closes, and Kai's presence disappears from within the house. His mother's footsteps backtrack, and I slide down in my dining chair.

"How can he do that?" it mumbles out of Milo in a breathy tone.

I look across the table to watch Milo scribbling a note across the page. "Huh?"

He looks up. "What?"

"You said something."

"Did I?"

"Yeah. Were you talking about Kai?"

Milo fidgets, averting his eyes. "I didn't mean to say that aloud. I guess I'm too frustrated."

"That was very composed frustration. Are you sure you and Kai are twin brothers?"

Milo laughs. "Been asking that for a long time. I just can't believe he's hanging with Tabitha."

"You don't like her?"

He shrugs. "I don't know her. I just can't believe he'd do it to you."

I rear back with a frown. "I'm not into Kai, if that's what you're getting at."

"No, I know that. I meant because she's mean to you."

"Oh." My shoulders slump forward. "Yeah. I don't know what he sees in her. To be fair, she's not as bad as the other two."

Milo shakes his head. "She's bad enough."

I bite into my bottom lip to stop myself from smiling. Why is it this brother saying these words? Why can't Kai see Tabitha for who she really is?

"I dunno," I say, straightening up. "There has to be something good about her. Kai wouldn't be with her otherwise."

Milo clears his throat and gives a slight nod. He lowers his head, giving his attention back to the page.

This is so awkward. I want to hang out with Kai and the other guys. I want things to go back to normal. Hanging with Milo is such a drag. But then there are those moments where it feels like I could dive head-first into a friendship with him. Ugh. I gotta nip those moments in the bud as soon as they bloom.

Being friends with Milo? Not a chance.

Milo lifts his head and catches me staring at him. "Are you stuck?"

"Huh? Umm, no. I mean, yes, actually."

Milo drops his pen and leans over the table. "Where are you up to?"

"Could you explain this section to me? I'm not sure if I'm getting it."

Milo grins. "Whoa. You're up to there already? Nice job."

"Oh, umm, thanks." Why am I blushing?

Milo gets up from his seat and rounds the table. I mumble some useless sounds, leaning away from him. He sits beside me, regardless.

As he explains the symbolism of this quote, I get a whiff of his cologne. Is that sandalwood? Whatever it is, it's delicious. The smell, that is, not Milo. I'm not thinking Milo is delicious. Oh my gosh, why am I convincing myself? I know I'm not into Milo. Now I've missed his explanation. *Again.* Oh, man. He's gonna think I'm so dumb! Ugh. Why can't I just pay attention instead of being distracted by this dang boy?

"Got it?" he asks dubiously.

"You saw me glaze over, didn't you?"

A breathy laugh puffs out of him. "You actually looked a little freaked. I know the language they use sounds daunting, but when you translate it into modern English, it gets easier."

"Can you go over the motivation again? Slower?"

He smiles. "Sure."

Okay, Jamie, stop thinking about how good he smells. Look at the page. Oh gosh, there are his perfect hands that put mine to shame. Is it bad that a boy has better nails than me? Although, according to Kai, I'm not even a girl.

Jamie! Pay attention!

I clear my throat, blink hard, and focus on Milo's words. His sweet, melodic voice that somehow makes all this hard stuff makes sense. My heart throbs and my skin heats as I focus on his deepening tone. I swallow hard as he taps the page.

"Got it?" he asks, hopefully.

I smile and am sure I'm now in full blush-mode. "Yep. Thank you so much."

"Anytime. You'll get this stuff. You're not dumb."

Is he in my thoughts, or did I say that aloud before?

"You keep looking freaked out," Milo comments. "Chill, Jamie. It'll all work out."

I swallow again. "Okay. Thanks."

Milo moves back to the opposite side of the table, and I exhale hard. *Geez,* I feel like I'm sweating. Why do my thoughts keep going down this road? Is it purely because I'm stuck with Milo? That can't be it. I'm with the other boys all the time. But hanging with them is by choice. Is that the difference?

It doesn't even matter what my first choice is anymore. My free afternoons are supposed to be at the skatepark with the guys or finding somewhere to kick a soccer ball around. If I have to stay with Milo, I might as well try to make the best of this.

"With Kai gone, we could work on your soccer skills," I suggest. I bite my lip and add, "Or, should I say, lack of skills."

"*Ha ha,*" Milo mutters. "Are you just saying that to get out of studying?"

"No, I want to finish this, but you also need more help. Aunt Maddy doesn't need me at the cafe, so I have free time to be here."

"Don't you usually hang out with the guys at the skatepark in the afternoons?"

I shrug. "Kai won't be there. The other guys are probably hanging out playing a video game."

"Well, if you're game to teach me again, I'm in."

We move onto my set of math problems, and I fight to stay conscious against Milo's hypnotizing scent. They are relatively similar to yesterday's homework, so once I tell the difference between dividing each side and minusing each side, he gives me the green light to leave the dining table.

"I'll head to the garage and grab a soccer ball," I say, launching from my seat. I'm well versed with the racks of sporting equipment lining the walls in Kai's parents' garage.

Milo leaves in the opposite direction, saying he'll change clothes and check on his cat.

When I collect a soccer ball, I slip out of my shiny black leather school shoes and put on a pair of Kai's old sneakers. They're loose, but surely more comfortable. I also grab one of Kai's sweatshirts and pull it over my crisp white blouse. I leave my shoes and blazer by my bag in the dining room and take the soccer ball outside.

While I wait for Milo, I kick the ball up and hit it with the inside of my foot. The ball lifts higher in the air and when it lowers; I hit it with my thigh. It bounces off and I strike with my opposite thigh.

"Whoa," Milo mutters, meeting me outside. "You're not making me try that, are you?"

I let the ball hit the ground and step on it to keep it in place. I laugh. "Somehow, I think it's above your coordination level."

Milo smirks. "Me too."

"Why don't you try dribbling?"

"Excuse me?"

I pass the ball to him, and to my astonishment, he stops it without tripping.

"Dribbling is where you run the field while maintaining control of the ball by kicking it ahead of you on each step."

Milo kicks the ball towards me, toe first, and it spins out. "Show me first."

"Boy, we gotta get you kicking with the inside of your foot, not your toes."

Milo groans. "It is so hard to care about these little nitpicks."

"I'm not nitpicking," I respond. "It's just technique. There's a wrong and right way. No in between."

"You're making this sound like math."

"Would it help you to think of soccer like math?" I ask, dribbling the ball across the grass.

Milo lowers on bended knees, watching me dribble. "Hang on, dribbling is kicking, right?"

I stop the ball and puff a laugh. "I knew there was a reason they call you a genius."

Milo stands tall with a dubious look. "Well, I'm no soccer expert, but wouldn't it make sense to teach me to kick before getting me to run and kick at the same time?"

It is a solid point. I roll my eyes and pass him the ball. "Good call."

Milo sticks his leg out to stop the ball, but the ball rolls between his legs.

I slap a hand over my forehead. "Oh, boy."

"Don't act like I should've stopped that," Milo says, retrieving the ball. "I only started practicing today."

"I don't get why you don't practice at home. If you know you're bad at it, why don't you put in work like you do your other classes?"

"Because my other classes are actually important."

I roll my eyes and walk over to him. "Whatever. Okay, let's work on your position when passing a ball. You want to be square on the ball."

He looks down at my body as I get into position beside him. "Square?"

His gaze gives me a chill and I shake out my limbs to compensate. "Think of it as a right angle."

He snaps his fingers. "Ah, got it."

"You want to aim your shoulder where the ball has to go."

"That part always trips me up. I can't coordinate my shoulder and my foot."

"Honestly, Milo, there's not a lot that doesn't trip you up."

"*Ha ha.*"

"Here, I'll show you." I demonstrate with the ball. "Aim behind the ball, angle your body, step onto the ball, and follow through."

"We may as well be speaking Spanish," Milo mumbles as I collect the ball.

"*¿No comprende, amigo?*" I say in a terrible Spanish accent.

"No, I take French."

Why did that just send a spark of energy through me? Every fiber inside me tingles. It's the ultimate rom-com trope to have the male lead dole out some French. But Milo isn't the lead in my love story. I'm still waiting for that guy to turn up in real life, instead of in the movies I stream.

I encourage Milo to practice passing, and it's varying degrees of bad. With some more pointers, he nears an almost good kick.

"Jamie," Mrs. Nelson calls from inside the house. "Your aunt has just pulled up out front."

"Okay, thanks," I call back.

Milo sighs. "Well, thanks anyway for your help."

I give him an unconvincing smile. "I think I'll be getting a better grade in math than you will in phys-ed. You're a better teacher than I am."

"I think I've proved over the years it doesn't matter who teaches me this stuff. I'm a lost cause."

I pat his arm for encouragement, but the maneuver comes off as awkward. "We'll give it another practice this week. You'll get it. Maybe. Hopefully."

Milo laughs. "Thanks for trying. I'll practice a little more before getting to my physics homework."

"*Yikes.* Physics sounds daunting."

He smiles. "It makes more sense to me than being out here. Theoretically, it should help me work out all this soccer stuff. It's all angles, thrust, and velocity. But it looks like I won't be an experimental physicist in the future."

"You're too smart for your own good," I say, heading for the back door. "I'm really lucky you're tutoring me."

When he smiles and waves goodbye, I enter the house, scolding myself for letting tingles run throughout my body.

Ten

The next day, I sit at the lunch table with the boys, listening to Tyler drone on about a sociology assignment. I don't want to pay attention to my own assignments, so I have zero interest in his complaints. I've pulled my chair out too far from the table to eat comfortably. I'm waiting for Kai to get here. He can drown out the sound of any voice.

"Oh, here she is," Lewis says in a breathy tone. He leans over the table with laser-focus.

Parker nudges him, saying, "Don't you even think about it."

There's only one girl they're ogling. I look over my shoulder, and sure enough, Yvette struts through the cafeteria. Even though she has the grace and beauty of a Scandinavian princess, my vision auto-focuses on the couple behind her.

Kai and Tabitha.

His arm is around her as they walk in time, smiling and laughing. Seriously, it's the time in the rom-com where the camera slows and focuses on their pearly whites and star-crossed looks in their eyes.

I straighten up in my seat, turned toward them. Yvette veers away, causing groans from Parker and Lewis. The groans get louder when she stops at a table and makes out with one of the footballer gods.

"What did you think was gonna happen?" Tyler says bluntly. "That girl is never single. You guys have gotta stop pining."

"Whatever," the boys mumble as they slump in their seats.

Yvette doesn't stay talk of the table for long when Kai and Tabitha land.

"Hi guys," Kai says with a large grin.

Tabitha is giggly, holding onto Kai's wrist that dangles over her shoulder.

"Is it okay if Tabby joins us?" Kai asks. His smile muscles quirk from being pulled tighter than I've ever seen.

"Sure," Tyler says, kicking out a seat close to me. "Hi Tabby."

Tabby waves as Kai pulls out another seat by me. "Hi everyone. Thanks for letting me hang out."

Kai sits beside me, sandwiched with Tabitha on his other side. Is this really happening? They've gone from lovesick looks across the cafeteria to being latched at the freaking hip?

"How was class?" Kai asks me, arm still hooked around Tabitha's shoulders.

"Umm..." I falter. I never stumble on my words when it comes to Kai. But how can I not be thrown? Sure, I saw them kiss, and he's talked about her a few times, and he ditched me last night for her... Oh my gosh. Is he falling in love with her?

Kai's eyebrows bounce up. "James? You okay?"

I clear my throat and fake a laugh. "Umm, yeah, bro. I mean, I was just thinking about how much of a dumb question that was. How was class? How do you think?"

Kai laughs, and this would feel easy, if not for Tabitha leaning forward and gaining my attention.

"Ah, Jamie?" she begins in a quiet, almost timid voice. "Like, aren't you failing? I thought you were supposed to be paying attention in classes?"

My chest rises and falls. My shallow breaths hasten. That wasn't timid at all. That's the same mean girl ploy I've heard a thousands times. They reel you in just to humiliate you.

"I…" It's like every thought evaporates from my mind. It's totally foggy in my skull.

Kai hugs Tabitha closer, saying, "As if she's gonna do a one-eighty and suddenly love school."

My chest eases. Yes, that's the Kai I know.

Tabitha keeps her eyes locked on mine. "But I thought she was being kicked out of school?"

"Whoa," Parker says in a low tone. "I didn't know it was that serious."

"They're not *kish…*" Even though I'm looking at Parker, I stumble on my words, feeling Tabitha's stare burning me. "Uh, I'm not get-ah-getting kicked out."

Lewis's eyes narrow at me. "What's with you?"

"*Duh,*" Tyler says, gesturing at me. "She's nervous because it's her last week at this school."

Kai splutters a laugh. "Where'd you get that info from? It's not her last week, and she's not getting kicked out. It's her scholarship she has to fight for because her aunt can't afford the school fees."

Tabitha hisses like she's touched a sizzling frying pan. "*Dang.* I couldn't imagine struggling because your family doesn't have money. I don't know how you do it, Jamie."

What kind of back-handed-compliment-insult was that?

"I…" My hands ball into fists. Thank goodness I break so many nails, or my palms would have five fingernail-sized piercings in them. The anger builds inside, and at this point, I'm directing it at myself. If Tabitha was one of the boys, I could've easily dominated with comebacks. Why can't I just lay into her? So what if she's a girl? Why does that freaking matter so much?

"It's not like she chose to be poor," Kai mutters.

My chin drops. Did he really just say that? Okay, Aunt Maddy and I don't have a fancy house, but it's not like we have to light candles every time the electric bill is due. Plus, the cafe is pulling more business since Maddy started catering outside events. That one society event we did was worth two months' revenue.

Kai knows we're not struggling. Why would he feed Tabitha's narrative?

"So have you stopped being a chicken and actually read that diary yet?" Kai asks, changing the subject as he picks up a handful of fries.

I glare at him, mortified at the matter-of-fact nature he blurted that out. Tabitha looks at us with piqued interest. Camila found a poster of my mother and milked it for everything it's worth. Can you imagine what would happen if her bestie reported back there's a diary from my mother?

Kai drops the fries, staring at me with confusion. "What?"

My eyes widen in the glare, and I nod at the intruder beside him.

Kai frowns and looks away from me, picking up the idle fries.

I look away from the table so I don't pick a fight with Kai. Bad feelings rampage inside me. I don't want to take out on him what's really meant for Miss Perfect.

My eyes wander the cafeteria, searching for a plausible excuse to escape my friends. Kylie, who works at the cafe, is sitting at a nearby table. She hunches forward, whispering behind cupped hands with her bestie. The girls are in their own little bubble and it makes my heart throb. If I had the courage to have a normal conversation with Kylie at work, maybe I could go over and say hi. Imagine how much easier life would be if I could escape to another table. Kylie and her friend aren't scary. I've never heard them say anything nasty about anyone. Maybe they'd even be sympathetic if we talked about my scholarship.

But why even daydream about it? It's not gonna happen. Anytime I attempt to talk to another girl, they look at me like I'm an alien. And the way I splutter and fumble around them, I don't blame them. It's just like when any of the boys stack-it at the skatepark. I point, laugh, and mock.

I guess I bring embarrassment upon myself. Why wouldn't the girls ridicule me when I make it so easy for them?

Tabitha's giggling brings my focus back to our table. The boys have their eyes on her, listening to her vapid story with bated breath.

I can't stand this. How dare she invade our space and hypnotize all my friends? Somehow, I've become an outcast. Heck, I feel more comfortable in my tutoring session with Milo.

Click. A lightbulb flashes in my mind. I pull my phone from my skirt pocket and open up my texts. I send a message to Milo. *"Hey. What are you doing?"*

It's a long-shot he'd look at his phone. The nerd probably escaped into a book.

Before I get down in the dumps, a reply pings. *"I'm just in Mr. Birch's classroom. Why?"*

Called it. *"I need help with something before next period. Do you mind taking a look at it?"*

"Sure. Come by."

I lift off my seat as if I'm set to launch mode.

"Whoa," Kai blurts. "What's with you?"

"I totally forgot about something for my next class," I lie. "I just texted Milo for help."

Kai's eyebrows push together. "You're leaving to hang with Milo?"

I roll my eyes. "Ugh. It's not like that and you know it. I need to keep doing my homework if I want my teachers to bump up my grades."

"Lay off her," Tabitha says, leaning into Kai. "You know the poor girl needs every bit of help she can get."

Does everything that comes out of your mouth have to be in that sarcastic tone? Ugh! Why can't I say it out loud?

"Fine." Kai sighs. "Go be part of the brainwashed masses and spew out the dribble these teachers expect us to learn."

"Thanks," I say through gritted teeth as I back away from the table. The other boys stare at me with dumbfounded faces.

Tabitha looks over Kai's shoulder while fondling his cropped hair. There's a vindictiveness as she smiles at me. As if she beat me for Kai's attention. Oh my gosh, does she think I'm her competition? *Eww.* What is with all these people thinking there's something going on between me and Kai purely because we're different genders? They're sick!

I back out of the cafeteria with little protest from my friends. Maybe they're too stunned for words.

I rarely walk the halls between classes. I don't have anything to do at my locker besides dumping my stuff until the next bell rings. So, I didn't realize how empty the halls get when it's not directly before or after a class.

It's a trek to Mr. Birch's classroom. He teaches all the super smart kids, so I've never entered this room before. The classroom door is closed, and I feel weird about opening it. So, I knock when turning the handle and pushing it slightly ajar.

"Yeah?" Milo says from inside.

"Oh, it's just me," I say, pushing the door further open and stepping into the room.

"Hey, I was surprised to get your text."

I'm about to reply, but I freeze instead. Milo isn't alone.

He's with none other than the Ashworth family heir. As in the family this school is named after.

Thomas Ashworth III. Or Ash, as everyone calls him.

He's the only boy who's ever made me clam up. I mean, his dad is a billionaire. It's crazy that we live in a world where he and I can attend the same school.

Well, I guess his family basically pays for my education. Except they don't want to if I don't pay attention in class. They have so much money they should just pay for it, anyway. They should pay for everyone's education. It would be a level playing field. Let everyone go to this school.

Although, maybe they could kick out the mean girls. That would be nice.

Milo gestures to Ash. "We were just working on something for physics. But I have a few minutes to look at whatever you need."

"Actually, Milo," Ash says, "I'll be going soon. My girlfriend texted, and she's heading over soon."

I've had nothing to do with Ash's girlfriend. I assume, to be this guy's girlfriend, she'd have to be ultra posh. Translation: stuck up. Isn't that the only kind of girl he'd be with?

"In that case," Milo says to me, "do you mind hanging around for a bit while Ash and I finish this stuff?"

"Oh yeah," I say, swatting a hand. "My stuff isn't that important. I was just freaked out about another teacher getting on my case. But I'm less worried now."

Milo smiles. "You'll be fine."

There's a sparkle in his eyes, and his smile makes my tummy flutter. I swear I've heard women say that line in a dozen rom-coms. But why the heck is Milo giving me these feels?

"Are you having issues with your teachers?" Ash asks me. "Which ones?"

I gulp. I've heard stories of him and his sister getting teachers fired over the silliest of excuses.

"Oh, it's not like that. They're not picking on me. Well, they are, but it's because I'm losing my scholarship."

Ash's brow lifts. "Oh, you're a scholarship kid?"

He didn't know that?

Yeah, why would he? He wouldn't keep tabs on who has scholarships. He's barely in classes, so I don't think he cares about what goes on in this school.

Speaking of which...

"So you're into this physics stuff?" I ask Ash. "I didn't peg you as studious."

The smile on Ash lips slides to the left in that effortlessly charismatic way. "I like things that make me think hard," he admits. "Otherwise, I get bored."

"Ah-huh," I say, not getting it at all.

"Hi, I'm here," a sweet voice calls.

I turn to the door as footsteps clip-clip into the classroom.

She takes my breath away. Her blonde ponytail swishes behind her head in time with the bounce in her step. I know she's Ash's girlfriend, because everyone at school is aware of that. Besides her relationship, I know zip about her.

As her eyes dart from me to Milo, and then land on Ash, she clasps her hands in front, her shoulders bunch high, and a pinkish hue graces her cheeks. It's as if she's nervous. Get real. She's probably attempting to appear humble in front of us mere mortals.

"Oh, am I interrupting?" she asks, pulling a blonde curl behind her ear.

"No, you're good," Ash says, stepping forward and curving an arm around her back.

He kisses her cheek and there may as well be love hearts in her eyes. There's your rom-com moment.

"Can you just give me a minute to finish up with Milo?" he asks her.

She nods as his arm falls off her. "Yeah, sure."

Ash motions at me. "Jamie's also hanging out until we're done."

She sucks in a breath and strains to smile at me. As Ash walks back over to the desk with Milo, she awkwardly waves.

"Hi," she mumbles.

Geez, girl, don't do me any favors by talking to me.

"Sorry, I know I've been at this school for a while now, but I don't recognize you from any classes."

I clear my throat and mutter, "Ahh, no, we…" Cue awkwardly dry cough. "I don't think… uh… umm, never mind."

"I'm Christie," she says. "Christie Klein."

I don't even want to talk to her, but I'm tongue-tied, regardless. I couldn't care less about what another rich kid thinks about me. But still, I stammer. "Jay… Jamie."

Christie smiles. "Do you go by Jay?"

Someone just hit me over the head, so I have an excuse to end this conversation. My face sizzles with embarrassment as I shake my head.

"Oh, okay," she says, maintaining the same happy smile. "Just Jamie then."

My eyes flick toward the boys. Milo is staring at me with a mixture of concern and confusion.

I swallow hard, hoping to get some moisture into my dry mouth. "It's Jamie West. If you're interested."

"It's nice to meet you."

"Sorry, it's a big school. I always find it hard to remember the name of the new kids." I side-eye Ash. "Despite whom they're dating."

Christie giggles. "Don't worry. I'm no one special."

I don't want to talk to this girl. Look at this fairytale she has with a billionaire's son. I really don't need to feel jealous of yet another couple.

Christie looks at me, turns to Milo, and then back at me. "So, Milo's your boyfriend?"

A laugh sputters out of me before I can control my reaction. I hold my belly, trying to mute the sound, but I've already attracted glances from the boys.

I clear my throat. "No. No way. He's my tutor."

"Oh, okay," Christie replies. "It just looked like we'd make a cute double date."

I grimace. "*Eww.* Really?"

Christie giggles. "Yeah, but I see you're not a fan of dating."

Geez. I gotta stop it with these disgusted faces and noises. Everyone assumes I don't want a boyfriend. I'm literally never gonna get one at this point.

"Are you okay?" Christie asks, examining my frown.

I shrug, clutching my elbows. "Yeah. I just came by for Milo's help with something. But it can wait until we have our actual tutoring session at Morton's Cafe."

"Oh, I've been meaning to try that place," Christie says.

"Really?" I ask with surprise.

"Sure," she replies. "It looks super cute. I heard they have awesome milkshakes."

I rub the back of my neck as I grin. "Yeah, we do."

Christie's eyes widen. "*We?* Do you work there?"

"Yeah, it's my aunt's cafe. Well, technically, I'm a part-owner, but I don't like thinking about that level of responsibility. Aunt Maddy agreed to keep me out of it until I'm eighteen."

"Wait. You're already a business owner at sixteen? That's impressive."

I shrug, smiling at the carpet. "I just inherited it."

Christie winces. "Oh, I'm sorry."

"Why?"

Her eyes widen. "Doesn't that mean someone died? And you said you co-own it with your aunt? Did your parents...?"

She looks severely freaked. She must have good parents.

I feel the boys' eyes on me, and I choose to joke, "Well, my dad might be alive."

Christie's expression morphs from freaked to horrified.

"I just..." My tongue is seizing up. "I don't know... I don't know my dad."

Her expression cranks back a few notches, although sadness coats her eyes.

"My mom is gone, but it was my gram's cafe." Sweat rolls down my brow. "She wasn't my real grandma, but that's a long story. Boy, I feel dizzy."

Christie reaches out and latches onto my arm. "Do you need to sit down?"

At that, the boys leave the desk and move over to us.

"I'm okay," I blurt. "Don't crowd me."

Everyone takes a step back.

A nervous laugh puffs out of me. "I've just never told another girl so much stuff about me."

Christie smiles and I note the confusion crinkling under her eyes. "Really?"

I shrug. "All my friends are boys."

"In that case, could we join you at the cafe after school?" Christie asks. "Would you mind?"

I smile at her and feel my nervousness washing away. "Not at all. You guys should come."

"Meet us at the limo and we'll go together," Ash says.

My chest constricts and I cough roughly. "Your limo?"

"Yeah," Ash says. "We may as well go together."

I look at Milo. He chews his lip and then shrugs.

"Jamie West and limo should never be in the same sentence," I say.

"I know how you feel," Christie says. "Going to school in a limo instead of a bus attracts a huge spotlight."

"Aren't you used to it?" I ask her.

She purses her lips and gives a slight shake of the head.

"We gotta go with them," Milo says. "Imagine how jealous Kai would be."

Something gnaws at my stomach. Kai told me he wouldn't drive Milo and me to the cafe because Tabitha wants a skateboard lesson. I'd pay to watch her fall on her butt. However, the more important takeaway is that Kai is ditching me for her again. Not cool.

I turn to Ash and smile. "Kai still brags about being online playing Shadow Quest at the same time as you."

"Oh, really?" Ash says, obviously having no recollection of it.

I nod, grinning. "He tried to recreate it so many times that soon, me and the guys started saying he made the whole thing up."

Ash shrugs. "I barely play that game."

The thought of texting Kai with a photo from inside the limo is too enticing to give up. "Okay, I'm in."

Eleven

"Hey, were you okay earlier?" Milo asks.

I shut my locker and give him a peculiar look. "What are you talking about?"

"With Christie and Ash," Milo elaborates. "You seemed a bit off, especially when you were talking with Christie."

My cheeks flush, and my stomach sloshes.

"Do you have a problem with her?" he asks.

I shake my head. "No, I don't know her."

"You just usually seem so cool and confident," Milo says. "I've never seen you act so nervous."

"It was nothing," I brush it off. "I guess I wasn't expecting to see them."

Milo nods reluctantly. "Yeah, okay."

Has he really never seen me splutter and stutter around other girls? Oh boy, it'd be a relief to know I'm not as obvious as I feel.

Milo and I walk the halls, pass through the foyer, and down the steps out of the school building. Before us, a limo sits idle. The back door is open and Milo beckons me to follow. My stomach sloshes again as Milo enters the limo.

Really? Are we seriously doing this? Driving to the cafe in a freaking limo?

I enter the limo and see Christie and Ash sitting on the seat that backs onto the partition between us and the driver.

Christie waves enthusiastically. "Hi guys."

We say hi back and Ash points a thumb at Christie, saying, "She hasn't stopped gushing about trying these milkshakes."

I clear my throat, hoping for words. I focus on Ash, and reply, "I hope they don't disappoint."

"I love anything sweet," Christie says with wild hand gestures. "Well, anything savory, too. Ash knows. He's caught me raiding the fridge too many times."

Ash smirks and kisses the top of Christie's head.

Okay, that was so adorable I could vomit.

"Did you tell Kai who you were leaving with?" Milo asks with a small smile.

"No," I say, pulling out my phone. "But I'm planning on making him jealous." I clear my throat and waggle my phone at Christie and Ash. "Do you mind if we take a selfie so I can tease my best friend?"

"Sure, but why didn't you bring her?" Christie asks.

My cheeks flush for a reason I'm not sure about. "Umm, he's a he. And he's choosing to be busy with his girlfriend."

"Oh, is it a new relationship?" Christie replies with a coy smile. "I can understand getting wrapped up in that."

I shrug. "I guess." I turn around in my seat and lift my phone high. "Everyone get ready."

Christie and Ash snuggle in behind me. As I frame us on the screen, Milo's face is notably absent.

"What are you doing?" I ask him. "Scooch in."

Milo fills with surprise. "Oh, really?"

I grin. "Seeing your face will help send Kai over the edge."

Milo smirks and scoots closer. I take three shots, hoping for a winner. One looks perfect and I send it to Kai without any context.

As Milo pulls away, I try not to focus on his body heat or the waft of his cologne. How is he pulling these reactions out of me? The boy needs to stop it.

It's only a short drive to Main Street. The limo pulls up outside Morton's Cafe and I feel super weird getting out. I hope no regulars see me and ask why I'm riding in the Ashworth's limousine. I can hardly comprehend how this happened.

Are Milo and Ash friends? How did nerdy Milo become friends with a billionaire? It can't be a love of math that brought them together.

Can it?

I show them inside and point out a booth. "Okay, you guys can take this booth and I'll get started on the milkshakes."

"Thanks, Jamie," Christie says sweetly as the three of them slide in.

"Umm," Aunt Maddy starts, giving a slight nod at the booth. "Why is Tom Ashworth's son in our cafe?"

"His girlfriend wanted to check it out." I nudge my shoulder their way. "She's the blonde over there. She's weirdly easy to talk to."

Maddy's mouth falls open as she grins. "What? Have you made friends with a girl?"

"I dunno if we're friends, but, umm, maybe."

Aunt Maddy cuddles into me. "Aww, baby, that's so awesome."

"Okay, okay," I whisper, wriggling out of the hug. "Don't make things weird. I'm probably two sentences away from doing that already."

"No sweat. Just act cool."

I laugh. "You're such a dork."

She pinches my cheek. "Takes one to know one."

"Come on," I say, beckoning Aunt Maddy toward the counter. "Christie wants to try a milkshake. They told me to surprise them with the order, so I was thinking we could make four different ones and add four straws to each shake. That way Christie gets to try all four."

"I'm prepared to make them everything on the menu," Aunt Maddy says, walking to the prep station with me. "Imagine if they love the food and want to use us for catering."

"I dunno if they know we do catering."

"Never a better time to let them know."

"Aunt Maddy, please don't embarrass me," I whine.

"Baby, there's no harm in putting it out there. Imagine working an event for the Ashworths." Maddy's eyes light up. "We'd never have to do another spot of advertising. The word of mouth would be epic."

"Let's just concentrate on making epic milkshakes."

Aunt Maddy opens the fridge by the prep station. "Sure. What flavors are we doing?"

"The Choc Peanut Butter Explosion is a must," I reply, readying the dry ingredients. "And who doesn't love the Strawberry Shortcake?"

"They need to try my favorite, the Salted Caramel Kettle Corn," Maddy adds. "Then it's either the Banoffee Mess or the Toasty S'more."

"Banoffee. We've already got a chocolate."

"Great. Let's get on it."

Maddy and I each work at a milkshake machine. Our milkshakes are legendary because of all the layers and ingredients we chuck in. We've perfected them over time so each one looks like an artwork. There's ice cream, fudge, sauces, sprinkles, candy, and so much good stuff to plop on top. Every mouthful bursts with happiness.

I walk ahead of Maddy and scoot into the booth, holding two shakes.

"Hi Milo," Aunt Maddy chirps as she lands at the table. "How are you?"

Milo smiles, murmuring, "Good, thanks."

"I'll put the Strawberry Shortcake in front of you," I say to Milo as I slide the glass toward him. "I know it's your favorite."

He tilts his head as he looks at me. "You remembered that?"

I shrug as my gut squeezes. "Sure, why wouldn't I? I mean, we have a lot of regulars with favorites that I remember."

Aunt Maddy smirks. "See, Milo. She is capable of memorizing facts."

Milo laughs, sliding the shake closer and aiming his lips at a straw.

"They all look amazing," Christie says, grinning.

"Hi, I'm Maddy West," Aunt Maddy says, placing the milkshakes down on the opposite side of the table. "I'm Jamie's aunt."

"Nice to meet you," Ash says as Christie slides a milkshake in front of him.

"You too," Maddy says with pep. "I've been dying to meet you guys."

Ash and Christie stare at her like she's shining bright headlights.

"*Psst*," I whisper out the side of my mouth. "Cool it."

Aunt Maddy giggles, waving her hands. "What I mean is, I wanted to meet someone from the Ashworth family. Even Ashworth family adjacent."

I groan. "Can you not?"

Maddy ignores me, leaning in. "Did Jamie tell you we also do catering?"

"Oh my gosh, Maddy," I cut through, "just leave."

Christie giggles. "It's cool. And no, I didn't know you catered. I can just imagine the looks on the society ladies faces if we had a garden party with milkshakes on this level."

Maddy winces. "No good?"

"I think it would make for a really fun party theme," Christie replies.

"Well, we do more than just milkshakes," Maddy says hurriedly. "We have a wide menu and can always create original dishes for the right event."

"*Aunt Maddy*," I groan. "Stop pitching. They're not asking."

Christies giggles again and Maddy pulls back.

"Okay, okay," Maddy says, surrendering. "I'll leave you guys to it. I hope you like the Salted Caramel Kettle Corn. It's my favorite."

"I'm a snacker," Christie admits, "so I'm sure I'll adore it."

I sigh. "Sorry about her. She just gets excited and loses her filter."

"Oh, please," Ash says. "Have you met my mother? I'd take your aunt any day of the week."

"She's the aunt who looks after you?" Christie says with surprise. "Was there a big age gap between her and your mom?"

Awkwardness quirks across my face. "Four years. My mom had me when she was sixteen."

Christie's mouth forms an o as her cheeks sink. "Oh."

"That would be tough," Ash comments.

I shrug. "She was the best mom."

Christie's face brightens. "I'm glad."

I gesture at the milkshakes. "We put in extra straws if everyone was to sample each."

Christie takes a straw of the Banoffee Mess in front of her. "You don't have to tell me twice."

The corners of Ash's eyes crinkle as he smiles at her. Goosebumps prick my shoulders. That's how someone in love looks at their person.

Ash tries the Salted Caramel Kettle Corn and deems it a winner. My ears prick to a soft cheer of triumph from Aunt Maddy as she wipes down a nearby table. Christie can't get enough of our last-minute entry, the Banoffee Mess. Overall, the milkshakes are deemed a success.

Inevitably, the boys fall back in physics homework talk on their side of the booth. Christie and I stay occupied with milkshakes as it becomes apparent we no longer have their attention.

"Sorry if I was weird back at school," Christie said softly. "I kinda assume people don't like me."

"Why would you assume that?"

She shrugs, twisting a loose curl. "Just habit. Ash is always on my case about judging people before I get to know them."

"I got the feeling *you* didn't like *me*," I admit. "But that would make sense to me. All the pretty, rich girls can't stand me."

"I don't know if I'd call myself either of those things."

"But don't you live at the Ashworth Estate?"

She nods. "Yes, but my family's not rich. At best, we're middle-class."

"That's not bad. It's still rich for a lot of people. It's way further up the ladder than a girl from Logan's Point."

"What's wrong with Logan's Point?" Christie asks. "Ash keeps prodding me to go hiking there."

"It's perfectly acceptable for adventuring, but it's unacceptable to live in. The town itself is rundown."

"Oh. You'd think people from Victoria Falls would pump money into its economy."

I smirk. "Then they wouldn't have somewhere to look down their noses at."

Christie giggles behind a cupped hand. "Sounds about right."

"What are you two talking about?" Ash asks.

"Logan's Point," Christie answers. "And why it's so-called *unacceptable*?"

Milo huffs. "It's so dumb. Just an excuse for people to be mean."

Tummy flutter. Again. Ugh. Chill out, stomach.

"I have to say it again. These shakes are amazing. Gosh, I can't believe I've never been here before," Christie says with amazement. "Meghan always likes going to Village Coffee at the other end of Main Street."

I swallow hard and fidget against the vinyl seat cushion. "Meghan? As in Meghan Fisher?"

Christie nods. "Yeah. You know her?"

A sour frown pulls at my lips. "Oh, I'm aware of her."

"Oh." Christie blows out a hard breath. "I always forget. She was a mean girl at Ashworth Academy before I moved here."

"It's fine. Let's just blow past the subject," I say, shaking my head.

"Hi kids," Coach Anders says with a wave as he strolls toward the counter. Everyone says hello back, and I can't help but grizzle.

"What was that about?" Ash asks. "Is there a problem with Coach Anders? Because if you need me to..."

"No!" I blurt, pushing my hands out like stop signs. "Coach Anders is the greatest teacher at our school. If you do anything, push the administration to give him a raise."

Ash smirks. "So, what was with the hostility?"

"He benched me from the soccer team."

"That's rough. What did you do?"

"Have sucky grades." I frown until a shiny idea pops into my head. "Hey, wait a minute. Can you help with that?"

Ash's eyebrows lift. "Help with what?"

"You're like the king of the school, aren't you? Can you make a call and get the school to stop threatening to take away my scholarship?"

Ash winces. "I don't think so. It'll set a dangerous precedent."

"Dangerous?" I question. "How so? All I need is for the administration to get off my back."

Ash shakes his head. "Ashworth Academy doesn't want to set a lazy academic standard. Sorry, you gotta put in the work."

"Says you," I protest. "You barely turn up to classes."

He smirks. "But my grades don't suck."

I groan and flop back in my seat.

Across from me, Christie frowns and mouths, "Sorry."

I shrug a response.

The conversation falls back to Milo and Ash's homework assignment. Christie leans into Ash, curling her arm around his bicep. When she dreamily rests her head on his shoulder, listening to the boys' conversation, it almost feels like steam will come out of my ears.

I didn't sign-up to sit across from a real life rom-com couple. They are super adorable together, especially when Ash runs his fingers across Christie's hand as he continues to talk with Milo. But I don't need to see any more cuteness when it comes to couples.

I excuse myself from the table, saying I need to check in with my aunt.

When I leave the table, I find Aunt Maddy talking with Coach at his table. He cups a mug of black coffee, listening intently to Maddy.

"Hawaii?" Coach says with surprise as he sits back. "Wow, what an escape."

"I didn't even know she needed an escape from life," I butt in.

Coach turns to me, greeting me with a small smile. "I know it's rough, kid. First time you two will be apart."

My shoulders slump and I step closer to Maddy. "It's gonna be totally weird."

"You know, if you need anything, you can always knock on my door at school," Coach says.

I bat my eyelashes and put on my sweetest smile. "I need to get back on the team."

Coach frowns. "That's not exactly what I meant."

I lift my hands innocently. "You said *anything*."

Aunt Maddy nudges me. "Stop being a troublemaker."

"You want me to stop being me?" I joke.

"Hey, I gotta go," Milo says, sidling up to us. "I know we haven't done any studying yet, but I have to get home before my grandparents arrive. If you need help with anything before classes tomorrow, we could always meet up before school?"

I shake my head. "I can't tomorrow. I have soccer practice."

Coach leans forward. "Maddy told me Milo is tutoring you, but it looked like a lot of socializing. Why didn't you study today?"

I shrug, guilt rising inside me as Coach stares me down. "I dunno. Christie and Ash wanted to hang out?"

"And how is that a valid excuse?" he presses. "I thought we agreed you'd prioritize your studies."

I huff. "Yeah, and I have..."

He cuts me off. "Doesn't look like it, kid. I think you'd better skip practice to catch up on homework."

"*What?*" I gasp. "That's not fair. You've already kicked me out of games. You can't take training away, too."

"You promised me you'd work harder when it came to your classes," he rebuts. "And I'm already seeing you slack off."

"Coach Anders, that's not really fair," Milo says in a low voice as he fidgets with the frame of his glasses. "Jamie has been working hard this week. I didn't tell Ash or Christie we were busy, either."

"Milo, it's not really the same when you're a grade-A student," Coach replies. "But I appreciate you sticking up for Jamie."

I grin eagerly. "So I can go to practice tomorrow?"

Coach smiles and shakes his head. "No, not tomorrow. We'll re-evaluate it next week. You need to keep focusing on classes right now."

I look up at the ceiling and groan.

Aunt Maddy slings an arm around me. "Toughen up, baby. You know he's right."

Milo waves, walking backwards. "Okay, text me where to meet up tomorrow."

"Bye Milo," Maddy says with a wave.

I huff and nod at him. "Yeah, okay. Bye."

Christie and Ash leave the booth as Milo heads for the door. Ash waves, following Milo out, but Christie walks toward us.

"Excuse me, Miss West," Christie says, joining us.

"Yes," Maddy replies eagerly. "Please call me Maddy."

Christie blushes. "Okay then. I just wanted to say, my mom is meeting with some society ladies about upcoming functions. I was wondering if you'd have a card I could pass along."

Maddy's eyes widen, and she hastily digs inside her apron pocket. "Yes, yes!" She plucks out a card and pen and scribbles on the back. "That's my cell on the back. Please get them to call that literally anytime day or night."

Christie giggles. "I'll pass on how eager you are."

Maddy bounces in place. "Please do."

"Aunty," I whisper out the side of my mouth. "Cool it."

Christie swats a hand. "It's totally cute." She tucks Maddy's card into her pocket. "Thanks so much for today. The milkshakes were beyond amazing. See you at school, Jamie."

A weird squeak comes out instead of a proper goodbye, but I cover with an enthusiastic wave.

Christie leaves the cafe and I help Maddy clear the booth.

"Whoa," Maddy murmurs, swiping a wad of cash. "That's a monster tip."

"*Geez.*" I gasp. "We need Milo to bring Ashworth in here more often."

Maddy hands me the cash. "Keep this. You might need it while I'm away."

"Are you sure? We usually split tips."

"Christie took my card with her, so I'm on cloud nine right now."

I pocket the cash. "Okay, if you say so."

The afternoon went slowly, with a dwindling number of customers. Coach left with one more lecture about studying over socializing. I gave him my best eye roll. I haven't been to the skatepark since Sunday, so I think that speaks volumes about my lack of socializing.

Kai texted back an hour after Christie and Ash left. *"What! You're hanging out with Ash? Without me!! How did this happen?"*

I took way longer than usual to reply. He needed to be taught a lesson. Just because he's with his girlfriend doesn't mean he should forget about his phone or the existence of his best friend. If he'd read the text right away, maybe he could've joined us for milkshakes. He should think twice about ignoring me.

It was a relief when we finally closed. The feeling didn't last long when I found out David would meet us at home. Like, come on, they'll spend a week away together. Won't they see each other enough?

I can't say any of these thoughts to Maddy, or she'll call me jealous again. It's just after seeing fairytale-worthy Christie and Ash, I'm just done with couples parading in front of me. At least when I watch a movie there's a layer of distance between me and the characters.

While we eat dinner, Aunt Maddy's phone beeps and vibrates on the kitchen counter. She gets up to look at it and her casual demeanor swiftly changes.

"Oh my gosh!" Maddy squeals at her phone. "It's a text from Christie. Her mom said there's an upcoming garden party that's not finalized. We could be a contender for catering!"

"Whoa. It really is who you know," I reply.

David gets up and cuddles up to her. "Congratulations, honey."

"Don't congratulate me yet," Aunt Maddy says, staring at her phone. "There's a lot of work to do with the menu plan and interviewing the organizers. It's a different plan for whether it's a sit-down meal, or walking horderves, or both." She lowers her phone with a devastated expression. "Oh my gosh."

"What is it?" David and I chime in at once.

Aunt Maddy's elongated face turns to David. "I can't go to Hawaii."

David puffs a nervous laugh. "What? Why not?"

Maddy raises her phone with urgency. "*Hello*? A huge catering opportunity has popped up and I need to put my best game plan together. How will it look if I'm on vacation instead of meeting with prospective clients?"

"But you don't even have a date or numbers yet," David replies. "There's no need to panic."

Aunt Maddy paces away from him, landing by the sofa. "How can you say that? This is a big break for me." She looks at me with anxious eyes. "For us. I can't risk this."

"Honey," David says softly, moving toward her.

"No," I say, halting David. "Let me."

I move over to Aunt Maddy, and she takes some steady breaths.

I take both her hands in mine and exhale hard. "Aunt Maddy, you should go to Hawaii."

She grips onto me tightly and whispers, "This is the part where you get to tell me to stay."

I frown. "I know. But if you stay, I know you'll regret it. I don't want you to feel like that."

"But this job could be huge for us. I can't risk losing it before my foot's even in the door."

"Aunty, we live in the digital age. You can use a video call for the meeting."

"But I can't virtually give them food to try."

"No, but me, Laura, Jake, and even Kylie can work on the food. You can be the virtual charisma."

Aunt Maddy shakes her head, eyes filled with worry. "I need to oversee what's being plated up if they're trying our food for the first time."

"No, Aunty, you don't. Trust us. If you tell us what to do, we can do it. We've got your back."

"Oh my gosh," Maddy murmurs. "Since when did you get so grown up?"

I giggle. "I guess the moment you got that text."

Aunt Maddy wraps her arms around me, shivering as her breath patters against my shoulder. "Thanks, baby. I trust you."

David's antsy presence lingers beside us. "So, Hawaii is still on?"

Maddy giggles, pulling out of the hug. "Yes, Hawaii is still on."

Oh crud. What did I agree to? Not only am I losing Maddy, but now I'm coordinating a menu plan? Oh well, at least it gives me an excuse to take time off from studying.

"I'll have Jake and Laura take the lead on all this catering stuff," Maddy says, swiping under her eye. "I don't want anything taking time away from your studies."

Ugh. Get out of my head!

I nod. "Okay. Sounds good."

"Speaking of, finish up your dinner so you can hit the books," Maddy says. "No movies tonight because you skipped tutoring today."

"If I hadn't done that, we wouldn't have this potential catering job," I protest.

Maddy smirks. "It's funny how things work out, isn't it?"

Ugh. I send my eyes into a massive roll and move back to my plate. I wonder how long I can drag out this meal.

Twelve

I expected a lecture from Maddy on the way to school this morning. Instead, she was too busy discussing her travel itinerary and all the things she needs to pack. That then morphed into needing to buy new swimwear and evening dresses. She then giggled, saying she wouldn't buy now. She'd wait and have a shopping spree in Hawaii.

A shopping spree. In Hawaii.

These are the things my aunt got excited about this morning.

Me. I get the luxury of a study session in the library while missing out on soccer practice.

Milo sits across from me, flipping pages. Every curl of paper makes my skin crawl.

I can't stand his face this morning. I tap my pen against the woodgrain of the table. I stare at him and rage boils inside me.

Milo's eyes leave his book and lock onto my pen. His gaze flicks up to me and his eyebrows lift.

"What?" I say bluntly, holding his stare.

He motions to the pen. "Must you?"

I tap the pen harder and to a faster beat. "I must."

Milo huffs, slouching in his seat. "You're in a mood."

"You think?" I snap. "I'm missing soccer practice and it's all your fault."

At that, he sits taller. "My fault?"

"Yes. You opened your big yap in front of Coach and made me look bad. We only missed out on studying yesterday because you brought your friends along."

Milo's eyes scrunch closed as he shakes his head, comprehending my words. When he stills and opens his eyes, he asks, "Is that how you saw yesterday?"

My hand throbs from smashing the pen against the tabletop, but my frustration won't let me stop. "I didn't at the time, or I wouldn't have let you sabotage me."

"Sabotage? Excuse me for letting you have a minute to make a friend."

I scoff. "What's that supposed to mean?"

"You and Christie were hitting it off. I thought you were having a good time."

The pen slips out my hand, greased up by my sweat, and hits the carpet below. I fold my arms and huff. "What's it to you?"

"Whatever," Milo grumbles, refocusing on the page in front of him. "I don't care. Let's just finish these notes for history class."

With his eyes off me, my rigid arms slacken to my sides. I watch him underline a paragraph in his textbook. Without my incessant tapping, the silence is deafening.

My clammy hands flex at my sides and an uncomfortable pain knots in my stomach.

Do I want him to care?

"So, are you gonna pick up the pen, or what?" Milo asks, not looking up.

My teeth grit as he continues to mark up the page. After that comment, no, I don't want to pick up the pen. I'm just gonna silent-treatment him. He won't get anything else out of me today. I'm so fed up with being stuck with him. I'm sick of memorizing all these useless facts. I'm itching to run drills, not recall dates of when wars started and finished.

Milo still hasn't looked up.

Does he not care if I pick up the pen? Is he fine with me just sitting here doing nothing? Won't he try to get me to work? What if him not doing anything at this exact moment is the reason I have to leave Ashworth Academy?

Would that make him happy?

Hot air puffs out my nostrils as I groan and snatch the pen off the carpet.

"Do you want to copy my notes?" Milo asks once my pen is back on the table.

He still hasn't looked up.

Fine. If he's not giving eye contact, I'm not speaking to him.

I look at the question prompts from our teacher, but the words blur. I sit the pen on the page and frown. I don't want to be here. I want to be out on the field. This is so unfair. If my family were rich, I wouldn't have to learn this stuff, and I wouldn't be benched.

Kai would never be treated this way.

I look back at Milo, who still copies from his textbook. Why does he care about this stuff? He's smart enough to pass his classes without all the extra effort.

Good to my word, I only replied to Milo in a series of grunts for the rest of our tutoring session. It put me in a bad mood for the rest of the day. I have put in well below minimum effort in all of my classes. When I leave geography class with Tyler, a zombie could drag themself into the hallway quicker than me.

Following Tyler into the cafeteria, I hear my name called. I halt before reaching any of the tables and see my teammates; Leah, Dominica, and Hayley, storming toward me.

"How could you?" Dominica snaps.

"Huh?" I squeak, feeling claustrophobic as they surround me.

Hayley whacks my shoulder. "How could you be so selfish?"

"I don't know... What are you...?" My eyes dart around them. Seriously. Why are they getting in my face?

"Coach told us you're off the team," Leah says and stamps her foot. "How could you do this to us?"

I fold my arms and look at my shoes. "I'm just benched."

Hayley groans. "You weren't even at training today."

"I... I just..."

"You had to study," Dominica cuts in. "Don't you think we all have classes too? But we work hard so we don't jeopardize our place on the team."

Leah steps in close and I'm blasted by the heat of her frustration. "Don't you get it, Jamie? *Team*. It's about all of us. Not just our individual needs."

"No, I get it... I just... It wasn't a big deal," I splutter. "I don't..."

"No big deal?" Leah's voice goes up an octave. "Since when is a soccer game not a big deal?"

Sweat drizzles my forehead and my heart pounds to a nervous beat. Of course, it's a big deal. Not playing is killing me. I wish I could say it, but their angry expressions have me paralyzed.

"Don't you have anything to say for yourself?" Dominica asks.

"Can't you even apologize to us?" Hayley asks, her eyes rounding as she pouts.

I stare at them, my mouth falling open as I mumble whispered nothings.

Dominica's eyes narrow at me. "What's wrong with you? Why can't you talk properly?"

Hayley huffs, averting her eyes. "She's so frustrating."

"Let's just leave," Leah says gruffly, turning away. "She can go back to sitting with all the guys."

Hayley's groan reverberates. "How does she pull that off? So many guys are drawn to her."

Dominica smirks. "That's the frustrating part."

As the girls move away, Leah grumbles, "I bet she doesn't see how lucky she is."

My mouth hangs open. As the girls disappear toward their lunch table, it finally puffs out of me. "Lucky?"

One, why did they start talking about me like I wasn't there? Two, are they jealous I hang out with guys?

A feeble excuse for laughter hums out of me. Now, that's a joke. Do they think I can easily get a boyfriend? Oh, please!

Okay, so let's recap. The Miss Perfects call me a tomboy loser who'll never get a boyfriend. Now my soccer teammates are jealous because I'm friends with boys. How am I lucky to be constantly friend-zoned?

Alternatively, Christie thought I was dating Milo. *Eww.* Did she really think Milo was the best I could do? It's because of him I missed training this morning and now my teammates hate me more than they already did.

Grrr! That's it.

I stomp my feet, curl my hands into fists to the point they sting, and march toward my lunch table.

"I'm going to practice with you guys after school," I blurt as I screech a chair out.

Kai jolts, dropping his sandwich. He looks up at me, asking, "What, like to watch?"

My eyes widen as I shake my head and plop down on the seat. "Nope. I'm doing drills with you."

"All right," Tyler cheers with a loud clap. "It's been ages since we kicked the ball around with you."

Kai's eyebrows twitch as he leans in. "Didn't your coach say you couldn't touch a ball unless he was training you?"

I shrug. "Screw it."

Tabitha leans around Kai. "Is it normal for a girl to play on the boys' team?"

I lean forward and scream at her, "Butt out!"

When a horrified look crosses her face, I sit back. But I almost slip off the side of the chair. Because I wasn't leaning forward. My throat isn't scratchy. Because I didn't yell.

It was a very vivid daydream.

And now, as per usual, everyone is staring at me, wondering why I still haven't spoken.

I slide on my chair, sitting properly, and thump my elbows on the table.

Kai nudges his lunch tray by me. "Hungry?"

When I reach for a fry, Tabitha clears her throat and says, "Ah, babe, I wasn't done."

A blush sweeps across Kai's cheeks and his eyes vibrate like he's making the hardest decision of his life. Keep the tray by his best friend or nudge it across to his girlfriend.

I roll my eyes and decide for him. I shove the tray across, muttering, "I'm not hungry."

"Word around school has made everyone hungry for milkshakes," Kai says. "Apparently, Ash's girlfriend can't stop talking about them. I still can't believe you hung out with them and didn't call me. You know how much I want to hang out with that guy."

"Why? Because we all bore you?" I tease, gesturing at our friends.

"No," Kai replies. "He can get anything at a snap of a finger. I've overheard all the epic things he and his buddies get up to on the weekends."

Tabitha curls an arm around Kai's bicep. "We'd make such a cute double date."

Kai's eyes light up. "Do you know his girlfriend?"

"I'm working on it," Tabitha says, her enthusiasm growing at the same rate as Kai's.

I have to look away before my eyes go into a rolling spasm. Although, it does fill me with a little glee that my time with the school's it couple has also made Tabitha jealous. That's a nice bonus I hadn't intended on.

The end of the school day could not come sooner. Kai's team always trains on Thursday afternoons and Saturday mornings before games. I change into my soccer uniform and tighten my cleats. Kai meets me by the girl's locker room and jogs down to the field to approach his coach.

"What's this?" Coach Lyle asks with his hands on his hips.

Could he grimace any harder at me?

"Jamie missed her practice this morning," Kai says. "Can she join us?"

Coach Lyle smirks and folds his arms. "What do you think this is? I don't let just anyone join my team. Plus, if you blew off your practice, what makes you think I'd give you the honor of training with my boys?"

"I didn't blow it off," I reply. "Coach Anders told me to work on an assignment instead of going to practice. Now, I've got itchy feet and need to run drills."

"Come on, Coach," Kai urges. "Let her train with us. She's better than half the guys here."

"Half?" I scoff. "Okay, I'll be modest and play along."

Coach Lyle rocks his jaw and then shrugs. "Okay, what do I care? Go on, you two, get going."

Without another word, Kai and I break out in a jog, gaining speed on the rest of the team, who run along the edge of the field. I get some strange looks from the boys on the team, but Kai and Tyler tell them to take a hike.

After a run and some stretches, Coach Lyle has us juggling balls. This couldn't be more perfect. Kai and I love competing against each other to see who gets the highest number and breaks our record. Kai once got to nine-hundred and fifty-three. It still blows my mind. I hate to admit he's better than me. That's why I never admit it aloud.

My best is seven-hundred and two. I've spent so many hours in my tiny backyard practicing, and I still can't get higher. Many days it's hard just to break two-hundred. Coach Lyle wants us to do one-hundred in a row without dropping the ball. Some of the guys struggle with the stamina and self-discipline needed. Kai, on the other hand, gives me a knowing look, trying for that elusive one-thousand reps. Somehow, I don't think Coach Lyle will let us dedicate the entire practice session to beating our record. We can't stay on school grounds for the number of hours needed to meet that feat.

Kai and I stare each other down as we start on our one-hundred. His cocky smirk is off-putting, and I swiftly change focus to the ball, keeping my knees lifting high. I get a nice bouncy rhythm, juggling the ball off one thigh, to the other, and repeat. It's Zen as I count each time my legs connect with the ball. My head stays steady, my gaze laser-focused, with the ball crossing my vision every second and a half.

After my ninety-ninth hit, I cheer, "One-hundred!"

Thrown off, Kai's ball ricochets off his right knee and hurtles toward Tyler. Tyler yelps, losing control of his ball too.

"Man, what gives?" Tyler whines, moving in a semi-circle to gain control of the two balls.

"Sorry, man," Kai says with a laugh, stopping the ball after Tyler passes. "I didn't expect Jamie to blitz me like that. I was only up to eighty-six."

I poke my tongue out at him. "Looks like you've gotta start over, bro."

Kai laughs. "Taunting isn't a good color on you, James."

I grin. "Since when has that stopped me?"

Five boys on the team can't get through one-hundred uninterrupted juggles, and Coach Lyle has them run more laps. The rest of us move onto the next drill.

Coach Lyle announces he wants to work on fake-outs. "It's all about footwork, misdirection, and juggling, like you've been practicing."

He then demonstrates a rainbow kick. He grabs the ball with his left foot and rolls it along the back of his right foot. Leaning forward, he pushes the ball into the air and kicks it over his head.

"Whoa," Kai breathes beside me.

"In motion, you want to push the ball forward first," Coach Lyle says, and then repeats the demonstration. He kicks the ball forward, runs on it, grabbing it and flicking it on the back of his foot. The ball becomes easily airborne and moves over his head.

I smile at Kai's eagerness to try the move. Happiness flutters inside me. My coach already taught me the move when I had excelled at the other drills he was teaching our team.

Kai dribbles his ball away from the group, finding space to work on the new move. I watch him recreate what Coach Lyle did. His tongue pokes out as he tries to get his footing correct.

"Uh, Kai," I say coyly. He looks up. "I think it's something like this."

I master the rainbow kick like it's the most basic of moves.

"What?" Kai asks, almost mad. "You can already do it?"

I flick my ponytail and roll my right foot over the ball without touching it, and then redirect with my left foot, passing it to him.

"Okay, you don't need to keep showing off your fancy footwork," Kai says, stopping the ball. He then flicks it onto the top of his foot, lifts it into the air, and then hits the ball with the inside of his foot. When the ball lands on the ground in front of him, he grabs it with his foot, rolling it under and keeping it locked under his foot.

"It's easy," I say, dribbling my ball up to him. I demonstrate the move again, reexplaining everything Coach Lyle already said.

"Okay, okay," he says, signalling for me to back off. "I got it."

Kai positions himself again and works out the mechanics of the move. The scar below his eye becomes more prominent as his focus narrows. Slowly, he rolls the ball up the back of his foot, anticipating the best time to kick it up and over. I cup a hand over my mouth, masking my silent giggle. I can't help remembering my time with Milo and teaching him the basics of the game. How are Kai and Milo identical twins? It makes no sense.

Kai has the right technique for rolling the ball up the back of his foot. He kicks the ball a few times, but not at the right trajectory to get it over his head. His expression is purposeful as he feels out the move. His next try, the ball successfully goes over his head. He cheers, "*Whoop,*" as he runs onto the ball in front of him.

"*Geez,*" I comment. "You picked that up fast."

He kicks the ball up, bounces it on his knee, and then onto his head. When he headbutts the ball, he replies, "Because I'm the best."

I'm not admitting it. I un-grit my teeth so it doesn't show on my face.

Kai continues practicing the rainbow kick until a truly satisfied smile graces his face.

"You wanna move onto something else?" Kai asks me. When I give a nod, Kai calls out to Tyler, "Hey Ty! Grab your gloves and we'll head down to the goal circle."

Tyler gives him a thumbs up and dashes to the sidelines for his gear. Tyler is their team's keeper, and he's exceptional at it. I can't wait to get a ball past him.

"You want to be defender?" Kai asks as we dribble down toward the goal posts.

I laugh. "Why? Do you need a challenge?"

"Oh, it's on," Kai teases.

When Tyler lands in front of the net, I position myself in front of him, ready to defend. Kai approaches with caution. At least that's how it appears. Kai loves a fake-out just as much as I do. His speed increases and he darts side to side with the ball. It's a simple trick to pull off, but defenders have tricks too.

I guess his moves correctly and manage to steal the ball. I flick the ball behind my foot and spin around to retake control, dribbling away from Kai. With enough space, I throw all my power behind a kick, shooting the ball out of the goal circle.

"Dang," Kai whines, chasing after the ball.

"Better luck next time," I tease, watching him collect the ball.

Kai rocks his jaw, locking eyes with me as he returns to the goal circle. I watch him intently, working out his next move. Kai goes again but passes the ball backward with his right foot. He rotates, angling his body to receive the ball with his left.

As he spins and circles around me to the right, I say, "So much for not showing off with fancy footwork."

He puffs a laugh as I press my body against his back. I jut out my foot to steal the ball, but he clips it and surges into a powerful midair kick.

Tyler defends the ball, passing it my way. When I get control of the ball, I zoom toward the top of the goal circle. Kai cuts in from the left, skidding to steal the ball. I get air under the ball and jump over Kai's foot.

"Nice one, James," Kai says, catching his breath.

I turn around and call out to Tyler. "Just forget I'm a defender for a sec!"

"Huh?" Tyler says, barely ready for my attack.

I angle myself, bend low, and swipe the ball hard and fast. It scuttles toward the goal posts and Tyler dives to catch it. He narrowly saves the ball.

"*Shoot,*" I hiss.

Tyler throws the ball back, and I take control. Kai comes in for the steal and our feet fight to take control. In the scuffle, the ball spins out, shooting left and nearing the goal circle.

I trip on my feet, attempting to spin and retrieve the ball. Kai makes a perfect getaway, keeping his balance and speed. He gains control of the ball, stopping it before it leaves the goal circle.

Kai doesn't turn around. Instead, he lifts one leg and bounces off the other, kicking the ball into the air. The ball swiftly flies over his head as Kai almost does a backflip. I've never seen him do a bicycle kick before. Someone, please help me pick my jaw off the ground.

The ball does a clean sweep past Tyler and hits the net.

"Dang, Kai. Since when can you do that?" I call out.

Kai swings around with a happy grin. "Just a little something I've been working on."

I still won't admit he's better. "Since when do you work on fancy tricks without me?"

"I needed something to one-up you with."

Wait? He thinks I'm the better one?

I smooth my hand over my ponytail and play it cool. "Well, I'm impressed. I bet it'll take me a lot less time to learn the move and perfect it."

"Are you saying I didn't pull that off perfectly?" Kai counters. "Because it was pretty near perfect to me."

"Since when is near perfect, perfect?" I tease. I wasn't insinuating anything, but how could I ever resist tormenting him?

Kai folds his arms, looking at me up and down. "I'd like to see you try it."

"Did you learn how to do it from a video tutorial?" I question. "I'd rather have Coach Anders teach me, so I don't break my back."

Kai puffs out a laugh and plants his hands on his hips. "Since when have you been too scared to try something new?"

I look around at the boys, running drills up the length of the field. Even though I've dreamed of switching to the boys' team for so long, I feel out of my comfort zone. I'm confident when I know the moves I'm pulling, but I don't want to try the stunt and fail. I don't want to be laughed out of here as an impostor and never invited back.

"Well?" Kai asks from the other side of the goal circle. "You gonna try?"

If there's anything worse than failing in front of a bunch of people, it's knocking back a challenge from my best friend.

I nod. "Okay. I'll give it a try."

"That's the way," Kai cheers. "Come over here. I'll teach you."

As I take a step toward him, a booming voice calls from the sidelines. "West!"

My skin grows icy cold. My shoulders stay rigid as I turn toward the voice.

Coach Anders stands on the sideline with his hands on his hips. His expression isn't stern enough to be mad, but he's definitely not happy.

Dang it. I'm so dumb. He always parks his truck in the west parking lot, which is right near the soccer field. Why didn't I think of that?

Duh. Because I literally didn't care and was dying to get out here.

A hand slowly lifts from his hip. He beckons me over and my gut plummets. What does this mean? Am I in big trouble? Like, officially off the team trouble?

When I stand there, motionless, he shouts, "Now!"

"James," Kai calls, jogging over to me. "I'll go with you. I'll talk him into going easy on you."

I shake my head and nod toward Coach. "No, I don't think that'll help right now. I'll see you later, okay?"

"Are you sure?" Kai asks with concern.

I give him a nod and then leave Kai and his teammates behind me. With every step toward my coach, a new knot forms along my back. Besides my aunt, he's the only adult I actually care about disappointing. And as I approach, it's clear that disappointment is all over his face.

"What do you think you're doing?" he asks in a reasonable tone.

"What?" I stammer, motioning behind me. "I just thought... Seeing as I missed this morning's practice... Plus, I caught up with studying..."

"Jamie," Coach says in a low tone that's wrapped in concern. "I was being serious when I said I didn't want you to touch a ball. You're a good player, I'll never deny that, but the sport consumes you. I need you to refocus because we can't afford to lose you from this school."

I dig my cleats into the ground as my gaze dips low. "Playing soccer won't make me lose my scholarship."

"But it doesn't help you keep it," Coach argues. "You have an academic scholarship and that's where you need to focus all your attention. I'm serious, Jamie. I need you to do better."

"I can't just snap my fingers and become a better student."

"But you can adjust your attitude."

I scoff and turn away from him.

"Come on, kiddo," he says, patting my shoulder. "Grab your gear and I'll drive you to the cafe."

"Can't I just finish the drills first?"

He frowns hard. "Am I talking to a brick wall or a functioning human?"

I huff. "Okay, okay. I'll get my stuff."

Coach doesn't talk on the car ride over to the cafe. At least he's smart enough to know he can't say anything without getting a snarky response. I clutch my elbows, squeezing my forearms against my ribs. The discomfort mixed with the gritting of my teeth is a good distraction from this hellish day.

"What's going on?" Aunt Maddy asks with concern. Her eyes dart from me to Coach, and then back to me.

"Are you going to tell your aunt what I caught you doing?" Coach asks.

I grumble. "Can we not make this seem like an earth-shattering big deal?"

"Jamie, what happened?" Aunt Maddy asks.

I huff and throw my arms up haphazardly. "I joined Kai for soccer practice."

Aunt Maddy's bottom lip drops, and she looks at Coach for further clarification.

"Jamie promised she'd only train with me," Coach says. "So, to find her with Coach Lyle's team was a broken promise."

"You joined Kai's soccer practice?" Aunt Maddy asks, pulling her phone from her pocket. "I thought you texted, you were studying with Milo at his house?"

I push down Maddy's phone before she opens the text messages. "You don't need to read it. We both know what I texted."

Aunt Maddy throws her hands in the air. "So, what gives? Why are you lying to me? And why are you going against what your coach asked you to do?"

I shrug, mumbling something that resembles, "I dunno."

"Worst of all, you're bailing on studying," Aunt Maddy says, heat rising in her voice. "What do you have to say for yourself?"

"Do you want me to say I messed up?" I raise my voice at her. "Soccer is the one thing I'm good at. I just wanted to feel good about myself for one moment on this crappy day."

Aunt Maddy's demeanor softens, and she runs the back of her hand against my cheek. "Why? What happened today?"

I groan and look away. "This whole week has been crappy."

"But you understand why you have to take your classes seriously?" Aunt Maddy asks.

I huff and give her a massive eye roll. "Yes. I'm not brain-dead."

"Jamie, I don't need this right now," Maddy says, her skin growing red. "You know I have to put in a lot of hours before I leave for Hawaii. I need to finalize a menu in two days, and I'm running out of time fast."

I pout. "I'm sorry to be such a nuisance to you."

Maddy gives an exasperated sigh and points to a table. "Can you please just do your homework?"

My shoulders slump and I lazily turn around. "Okay."

As I scuff my way to the table, I hear Aunt Maddy say behind me, "I just feel like it's all my fault, Brent. I've never asked her to do her homework before. I didn't expect her to be a smarty-pants, but I thought she'd at least coast through."

"Hey, it's a big deal becoming a guardian. You're doing your best. Plus, you two have this business on your shoulders. Trust me, you're kicking butt."

"Thanks," Maddy says with a happy sigh. "Can I get you a coffee?"

"I'd love one," Coach replies.

Thirteen

Thank goodness it's Friday. And I'm out of a classroom! Although I'm stuck teaching Milo, AKA Mr. Hopeless-Case, how to play soccer. At least I'm out on the field. I hate being cooped up inside all day. Why can't they mix it up and have English or history outside now and then?

Milo is getting out of his head. His class assignment in phys-ed is next period. If he can just remember to let his body do the talking, he might stay coordinated enough to get a good grade. I'm sure it's only a pass/fail grade, but if he continuously trips over his own feet, I don't see him passing.

"Do you feel more confident?" I ask with hope.

Milo stops the ball and his shoulders slump forward. "When it's just you and me, I feel less awkward. But just thinking about being in class, around the other guys, and my teacher's eyes scrutinizing me, it freaks me out."

"You're always telling me not to freak out with my classes. What has you so spooked about this one?"

Milo shrugs. "Years of history."

My stomach wobbles. "But you feel okay around me?"

He smiles, and the sun sparkles against his glasses. "Yeah. I don't know why."

I rub behind my neck and smile at the grass. "Oh."

"*Crap*," Milo hisses.

I look up to see his horrified expression. "What is it?"

Milo's eyes focus behind me, and I watch his throat constrict as he gulps.

I turn around and almost lose my balance as Coach Anders strides toward us.

"Are you serious, West?" he says in an I-mean-business tone.

"It's not what it looks like," I yelp, holding my hands out.

"Didn't I get through to you yesterday?" Coach asks, landing in front of us with a pointed stare.

"What happened yesterday?" Milo asks.

I open my mouth to speak, but embarrassment and shame clams me up.

"I caught her on the field, training with the boys' team," Coach says, with a smug smirk as he folds his arm.

Surprise lifts Milo's facial features. "I thought you said you were helping Maddy yesterday."

"Well, well, Jamie." Coach leans into his smugness. "Who haven't you lied to in the past twenty-four hours?"

I groan and roll my eyes. "It's not a big deal."

"I think your aunt would disagree," Coach says. "And don't forget, I knew your mom. I never knew her to be a liar. What do you think she'd say about this?"

I frown and my shoulders slump. "Don't bring her into this."

"Why, Jamie?" Coach questions. "Because she'd be disappointed?"

"She wouldn't be if she knew the truth," I reply, standing taller. I look at Milo and then back at Coach. "We weren't just fooling around. I'm teaching Milo some techniques."

"It's true," Milo pipes up. "I asked Jamie to give me some pointers."

Coach gives Milo an incredulous look. "And why would you do that?"

"Because, if you haven't noticed, I suck," Milo replies bluntly. "The class is huge, and I feel like I get lost in it. It doesn't seem to matter if I do well during class or not. Until it's report card time."

"Regardless of your soccer aptitude," Coach responds, "you have a brother capable of teaching you."

Milo fidgets, looking at me and then at his feet.

"Okay," Coach sighs. "You didn't want to go to your brother, but going to Jamie during this time wasn't the best decision."

"I'm studying with her every day," Milo replies. "I didn't think there'd be any harm."

"Phys-ed is the only class he's flunking," I say. "He wanted to be better, and I thought I could help."

"My class assignment is today," Milo says. "After today, I won't have any reason to kick a ball around with Jamie."

"Show me what you've got," Coach Anders says to Milo.

With a nervous exhale, Milo pushes his glasses back up his nose.

"Go on," Coach urges, staring him down.

I roll the soccer ball under my foot and nudge it over to Milo. He stumbles, trying to stop the ball, and it's painful to watch. The way he fidgets behind the ball looks more like nerves than poor technique. He had this before. Why does Coach watching throw him off his game?

Coach asks Milo to dribble the ball away from us and then kick it over to him. The ball gets away from Milo. When he regains control, he trips over it. When he aims at Coach, it's easy to see it won't reach him. Milo's shoulders aren't square and he's not looking ahead before he strikes. The ball lacks power behind it and bounces as it veers to the left.

Coach strolls toward the ball and picks it up. "Okay, I want you two to see me after school."

"What for?" I blurt.

"Looks like you'll both need some help to boost your grades," Coach replies. "I'll have a new assignment ready for you. You can collect it after your last class."

"Another assignment?" I complain. "You can't be serious. I already have a ton of extra homework."

Milo dawdles back to us, a frown drooping on his face.

"Your class is today?" Coach asks Milo.

He nods. "Next period."

"We haven't been goofing around," I tell Coach. "He's done so much better than that. He was just nervous." I look at Milo and sigh. "What happened?"

He lifts his hands and shrugs.

"Will you see me after school?" Coach asks him.

Milo nods.

"Good," Coach says. "Now, go run five laps of the field."

Milo's eyes pop behind his frames, and his Adam's apple bobs.

"I'll go with him," I offer in an attempt to sweet talk Coach.

He smirks at me. "It's not a punishment for you. I want you to get your butt to study hall and start on your homework."

I grimace. "What? But I..."

"Now, West. Or would you prefer detention?"

I lift my hands and back away. "Okay, okay. I'm going."

I glance at Milo, and he shrugs with a tentative smile.

"Nelson, did I stammer? Why aren't you running?" Coach barks, interrupting our moment.

Milo jolts and turns around. "Yes, Coach."

As Milo starts on his first lap, I trudge my way back into the school building and my awaiting geography homework.

I can't help thinking about Milo for the rest of the day. Kai is in the same phys-ed class, but bringing up his brother will seem totally weird, so I don't ask. It's already a given that Kai was the star of the class, so there's no good segue.

My last class for the day is history. I try to keep my eyes forward, but I can't help glancing in Milo's direction. He doesn't notice me the first two times, but on the third look, we lock eyes.

I squeak a gasp and face front.

What the heck was that noise? Oh geez, now my face is heating up.

"Jamie," our teacher calls out.

Crap. Will he ask why I'm all embarrassed right now?

"Can you tell me the significance of 1791 to American history?" he asks in a tone that presumes I wasn't listening.

Well, I wasn't listening. But I've memorized so many useless dates this week, an answer leaves my lips like muscle memory. "That's the year the first ten amendments were added to the Constitution."

His brow lifts, and he smiles. "Correct. And what are they called?"

"You mean, The Bill of Rights?"

"Perfect," he responds. He then picks out other students to name the amendments.

I slouch in my chair, happy to have the spotlight off me. Without thinking about it, I roll my head in Milo's direction. Our eyes lock and smile lines crinkle inside his frames. My heart warms with a flutter. I smile back.

When the bell rings, Milo is up in a flash. He carries his books over to my desk.

"Yeah?" I ask, looking up at him.

"I want to walk with you to see Coach Anders," Milo says. "I'm not walking into his office alone."

I shrug and stand up. I gather my books and reply, "Okay, fine with me."

When we get into the hall, we pass a few classrooms in silence. He hasn't told me how the class went, so it can't be good news.

"So." I bite my lip. "How was your phys-ed class?"

Milo scuffs his shoes along the tiled floor. "If you thought I was a hopeless case in front of Coach Anders, you don't want to know."

"Why were you so nervous in front of Coach?" I ask Milo. "All he wants to do is help."

Milo huffs. "I don't know. It was just easy when it was only you and me."

"I don't see why."

Milo digs his hands into the pockets of his trousers. "Thanks for sticking up for me, anyway."

"It's fine. I didn't want Coach to think I was using you as an excuse to get in some soccer practice." I roll my eyes. "Not that he saw anything that proved I was teaching you."

"We don't know how long he was watching us before he called out."

"After catching me training with Kai, I doubt it took him much time to pull the plug."

"Why did you do that? We could've kicked the ball around at my place if you wanted."

"It's not the same. I was angry that I'd missed practice, and then some of my teammates laid into me about jeopardizing the team. I just wanted to get back out there. With a team."

We get our backpacks from our lockers and make our way to Coach Anders's office. He shares it with two other coaches, one being Milo's phys-ed teacher, which accounts for him still acting nervous.

I knock on the door and push it open as Coach Anders says, "Come in."

When we see he's the only person inside, Milo exhales, and his body language loosens.

"Good, you're both here," Coach says with a happy grin. There's a distinct glint in his eyes. It's the same spark he has right before he tells us to run super hard drills.

Oh gosh, just what does he have in store for us now?

Coach reaches behind his desk and lifts something up. "Meet your new assignment."

A baby carrier lands on his desk.

"Huh?" Milo and I respond at once.

"Say hello to your infant simulator," Coach says, turning the carrier so we can see a freakishly realistic baby sitting inside.

"I don't get it," I mutter.

"You two will care for this baby for the next forty-eight hours. I'll pick him up on Sunday during your shift at the cafe," Coach explains.

Milo gives me a dumbfounded look, and then says to Coach, "You want us to carry a doll around for two days? That'll make up for our grades?"

Coach slides two wrist bands across his desk. "You'll each wear one of these. They monitor your interaction with the baby. The good and the bad. This isn't just a doll, it's a real-life robotic simulator. It will cry, need feeding and changing, and also comfort."

"How the heck am I supposed to look after a baby while juggling all my classes and working at the cafe?" I ask, feeling a monster headache setting in.

"Obviously your phys-ed class marks aren't an issue," Coach says to me, "but this can count toward your health class marks. A boost in that class will help raise your grade average. Are you willing to make that happen?"

"Yeah, I guess. But..."

Coach cuts me off, saying to Milo, "This assignment has enough physical components that Coach Lyle and I have agreed this assignment will count towards your phys-ed criteria. If you complete this task successfully over the next few days, you won't have to worry about the lack of skill you've shown over your past phys-ed assignments."

Milo fidgets with the left earpiece of his glasses, thinking it over.

"You can each take one night to look after him," Coach says. "Jamie, you can take him home tonight, and then Milo can cover Saturday night."

"But that doesn't give me a night away from it," I protest. "I'm staying with him this weekend."

Coach looks between us, and Milo says, "Jamie's staying at my house while Maddy's away."

"Then this should make it easy for you two to work together," Coach replies. "Hopefully better than your last project. Milo's skills didn't exactly shine today."

"He shouldn't be punished for not being a sporty person," I say. "Not that I'm trying to say I should be punished for not being academically gifted."

"You haven't been giving your schoolwork your full attention," Coach says. "I know you're smarter than you give yourself credit. I want you to prove it to yourself."

I screw up my face. "What does that mean?"

"What everyone has been telling you all week. Focus up," Coach says. "But instead of doing it because everyone is telling you to, do it to prove to yourself you can."

I wince. "That would be easier if I cared about schoolwork."

Coach laughs. "I think by how much effort you've already put in shows you do care. Deep down. Okay, maybe deep, deep down."

I smooth my hand over my ponytail and exhale slowly. "Okay, if we do take on this assignment, what exactly is involved?"

"I've sent a full guide to your emails on the student portal," Coach says, pulling the robot baby out of the carrier. "Once we activate him, he will act like a real-life baby. He will cry in different volumes and pitches, and over time you will need to work out what each cry means. He will need to be fed, and held, and even need a diaper change."

"*Gross,*" I whine.

Coach laughs. "He doesn't take in or expel liquid. It's just a simulation." He lifts a bag. "Inside is his bottle and diaper. They have sensors in them to recognize the baby is getting what he needs." Coach holds the baby by the ankle. "The sensors will pick up abuse and mishandling. No holding him incorrectly. You need to cradle him, supporting the neck. Even in the car, you need to ensure you strap in the carrier. The baby must be secure so his head doesn't bop around."

"And you said we have to look after him overnight?" Milo asks. "But there's an off switch, right?"

Coach smirks, enjoying this a little too much. "There's no off switch. Once he's activated, he doesn't turn off until the forty-eight hours are over." He motions to the wristbands. "Ready to get started?"

I give Milo an uneasy look and he shrugs. "It'll help your grades."

I wince. "But it's looking after a baby."

Milo grabs a wristband. "How hard can it be?"

"That's the spirit," Coach says. "Plus, Jamie, it's one assignment closer to getting off the bench."

"Ugh. Fine." I swipe the orange wristband and clasp it around my wrist. It pops when clicked in place. The top button completely suctions over the bottom button.

"Here we go," Coach says, activating the baby. "Good luck."

Coach moves to hand me the baby, but I recoil. "*Eep.* I don't want it."

Milo laughs, moving over to Coach with bent and ready arms. "I'll take it."

Milo cradles the baby, and I watch as Coach shows the proper way to support his neck. Oh my gosh, this is so crazy. We are talking about this thing like it's real. It's a freaky plastic doll.

The baby makes a gurgling sound and Milo jolts. "What was that?"

"It's one of the sounds you'll need to become familiar with," Coach replies. "But I'll give you a freebie. That's a happy sound."

"Why does the school even have this baby simulator?" I ask Coach.

"We have twelve," Coach replies. "They're for students enrolled in the early childhood development class. They are also available to health classes, but we haven't added it to the curriculum for a couple of years. We were unhappy with what messaging it was actually providing for the class."

"But you're happy for Milo and I to deal with this?" I question.

"You two are smart and capable young adults," Coach says proudly. "And you can contact me via the student portal if you need any help or support.

Now, I've got to get going across town. I need to help out at the senior football game."

Milo gently places the baby in its carrier, and I sling the baby bag over my shoulder.

"You two will be fine," Coach says, walking us out of his office. "Just make sure he stays alive."

I give him a horrified look. "Does that mean we can kill it?"

Coach pats my shoulder. "Just make sure he gets what he needs."

"Oh, brother," I say glumly. "This will be tough."

Coach laughs. "I wouldn't exactly call it a piece of cake. He will need a lot of attention. And, by the way, the wristbands are tamper-proof, so there's no getting them off until Sunday afternoon."

Milo flexes his arm, hanging the carrier inside his elbow. "It's okay. We got this."

"It goes without saying, you don't need to be at the game on Saturday," Coach tells me.

The wind is knocked out of me. "What? But you've always said, even if we're a benchwarmer, we need to show up at every game or there are consequences. Like keeping us out of future games."

"There are always exceptions," Coach replies. "Like when Dominica missed a game for her grandfather's funeral. Your grades are important enough to miss a Saturday morning of bench-warming."

"But I can watch a robot baby and sit on the bench at the same time."

Coach shakes his head. "No. You can look after the baby and also complete your other assignments."

I give him a defeated huff and slump forward.

"See you Sunday," Coach says.

I frown and wave. "See you Sunday."

"I'll order an extra-large pancake stack to make up for your tiring weekend."

"It's funny how after we strapped on these wristbands, you started skewing this assignment to the negative."

He laughs, waving me off. "You'll be fine. I promise."

I catch up to Milo, thankful the hall is emptying as he carries this baby carrier with zero context.

As we walk through the foyer, I glance at the carrier and ask, "Are you okay carrying that?"

"Yeah, it's fine."

"Even if we walk to the cafe?"

"Yeah, it's no sweat," Milo answers. "At least we'll be in the same house for most of this assignment."

"Yeah, but I was hoping when I wasn't working, I'd be at the skatepark with Kai."

"Maybe you can take him with you?" Milo suggests. "It can't be as hard as Coach Anders made out."

As if on cue, the baby makes another gurgling noise.

I shudder. "I don't like that it makes noises unprompted. It's so freaky."

"All we have to do is interact with it. At least we don't have to write a paper."

I nod. "That is a bonus."

We walk across the front lawns of the school and head for the footpath, which leads toward Main Street.

Kai, Parker, and Lewis hang by the fence and immediately spot us.

Kai laughs at the sight of us. "What's this? Why do you have a baby carrier?"

"It's my new assignment," I reply. "I'm paired up with Milo."

"Huh? Since when?" Kai asks, confused. "What class is this for?"

"It's extra-credit to make up for other assignments we didn't pass," Milo says.

Kai stifles a laugh. "What, like not being able to kick a ball straight?"

"Wait, they can just give you a baby assignment?" Parker says with alarm. "How bad do your grades need to be to be dumped with this?"

Lewis nudges him and motions at Milo. "It can't take that much if Milo has the assignment."

Milo shakes his head, his gaze low as he tries to ignore the boys. "We'd better go," he murmurs to me.

"We're just waiting for Tyler to catch up and then we're heading to the park," Kai says. "You coming?"

I motion to the carrier Milo is carrying. "Hello? I just told you I have a new assignment."

Kai shrugs. "So?"

"I can't just ditch it," I argue. "It has motion sensors for if I'm around or not."

Kai winces and points at Milo. "Let him do it. It's not like it wasn't obvious he'd fail that phys-ed assignment. He knew what he was in for."

I was blaming Milo for this mess because hanging out with Christie and Ash led to me missing a tutoring session. But really, it's all Kai's fault. Him and his obsession with Tabitha Jones. If they weren't so barf-inducing, I could've stayed at my lunch table and never spoken a word to Christie. Everything would've gone along as per normal. I'd be hanging with my friends and only dealing with Milo in small doses.

I've just mentioned I wanted to spend my weekend with my best friend at the skatepark, but as if that'll happen. How many times this week has he already blown me off for Tabitha? How could I expect this weekend to be any different?

"If you knew he'd fail, why didn't you teach him something?" I ask Kai.

Kai screws up his face. "*Pfft.* I've known this guy long enough to know giving him pointers is a lost cause."

"*Pfft.*" I bat a hand, turning away from Kai. "Whatever."

"Whoa. What gives? Are you dissing me, Jamie?" Kai asks, stepping up to me. "What? Are you blaming me for this stupid baby project because I didn't help Milo? I don't even understand why you two are paired up for this."

I turn around and smack into Kai's chest. I step back with a huff. "Milo's in this because he cares about his grades. I'm here because, unlike some people, I have to study to stay in school."

"James, stop being all huffy with me," Kai says, opening his arms wide. "I was just kidding around with you. Come on, give me a hug."

I take the carrier from Milo. "Sorry, my hands are full."

"James, what the heck?" Kai asks, dropping his arms to his sides. "Are you really mad at me?"

"No," I say, pacing away from them. "I'm just mad."

As I continue at a hurried pace, Milo's heavy footsteps chase behind in order to keep up.

"Hey, are you okay?" he asks, reaching my side.

I don't give him a response. Instead, I continue in my angry march. Hot, sticky sweat coats the back of my neck and clings to my shirt collar.

"Let me take that," Milo says, reaching for the carrier.

"Fine," I mumble, relinquishing control.

My mind blackens as I try to calm the storm of emotions swirling inside of me. I look down at the baby carrier, and then up at Milo's face. It's becoming increasingly harder to comprehend the topsy-turvy nature of my life.

Fourteen

Our walk to Main Street was mostly silent. Periodically we'd check on the baby. It was eerily quiet, and we didn't know if it was a good or bad sign. Coach said we needed to identify different cries, and so far we'd only heard random gurgling.

When we enter the cafe, Aunt Maddy double-takes at the carrier. "Umm. What is this?"

Milo flips it around so Maddy can see the fake baby.

"Coach Anders wants us to look after it all weekend," I explain. "It's an extra credit assignment for the both of us."

Aunt Maddy grins at the baby and fights to hold back a laugh. "So, you two sixteen-year-olds have to look after a baby? Okay, cool."

"Why do you look like you're enjoying this concept?" I question.

Aunt Maddy smirks. "It's just ironic."

I pout. "Why? Because of Mom?"

Maddy's face brightens as she nods.

"But, come on," I say, latching onto my hips, "you can't be for this impromptu assignment. It's your last night, we're still working on the catering menu, and I have a ton of other homework."

Aunt Maddy finally lets her giggles out. "Oh, I'm more than fine with this. My problems are nothing compared to when I was twelve and helping care for a real-life baby." Maddy leans down and plucks the fake baby out of the carrier. "Besides, this one hasn't even made a sound."

Cradled in Maddy's arms, the fake baby gurgles.

Maddy giggles. "Oh, so he does work."

Milo shows off his wristband. "He's active for forty-eight hours and these bands monitor how we interact with him."

"So, you really think it's cool that Coach lumped us with this assignment?" I ask.

Aunt Maddy grins. "I'm just sad I won't be able to see all of this play out. You are so spoiled, Jamie. I can't imagine you devoting forty-eight hours to looking after someone else."

My jaw drops and I let out an indignant gasp. "Spoiled? Me?"

"It's not your fault," Aunt Maddy replies. "Lily and I agreed we never wanted you to struggle for anything."

My stomach sloshes like any time Mom is brought up.

Aunt Maddy offers the baby to me and I recoil. Luckily, Milo goes in for the handoff.

"I'm just going to sit in a booth with Milo," I tell Aunt Maddy. "We need to read through the guidelines Coach sent us. Then I'll be free to help you with the catering stuff." I turn to Milo. "Is that cool?"

Milo nods. "Yeah, I can look after him now, seeing as you're taking him tonight."

Aunt Maddy giggles. "Oh good. I do get to see some of your suffering."

I groan. "Aunt Maddy, you are enjoying this a little too much."

Milo sets the baby back in the carrier and follows me to the booth. When we sit, Milo takes out his phone, opening the attachment Coach sent. He reads through the first lines of description, which mention the wristbands, proper care versus mishandling, and sensor-enabled diapers and bottles.

After he reads the part about the different sounds the baby emits, he grimaces as he continues, "...And although your baby might cry when he or she needs a diaper change, in some cases, the baby will emit an odor, signifying he or she needs changing."

"Ugh. Gross." I wince. "It farts?"

Milo laughs. "Coach said it was realistic. It also says after feeding it needs to be burped, which sometimes is a short process, but sometimes can be lengthy."

"Lengthy? That sounds ominous."

Milo flips his phone to show the screen. "There are diagrams on how to do everything."

"I'm already exhausted thinking about it."

"It says one of the first things we should do is name the baby to establish a bond," Milo says. "Should we name him now?"

"We should just call him Baby, like my mom did for me."

"What do you mean?"

I smirk. "My name was literally Baby West for the first six months of my life."

Milo laughs. "What? How is that possible?"

"That's how long you legally have to name a child. Mom said she already had too much responsibility, and naming a human was over her limit."

"Whoa. I can't imagine being that stressed out."

I look down at the baby and shake my head. "Neither can I."

"Is that why Maddy calls you baby?" Milo asks.

I smile and nod. "She bonded with me as Baby while she babysat when Mom worked nights. She likes it, no matter how many times I tell her to retire the nickname."

"Seems like both your mom and your aunt had to work really hard."

"Yeah, I guess that's why Maddy laughed when she saw this thing. Our lives are easy now compared to when I was born."

"Hey, he's a baby, not a thing," Milo jokes. "Anyway, the assignment says we should name our baby."

"*Eww.*" I grimace. "Don't use the words *our baby.*"

Milo laughs, showing me his phone screen. "It literally says that, though."

"I don't want to think of this thing as my baby," I argue. "I especially don't want any weird images in my mind of this somehow being our baby."

Milo's face screws up, causing his glasses to slide. "Why would you think like that? The baby's fake and this is an assignment."

"Maybe the wording hits me harder." I shrug. "I dunno."

"So," Milo draws out the word. "You don't want to name it?"

"You can. I don't care what you call it."

Milo takes the baby out of the carrier. "Shouldn't it be a team effort?"

"No, I'll give you full control. Naming a baby isn't something I want to do."

"Because of your mom?"

I shake my head. "No. It just feels off."

"He can just be Baby, if you prefer."

"No, name him something, so it's not confusing."

Milo tilts the baby in his arms so I can see his face. "Don't you think he looks like a Gandalf?"

I splutter a laugh. "Like the wizard?"

Milo grins. "Yeah."

"He's a baby, not ancient."

"Maybe if we give him a magical name, he'll be a good baby for us."

I pinch the bridge of my nose as my shoulders shake from my laugh. "Oh Milo, you're such a nerd."

"So, is that a no on Gandalf?"

I laugh and can't help but smile at Milo's silly suggestion. "No, let's go with it. We have baby Gandalf."

Milo sits back with a happy grin. "All right, awesome."

Oh my gosh, Milo looks so adorable cradling that baby. Whoa, wait. Adorable? Milo? No, I'm just in a good mood because of the baby's wacky name. That's it. I don't think Milo's cute. It's his suggestion that was cute. Not that Milo was being cute. Ugh. *Jamie, stop going round in circles!*

"Are you okay?" Milo asks, looking up from the baby.

"Yeah," I say, swatting a hand as if I'm cool as a cucumber. "Just got a million things running through my head."

He nods. "I know. This isn't ideal timing with your aunt going away."

"I still have her help tonight."

"So you'll be okay taking him overnight?"

I nod. "Yeah, I need the boost in grades the most. Plus, I feel like I got us into this mess."

"We wouldn't have been out on the field if I hadn't asked you for help."

"You heard about yesterday. I would've found a way out there, with or without you."

"I'm sorry you're off the team," Milo says sincerely. "I know I'd hate it if I was banned from doing something I love."

"I don't think you have anything to worry about. No one will ban you from reading anytime soon."

Milo smirks and looks back down at the baby. "Yeah, that's all I do for fun."

Before I can ask him to elaborate, because I literally don't know any of Milo's other hobbies, Aunt Maddy comes over.

"How's everything going, guys?" she asks, bending at the knees by Milo's side. "Are you comfortable holding him?"

"Seems okay at the moment," Milo replies.

Aunt Maddy checks how Milo holds the baby and nods her approval. "Nice. His neck is all secure, and he looks cozy. Does the little guy have a name yet?"

At that, Milo and I burst into laughter.

"What?" Maddy asks, standing tall. "What did I say?"

"You tell her," Milo says, grinning at me.

"Gandalf," I tell her, unable to keep a straight face.

Surprise takes over Maddy's expression. "As in, Lord of the Rings?"

"Yep," Milo and I reply at once.

Aunt Maddy giggles. "Okay, very unique. Jamie, can you come with me? Milo looks like he has things covered now."

"Yep," I say, sliding out of the booth. "Call out if you need help."

"We'll be fine," Milo says, freeing a hand to wave goodbye.

I wave back. "Bye bye, Gandalf."

Aunt Maddy giggles as we walk away. "Ridiculous."

I laugh with her. "I know. But what do you expect from a guy who named his cat after Batman's butler?"

Aunt Maddy looks at me strangely. "Are you serious?"

I grin, nodding. "Mhmm. That's where Alfred's name came from."

"Oh my gosh, that's too much."

Aunt Maddy shows me her progress with the catering menu. She walked me through the concept last night after we closed the cafe. Now, she's put much more work into it. Clearly overcompensating because she won't be at the meeting in person.

Mrs. Fisher, the head of the organizing committee, arranged a menu tasting on Monday afternoon. Again, Maddy wanted to come home from Hawaii after the weekend. It took all my strength not to encourage the idea. There's only so long I can continue being selfless.

When we catered the other society event, it was on a bigger scale than a simple garden party. Nevertheless, Maddy tells me she wants us to make a mark. She wants the food to be the star, forcing every guest to take a card for their next event.

We're about ten minutes into work when the distinct cries of a baby break our concentration.

"Jamie," Milo calls from the booth, craning his neck. "Come here and work out this cry with me."

"Aunt Maddy, will you come with me?"

Maddy stifles a giggle and nods. "Sure."

When we get to the booth, Gandalf is fussing with whimpering noises. Before I can make a suggestion, he lets out a high-volume wail that cracks into a hysterical cry.

My hands launch over my ears. "Good lord. What is he, Satan spawn?"

"Has he been fed yet?" Aunt Maddy suggests.

I slide over to the opposite side of the booth to grasp the baby bag. I pluck the bottle from inside and hand it to Milo. "Here."

Milo takes it. "You don't want to try it first?"

I can't hide my freaked-out expression. "No way."

Milo laughs, cradling the baby and pressing the nip of the bottle to his mouth. A happy suckling sound emits from the baby.

"*Phew,*" I breathe out. "The crying stopped. Thanks, Aunt Maddy."

"It's no problem. I'm guessing after his bottle, he'll most likely need changing, and then sleep," Aunt Maddy replies.

"How do I know if he's done?" Milo asks.

Maddy bites her lip in a devilish way that Milo doesn't catch. "Try taking the bottle away."

Milo does and Gandalf lets out an ear-piercing scream.

"*Geez,*" Milo yelps, putting the bottle back.

Maddy holds her belly, laughing. "When he doesn't do that, that's when you know he's done."

"That was just mean," Milo says.

Aunt Maddy pats his arm. "Sorry, kid. You'll figure this out."

Defeatedly, Milo lets out a chuckle, looking down at the baby in his arms. "Thanks."

"Oh, I'm having a flashback," Aunt Maddy says softly, cupping her mouth as she watches Milo with Gandalf.

"What do you mean?" I ask curiously.

Maddy shakes out of it. "Oh, no, nothing. It felt like déjà vu. Are you okay, Milo?"

He nods. "Yeah, I'll call out if I need more help."

Aunt Maddy beckons me to follow, and we head back to the prep area.

"Remember to burp him when he's done," I say, moving away from the table.

Milo raises an eyebrow as he watches me walk away. "Are you sure you don't want to get involved?"

"No, you got this," I say mischievously.

Milo shakes his head and returns his attention to Gandalf.

A while after I help Maddy finish the last pieces of the catering menu, Gandalf has been successfully fed and burped. Milo tried to put him back in his carrier, but Gandalf kept fussing. Aunt Maddy suggested Milo try his best to hold him close and soothe him to sleep.

It's then that Kai walks through the front door.

"What happened to the skatepark?" I ask, walking up to him with folded arms.

"I wanted to make sure we're cool," Kai says in a low tone. His eyes have dulled and the corners of his mouth drag down.

I sigh, exhausted. "We're cool. I'm just mad at my situation. I took it out on you, and I'm sorry."

Kai pulls an arm around me, and I lift my chin onto his shoulder. "Don't be sorry. I know I've got it a lot easier than you. You just always kid around about stuff. I didn't realize you were struggling."

I drop my chin, and Kai's arm unravels. "I have to care about stuff that I never have before. It's weird."

"At least you're staying with me for the next few days. We'll play video games, go to the skatepark, and just be normal."

"Just because it's the weekend, and I won't be with Aunt Maddy, doesn't mean I can slack off. When I'm not at work, I have to do my homework assignments."

Kai groans. "Boo."

"This is what I'm talking about, Kai," I complain. "This is make it or break it for me. Without my grades improving, I'm out of Ashworth Academy."

"I know, I know," he mutters. "But we can squeeze in a bit of fun time. Can't we?"

I hold my thumb and index finger slightly apart. "A bit."

Kai pats my back. "That's my James."

I turn back to the table and walk over to Milo and Gandalf. "I can take over," I say. "Seeing as your ride is here."

Milo stands up, cradling the baby. He carefully pulls Gandalf away from his body and hands him over like he's glass. I bow my arms, ready as Milo places the baby down.

"Why are you two acting like it's a real baby?" Kai asks. "You know it's fake, don't you?"

"*Ha ha,*" Milo says sarcastically. "He has sensors that pick up any mishandling. We have to treat him like he's real. That's the assignment."

"*He?*" Kai jokes. "Dang. You do really think he's real."

I grin at Kai. "He is real. He's our baby Gandalf."

At that, Kai claps and throws his head back with laughter. When his head lowers, he wipes under his eye. "Oh gosh, James. What a name."

Milo slings his backpack over his shoulder and moves toward his brother. "Thanks. I thought it sounded good, too."

Kai's smile disappears as he watches his brother move toward the front door.

"Bye, Jamie. Text me if you need help," Milo says with a wave. "Bye, Maddy."

Aunt Maddy waves from the counter. "Bye, Milo. See ya, Kai."

Kai flicks his car keys around his finger and he looks me up and down with the baby. "Yeah, I'll see ya." He shakes his head as he turns around. "You holding that baby looks super weird."

"Thanks," I reply. "It feels weird. See you tomorrow."

Kai waves with his back turned. "Can't wait."

Aunt Maddy walks over from the counter as the boys leave. "So, do you think you can work while looking after a baby?"

"Ah, no," I say bluntly. "How the heck will I do my homework?"

"He'll sleep," Maddy says matter-of-factly.

I roll my eyes. "Why hasn't he done that yet?"

Before Maddy can respond, a bad smell wafts up, causing our noses to crinkle.

"*Eww.* What the heck is that?" I ask.

Aunt Maddy giggles, cupping her nose. "That would be your baby."

"*Gross.*"

Aunt Maddy grabs the baby bag and beckons me to follow. "Come on. We'll take him into my office and change him."

"Will you do it?" I ask, following.

"*Pfft.* I think those who think Gandalf is an appropriate baby name will do the changing."

"Milo named him. Dang it. He would leave right before this happened."

"You can get him back tomorrow," Aunt Maddy says as we round the counter and move across to her office. "When you're at his place, you do the feeding, and he can do the changing."

"He can do the whole lot," I say, placing Gandalf down on the table.

Thank goodness he doesn't actually do anything in his diaper. I have no idea how Maddy remembers how to change diapers after so many years. She must've done so many for me while Mom was working three jobs to take care of us.

Once Gandalf is changed and settling into sleep, I text Milo. "*You wouldn't believe what Gandalf did when you left! He let out this disgusting smell,* and *I had to change his diaper.*"

Milo texts back. "*LOL. That'll teach you for not getting involved sooner.*"

"*Nope. It should've been your diaper because you fed him.*"

"*Did you want to deal with the screaming?*"

"*Still. It was bad timing for you to leave.*"

"*LOL. I promise to do some diapers tomorrow.*"

"*Oh, don't worry, you will be.*"

"*Make sure you text me if you need anything. I can always ask Mom to drive me over.*"

There's a tremor in my hands as I text back. *"I have Aunt Maddy. Thanks though."*

"No problem."

The tremor spreads up my arms and into the arteries, leading to my heart. If I were paired up with Kai, he'd make any excuse to ditch the baby. How is Milo so thoughtful?

Fifteen

At home later that evening, Maddy gets a call from Coach. She nods along, agreeing to things, and soon she's smiling.

Maddy smirks, lowers her phone and hits a button. "Can you repeat that, Brent? I want Jamie to hear."

I click my tongue as Coach's mild laughter comes through the phone speaker.

"Hey Jamie," Coach says. "I was just checking in to ensure Maddy was okay with this baby simulator being in the house."

"And?" Aunt Maddy says in a leading way.

Coach laughs. "*And,* I wanted to make sure Maddy let you do the work on this assignment. I know it must be tempting to let her take over when the baby cries."

I snort like I'm insulted. "As if I'd do that."

"Yes, because you didn't get this assignment because you slacked off on your other ones," Coach says sarcastically.

I groan. "Ugh. Whatever."

"Don't worry," Coach says light-heartedly, "I also called to stop Maddy from letting her instincts takeover and doing the assignment for you."

My eyes narrow at Maddy. "What does that mean?"

"That she's a natural with babies," Coach replies. "I remember how Grams would gush about her any time I went into the cafe when you were little."

Aunt Maddy leans over and pinches my cheek. "Well, how could I not take care of her? She was so gosh darn cute."

I steal my face away. "Oh my gosh, stop. You're so embarrassing."

Coach laughs. "So, are we good here?"

"Yes, Brent," Aunt Maddy replies. "I won't take over, and Jamie will take responsibility."

"Yeah, sure, whatever," I reply.

"You can reach out through the portal if you get really stuck," Coach says. "Just try to stay calm and work out all your options to soothe the baby. It might get tense overnight."

"Tense?" I ask, seizing up.

"The simulation continues throughout the night," Coach replies. "It'll feel more difficult when it's interrupting your sleep."

Aunt Maddy giggles. "Ah, you're gonna have so much fun."

"Thanks, guys, for putting my mind at ease," I say, folding my arms.

After dinner, Maddy and I watched two rom-coms back to back. She had banned me from watching, so I'd have more study time. But considering she'd be leaving me for seven days, she kicked the harsh vibes.

Besides, she knows I'll be staying under Mrs. Nelson's roof, and she can be strict at times.

At 12.30 a.m. Maddy left for her bedroom, asking me for the millionth time for good luck on her trip. Now that she doesn't have to concentrate on me or work, the thought of being on the plane is freaking her out.

When Maddy left, Gandalf started up. He'd already had a bottle during movie one, and a changing during movie two.

"Do you need me to come back?" Aunt Maddy calls out.

"No, I got it," I say, picking up the fake baby. "You just get some rest."

"Okay, love you," she calls and then closes her door.

I cradle Gandalf close to my body, and his cries turn into a soft whimper. With a few rocks, he settles back to sleep.

Phew.

I put him down in the carrier beside the bed, and get myself comfy, ready to drift off to sleep.

2.00 a.m.

Gandalf's annoying cry pries me from my sleep. I rub my crusty eyes and pull myself to the edge of the bed. I peer over at the fussing doll and my head pounds.

"Seriously?" I whisper harshly. "What do you want?"

The cry gets louder. When he raises the volume, that usually means a bottle.

I groan and drag myself out of bed. "Okay, you little monster, if I do this you have to promise not to cry again until 9 a.m."

I get the bottle from my desk and scoop Gandalf into my arms. It takes ten minutes for him to be satisfied with the bottle. I have to admit, the suckling noises were kinda cute.

The worst part is the burping. It takes ages! And I never know what kind of pressure is correct or leaning toward abuse. Aunt Maddy said it has to be hard, but Coach said mishandling will lower my grade.

Eventually he burps, allowing me to place him back in the carrier without him whimpering.

3.15 a.m.

I'm pulled out of a dream where I'm rollerblading up a steep ramp, about to get airborne. I'm so confused as to why I'm awake. The screeching noise in the background comes into focus, and my blood boils from the sound of Gandalf.

"Ugh. I hate you!" I groan.

I pull him out of the carrier and plop him on the bed. I probably used too much force, but it's the middle of the freaking night, and I enjoy my sleep.

"What's wrong with you this time?" I mumble sleepily.

He makes that uncomfortable, cut-off cry, and I think it means diaper change. I guess it makes sense since he recently ate.

In my dopey state, I somehow manage a quick change and get him back in his carrier. He makes more whiny sounds, so I rub my hand against his stomach as I faceplant my mattress. I doze off at the sound of him gurgling.

4.25 a.m.

I wake up with searing pain in my hands. My fists are so tightly wound, they're difficult to unravel. My jaw hurts from grinding my teeth. My stomach is cramped from raising my knees into the fetal position.

My unconscious self tried so hard to keep me asleep, but I was no match for Gandalf's cries. His pitch is crazy high and the sobs vary in length.

"Oh my gosh," I whimper, verging on tears. I pull him onto the bed. "Why won't you stop crying?"

The baby continues to fret, and my first instinct is to cover his mouth. It barely mutes him. I can't have him waking up Aunt Maddy. But maybe I need her. Or a priest to perform an exorcism.

I hold the baby close, hoping some rocking back and forth will soothe him.

His cries persist.

"Come on, Gandalf," I whisper harshly. "You've already been fed and changed. What is it now?"

As he continues to cry in my arms, my tears stream. A mixture of sleep deprivation and running emotions. My head is a jumble of thoughts and I can't think of what my next step should be.

I don't know how he could help, but I pick up my phone and text Milo, anyway.

"Gandalf won't stop crying."

"I think he's possessed."

"OMG why won't he stop?"

"I can't do this anymore. I want to find an off switch."

Each time I texted, I told myself it'd be the last time. However, my scattered emotions wouldn't let me stop. My teeth chatter as the feeling of helplessness ripples through me. Somehow, writing to Milo comforts me.

When I'm about to text another rambled message, my phone buzzes with an incoming call from Milo.

I hit answer and lift the phone to my ear.

"Hello?" It comes out like a wounded whimper.

"Jamie, you sound so sad," Milo whispers through the phone.

"I can't believe you called," I whisper back.

"It seemed like you needed help. Is looking after him too much?"

I roughly swipe my weeping eyes with my sleeve. "I just don't know why he won't stop. I've done everything he could possibly need, and he keeps crying every hour."

"What does everything mean?" Milo asks. "Feeding, burping, changing, cuddling?"

"Yes, Milo!" I yelp. There's a moment of silence on the line until I sigh and add, "Sorry for snapping. I'm just losing it."

"Don't be sorry," he says in a soothing tone. "I'd go insane too if I kept getting woken up and couldn't fix it."

My teeth chatter as I hold back a sob of frustration. "I just don't know what else to do."

"Have you asked Maddy for help?"

"I don't want to wake her," I admit. "She's going on her first ever flight tomorrow, plus it's her first time out of the state. She's nervous enough about her trip and leaving everything behind. I don't want to stress her out by taking away her sleep."

"Do you want me to come over?" he asks. "I could call a taxi."

"No, don't do that," I reply, appreciating the gesture. "I shouldn't have woken you up."

"Don't be silly. It's my assignment too. If you're up, I'm up too."

I let out a faint giggle. "Don't say that, or tomorrow night I'll have to stay up when it's your turn."

"Hopefully, he'll be a better baby tomorrow night."

"If I were paired up with Kai, he never would've called. He'd tell me to stick Gandalf in a closet and then get online to play a game with him."

"If Kai ever had to do this assignment, I pity the poor person paired up with him. He blows off everything."

"That's usually what I like about him. But now he doesn't get how important it is that I do well in my classes."

"Well, you sure told him this afternoon in the cafe. He was quiet on the drive home."

I'm taken aback. "Really? He didn't talk himself around in circles?"

"No. He just sat behind the wheel and seemed to be thinking hard as we made our way home."

"Huh. Well, that's something."

"Look, I know it's not much, but I hope you know I've got your back." He sighs and I hear a rustling as he shifts in bed. "I know what it's like to put your all into your schoolwork. You've got me to talk this stuff through with. That is, if Kai won't be there for you."

"Thanks, Milo." I awkwardly clear my throat. "But I'm sure Kai is coming around. It's just been a big change in our usual dynamic."

"Yeah, sure."

Not to mention Tabitha clawing her way into his life. Ugh. I still can't comprehend how that happened.

I shake out of my nagging thoughts and listen for noises coming from Gandalf. "He's so quiet," I whisper into the phone. "You should go back to sleep. I can handle this."

"Are you sure you'll be okay?" he asks tenderly.

I nod against the phone. "Yeah, he seems to have settled. Maybe the trick was being on the phone with you."

A murmured laugh comes through the phone line. "Okay then," Milo says softly. "Remember to call me back if he starts screaming again."

"Okay, I will."

We hang up and I slump against the bed, breathing out slowly. Wow. I hope Gandalf feels as at ease as I do.

I drift back to sleep without another interruption until 6.00 a.m. Aunt Maddy traipses around the house, gathering last-minute items for her trip.

I groggily get out of bed and carry Gandalf out of the room with me.

"Wow, you look bright-eyed," Aunt Maddy jokes as I meet her in the hall with half-closed eyes.

I gesture at the baby. "He kept me up all night."

"Aw, poor baby," Maddy says insincerely. "Can you get dressed? I need to drop you at Kai's house by 7.00 a.m."

"We have plenty of time," I say hoarsely.

"Not really," Aunt Maddy says, tipping into panic mode. "It takes twenty minutes to get there on a good day. You know how much of a fight it can be against the soccer traffic."

"Okay, okay," I say, turning back into my bedroom. "I'll get dressed way too early just to please you."

"Thank you," Aunt Maddy says in a high pitch as she paces back to her bedroom.

I lethargically change out of my pajamas and into sweats. When Gandalf fusses, and I dig into his bag for his bottle, a shrill gasp sounds from Aunt Maddy's room.

"Maddy? Are you okay?" I call out.

"Holy cow!" she shrieks, bounding toward my bedroom. I meet her in the doorway where she's holding up her phone. "David has to go into the office to deal with something urgent." Maddy shudders, gripping the phone tighter. "We're not gonna have enough time to drop you at Kai's house and come back this way to go to the city."

I grab her shoulders. "Aunty, chill. We can handle this. What if we drive to Kai's and David meets you there?"

"But what about my car?"

I shrug. "Leave it there."

Her skin becomes a duller shade of pale. "Oh my gosh. Maybe I just shouldn't go."

"This is just your nerves about the flight and being away from home talking," I say soothingly. "It'll be fine. Let's just pack up our gear and get going."

To throw a spanner in the works, Gandalf lets out an ear-piercing scream.

"Ugh. He's dying for his bottle."

"Okay, I can handle this," Aunt Maddy says, fanning her face. "You've got so much stuff to deal with already. You don't need to pull your aunt off a ledge. Thanks, Jamie."

I kiss her cheek and back away to the crying fake baby. "You'll be okay."

"I hope you will be," she says, leaning against the doorframe.

I smile through a yawn. "I will be."

Aunt Maddy's hysterics continue throughout the house as she second guesses what she packed and what she might've forgotten. I finally get her out of the house by reminding her Hawaii has stores.

On the drive into town, her clammy hands squeeze the steering wheel and her knees bounce to an anxious beat. Fortunately, when we arrive at Kai's house, David pulls up outside.

"I didn't think I'd beat you here," David says as we get out of the car.

"She was panicking," I tease.

"Oh, honey, why?" David coos, wrapping his arms around Maddy and kissing the top of her head.

Barf.

Ugh. I gotta stop doing that.

"This trip is a big deal," Aunt Maddy says, leaning against David for support. "Plus, I'm nervous about leaving Jamie."

"I'll be fine," I say and the pair break apart. "Kai's family are like my second home. They'll take care of me."

Aunt Maddy hugs me. "Please keep doing your homework and pay attention in classes."

"I'll do my best."

Aunt Maddy grins, pulling back. "That's all I ask."

"Okay, hon," David says. "I'll grab your bags and then we'll head off."

I move to the trunk at the same time as David to collect my bags. I want to ignore him when he asks if I need a hand. Instead, I let him help and give him a smile. Heck, he's taking my aunt on a getaway. I know he's good to her, and I want to ensure he stays good to her. Just because he's not my type doesn't mean I should continue being curt with him. To be completely real, he's never done a thing wrong to me. I think I've just enjoyed making faces at him. I need to work on cutting that habit. Even though it's fun.

I thank David, and then see Maddy get Gandalf's carrier from the backseat. I realize, for a brief moment, I'd forgotten his existence.

Aunt Maddy helps me walk my gear and my fake baby to the door. I want to send her packing after I ring the doorbell. Her jitters come back in full force, waiting for someone to answer the door.

"Why don't you take off?" I suggest. "Everyone's out watching Kai's game, and Milo's probably upstairs. He'll take a few minutes to open the door."

"No, I can't leave until you're inside."

"Aunt Maddy, please," I whine. "I'm afraid your nerves are contagious."

She kisses the side of my head and squeezes my shoulder. "Okay, baby, I'll get going. I'm so proud of you. Do well this week."

"Have fun on your trip. I truly mean it."

Aunt Maddy grins, backing down the garden path. "Thanks, we will."

Ugh. *We.*

Seriously, I gotta stop grimacing at the thought of Mr. Stuffy. She's crazy nervous because she likes him so much. I gotta practice being happy for her, plain and simple.

David's car fires up the moment Milo answers the front door.

"Hey," he says in a somewhat croaky voice.

"Did you just wake up?"

He adjusts his glasses, stifling a yawn. "Yeah. Stayed up too late reading."

"*Nerd,*" I cough.

Milo smirks and picks up Gandalf's carrier from beside my feet. "It had to be a better night than you had. This guy kept you up all night, huh?"

I blow out a hard breath and grab my two duffel bags. I follow Milo inside as he carries Gandalf and the baby bag. My nostrils twitch as my eyes drift along Milo's shoulder blades. How does he smell so good first thing in the morning?

Jamie, no. What are you thinking? Stop it.

I drop my bags and shake out my hands. "Sorry again about texting you in the middle of the night."

Milo shakes his head. "I already told you; you don't have to be sorry about that."

I rub my temples. "Man, my head is throbbing."

"Yeah, you look super tired. So, having a baby isn't the greatest?"

"He's an absolute monster." My gaze lands on the invitingly comfy couch. "Do you mind if I take a nap?"

"Not at all. Did you want to go to my room?" Milo asks, sending a thumb over his shoulder toward the stairs. "Mom already changed the sheets for you."

I slink around the couch and flop onto the pillowy soft cushions. "Nope. I'm good right here."

"I'll take your bags upstairs for you."

"Oh." It takes me off guard because it sounds so gentlemanly. "Okay, thanks."

Milo smiles. "No problem."

I settle on the couch, and my crusty eyes close immediately. My body relaxes without the threat of Gandalf's nearby cries.

Sixteen

My stomach grumbles so hard it wakes me up. The house is quiet, which means everyone is still out, watching Kai's game. It's gotta be around midday, maybe a bit later. I look over the back of the couch and see no sign of Milo.

I make my way upstairs and hear narration coming from the TV. I step onto the second-floor landing and find Milo, chilling on the couch with Gandalf reclined beside him.

"Wow, you two look comfy," I comment.

Milo laughs. "I figured it was okay because he hasn't fussed."

I place my hands on my hips and sigh. "Don't tell me he hasn't cried while I've been asleep. He's supposed to drive you crazy and then be asleep when I'm up."

"It's okay, I'll look after him today," Milo says placatingly.

"It's not fair." I pout, sitting on the couch beside them. "How come you have the magic touch? Even with just a phone call you put him at ease."

"I think it's just dumb luck and good timing."

I look at the screen and frown. "What the heck are you watching?"

"It's a documentary on the Mayans. I like finding out how ancient civilizations made things work."

I blow out a breath. "This'll put me back to sleep."

Milo laughs and lifts the remote. "Well, what would you be watching?"

Something with a head-over-heels love story. "Nothing," I say, flicking my hair over my shoulder. "I'd be crushing it on Shadow Quest."

Milo groans. "Dang. Kai is always playing that game. I'm so over hearing the guard say, 'You'll never pass.' Kai can't pass that level, and it's driving me bonkers."

I steal the remote from Milo and flip to the channel for the gaming console. "What if I pass the level now and then you won't hear the same game chatter anymore?"

Milo smirks. "Until he gets stuck on the next level for eternity."

I boot up the game and sit back with the controller. "I'm here for a few days. Maybe I'll finish the entire game during my stay."

"While that'd be hilarious because it'd annoy Kai," Milo replies, "I doubt my mother will let you anywhere near video games. She's already said she'll be on you like a hawk for Maddy's sake."

"*Boo*," I hiss. "Your mom is such a party pooper."

A knowing smile graces Milo's lips, and he sets Gandalf in his carrier.

I shrug. "Let's see how far we get before she gets home."

Milo's eyebrow raises. "You want me to stay and watch?"

I bite my lip, suddenly feeling foolish. "I thought you might, but if it's too boring..."

Milo grins and settles back on the couch. "No, I'm happy to stay."

I tap the controller through all the menu options. "Maybe I'll even teach you how to play."

Milo snorts. "Because teaching me soccer was such a great success?"

I shrug, a teasing smile tugging my lips. "I need a challenge, and even though Kai finds it so hard, this game isn't it."

"*Burn.*"

I look over at him, and something about him appears different. I've never really seen him relaxed on this couch before. Usually, he slinks past to his bedroom, avoiding insults from Kai or the other guys. It's nice seeing him so chill.

"What?" he asks softly.

I smile and look back at the screen. "Nothing. Just never heard you say burn before."

"I know, it was weird," he says jokingly. "But it felt appropriate."

I nod as the level begins. "Very appropriate."

My thumbs tap buttons from muscle memory. I'm only good at this game because I waste time playing at Kai's. We crash on the couch and play video games until we're comatose. At home, however, I endlessly stream rom-coms to pass time. The boys assume I spend that time still playing, gaining skills, and that's why I beat them. If they had any idea how little I play outside of this house, they'd be as ragey as Camila.

No boy likes admitting a girl is way better than them, especially when she practices less. No wonder they think of me as one of the boys. It's less of a threat to their manhoods. I guess that's why I'm not attracted to any of my friends. That kind of thinking isn't exactly attractive.

I hold the controller out to Milo. "Come on, you give it a try."

He holds his hands up like the controller is a gun. "No way. I'll suck at it and ruin your progress."

"I just passed a save point," I reply, swirling the controller. "You literally can't mess up."

Milo gives me an uneasy look. "I dunno. I'm really fine with just watching you."

"Go on," I encourage. "It'll give me some entertainment. I don't have any of the other guys around to poke fun at."

Milo huffs. "So you just want to tease me?"

I sit back, composing myself. "No, I don't want to tease you. I genuinely think you'll find it fun."

Milo stares into my eyes and a rush of goosebumps fly down my arms.

He takes the controller and his fingers brush past mine, sending a thrilling spark inside me.

"Okay, I'll try," he says, looking over the controller. "So, what buttons do I press?"

I quickly go over the controls and the game mission. As Milo moves the character around the environment, I give him pointers and tell him what to look for up ahead.

It takes so much strength to hold back my laughter the third time his character respawns after dying.

"It shouldn't be this easy to fall into those pits," Milo complains, pointing the controller at the screen.

"Mhmm," I mumble, rubbing my lips to hold back the laugh.

Milo looks at me and rolls his eyes. "Oh my gosh, just let it out. You look like you're gonna burst."

I swallow hard and shake my head. "Nope, I'm good."

"Well, what am I doing wrong? How can I avoid those pits to hell?"

I hold up my hands like the answer should be obvious. "Walk around them."

Milo groans. "But then there are spikes and hanging swords in the way. And if I go left, there's an ogre-looking-thing that wants to kill me with an ax."

"You do realize you need skills to play video games," I say. "It takes practice just like everything else."

"I have no idea how you don't give up after one try. If it were my console, it'd already be in the trash."

"Geez, such a defeatist." I click my tongue. "What would you say to me if I threatened to throw my copy of King Lear in the trash?"

Milo huffs. "To take a breath and keep working at it."

I lean closer and pat his upper arm. "You haven't let me give up yet."

Milo looks down at my hand, and I notice his Adam's apple bob. When his hazel eyes look into mine, an electric charge hums between us. I should lift my hand off him, but I seem unable. Or unwilling.

"I won't let you because every day I see you improving."

When my lingering hand starts squeezing his arm, I pry myself away. "Sorry," I breathe.

Milo smiles. "Don't be."

My eyes haven't shifted from his eyes. I don't know if it's his glasses or not, but I swear Milo's eyes are more green than Kai's. I thought identical twins would have the same colored eyes. But maybe it's a symptom of Kai taking up all the room in the womb. I'm still so annoyed about Kai doing that. Still, to this day, Kai takes up most of the space in their lives. That's why it's so rare to see Milo chilling in this living room.

Milo's lips part, maybe to say something, maybe to...

"*Ahhh!*" the video game character screams, pulling our attention to the TV screen. We witness the last moments of an assassin elf swinging his blade.

"Oh man," Milo laughs, slumping against the couch. "Even when I'm not paying attention, I manage to kill my character."

And at that, any hope of keeping my laughter to myself disappears. A barrelful leaps out of me, forcing me to hold my gut as I fold in on myself.

Milo joins in laughing, swiping a hand under his glasses to wipe his eyes. His shoulders jiggle as he laughs and I can't help thinking how dang cute his smile looks.

As whispered laughter hiccups out of him, Milo attempts another try. My eyes shift back and forth from the screen and Milo. There's determination in his eyes and his tongue slightly pokes out as he goes for it. His character runs past two pitfalls and avoids a row of falling swords. And just when he gets further than he'd ever gotten, a trap door swallows him whole.

Milo drops the controller and we both burst into thunderous laughter.

"Oh my gosh," I say, straining for breath as I keel over giggling, "you have the worst video game luck."

Milo wheezes, planting a hand over his chest, and his glasses slide down his nose. "I officially give up."

I giggle and pat his knee. "I think that's fair. You gave it your all."

Milo sniggers and places his hand over mine. "Thanks for not saying I just suck."

I bite my lip and soak up the warmth from his hand. When he releases me, I pull my hand to my lap and smile. "You didn't suck."

Heavy footsteps sound up the stairs. Kai walks onto the landing, dumping his bag with a huff. Grass stains cover his soccer uniform and his chest heaves. He looks at the TV screen and then back at us.

"What the hell, James?" Kai asks, scrutinizing us. "You don't show at my game, but you're playing Shadow Quest with *him*?"

"What's the big deal?" I ask, sitting taller.

"I thought you were supposed to be studying," Kai says. "If you wanted to slack off, why weren't you hanging with me?"

"Give me a break," I mutter and gesture at Gandalf. "This thing kept me up all night."

"Ever heard of an off switch?" Kai argues.

"It doesn't turn off, genius," Milo scolds.

Kai rolls his eyes and swats a hand at his brother. "Don't you start with me."

After Kai marches into his room, shutting the door behind him, I whisper, "He's in a mood. They must've lost."

"That would be a good excuse for his grouchiness," Milo replies. "But he's always like that with me."

"Everyone must've come home while we were laughing. I haven't seen your grandparents since they've been here." I get off the couch. "I'm heading downstairs."

Milo follows, carrying the baby carrier. I fly down the stairs, eagerly outpacing him.

"Oh, Jamie!" Grandma Nelson says excitedly, throwing her arms toward me. "Hello, sweetheart. We've missed you."

I rush into her arms, giving her a hug. "I've missed you too."

"We were worried something had gone wrong with Maddy's trip when we saw her car out front," Mrs. Nelson says, carrying a tray with a jug of coffee and a set of mugs.

"She said she's sorry for leaving the car here," I reply. "Her boyfriend got held up. They ran out of time to drop me off before heading toward the city. The car key is on the counter if you want to move it."

Mr. Nelson waves a hand. "It's fine where it is. Our cars fit in the garage, so it's no trouble."

"Oh my gosh," Mrs. Nelson says with a laugh, placing the tray on the coffee table. "Is this the baby?"

She holds a hand over her growing grin as she peers over the baby carrier. Milo sets it on the couch and gives an embarrassed smirk.

"Wow, it is lifelike," Mr. Nelson remarks.

"In your day, they gave you a sack of flour to look after," Grandpa Nelson says. "Now the kids have to deal with something that cries."

Grandma Nelson curls an arm around Milo's arm. "Does it eat and go potty too?"

Milo nods. "Yes, but it's simulated. There's no actual food or mess."

"He does fart and burp though," I add. "He can be a stinky little baby."

The parents and grandparents all laugh, delighted at the thought of the fake baby emitting nasty gasses.

As everyone takes a seat amongst the couches and armchairs, I ask, "So, how was Kai's game?"

"It was rough," Mrs. Nelson says through a tight expression. "They lost three to one. Kai took it pretty hard."

I look over my shoulder at the stairs. "I should go talk to him."

"Give him some time to shower and cool off," Mr. Nelson suggests. "He was pretty agitated during the drive home."

"Are you hungry, Jamie?" Mrs. Nelson asks. "There are sandwiches on the kitchen counter. Go help yourself."

My gut spasms as I walk into the kitchen. Now it's not only hunger plaguing me. Guilt eats away at me because I didn't ask Kai how he was when he walked upstairs. I was having so much fun with Milo. Kai's game wasn't a priority.

Milo.

A new feeling washes through me. Milo had me laughing so hard. I relive the moment his hand slid over mine. I swear, he looked at me as if he were going to kiss me. At least that's how characters in movies act before a first kiss.

I walk back toward the living room with a half-eaten sandwich, and my eyes drift to Milo. He's busy talking with his grandpa.

Did he want to kiss me? Did he feel the same surge of energy I felt?

And why did I feel that way? Why do I keep fantasizing about him?

I don't want to kiss Milo. Do I?

"Have you settled into your room, Jamie?" Mrs. Nelson asks. "Milo said he'd have it ready for you when we left this morning."

"Ah no, actually," I reply, swallowing a bite. "I haven't gotten that far yet."

Grandma Nelson pats my back. "Sorry we took your usual room, dear."

I giggle. "That's okay. You got to it first."

Gandalf fusses in his carrier, and ten seconds later, lets out a shrill cry.

"Good lord," Grandpa Nelson blurts. "That thing's got some lungs on him."

I finish my sandwich and move toward Gandalf. "It means it's bottle time."

Milo lifts the carrier before I get to it. "His bag is still upstairs."

"Milo, make sure you get Jamie comfortable in your bedroom while you're upstairs," Mrs. Nelson says. "I don't want her feeling awkward during her stay."

"Yes, Mom," Milo mutters. "I already took her bags up. It's fine."

I smile and nod. "Yeah, I'll be fine. See you all later. Hopefully, he'll sleep after this."

Grandpa Nelson chuckles to himself. "Will it be farting and burping time next?"

Milo and I both let out a groan, which sends the parentals into hysterics. We wave goodbye and head back upstairs.

"Shall we feed him in my bedroom?" Milo asks. "Or, your bedroom, I guess."

"Let's call it your bedroom. I don't want to feel like I'm stealing your space."

Milo smirks. "You kinda are, though. Anyway, I'll show you your space."

Seventeen

"I cleared most of my stuff from the desk so you can work," Milo says, lowering the baby carrier to his bedroom floor. "There's some space in the wardrobe for you to hang your clothes, and the bed sheets and cover are all fresh. I hope it's not super weird for you to stay here."

"I feel bad for kicking you out of your space," I say with genuine remorse.

When I spy the action figures, D&D miniatures, and other nerdy pieces lining the bookshelves on the wall, I can't help smirking.

"I don't mind giving you my room. It's sharing with Kai that feels like punishment."

I look down at the pristine carpet without a piece of fallen clothing. "He's not exactly a neat-freak like you."

"I think *freak* is a bit strong."

I grin, unable to resist teasing him. "How will you react if you walk by and I've littered the floor with clothes, cleats, rollerblades, and a soccer ball?"

Milo sucks in an apprehensive breath, his chest expanding. He deflates, avoiding eye contact. "It'll be fine. I can clean once you're gone."

I giggle. "Worried about my cooties?"

He looks back, a faint pink hue coloring his cheeks. "No."

Unintentionally, I rub my lips together. My eyes run along the frames of his glasses and lock onto his welcoming hazel eyes. I clear my throat and move toward my bags.

"I should get a start on my homework," I say, lifting the bag with school gear inside and shifting it closer to the desk.

"Oh, I almost forgot to grab this," Milo says, lifting a book from the desk. He tilts the cover, showing me the title. "I got it with your gift card."

"Oh, cool. Do you like it?"

"Yeah, it's interesting. It's about Hatshepsut. She was an Egyptian pharaoh, but something happened to her and most of the carvings and statues about her were destroyed," Milo explains. "Pieces of her life are still being put together, so I can't get enough of finding out more about her."

I smile at the excitement buzzing off him. "I'm seeing a pattern. Learning about ancient civilizations gets you intrigued."

Milo tucks the book under his arm. "It's just so different from everyday life. I like escaping into history." He motions at my books. "Do you want help with anything?"

"No, I'll be fine. If I get time away from the baby, I should be able to knock out one assignment."

Milo picks up the carrier housing Gandalf and moves toward the doorway. "Okay. Good luck."

"Thanks," I say as he disappears into the living room.

When Milo descends the staircase, I get ready to work. I set my laptop on the desk and as well as a wad of books. I search through the pile for my history notes, and stumble on my mom's diary. I don't even know why I packed it. I still haven't read a full page. Maybe I'll get rid of these jitters and crack it open once the baby project is over.

I set the diary aside and position my history textbook and essay notes next to the laptop. I figure the best option is getting the most boring assignment out of the way first. It's just reciting facts. Math takes too much brain power and definitely requires Milo's help. And decoding what's going on in King

Lear still stresses me out. I can't wait until we move onto another book that actually uses normal English.

I look over my history notes. There's a lot of underlining and highlighting, but not a proper timeline for my paper. Before I start typing, I grab a pen and sit on the bed, making a plan in my notebook of what order to discuss each historical fact. If Milo thinks history is fun, maybe I can get into it too.

I take my time, carefully writing each line with purpose. There's a tingle in my fingers as I grip the pen. I've never felt this level of pride about homework prep before. It's oddly satisfying.

After half a page, I drop the pen when I hear Kai's door opening and footsteps moving across the upstairs living room. "Kai?"

He grumbles and his footsteps near the bedroom. "Yeah?" he asks, slumping against the doorframe with his hands in his pockets.

"You lost," I say, matter-of-factly.

He huffs and pulls out a hand to wipe it across his brow. "Yeah. I was off my game today. Worse of all, Tabby was there to see it."

"*Oof.* You don't think...?"

He scrutinizes me. "What?"

I can barely contain my smirk. "That she's a bad luck charm. You know you should've won against that team."

Offense covers Kai's face. "How could you say that?"

I shrug, sitting cross-legged on the bed. "I dunno. Just a thought."

"She's my girlfriend, Jamie. I'm nuts about her, and you call her a bad luck charm?"

There's an ache in my heart. "How am I supposed to know how much you like her? You never talked about her before you made out with her on your birthday."

Kai pulls off the doorframe and folds his arms. "How could I talk to you about my crush? You couldn't give me tips on how to approach her or find out if she liked me back. You can't even talk to girls."

It's like being hit in the chest with a baseball bat. I pant for breath as he watches me with dismissive eyes.

"Come on." Kai shrugs. "It's not like I'm wrong. You're not exactly a girl's girl. When I need help to find something fun to do, or someone who can challenge my soccer game, then I turn to you."

I slide my legs off the bed and sit on the edge. "You didn't think I'd be cool with you dating Tabitha?"

Kai walks into the room, stopping a foot away from the bed. "Am I wrong? You haven't exactly been taking it well."

"Because you hid it from me. And now she's at our lunch table. It was a shock."

Kai sighs. "I get that. I should've given you a head's up. My bad."

I nod. "I'm sorry I wasn't at your game. Coach Anders told me to miss my game to focus on this baby project and my other assignments. To be honest, I slept most of my time here."

Kai grins, sitting on the bed beside me. "That baby really kept you up all night?"

"It was torture. I was losing it so much I cried."

Kai bursts into laughter. "What? Ha! Classic. James cried like a baby."

I nudge him. "Hey! It wasn't funny."

"Yeah, it's hilarious. You never cry."

I click my tongue. "At least your brother was supportive."

"Ugh." Kai grimaces. "You two are getting way too close. It's gross."

I slide across the bed, getting space between me and Kai. "Gross?"

"It's like seeing a lion and a gazelle hanging out," Kai replies. "Shouldn't one be killing the other?"

"So, I should kill Milo instead of letting him help me with my homework?"

Kai rests his arms behind him as he looks up at the ceiling. "All I'm saying is, it's weird you two are hanging out when it's not studying."

I nod. "Yeah, it is."

"*Phew.*" Kai stands from the bed. "I'm glad you didn't get a head injury and start thinking Milo's your friend. Come on, let's get out of this room. I can smell that dang cat without him even being in here."

"I really should work on my history paper."

Kai's nostrils flare. "Seriously? I thought this weekend would be epic. My best bud is over and we should be out at the skatepark or hiking at Logan's Point. Or even just playing a video game."

"The weekend isn't over. I have a mountain of extra work from every teacher and I need to get it off my plate."

"You're staying in here?"

I shrug. "I guess."

He groans, scuffing toward the doorway. "It's not bad enough I have Milo's crap taking up space in my bedroom. Now you're hanging out in *his* room. This is not my idea of a fun weekend."

I roll my eyes. "Oh my gosh, Kai, just get out."

He turns back at me with inflamed eyes. "Excuse me?"

"I'm sick of all your complaining," my voice raises. "I'm the one getting kicked out of school. My aunt is away, and I still have to work at the cafe while finishing all this homework. I'm sorry I'm not as privileged as you!"

His shoulders slump, and shame droops his face. "Crap, James. I'm sorry. I just hate how everything's changed. Things used to be so easy when we'd hang out. This week has sucked. I've barely seen you."

I get off the bed and hug him. "I just need your support right now. Don't you realize how hard all of this has been?"

He sighs against the nape of my neck. "No, I get it. I just miss hanging out with you."

I smile and pull away. "Just give me an hour to study and then we can hang out."

Kai backs away. "No, I'll leave you to it. I'll give Tabby a call and hang out with her, so I won't bother you anymore."

"No," I blurt, and it stops him in his tracks. "Ahh, I mean..." I look around the room and then move to the desk and pick up my mom's diary. "I've still been too chicken to read this. Want to check it out with me?"

Kai moves closer. "Is that the diary?"

"Yep. I've flipped a few pages and liked looking at her handwriting, but I haven't actually read it. Aunt Maddy's warning put me off."

Kai winces, tapping the soft cover. "Do you want to find out who your dad is?"

"I don't know. I mean, just because I read a name won't mean that I know him. He still won't know I exist."

"What if it's messed up inside?'

I open the cover and exhale slowly. "That's why you're here."

Kai laughs. "To hold your hand, you big baby."

I sit down on the desk chair. "That's right."

"Okay," Kai says, sitting down on the bed, "let's do this."

I giggle at the first page. "Whoa. She's pissed."

"Huh?"

"My mom is angry at some guy. She loved his hair, but he got a buzz cut and now she's livid." I grin and clear my throat to read aloud. "*How could he do this? I loved running my hands through his long, thick hair. I can't even look at him now. I stormed off, calling him Buzz. I don't even know if he cared.*"

Kai smirks. "Geez, if a buzz cut is the worst thing he did, maybe your mom just had crazy high standards."

"Mom had a few boyfriends. She probably dumped him for someone else." I skim a few more lines and then read aloud again. "*He told me the nickname has spread through the football team. Everyone is calling him Buzz. Wow. I can't believe my influence has spread through Ashworth Academy. Someone pinch me.*" I lower the diary as my mouth hangs open. "What?"

"Your mom was dating someone who went to Ashworth Academy?" Kai questions. "Did you know she knew anyone from our school?"

I shake my head, bewildered. "No way. I know she did everything she could to get us to Victoria Falls. Aunt Maddy said they didn't know anyone until Grams took us in."

"Maybe your aunt didn't know about this guy," Kai suggests. "Maybe your mom kept him a secret."

My stomach wobbles with worry. "Oh boy. What if this guy is some kind of sick low life?"

"Read on," Kai urges. "We don't know anything yet."

I sit the book on my lap, close my eyes and breathe out. "This is why I haven't read this yet." I open my eyes and my vision of Kai is blurry. "I'm so scared of finding out what my mom hid from us."

Kai gets up from the bed and moves across the room. He takes the diary and sets it on the desk. He plucks me at the elbows, encouraging me to stand.

As I stand in front of him, he rubs my back and says, "You don't need to do this right now. Like you said, you've got a million things going on. You don't need to pile this on too."

My breath comes out shaky as I lean my head against Kai's chest. "I just wish it wasn't some massive secret. Couldn't she have told Maddy? Then I'd know if I should be scared or not."

"Maddy was a kid back then."

I rub my temples and sigh. "My head really freaking hurts."

Kai takes a step back, propping me up by the shoulders. "Do you need another nap?"

I smile. "Maybe reading my American history textbook will put me right to sleep."

A soft laugh hums out of Kai and he edges back to the doorway. "I'll leave you to it. Hit me up before you go reading the diary again. Yeah?"

I nod. "Yeah."

"Catch ya," he says with a wave. He disappears out the door and soon his rapid footsteps thunder down the stairs.

I slump onto the desk chair and move Mom's diary to the side. I shudder at the thought of my dad hurting my mom. I just wish I already knew what went down. Maybe if she were here, she would've already told me. Oh geez, Mom, I wish you were here.

"*Meow.*"

I jolt in my seat, turning to the door where Alfred wanders in, waving his thick fluffy tail in the air.

"What are you doing here?" My legs tense as he moves my way, meowing again. "Oh no you don't. Stay back."

Alfred meows and rubs himself against my legs. I wince as he purrs, vibrating against my legs.

"*Eww.*" I squirm. "Get away from me."

Alfred brushes his ginger fur against me one more time and then waddles over to the bed. In one fluid motion, he leaps onto the bed. He pads around the center of the bed cover and plonks himself down in a half moon shape.

"Thanks a lot," I muttered to the cat. "Those sheets were just washed."

I turn back around on the chair and pull my laptop toward me on the desk. I keep telling everyone I need to knuckle down and get this done, but saying it is a heck of a lot easier than doing it.

An hour into my essay draft, there's a knock on the doorframe. I turn to see Milo poking his head in.

"Hey, is Alfie in here?" he asks.

I huff, throwing a thumb back at the bed. "Yeah. He made himself at home over there."

Milo walks in, planting the baby carrier onto the carpet. "Gandalf's stressing me out, so I need some kitty time."

"I'd rather deal with the baby than the cat," I murmur.

"What's your problem with Alfred?" Milo asks, scratching the cat under his chin. "What'd he ever do to you?"

"I just don't like him," I say, wincing. "Can you get him off the bed?"

"It's a bit hard to break his routine. He knows he's always allowed to be here," Milo says, brushing the fur along Alfred's body. "Usually, you guys are out on the couch making a racket with the TV blaring. It's your fault he comes in here to hide."

"Ugh. Well, if it's my fault, shouldn't he be hiding now?"

Milo smirks. "It was quieter with you than hanging with me and crying Gandalf."

I turn to the baby carrier and sneak a peek at Gandalf. "What did he want now?"

"I fed and changed him," Milo replies, walking back to the baby carrier. "I'm guessing it's sleep time."

"Did you burp him?"

"Yeah, but nothing happened."

"Remember what the guide said? Sometimes it takes ages."

Milo picks up Gandalf and rests him against his chest. "Maybe he doesn't need to be burped every time."

I stare at him with tired eyes. "No, he does. You need to persevere."

Milo groans, patting the baby's back. "So boring."

"Get a grip. At least it's not three a.m."

I turn back to the desk and Milo asks, "What are you working on?"

"My history paper."

"How are you doing with memorizing the dates?"

"Huh? I'm not. I'm just writing them down as they come up in my essay."

"You know how Mr. Duncan likes to give pop quizzes," Milo says, bouncing Gandalf as he pats his back. "You need to know the dates, important document names, and the figures in power."

I groan, collapsing against the chair as I look up at the ceiling. "I can't handle all this crap in my head. Every teacher wants me to memorize endless notes. When does it end? I can't do this."

"Hey, hey," Milo coos, getting off the bed and edging closer. "Don't spiral. You already have all your information for your paper. Maybe if we just go through it one paragraph at a time, it'll be easier to digest."

"I don't want to do that," I say, defeatedly. "I just want to finish the paper and move onto the next subject."

"But history is one of the classes you need the grade boost the most," Milo says with concern. "You know, acing a few pop quizzes will be beneficial."

I pout hard. "Milo, I don't wanna."

"You didn't choke in class when Mr. Duncan asked you about the Bill of Rights," Milo says with growing confidence. "Jamie, you've already got this. Back yourself."

I get off the chair and pace between the desk and the bed. "I'm just sick of this. I feel like I'm doing so much work but only forming a dent in everything that's due. Kai already gave me a hard time about not hanging at the skatepark, and I just wish I was there."

"Hey, don't let Kai derail your progress."

"I'm not. I just want to grab my blades and get out of this house." I move over to one of my bags and pull down the zipper, revealing the rollerblades. "I packed them like an idiot. Your mom won't let me take them out because Aunt Maddy doesn't want me wasting time."

"Would getting on them help clear your head?"

"I guess."

Milo grins. "Then you should grab them and we should head out."

I give him a dubious look. "You want to go to the skatepark with me?"

Milo laughs. "No. How about the backyard? Get on the rollerblades and I'll fire questions at you. Maybe the change of scenery and having something else to do will help clear everything else out of your mind."

I grab the blades. "Do you think it'll work?"

"Whenever I'm trying to solve a hard math problem, I grab a stress ball and walk around the house. Somehow, it helps me find the answer."

"Well, I'm pumped to get these bad boys on. But Kai was already annoyed that we were playing Shadow Quest together. I think he'd boil over if he saw me wearing my blades and hanging out with you."

Milo shakes his head. "Kai left."

I almost drop my rollerblades, fumbling to keep hold of them. "What?"

"Yeah, he left a while ago," Milo says, hanging his thumb over his shoulder. "I think he's with Tabitha."

My mouth hangs open and there's a stabbing pain in my heart. He knew I was dealing with a lot and panicking over the snippet I read in Mom's diary. And then he left me to be with *her*. How could he just take off like that? Oh, and I will be so angry if he breathes a word about the diary to Tabitha. I still can't believe he just blurted it out in the cafeteria that day.

I grab my phone and send Kai a quick text, explicitly telling him to keep the diary a secret between us. I put down the phone and let out a frustrated sigh.

"Okay," I say, bundling the rollerblades under my arms. "Let's do this."

When we get downstairs, Milo's parents are busy in the kitchen, while the grandparents read on the couch. We sneak outside so Mrs. Nelson doesn't lecture me about going back to the desk. If this works, maybe she'll cut me some slack during my stay. Crazier things have happened.

Once I'm strapped in, nervousness ripples through me. "I feel like I'll blank on this stuff. I marked up the textbook, but that was only so I could quickly jot down my notes for the essay."

"Come on. You know this stuff." Milo sways Gandalf in his arms, trying to lull him to sleep. "You're not dumb. You've just never seen it as important before."

Mom's diary floats around my head. She was so excited about something she made up had gathered traction at Ashworth Academy. Aunt Maddy has told me so many stories about Mom dreaming about that school, wishing she and Maddy could've enrolled. I can't let Mom's dream die.

"My mom worked her butt off so I could go to this school. I won't let her down just because I can't be bothered to do the work." I blade along the paved path lining the porch, stretching my fingers as I glide. "Hit me with it."

"Okay, when was the industrial revolution?"

"1876 to early 1900s."

"And what did it come off the back of?"

"The Civil War."

"Which started when?"

I blank. I take two stretches of the porch, back and forth, before it hits me. "1861."

"Nice," Milo cheers, pacing along the patio as he bounces Gandalf in his arms. "And what are three things that came from the industrial revolution?"

"Umm, the railroads." I take a few more glides along the pavement as I think back to my essay talking points. "Immigration…"

"You got it," Milo whispers.

"I dunno," I say, shrugging my palms upward as I blade past Milo. "Industry expansion? Like factories and machinery, and longer working hours."

"For pulling it off the top of your head, I think that's a good answer," Milo replies. "You just might want to put it more eloquently in your paper."

"Hey, at least I could remember something."

"You remember heaps, Jamie. You should be proud of yourself."

"Give me another one," I say, gaining speed on my rollerblades. "I'm feeling on fire at the moment."

"Should I have had you on rollerblades for all your tutoring sessions?" Milo jokes.

"You could try them, if you want."

"Oh, no way. After how well I went at learning soccer and that video game, I think I'll pass."

Milo quizzes me on colonial settlement and the Great Depression. Some facts come to me right away, but many I fumble and need him to prompt the answers.

Milo stops asking questions when his head tilts side to side, checking on Gandalf. "I think he's asleep," he whispers.

"But I didn't hear a burp."

Milo's eyebrows rise as he looks down at me from the porch. "Who cares? He's asleep."

"You cut a corner. Now he won't sleep through."

"You had him one night and suddenly you're an expert?"

I sit against the porch to take off my rollerblades. "Stop arguing and put him in his carrier. Or he really will wake up."

I gather my rollerblades and follow Milo inside.

"Thank you for making me do that," I tell him. "It was really fun to have an excuse to get back on my rollerblades."

"No sweat," Milo says with an adorably infectious smile. "I'm glad I could prove you know this stuff."

My heart flutters. "I can't believe how much you have my back in this. You don't have to be helping me, you know."

He nods. "I know. But I wanted to help."

I'm dumbfounded. "Why?"

Milo shrugs and walks ahead with the baby. "Because I like you."

Eighteen

Kai isn't home for dinner. Apparently he texted his mom, saying he was taking Tabitha to a fancy restaurant. Like, seriously? I'm the one dreaming about rom-com scenarios, and Kai is the one living them. What kind of world is this?

Although Kai not being home is kind of a bonus. If he saw the puzzlement creasing my face right now, he'd know something is up.

I just can't get Milo's words out of my head,

Why did he say he likes me? Obviously just as a friend, but still. I've known him for years, and I'd never say we've been friendly toward each other. If he'd never started tutoring me, I never would've seen this side of him. This soft, gentle, encouraging, and thrilling side that makes my insides do strange things.

But he chose to tutor me before this closeness happened. Surely his mother made him say yes when Aunt Maddy approached them about tutoring. He told me he wanted my help with soccer as a trade. Now he says he did it because he likes me.

Why would he possibly like me?

This makes no sense.

Ugh.

During dinner, Milo is wrapped up in conversation with his grandpa, so it's impossible to get a read on him. That is, until the conversation at the table changes.

"I just think it's so cute that Kai took Tabitha out tonight. He must be smitten to take her on a proper date," Mrs. Nelson says. "Anytime I want to take the family out somewhere with a dress code, he gives a massive protest."

Grandma chuckles. "I remember when you two were newly dating. It's nice to hear Kai is being so adoring."

"*Pfft.*" It sizzles out of Milo.

His dad looks at him pointedly. "What was that, son?"

Milo looks up, face paling with regret. "Huh? What? No, nothing."

"Don't give us that," Mrs. Nelson says sternly. "Out with it."

Milo glances at me, and I gulp in response. Usually, I hate it when Milo blurts out Kai's whereabouts. But, right now, Kai isn't exactly in my good books.

"Should we be concerned?" Mr. Nelson asks. "You're giving us that look like Kai has lied."

Milo shrugs, looking down at his plate. "I just think it's bogus that he'd be at some restaurant."

Mrs. Nelson leans in. "And where do you think he'd be?"

Milo fidgets in his seat, visibly uncomfortable. "I overheard him talking on the phone. He mentioned Dead Left Cliff."

I grind my teeth. Dead Left Cliff isn't a place for the faint-hearted. We've gone there a few times and dared each other to get too close to the edge. It's a place for me and the guys. I severely doubt Tabitha would be into it.

Mrs. Nelson slaps the table top in frustration. "That boy. How many times have we told him not to hang around there at night? I knew once he started driving, he'd stress me out further."

Mr. Nelson squeezes his wife's shoulder placatingly.

"He might not be there," Milo offers. "I don't know for sure."

"Oh, please." His mother smirks. "How often are you wrong about what your brother gets up to?"

Milo sits back in his chair, sighing. The frown on his face seems genuinely remorseful.

Is he always like this when snitching on Kai? Does he try to resist, but his parents get it out of him because he has a bad poker face?

After dinner, Milo is uneasy with me. He doesn't make eye contact when he asks if I could watch Gandalf so he could take a shower and finish his calculus homework. No doubt he's nervous that I'll text Kai, letting him know Milo ratted him out. Lucky for Milo, I'm beyond caring about what Kai is up to tonight.

Mrs. Nelson suggests I go back to my homework, too. I know better than to mess with her on my first night here.

Once Gandalf and I were upstairs in Milo's bedroom, Aunt Maddy called. *Geez*, I had no idea how much I already miss her. She could hear it in my voice and gave me permission to blow off some steam with one of my favorite rom-coms.

Milo needed at least an hour to work on his homework, so it was probably enough time to sneak in a quick ninety-minute movie. Kai wouldn't even be home by the time the credits roll.

I pick Aunt Maddy's favorite movie, Never Been Kissed, and curl up under the covers with the laptop resting on my thighs. I hug a pillow, hearing Aunt Maddy's voice in my head reciting the lines the characters say. A happy warmth spreads through me, and by the time the movie is halfway through, my sadness has drifted away.

"Hey, you want me to take him?" Milo asks, walking into the room.

His sudden arrival causes me to jump. My fingers fumble as I hurriedly pause the movie.

"Are you all right?" Milo asks with caution, halting before he reaches Gandalf.

"Mhmm." I slink under the covers as embarrassment flames my cheeks.

"What's with you? You're acting like you're watching something you need to be over eighteen to access."

"Oh lord, no." Mortifying. I lower the laptop screen and tilt it further away from Milo's gaze. "It's nothing like that."

Milo grins. "Then why are you turning it away and looking so pale?"

I huff and avert my eyes. "Because it's super embarrassing."

Milo laughs and walks over to the bed. "Now I gotta know. What makes Jamie West so embarrassed?"

"No, don't," I squeak, holding the laptop screen against my body.

Milo raises his hands and backs away. "Okay. Sorry if it's private. I didn't mean to make you uncomfortable."

I sigh and release the laptop. "Now you're gonna think it's something way worse than it is." Reluctantly, I turn the laptop to face him and hit play. "This is my dirty secret."

His brow furrows and his palm raises. "I don't get it."

I deadpan him. "It's a rom-com."

"And?"

"I binge watch them. I fixate on the characters and live vicariously through them."

"Is that bad?" Milo asks, totally not getting it. "Don't most girls watch these movies?"

"But I'm not most girls," I mutter, crossing my arms. "At least, I'm not supposed to be."

Milo steps toward the bed and perches on the edge. "What are you saying?"

"I hang out with the guys," I say softly. "I'm the tomboy. I'm not supposed to like girly stuff."

"Does it matter?"

I slide the laptop onto the bed and hug my knees. "The guys are my only friends. If they find out I like this stuff, they won't want to hang out with me anymore."

"That's crazy," Milo replies. "Have they actually said that?"

"Well, no, but that's because I've never brought it up." I tap the laptop. "This stuff is just between Aunt Maddy and me."

"It's not the guys, is it?" Milo whispers. "You're worried about Kai."

I swallow roughly. "He likes the version of me he knows. And it's not just him. I like the dynamic between us. I don't want to ruin it. Please don't say anything to him."

"I won't. But you shouldn't have to hide things you like to stay friends with someone. Isn't he supposed to be your best friend?"

I nod, my mouth drying.

Milo blinks behind his round framed glasses. "But you told me?"

I chew on my nail. "I guess you seem less judgmental."

Milo stares deeply into my eyes, his glasses slightly dipping down his nose. He clears his throat and sends his attention to the laptop. "So, what's this movie, anyway?"

"It's called Never Been Kissed. Heard of it?"

"Never."

"It's Aunt Maddy's favorite. She called before and said they landed safely and were heading out to dinner. Playing this movie made it feel like she's here with me."

"Aw. It's the first time you two are really apart, huh?"

My lips press together firmly as I nod at the screen.

Milo's hand rubs my shoulder. The unexpected action causes me to tense and then relax as goosebumps form under his fingers.

"You'll be okay," he whispers.

I turn to him and smile. "Thanks."

His eyes fixate on mine with more urgency than last time. I suck in a breath; the apprehension getting to me just as much as it does for Josie on screen. I wet my lips and my eyelids lower. Without a second to rethink it, Milo's lips press onto mine.

It's like thousands of tiny fireworks tingling against lips. His kiss has strong pressure, mild suction, and a dose of hunger. As his head tilts, my lips part against his lower lip. The fullness of his bottom lip plucks into my mouth with an enjoyable sensation. As I release it, Milo takes control of the kiss, amping up the pressure and suction. A small moan seeps out of me as the tip of his tongue swipes my lip.

He pulls away and I rub my lips together, tasting the kiss all over again. I open my eyes as Milo fixes his glasses. The word wow wants to leap out of me, but I stop when Milo's face grows sunken. His complexion dulls, and he scoots back on the bed.

"Ahh," he stammers, getting off the bed. "I just came in here to get Gandalf. I'm free to look after him now."

Still spinning from the kiss, I utter, "Okay."

Milo steps across the room and picks up the baby carrier. "Yeah, okay," he mumbles awkwardly. "I'll see ya."

He leaves the room and I sit back against the wall. A weighted breath puffs out of me. I smile as I rub my lips together. We kissed.

I look back at the laptop screen and wink at Josie. "I've been kissed."

I rub the middle of my chest, unnerved by how fast Milo made his getaway. What was with that? He made the first move, didn't he? I don't feel like I lead him on. His lips pressed against mine first. He initiated, so why did he leave?

I rub my temples and sigh. *Stop overthinking this, Jamie.*

At least it answers my questions about him liking me. Well, I think it does. Beside the abrupt exit.

I sit up and close the laptop. I shake my head and can't contain my smile.

Who cares what it means? I freaking had my first kiss!

Ninteen

While I finish typing my history paper, I can't help hearing Kai and Milo bickering in the other bedroom. A bathroom divides us, but it doesn't stop—Kai's voice, especially—from invading my space.

It actually makes me grin. I shouldn't be feeling so happy about my best friend being miserable. But he's been acting really sucky lately. If my staying here is causing him friction, then good.

I get up from the desk and walk to the doorway as Kai stomps into the living room.

"How was your evening with Tabitha?" I ask in a salty tone.

"It was the only highlight of the day," Kai says bluntly.

"Were you even at a restaurant tonight?"

"Wow, you're starting on me too. I already got enough heat from Mom and Dad." Kai runs a hand over his head, agitated. "Going out to the cliff was just an idea. Tabby wanted to go out for dinner, so I did what she wanted."

I huff. "Lucky her."

Kai groans. "Then I come home to my room practically turning into a library. He's totally raging on me because I wanted to turn music on in *my own bedroom.*"

"He's given up his space too," I say, clutching my elbows as I lean against the doorframe.

Kai huffs as he perches on the arm of the couch. "What are you doing sticking up for him? You're supposed to be on my side."

"I saw a different side tonight. Your parents forced him to spill info on you."

"Milo's a traitor, you know that. Or are you suddenly Team Milo?"

I pout, flashes of my first kiss running through my mind. Does this now make me the traitor? "I was just trying to say I feel guilty for taking over his space."

Kai rolls his eyes, gets off the couch, and walks over to me. "Don't get sad about it. I'd kick my brother out of the house to keep you here."

I laugh and let him side hug me. "I don't want Milo out on the streets."

Kai smirks as he pulls back. "Yeah, because Mom would never get off my case."

I fake a smile. "Yeah, that's why."

"Has she been giving you a hard time about studying?"

I shake my head. "Not really. I'm doing it regardless because there's so much to do."

"It's making you so boring."

I step back into the threshold of Milo's bedroom. "Why do you care? You have Tabitha to hang out with. Apparently, she's the only person who's made you happy today."

"That's because my best friend isn't being herself and sneaking out with me."

"Because I need to grow up and do the work." I almost yell it. "*Geez*, Kai. What are you not getting?"

He shrugs and turns away. "I just can't wait for it all to be over and for things to go back to normal."

"My scholarship will always be based on my academic record. I need to keep this up to stay in school."

"So, you'll turn into one of the brainwashed masses and keep regurgitating the crap they force feed us in school?"

"I'm sick of feeling dumb," I admit. "I never realized it before because I never paid attention. But now that I'm learning stuff, it's a massive struggle. I just feel like an idiot. I'm sick of feeling behind. It's embarrassing when Milo's teaching me and I just don't get it."

Kai sniggers. "You want to impress Milo?"

I grip the door hard and step back. "No. I want to impress myself." I slam the door hard, vibrating the bedroom walls.

Why is he being such a butthead? I guess it's worse because this is the first time in our friendship that we're not on the same page. I mean, sure, I'd love for things to go back to normal. I freaking love hanging out with Kai and having fun. But until my grade average is higher, I can't strike that balance.

I move back to the desk and pick up the diary. I smooth my hand over the cover and smile. "I'll make you proud, Mom."

I take a deep breath and open the diary. I skim through her talking about Buzz and how she wishes she could see him more. He lives in Victoria Falls and she can't afford to drive over often enough. He's a running back on the football team, and training has gotten intense, leaving no room for her.

Hmm. Maybe I should get Kai to read that and see that sometimes other obligations get in the way of relationships.

My fingers tremble around the page when Mom talks about another guy named Trigger. What kind of a name is that? She's into his leather jacket and the fact his hands are blackened and smell of grease from working on cars all day. She hasn't said anything bad about him yet, but I'm bracing for the worse.

When I was really little, Mom told me stories about her parents. Her dad spent most of their money on alcohol, and one day took off. Her mom then met Maddy's dad and there was hope that things would change for the better. But once Maddy was two-years-old, her dad started hitting their mom.

I'm so lucky to have my mom. She might not be with us anymore, but she did her darndest to get Maddy and I out of that house. Her mom was complacent in her toxic life. I love that my mom had strength and integrity. People like Camila want to taint her memory and put her down because of the things she did for money. But Lily West would've done anything to provide for us.

She's still listed as a missing person. With what her dad did and how much she struggled, the cops wholeheartedly believe she escaped her life. But she'd never leave us. In the past, I never let myself think about it. Now, I want to find out what happened to her.

I look down and skim through Trigger's introduction of Trigger. This guy could be my dad. He could've been the last person to see my mom alive. I shudder at the thought. Aunt Maddy told the cops about Mom's known associates when she first went missing. Surely, they interviewed this guy? But if he said she ran away, maybe they believed him.

My head feels so full that finishing my paper seems like a way to chill out. I read over my draft several times before emailing it to Milo. I type a short message along with the attachment. *"Can you point out any paragraphs I need to expand on? I think it's good, but it might not be good enough for Mr. Duncan."*

While I wait for Milo's reply, I scroll around on the school portal. There's a message from Coach Anders. *"Everything okay with the baby simulator?"*

I crack my knuckles and type a reply. *"Last night was rough! But Milo and I have been working well together and today seems okay."*

My mind drifts back to that kiss. Will Milo even look at my email after the way he hurried out of here? Will we ever talk or make eye contact again? Our hands even brushed together several times today. I don't want to lose that. Not over a silly kiss.

Well, if I'm honest, I want more of those silly kisses.

Why did he have to run off like that?

Before I can spiral, a reply pings in my portal messages. From Milo.

"It looks good. Paragraphs 3 & 4 seem a little rushed, so maybe tidy those up. Overall, it looks like a solid B."

A B? Oh my gosh! Aunt Maddy will be stoked. I can't wait to show this off to her.

I rub the space on my chest over my heart. He read my essay right away. Things are still okay.

Thank goodness!

I still need Milo's help with math and English, but I don't want to push it. He's working on his own assignments while looking after Gandalf and dealing with Kai's mood. I sit back on the desk chair and turn my head toward the wall shared with the bathroom. My eyes squint as I try my best to prick my ears. I wonder if Gandalf is fussing. Hope Milo knows to ask for help if he needs it.

I turn back to my laptop and reply to Milo. *"Thank you so much! I doubt I'll get a B, but it means a lot. How are things with Gandalf?"*

His replies hits two minutes later. *"I've fed him now, just rocking him against me as I type. Don't worry, I won't cut corners this time."*

His answer makes me laugh. I enjoy that there's still ease flowing between us. However, it gives me pause. Are we ignoring that the kiss happened? Did it happen? Did I go crazy and imagine it? Was it just a higher level of fantasy and he ran out of the bedroom purely because I was comatose and drooling?

Oh my gosh. This is so embarrassing.

No, I didn't imagine it. The kiss must've sucked and now he's ignoring the subject.

Dang. It really felt good to me. I'm probably worse at kissing than him. Yet another thing he'll have to teach me. Hmm. Kissing lessons don't sound like a bad idea.

"If he gets annoying, you can drop him off with me. I don't mind."

"It's all good. You've already done a lot."

I close out of the school portal and stare at my King Lear notes. I push them aside. So not in the mood. Through my bedroom door, I hear the blasts and catchphrases from Shadow Quests coming from the TV. Should I go out and play with Kai to bury the hatchet? It'd be better than getting up in the morning and having harsh awkwardness between us.

I get off the chair and move to the door. I turn the door knob slowly and pull the door open without a creak. I spy the back of Kai's head over the couch and hear him talking. His voice is low, and it takes a while to work out what he's saying.

That is until he mentions dinner. Holy cow. He just spent the whole day with Tabitha, including a dinner date, and now he's on the phone with her?

I close the door and storm over to the bed. I plonk face first and tug the covers over me. Screw this. He should've knocked on my door and made up with me. He chose to chat with her instead of making things right. He says he misses me, but he doesn't act like it. He's the one who's changed for the worse.

My angry thoughts spiral in my head until darkness consumes me into a lulled sleep. I wake up groggily with the overhead lights still on. I check my phone.

2.30 a.m.

I pull myself out of bed and stagger to the light switch. When I flick them off, I notice light seeping in from under the door. I open the door and see the TV on with no sound.

"Huh?" I mutter as I tiptoe across the carpet. As I round the couch, I find Milo lying on his back with Gandalf resting on his stomach.

"Oh, hey?" he whispers, tilting his head questioningly. "Did I wake you?"

"No. Well, I don't think so." I rub my tired eyes. "What are you doing up?"

"Gandalf was crying, and Kai was about to rip both our heads off. It was safer to come out here."

"I'm sorry he's kept you up. Do you want me to take over?"

Milo sits up, fixing his glasses. "No, I'm good. You should go back to bed."

"I feel bad." I sit on the opposite end of the couch. "If you're up, I should be up too."

"We're trading off. You already did your night."

"But I also woke you up." I smooth back my wild bed hair. "You calmed me down."

Milo smiles. "Well, if you want to stay, I won't stop you."

"Coach emailed me last night," I say. "He'll be at the cafe at 10 a.m. to take Gandalf. We don't need to do the full forty-eight hours. He must feel sorry for us."

"Hallelujah." Milo huffs. "Not that I won't miss the little guy, but he's so much work."

"Agreed. I don't know how my mom did it. Aunt Maddy said she was a natural and loved being a parent. I don't want to do it for another twenty years."

"But you would have kids?"

His question takes me aback. "Oh, well, umm. I don't know. Maybe. Ask me again in a decade or two."

He sniggers. "Okay."

Milo rubs Gandalf's back gently and I can't help focusing on every detail of his hands as my eyes become accustomed to the dark.

"What are you thinking about?" Milo whispers.

I break out of my stare. "Huh?"

"You looked deep in thought."

"Oh." I tuck my hair behind my ears. "Just thinking about a dream I had."

"Good dream?"

I clear my throat and search for his eyes in the dark. "It felt real. Has that ever happened?"

"Yeah, I guess."

"Or when something happens in real life, and you can't tell if you imagined it."

Milo shifts against the couch, fidgeting with his grip on Gandalf.

I lean closer. "I didn't imagine it, did I?"

He gulps. "What?"

Clamminess coats my face and neck. My voice is shaky when I whisper, "The kiss."

He blows out a hard breath. "Sorry."

"Why?"

"I shouldn't have…"

"But I liked it."

He pauses for two beats. "You did?"

"It was electrifying."

He laughs, scratching the side of his head. "Oh. I figured you'd regret doing it."

My stomach twists. "Why would you say that?"

He chews his bottom lip and turns away. "Because I'm not good enough for you."

I gasp, my chest aching. "Did you really just say that?"

He turns back to me, quiet.

"Milo, you've been more encouraging and supportive to me in the last week than some of my friends have been in years." I rub my chest, losing some tension as the warmth spreads. "I've been having so many thoughts about you I couldn't control. Believe me, I wanted to kiss you."

His mouth falls open. "Really?"

A soft giggle pours out of me as I cover my face. "Okay. Maybe I've spent a lot of time fighting these feelings. But, in the moment, it felt so dang right."

He lowers Gandalf to the couch cushion and slides closer. He scoops up my hand and looks deeply into my eyes. "Jamie, I've liked you for longer than I can remember. After we kissed, I got scared. You've never noticed me before, so I figured you'd ridicule me or yell and make a scene."

I wince, gritting my teeth. "You thought I'd do that?"

"I freaked out. Besides, it's how you and Kai usually act when something you don't like happens. Admit it, we've been nothing close to friends."

"Well, no. That's a given."

He drops my hand. "Even this past week. We'd have moments where I thought we were getting closer, but then you'd snap and pull away from me."

"Sorry." I frown, feeling the sadness weighing me down from within. "There were a ton of conflicting emotions going through me." I huff and look over my shoulder at Kai's bedroom. "I don't want anything to affect my relationship with Kai."

"He already gives me a hard time. I don't think I could handle his tirade if he found out I kissed you."

I shrug. "He doesn't have to know."

He double-takes at me. "Huh?"

I giggle, digging my fingers below my bottom lip. "I liked kissing you. I wouldn't mind doing it again."

"In secret?"

"Would that be so bad?"

"Just the thought of it gives me anxiety."

I lean closer and whisper an inch from his lips. "You should try rebelling now and then."

Before he can respond, my eyes close and I press my lips against his. It takes a beat or two until he kisses back. His hands run up my arms and grip my shoulders. I pull a hand around his neck and comb my fingers into his thick hair. Our lips slip and it causes a soft moan to expel from both of us. His arms pull around my back, forcing us closer together. My body temperature spikes and I increase the suction in our kiss.

As my other hand brushes against his cheek, Gandalf cries from behind Milo. We break apart and Milo turns to pick up the fake baby.

"Way to kill the mood," Milo jokes.

I giggle, sitting back on the couch and hugging my knees close to my chest.

Milo rocks Gandalf and the cries decrease in volume. "So, what does this mean?" he asks. "We've kissed. Now what?"

I raise my palms upwards. "More kissing?"

His eyebrows raise. "That's it?"

I sit up. "I like how things are between us. I think we have a good thing going. We're amicable and there's obviously something between us. Can't we just be friends who kiss?"

"Is that all you want?"

The clamminess spreads down my back. No, I want a boyfriend. A boyfriend I can show off. A boyfriend that won't ruin all my other friendships.

I nod. "For now. Is that okay?"

He smiles. "I can't go back to not kissing you. I'm in."

I lean in and kiss his cheek. "Thanks, Milo." I get off the couch and move back toward the bedroom. "Good luck getting him back to sleep."

He watches me from the back of the couch. "You're leaving?"

I pull the door behind me and say, "If rom-coms have taught me anything, it's leave them wanting more."

Twenty

Electricity buzzes under my skin as I lie in bed this morning. Flashes of midnight kisses on the couch with Milo flicker through my mind. I rub the goosebumps from my arms and pull down the bed covers. I rock my jaw, feeling the stretch from too much grinning during my sleep. From the way my smile muscles ache, I'm guessing I was grinning all the way through my dreams until my alarm woke me up.

I sit on the edge of the bed and smooth back my wild bed hair. I giggle, remembering Milo's adorable face as I walked away in the middle of the night. How will we act around each other this morning? Will it be awkward? Oh man, what if everyone can tell we've kissed? Will my face give it away?

Maybe I should avoid eye contact with Milo altogether. I'll at least keep our communication to a minimum. While it's still unexplored territory, I want to keep this a secret from Kai. He can't handle me being platonic with his brother. I have to keep this thing between me and Milo on the down-low until I can fully comprehend and explain it.

Me and Milo. It's surreal I'm even contemplating something romantic with this boy. Yet, it's beyond that. We're affectionate, close, and he makes me grin like a total goofball. How in the world does Milo Nelson have this hold over me?

I scuff across the bedroom, slip into a fluffy pair of slippers, and make my way to the bathroom to get freshened up for my workday. As I reach for the bathroom door handle, it turns. The door swings open and I'm face to face with Milo.

My insides melt down to goo, and I lean to the side. "Hi," I whisper pathetically.

His teeth graze his bottom lip as he smiles. "Hey."

I run a hand through my hair and my body temperature sizzles. "How are you?"

"I'm good, considering I didn't get much sleep last night."

"Gandalf kept you up?"

He folds his arms and looks down and to the side. Nervousness twitches the corners of his smile. "Ah, more like thoughts of someone else had me up all night."

Self-consciously, I tug at the neckline of my pajama shirt. "Oh. Umm. Okay."

Milo puffs a murmured laugh, smoothing down his t-shirt and fidgeting in his stance.

While my mind blanks on anything to add to the dwindling conversation, Kai's bedroom door bursts open beside us.

Kai walks out and double-takes at us. "Milo, grow a brain. Get out of Jamie's way."

As Kai cuts through the upstairs living room and then makes his way downstairs, Milo and I awkwardly pass each other in the bathroom doorway. We mutter nonsensical things, trying to act cooler than we are. I wave goodbye and close the door. The silence in the cream-tiled bathroom allows my heart to pound in my ears.

That was torturous.

Kai's interruption sent my head spinning. My heart can barely keep up. I exhale a steadying breath, pull a towel from the cupboard and rest it by the bathtub. I run the water in the shower and peel off my pajamas. Once steam billows off the water, I jump in, ready to wash off the awkwardness so I can get to work with a refreshed mindset.

After my shower, I make my way downstairs with my laptop bag. Last Sunday, all I could think about was leaving work so I could hang with Kai at the skatepark. This Sunday, I'm taking my homework with me so I can work on it during quiet periods during my shift. The likelihood of that is low, considering Pancake Stacks Sunday is our busiest day of the week, but you never know. I'd rather feel prepared.

Yeah, seriously, who am I?

Chirpiness bounces off the walls as family members move about the kitchen, dining, and living areas. Not only are Kai's parents driving me to work, they're taking their family out for breakfast at our cafe.

Grandma Nelson wraps me up in a hug the moment she sees me. While she squeezes and sways me, I spy Milo chatting with his grandpa. Gandalf's baby carrier is slung over his forearm. I peel myself away from Grandma and clutch the handle of the baby carrier.

Milo gives me a questioning look, and I say, "I'll take him from here. You look like you could use a rest."

Milo smiles, rubbing his red-lined eyes as he lets me take possession of the baby carrier. "I don't know how parents function," Milo says, yawning.

Grandpa chuckles. "This fake baby is a miracle worker. Gives kids appreciation for their parents."

"He means parents of newborns," I say. "Once kids can walk and talk, they're not as much effort."

Grandpa and Grandma burst into wild laughter. Grandma wipes under her eye, grinning from ear to ear. "Don't let Grace hear you say that. It'll be your head."

"Okay, everyone ready?" Mrs. Nelson calls out, striding out from the kitchen with an almighty clap. "We need to take two cars. Where's Steve?"

Mr. Nelson jingles his car keys from his comfortable armchair. "Just reading the news while I wait for everyone."

Mrs. Nelson huffs. "Yes, honey, you're always ready. Where's your wallet?"

"It's right..." Mr. Nelson gets up from the armchair and moves toward the rear of the house to his bedroom. "I'll be right back."

"Remember to pick up your cell while you're in there," Mrs. Nelson calls after him. Kai exits the kitchen, as his mother continues, "Okay, Kai's taking his car because he wants to drive Tabitha in. Dad will take the sedan so Grandma and Grandpa are comfortable."

Kai eyes his mom. "And you're going with them?"

She pinches the tip of Kai's nose. "I'm going with you, darling. I want to meet this girl's parents."

Kai frowns. "At eight in the morning?"

"That's the time we're all meeting her," she replies.

Kai shrugs. "Fine, whatever."

My hands tingle in suspense. "Ahh. Tabitha's coming to my cafe?"

Kai grins. "She'll love it. Plus, it'll give you two a chance to hang out outside of school."

"Jamie's not there to socialize, she's there to work. Don't distract her just because her aunt's away." Mrs. Nelson beckons everyone toward the garage. "Okay, let's go. Jamie can't be late for work."

Milo gestures to the baby carrier. "We can't all fit in Dad's car. The carrier needs to be strapped in or it'll register as abuse."

I lift the carrier, making sure not to knock Gandalf. "We haven't done all this work to fail at the last minute. I'll go with Kai."

"No, you'll be late if you come with us," Mrs. Nelson says as her husband wanders back to us. "Milo, you'll come with us. Honey, make sure Jamie's baby carrier is fastened tight in the back seat before you take off."

"No problemo," Mr. Nelson says, leading the way to the garage.

Kai follows, pulling on a bomber jacket. "Today, Milo."

Mr. Nelson chuckles. "Kai, you're a nervous wreck. Take a breath."

Milo shoots me a look as he walks to the garage door. The apprehension in his eyes mirrors the dread seeping into my stomach.

I. Do. Not. Want. Tabitha. Jones. In. My. Cafe.

Should I get a sign made and stick it on the front door of Morton's Cafe? Ugh. Seriously. Why do they have to do a meet and greet at my family's business? Can't they do it here while I'm at work? I don't want to witness this. Plus, I don't want someone who torments me in the school halls to enter the space where I work. All those people are supposed to stay at Village Coffee on the other end of Main Street.

At the cafe, I seat Mr. Nelson, Grandma, and Grandpa at the long stretched table reserved for them. I leave Gandalf with them and walk behind the counter. I pull on an apron and my hands tremor as I yank on the ties and twist them around my middle.

"Hey, sport," Jake says, viewing me from the food pass. "You okay? Looks like some angry tying there."

I drop the ties of the apron and flex my fingers. My knuckles crack from the furious hand movements. "I'm fine."

Laura comes out of the kitchen. "Kylie took tables one through ten so you could have the section with your friends."

My gut plummets. "No."

Laura blinks at me. "Excuse me?"

I shake my head. "Sorry. It's just I'd prefer not to serve them."

"Since when?"

I cover with, "I'm already seeing too much of them. Who knew living with your best friend could be too much of a good thing."

Laura laughs, picking up a coffee pot. "Well, too bad. Kylie's already started and you know how confusing it can get when we swap tables. I'm sure you and your bestie can handle it."

I fake a smile and ready my station. Lucky for the other tables in my section, they're about to get a whole lot of attention. I'm willing to do anything to avoid Tabitha's snarky comments.

I start Mr. Nelson and the grandparents on coffee while they wait for the others. Gandalf gurgles while I stroke his stomach. It's weird to think he'll be gone in a few hours.

For the next fifteen minutes, I busy myself with tables until the distinct noises of Kai and the others bustle into the cafe. My back seizes and I carefully look their way. My gaze stays low, scared to look her directly in the eyes. I've barely seen her outside of school, so I don't know if her vindictiveness is better or worse in a different environment. A twinkle of hope lights inside me. Maybe it'll be better. There has to be a reason Kai keeps gravitating toward her when school finishes.

Everyone at the table makes a fuss, leaping up to welcome Tabitha with hugs. While they huddle together, I edge toward the table to collect Gandalf. With all the focus on Tabitha, I don't want him to get neglected.

"You can leave him here," Milo says softly, moving toward the other end of the table. "I'm happy to watch him while you work."

"It's okay," I say with a smile. "I'll put him behind the counter. Things at your table might get a little preoccupied."

He shakes his head. "I won't though."

I lean in and whisper. "I know your mom, though. She'll drag you into the conversation whether you like it or not."

A faint laugh slips out of Milo. "Okay, you take him. Getting up to check on him will give me a good excuse to leave the table."

I nod and can't help eyeballing the group. I wonder how it went meeting her parents. I zero in on Mrs. Nelson. She's usually a good judge of character. Can she see-through Tabitha?

I look back at Milo, about to ask how the drive over here went, when the family disperses around the table. I jump when Mrs. Nelson asks me for coffee. Without looking up, I take Kai and Tabitha's drink orders. Kai orders a Toasty

S'more milkshake for her, saying she'll die and go to heaven. I could arrange that. There's rat poison locked away in the office.

I ask Milo if he'd like his usual, and he replies with a coy smile and slight nod. No one notices the lingering stare we share, too busy asking Tabitha for her life story. It's super weird. Usually, especially with Grandma and Grandpa around, I'm the center of attention. Now, as I serve drinks, take the breakfast order, and serve it, I'm invisible.

This has never happened before.

I've never been invisible to anyone with the last name Nelson.

My eyes burn holes into the back of Tabitha's head. She's the invader. Her evil plan is to turn them all against me. Why didn't I see this coming? She won't insult me in my workplace. She's torturing me by making me watch her take away my second family.

Thank goodness for the other tables. I put the Nelsons out of my mind as I take orders, serve food, and clear away dirty plates. Every time I go in and out of the kitchen, I check on Gandalf, who pleasantly lies in his carrier.

When my section gives me a break, I lean against the counter for a breather. Kai pivots his head, looking for me. When he spots me, he grins eagerly and excuses himself from the table. As he walks toward the counter, I watch behind him. Tabitha turns with her mouth ajar, wary of her boyfriend leaving her for me.

Yes! Internal fist bump.

Kai leans against the counter beside me. His heels bounce with nervous enthusiasm as he looks back at the table. "It looks like it's going well, right? The fam seems to like Tabby. Don't you think so?"

"Yeah, I guess. From what I can see. I'm too busy working to keep tabs on things."

"You don't care if today goes well?"

"Why did she want to come *here* to meet your family?" I ask begrudgingly. "Tabitha and her friends have never come here before. I figured it was beneath them."

"What can I say?" Kai replies. "Once word got around that Ash and his girlfriend loved the shakes here, everyone wants in on the trend. This place will be the new *it* place."

I roll my eyes. "Wow. Aunt Maddy will be thrilled."

Kai pinches my cheek. "Cheer up. More business equals more ways for your aunt to pay your school fees."

I fold my arms and frown. "So I don't have to study anymore?"

"So we can get back to having more fun together."

"You know I want that, too. But whenever I have downtime, you're with Tabitha."

"Not today," Kai declares. "Tabby's around now, but I don't need to see her for the whole day. I'll take her home after breakfast and I'll be totally free when you get off work. Let's hang out at the skatepark. Just you and me."

"What about the other guys?"

"What about them?" Kai says as sincerity twinkles in his eyes. "I just care about chilling with my best bud. I know it's weird that I have a girlfriend now, but it doesn't make you any less of a priority in my life."

I fold my arms, slightly turning away. "Well, it sure has felt like that the past few days."

"It's just new," Kai replies. "I'm working out the balance. I'll make it right. I promise."

I drop my arms to my sides. "Okay. I believe you."

"So, you'll take a break from the books?" Kai asks with hope. When I nod yes, he adds, "Awesome. I'll pick you up from here with your blades in the trunk of my car. We can hang out as long as you want."

I grin and pat his shoulder. "Sounds perfect. Thanks, bro."

Kai walks back to the table and a wealth of good vibes bubble inside me. There's pep in my step as I refill coffees in my section. I'm broken out of the bubble when my ears prick to Gandalf's cry. I know that bottle cries the best, and I move back to the counter.

I pull his bottle out of the bag and press the nip to his mouth. He suckles away happily and I let out a content sigh.

"Is this the baby?" a soft voice asks behind me.

I turn around and jolt backward. Tabitha stands before me, craning her neck to sneak a peek at Gandalf.

"Yeah," I say, turning the carrier. "Coach Anders will be in soon to pick him up."

"And it's actually been like having a real baby?"

I nod. "Complete with crying, nappy changing, and burping."

"*Eww.*" She giggles behind a cupped hand. "I hope I never have to do this assignment. I couldn't imagine doing it for real. Kai said your mom was our age when she had you."

I stiffen and my stomach wobbles. "Yes."

She curls her hands into her hair, looking off to the side in wonder. "I couldn't imagine. Did she cope, or is that why she left? She's a missing person, right?"

"She didn't leave," I blurt, raising my voice enough it engages the two closest tables. "My mom loved me."

Tabitha's eyes grow circular as her mouth falls open. "Oh my gosh, I didn't mean anything..." She slaps her forehead. "Geez, I'm such an idiot. I'm sorry."

I look her up and down and find her genuine enough. "It's fine," I mutter.

"Look, that picture that Cammy found," Tabitha rushes her words, "I didn't have anything to do with..."

"Don't!" I cut her off, holding up my hands like stop signs. My eyes water and I use all my strength to not let my voice quiver. "I can't hear it right now. This is where I work and my coach will walk in any minute now."

Her bottom lip quirks as she pouts. Her eyes droop as she backs away. "I'm sorry," she mouths, moving back over to Kai.

I watch her sit by Kai, who's in deep conversation with his dad and grandma. When he notices Tabitha, he double-takes. His hand rests on her shoulder and his head dips low. I can tell he's whispering, "Are you okay?"

I stretch my back, feeling every knot cause more tension. I look across the Nelson table and almost lose balance when I land on Milo, whose eyes lock with mine. Was he watching the entire time Tabitha was over here?

He scoots his chair back and moves my way. I press my shaking hands into my churning stomach. He stops short of the counter, taking me in.

When he says nothing, I blurt, "Yeah?"

He lifts his palms up. "Everything okay? It looked intense over here."

I smooth my hands over my hair and press them against the back of my neck. "I can't deal with her here," I whisper harshly. "Why is everyone cool with her being here?"

Milo steps forward, as close as he can get with the counter between us. "I'm not."

I blink too many times, wishing he'd turn into a prince and carry me away. "What happened during the car ride over?"

Milo leans his elbows on the counter as he sighs out. "I had to sit next to her because Mom was riding shotgun. Kai would keep hounding me to talk to Tabby, but I couldn't say more than hi. I just can't forget the way those girls treat you. It's insane that Kai can."

I hug my waist as my knees knock. "You think Kai doesn't care that Tabitha's friends say messed up things to me?"

Milo peels off the counter. "Or he's oblivious to it?"

"She just tried it again," I murmur, wiping under my eye. "She was about to bring up the picture of my mom. I'm surprised more people didn't hear me yell."

Milo throws a thumb over his shoulder. "Do you want me to ask Kai to take her home?"

I shake my head. "No, I don't want to make a scene. Your dad will ask for the bill soon, anyway."

He nods and clutches his elbows. "Kai said you're hanging at the skatepark after work?"

I bite my lip and nod. "Just for a little bit. I told your mom I brought my laptop, so she didn't think I was totally ditching my assignments."

Milo fidgets in his stance, glancing around the prep station behind me. "No, that's okay. I was just checking because my friends usually come over on Sundays while Kai is out with you. I just didn't know if you'd come back home to study, or were expecting me to be free. Not that I'm saying you and I would do anything... Well, not that we can't. I just..."

"Milo," I cut him off. "Stop rambling. It's fine. I'll be with Kai for a few hours, as per usual. What do you and your friends do on Sundays, anyway?"

"Something you and Kai would no doubt ridicule us for."

I puff a laugh and shake my head. "Okay, I get it."

Over Milo's shoulder, I see the front door of the cafe open. My stomach wobbles. Coach is here. I pick up the baby carrier and motion to Milo.

Milo spots Coach, swallows hard, and then looks down at Gandalf. "This is it, little buddy. Time to part ways."

"Oh, man." I pout. "Don't say it like that. It sounds sad."

Milo fidgets with his glasses as he tilts his head, watching me. "Aw, cute. You're going to miss Gandalf."

"Shut up." I laugh. "Am not."

Milo squeezes my shoulder. "Who knew Jamie West had such a tender heart?"

I groan and push past him. "Stop it. Let's get this over with."

We meet Coach at a small table in my section. He watches us intently. No doubt trying to figure out the weird energy flowing between us.

"How'd you two do?" Coach asks, carefully looking between Milo and me. "You survived?"

I hand the baby carrier over to Coach. "Two days was more than enough."

Coach chuckles, resting the carrier on the table. He picks Gandalf up and deactivates him.

"Does he only have one setting?" Milo asks, gesturing at the fake baby. "Because last night was rough. How is anyone supposed to concentrate on any other assignments when this one is constantly screaming for attention?"

"It's a wonder parents ever get anything done," Coach says sarcastically.

"That's the same attitude all adults have," I say bluntly. "Is this why you don't have kids, Coach? Did you have to do this assignment when you were at school and it turned you off for life?"

Coach gives me an exasperated sigh. "I just got a flashback of Grams asking me when I was ever going to find a nice girl and settled down."

I giggle. "I'm surprised she didn't set you up with Mom."

Coach smirks. "Wasn't for lack of trying."

I smile and nod. "Sounds like Grams."

Coach beckons for our wrists. "Hands up, kids. I'll take those wristbands now."

"Freedom," Milo jokes as Coach uses an indented metal tool to remove his wristband.

Coach takes mine, and it feels oddly unsettling. It dawns on me Gandalf won't cry again. He won't even be called Gandalf. He'll be put back on the shelf until a new pair of students are up for the challenge.

"In all seriousness," Coach says, "are you two okay? I know it couldn't have been easy."

"I'm okay," I reply. I nudge Milo and try to hide my bashful smile. "He was a big help."

Milo lifts his hands, taking a step back. "I'd have been lost without Jamie. It was all her."

"Team effort?" I offer.

His smile slides to the right. "Sure thing."

Coach gives us an approving nod. "That's great to hear. I'll upload the data tomorrow and add your extra credit to your records as soon as I can. Jamie, I'm sure it'll give you not only a grade average boost, but a confidence boost too. I hope you're beginning to see your potential."

I dig my hands into the pocket of my apron. "Yeah, I am. I've been taking my homework a lot more seriously. I mean, ask Kai. He's so sick of me studying all the time that he's started calling me a nerd."

Coach's head falls backward in laughter. "My goodness, I never thought I'd hear the day." He wipes under his eye, steadying his breath. "Your mom would be so proud right now."

Instinctively, I sniff hard. "Thanks," I whisper tightly, careful to not let emotion shake my voice. "I know how much she wanted me to have advantages. I just never realized I was ignoring them before."

"You're sixteen," Coach says tenderly. "Give yourself a break."

"Thanks. Your usual?"

Coach nods. "Please."

"Thanks again, Coach," Milo says with a wave as he turns away from the table with me. "Phew," he whispers. "We're done."

I bite my lip, looking up at him. "I think we did okay."

He lifts his hand, angling for a high five. "We nailed it."

"Goof." I laugh and indulge him in a high five.

Milo goes back to the table, and Mr. Nelson meets me at the counter to pay the bill. He confirms Kai will pick me up at the end of my shift, and then rallies everyone to the vehicles.

Kai gives me a side hug, annoyingly asking me again if I think everything went okay between Tabitha and his family. When he finally believes my third, "yes," he moves toward the front door. I smile, waving back at Milo as he leaves. The smile fades when Tabitha gets in on the waving.

Seeing her walk out the door did not come soon enough.

"All good, kiddo?" Coach asks as I near his table.

I plonk on a seat across from him. "I'm exhausted."

"It's good to see you put so much effort into something that's not soccer."

I wince. "How'd they do?"

"It was rough. I won't sugarcoat it."

I slam a fist onto the table. "Why did you bench me? I could've handled studying and playing."

"And how would you have learned how important studying is if I didn't set boundaries and give you repercussions?"

"It's not up to you," I argue. "The principal can give me detentions, suspensions, or expel me. Why is it up to you?"

He leans over his coffee. "Because believe it or not, I care about you."

I fold my arms, sinking lower on the seat. "Well, thanks, I guess."

"I want you to do better so you can get back on the team. Take it as an extra incentive that they *really* need you."

I blow out a hard breath. "They already hate me for missing practice. I can just imagine what they'll say on Monday morning."

"They just need to put in as much practice as you're doing with studying," Coach says with a wry smile. "I need more than one star player."

I laugh and stand up. "Thanks, Coach. I needed an ego boost."

"It's true, kid. You're my star." He opens wallet and places some cash on the table. "A little extra for all your effort."

My heart swells. "You didn't have to do that."

He stands and pats my back. "You're doing good, Jamie. Keep it up."

I thank him again, and he leaves the cafe. I pick up the money and move behind the counter. I close out his table, pocket his generous tip, and tell Laura I'm taking a break.

After whipping together a loaded sandwich, I seclude myself in Aunt Maddy's office. Kicking back in her desk chair with my feet on the desk, I stretch my arms above my head and listen for a crack in my back.

"*Ahh.*" It purrs out of me with relief.

I slip my feet off the desk and pick up my sandwich. With a big bite, I flip through the notes I brought with me. I stop on Mom's diary. This book has become a security blanket. Keeping it close has me feeling protected. There's been such a disconnect between me and Mom's presence for the past few years.

Now it's like she's back and telling me all her secrets. I'm weirdly missing Gandalf right now, and I need one of her stories.

I flip through Mom's diary and stop on a page framed with hand drawn love hearts. My heart pitter-patters, and I read over what she wrote.

I've never loved a single living thing more. I can't believe how natural and fulfilling it feels to hold my baby girl in my arms. All I want to do is to protect her from the hideousness of this world. I see every time someone gives me a disgusted look for being her mom at such a young age. It's every time I leave the house with her. I never want my baby to be looked at like that. But at least I know I can be strong and have her back. I won't let her be teased and ridiculed and hurt. I will take it to protect her and Maddy. I don't want either of them to suffer. I will take all the hits for them.

I swipe at my watering eyes, but it doesn't stop the stinging tears from erupting. I suck in a ragged breath. *Oh, Mom.* I know you tried your best.

She didn't even know how little time we'd have together, and she still made up for it. Aunt Maddy and I are doing fine. I could live without the bullying at school, but I think those girls are lucky my mom's not around to flush their heads in a toilet bowl.

The imagery makes me chuckle, and I wipe my eyes clear.

Love comes to life from her handwriting on the page. It truly makes me glad Gandalf was a simulation that lasted only two nights. It's unfathomable to be so loyal and protective of another person for the rest of my days.

I put the diary aside and pick up my phone for a mindless scroll. Before I can think about which app to open, my attention zooms in on a text from Kai.

"Hey, Tabby wants to watch a movie. Our session time is in twenty minutes, and it runs for two hours. Let me know where you'll be after work and I'll pick you up after I drive her home."

My hand shakes as I grip my phone. Pain radiates down my neck from gritting my teeth so hard. Never has the phrase 'blood boiling' meant more. I drop my phone onto the desk, afraid I'll snap it in two. I swipe my clammy hands against my apron and let out a furious, yet muffled yelp. Steam hits my face as I snort hard.

Did I imagine it, or did he not beg me to hang out with him the minute I finished work? He promised to find a balance between me and his girlfriend. However, the minute she has him alone, he goes back on his word.

I snatch my phone and hurriedly text a response. *"Don't bother. I'll stay home after work."*

"Don't be huffy. It'll only be an hour, maybe 90 mins after your shift."

"That is until she decides she wants to do something else with you. Don't make me any more promises you can't keep."

"I'm sorry. I didn't think it was a big deal. Do you want me to cancel on her?"

Ugh. So I can look like the bad guy? *"No."*

"Thanks, James. I hope one day you find someone and understand how your mind gets wrapped up in wanting to spend time with them."

I slide the phone into my pocket. My lips rub together as memories of Milo flood my mind. Okay, Kai. Maybe I'll follow your lead.

Twenty-One

Time stood still on the approach to 2 p.m. It didn't help that I had to spend most of the time with a frosty Kylie. I'm unsure where Kai's parents will be. As far as they're concerned, Kai's picking me up, so they could've made plans to go out of town. With my fingers crossed, I dial the landline. Grandpa Nelson answers the phone with a jovial bounce in his tone.

"I'll be there in a jiffy," he says with no qualms about picking me up from work.

When his gray sedan arrives out front, I wave goodbye to the crew and book it outside.

"Has my grandson become forgetful since turning sixteen?" Grandpa jokes on the drive home.

"Just mixing up his priorities," I reply as diplomatically as possible.

"Well, you won't have to waste your afternoon with me and Grandma," he replies, turning a corner. "Milo and his friends are playing a game in the dining room."

"You mean in the living room?"

"No, it's at the table. Some kind of big board game with lots of figurines taking up space." Grandpa throws a hand in the air with an exasperated splutter. "Beats me what it is. Looks complicated."

I smirk, tapping my fingertips together. "I'll have to take a look."

We arrive home and Grandpa Nelson parks in the garage by Mr. Nelson's car. Mrs. Nelson's SUV and Kai's car are both absent.

"Grace and Steven are both out," Grandpa informs, referring to Kai's parents.

"Kai's at a movie with Tabitha," I tell him. "I suspect they'll stay out all day together, just like yesterday."

Grandpa chuckles as we make our way into the house. "He sure is smitten with that girl, isn't he? Pretty little thing, she is, and quite a lovely personality."

Geez, who'd you meet, Grandpa? "Yeah, sure."

"Do you spend a lot of time with her at school?"

Just when she and her friends are calling me names before, during, and after classes. "Sometimes."

Grandpa pats my back. "Helps when you're friends with the person your friend is dating."

I don't respond because my fake niceness is stretched too thin.

Grandpa turns into the living room where Grandma waves from the couch over a novel and cup of coffee. I wave back and continue toward the rear of the house, where excited chatter grows louder.

As I approach the dining room, the shouting across the table isn't any easier to understand. Milo's friends argue about rules and lore as they gesture at pieces strewn across the table. I tilt my head as I stand a few feet away from the table, trying to get a handle on what exactly I'm looking at. Milo has his back to me, one friend sits adjacent at the head of the table, and the other friend sits opposite Milo.

The friend sitting opposite grows mute the minute he notices me in the room.

"Umm, hi?" I say with a hint of laughter.

Milo turns and gives me an uneasy look. "Oh, hey. What are you doing back?"

"Ah, I live here at the moment. Remember?" I tease.

He rolls his eyes. "I thought you were going to the skatepark with Kai."

"He ditched me." I saunter toward the table and glance over the gameboard, filled with mountainscapes, caves, rivers, and land borders. Different colored, shaped, and sized figurines take over quadrants of the board. "What's all this?"

The boys shift away from my gaze, making noises but not actual words. In front of them are cards, dice, and other tokens. I pick up a card from Milo's pile and inspect the front and back.

He snatches it from my grasp. "It's called Draikin Crusades and we're in the middle of a game."

I rest a hand on the back of Milo's chair and pop a hip as I watch the other two boys squirm in my presence. "Well, don't let me stop you. I need to unwind after my shift and this might be just the entertainment I need."

Milo's eyes narrow, scrutinizing to find my intent. "Not buying it. You can go upstairs and play a video game."

"I'm bored with them."

Milo divides his cards and places half of them in front of the empty seat beside him. "If you're sticking around, you have to play."

Frustrated groans erupt from the other boys.

"But you're in the middle of a game," I reply, backing away from Milo.

Milo shrugs. "You play, or you leave."

"She can't play," one of the boys whispers harshly. It's John Hughes from my math class.

"You're dividing your army and loot," the other boy, Ryan, says to Milo. "We're not giving her anything."

Milo smirks. "It's no big deal. I'll still win."

Intrigued by the competitiveness shining through Milo, I pull out the chair beside him. "Okay. How do I play?"

Milo gestures at his friends. "You know John and Ryan, right?"

"Yeah, hi," I say to the guys, having rarely spoken to them before.

"Hi," they reply in sullen tones. It's beyond obvious how much they don't want me around, but I don't care. I block them from my view, sending all my attention directly at Milo. I'm magnetized to his radiating confidence as he explains the game pieces and which player occupies which space on the board.

I took none of it in, but it's a game. How hard can it be? It's not even on a TV screen. I bet I beat these boys as easily as I do my friends.

John and Ryan snigger together when they inspect the cards, land, and army Milo gave me. I watch the boys, glance at Milo, look down at my game pieces, and then back at him.

"Did you give me your rejects?" I ask Milo.

Even though he's being sneaky, his smile is too dang adorable for me to be mad. He taps his cards and shrugs. "You didn't think I'd give away anything important, did you?"

I giggle. "You butthead."

He laughs. "Hey, you're joining the game late. It's your loss."

John and Ryan exchange glances as Milo and I laugh together. Their brows furrow as they decode our dynamic.

"Sabotaging someone is almost like cheating." I look at John pointedly. "You'd know about cheating. Wouldn't you?"

John's expression falls, muttering wounded sounds.

Milo shifts in his seat. "What are you talking about, Jamie?"

It makes sense Milo wouldn't know about John cheating on his math homework. They wouldn't be friends otherwise.

"Never mind." I clear my throat, straighten up, and scoop a pair of dice in my hand. "Okay, what number do I want to roll?"

Milo points a finger, circling an area on the board with ridged mountains. "Only a nine or higher will get you out of that mess."

I clasp my hands together, shaking the dice inside my palms. I drop the dice onto the table and find a two and a three staring up at me.

The table erupts in laughter. My eyes slit as I look around at the boys enjoying my failure. Milo instructs me to pick up a card. When I turn it over, more laughter occurs. I already have two of these cards in my pile, which were deemed terrible picks.

"Maybe you guys think no one can win when occupying this area," I say as the laughter dies down, "but you've never seen me play."

John rolls the dice. "Yeah, and you've never played, period. You can trash talk all you like. It doesn't mean you can change the way the game works."

Ryan quickly makes his move after John. He rearranges his army and invades one of John's domains. "And you have a tendency to forget to cover your weak points."

John groans. "What the heck? I hate you."

Milo laughs. "It's your own fault for leaving yourself wide open. You know Ryan will always swoop in when you don't evenly disperse your warrior orcs." Milo rearranges his cards and examines the board. He then nudges me, saying, "The good thing about your crummy hand, is I don't think you need to worry about anyone invading."

I grin. "That's a good point. I can just work on moving onto other territory."

John scowls at me. "Don't even think about it."

Milo makes his move, and nothing seems to change on the board. But considering the ease in Milo's body language, I'm guessing he's planning a low-key strategy which will pay dividends later. I pull at my shirt collar. Oh boy, his air of cool confidence is really making my blood pump harder.

As the game continues, I make some ground. However, anytime I try to conquer, I'm swiftly knocked back a peg or two. Milo tries to give me pointers, but the other two guys shoot him down, constantly repeating, "This is war."

The seriousness about this silly tabletop game has me in stitches. Milo continues to conquer more ground, building his army. The other two boys complain, but Milo keeps his cool. Seriously boy, could you sizzle any hotter?

"Hi there, Kai. How was the movie?" Grandpa's voice echoes from the living room.

The distinct click of the garage door closing follows. "It was good, thanks. Is Jamie around?"

"In the dining room with Milo."

My back seizes, and my lungs constrict. I squeak, forcing oxygen in as I turn my head on a stiff neck. From the corner of my eye, Milo notices me rapidly shifting into freak out mode.

Oh my gosh, this was a huge mistake. Kai can't catch me playing this game.

Kai enters the room and immediately holds his belly in laughter. "Oh, good lord. What do we have here? The nerd brigade and their dweeby tabletop game?"

Milo huffs at his brother. "Can't you just move along?"

"James, what are you doing?" Kai asks, ignoring his brother as he moves closer to me. "Are you actually into this weird game?"

He gives me the look we normally share. My best friend mocking me for something this lame is cringe-inducing.

An indignant snort pours out of me as I leap off the chair. I push away from the table, grimacing as I shake out my shoulders. "As if. What do you take me for? Some kind of loser?"

Kai laughs as he hangs an arm around my shoulders, guiding me out of the dining room.

My back cramps with knots. Regret fills me with queasiness as the word loser ricochets around my head. Why did I say it? It just slipped out as if it were on autocue. I just didn't want Kai to give me a hard time. The easiest thing to do is deflect.

Ugh. I just walked out on Milo after dropping the L-bomb. My heart breaks. I feel like crap as I march up the stairs with Kai.

"Did you hear me, Jamie?" Kai asks as we hit the upstairs landing.

"Huh?"

"I said I'm sorry," he replies. "For like the millionth time. Are you really that grumpy with me?"

"Oh, no. I'm over it," I say, flopping on the couch. Kai hanging out with his girlfriend is small potatoes compared to what I just did to Milo.

"Good," Kai says, crash landing beside me. "Because we still need to hang out."

I rub my temples. "I just wanna nap."

Kai reaches down beside the couch, unplugs a cord and then lifts the drone I got for his birthday. "Come on, let's get out of here. The drone's all charged up. We'll head out to Logan's Point and fly it around."

I hug my waist. Since reading Mom's diary and the ugly words that came from Camila's lips at school, it's the last place I want to be. "I don't want to go to Logan's Point."

"That's cool. How about the mountains just outside of Logan's Point? Imagine the views out there."

I smile at his animated excitement and agree. "Okay. I've been dying to take it out ever since we picked it up at the store."

"Awesome. Let's go." Kai hitches the drone under his arm and gets off the couch. "It's a bummer we can't go out to Dead Left Cliff. Since Milo couldn't keep his yap shut, Mom's been grilling me about going out there."

Sick of hearing Kai blame things on his brother, I brush him off. "Yeah, yeah. Whatever."

After quickly changing into denim shorts, a black t-shirt, and tying a green hoodie around my waist, I meet Kai downstairs, avoiding the dining room as we make our way into the garage. From the quietness downstairs, I gather the game has been packed away.

"Who brought you home?" Kai asks as he backs down the drive.

"Your grandpa."

"Okay, good. I was hoping I didn't leave you stranded."

"Would it have mattered? You'd already bought your movie tickets, right?"

"I figured Jake or Laura could've driven you home."

I side-eye him. "While Aunt Maddy's away on the busiest day of the week?"

He groans. "I dunno. Why is this turning into another fight?"

I sigh, sinking against the leather seat. "I don't know. I don't want to keep fighting with you."

He smiles. "Good. Me neither."

The car rolls through Main Street and we pass the neighborhoods leading out to Mountains Road. Kai loves taking his car out here because there are so many twists and turns on the road as we climb the mountains.

"Anyway," Kai pipes up. "Why were you playing that game?"

I fidget in the seat. "They were entertaining to watch."

Kai laughs. "*Ha.* I see. You were mocking them."

I rock my jaw, searching for the right response. "I wasn't taking it seriously. Let's put it that way. Besides, it's basically the same as the games we play. Except, they don't get to watch a heap of speed-runs on how to finish a level. Their games are random, depending on what number they roll, and what cards they draw."

"*Pfft.* Whatever. They're not the same."

In some ways, the twins are more alike than I care to admit. "How was the movie?"

Kai smirks, shaking his head. "Some chick flick. I would've rather eaten gravel. Dang, James. You've no idea how awful those things are."

My stomach flips. "Yeah."

"But hey, Tabby liked it, and I got to have my arm around her the whole time." He chuckles. "Block your ears. *Ha.* We even made out a few times. Saved me from the boring bits!"

My insides twist in distress. I am simultaneously jealous and offended. The mix of emotions is causing extreme havoc in my body.

Kai tilts his head to gain a better view of me. "You okay? You look like you're in pain. Geez, did the mention of making out in the movie theater make you sick?"

He had a total rom-com moment, while watching a rom-com, and it's all a total joke to him. Plus, he's convinced I'd hate every second of it. How am I supposed to partake in this conversation? Do I just blurt out that I'm actually obsessed with romantic situations? That I'm jealous he's the one going out on dates? If I did, would he slam on the brakes and ask where his best friend went?

"James, what's going on? You're freaking me out."

I swallow hard and wipe my clammy forehead dry. "Sorry," I breathe. "I think I drank one too many milkshakes in Aunt Maddy's office today."

Kai slows the car's speed. "I'll take the bends easier so you don't hurl."

I give an unconvincing smile. "Thanks."

After five minutes of silent driving, Kai parks in a parking bay on the mountain's edge and at a high altitude. He gets out and retrieves the drone from the back seat. "Ready, James?"

I get out, smoothing a hand over my swirling stomach. "Mhmm."

He fires up the drone, and watching it swirl around in the sky is a good excuse to stay silent. As I watch it circle above us, my mind clears. Maybe I was right to always avoid talking about dating with Kai. My head has never been such a mess.

As the drone flies over the valley below, Kai leans against the railing. A relieved exhale pours out of him. "Man, I'm so glad this morning went well. It wasn't my imagination, right? Everyone loved Tabby?"

I nod, resting on the railing beside him. "Your family only said nice things about her."

He puffs out a laugh. "I've never been so nervous."

"Really? Why were you so nervous?"

"Because I really like her."

I stare at him, seeing genuine admiration in his expression as he thinks about Tabitha. "I don't mean this to sound rude or anything, but why do you like her?"

He turns to look at me. "Huh?"

"What do you like about Tabitha? You've never actually told me."

He smiles and pushes off the railing. He stands taller as he brings the drone in. "There's so much to like about her. She makes me feel calm. She doesn't judge me. Above all, she's kind, considerate, and loyal. What more could I ask for in a girl?"

My mouth sours with disgust. Does he own the ultimate pair of rose-colored glasses, or what? The words he described are the total opposite of what I'd call Tabitha Jones. Are Milo and I the only two people to see her as she truly is?

I give my delusional friend an uneasy smile. "You really think she's like that?"

Kai lands the drone on the dirt in an empty parking space. He takes one hand off the controller and squeezes my shoulder. "I know you're still warming up to the idea of me having a girlfriend, but give her a chance. You'll really like her, James. I promise."

There's the second broken promise he's given me today.

"Sure," I say, taking the controller. "Whatever you think."

"Don't crash it," Kai says, looking down the ravine. "I ain't climbing down there to rescue it."

I nudge him as the drone soars into the sky. "Excuse me. You're the one who totaled your last drone. I'm a good driver."

"Unless it comes to passing your driving test," he teases.

I nudge him harder, sending the drone haywire.

Kai fights for the controller. "Hey, you crazy person. Look out!"

I get the drone back on course, plucking the controller from Kai's grip. "Stop panicking, you baby."

"Speaking of babies, I'm so glad that thing is finally out of the house."

I grin. "You mean Gandalf?"

Kai groans. "Oh my gosh. It's hellish enough sharing my room with Milo, but having that screaming smelly thing around sent me through the roof."

I snort. "Geez, Kai, you're so dramatic. Gandalf was not that bad. I even miss the little guy."

Kai scoffs. "You do not."

I shrug, bringing the drone back toward us. "I kinda do."

"You freaky weirdo."

I laugh and land the drone. "Give me a break. It was extra credit I severely needed."

"I doubt you needed it that badly. You've been studying day and night. If you're still failing after all that work, there's no hope for you."

I shove the controller at him. "Well, thanks."

"I wasn't being sarcastic. I really mean you've been working hard and it should pay off."

I cross my arms. "And what if it doesn't? I'll be too dumb to function?"

"You're so touchy about this school stuff." He grabs my shoulder, giving me a slight shake. "James, you're not getting kicked out of school. You're too stubborn to let that happen." He smirks. "I know that because you're exactly like me."

I blow out a hard breath. "Kai, I really don't want to leave Ashworth Academy. The thought petrifies me."

He nudges me and then picks up the drone. "It's not happening, Jamie. I'll protest harder than I've ever done if they even consider tearing up your scholarship."

I giggle, easily picturing the scene Kai would create. "Okay, bro, I believe you."

"I got you." He grins, giving me a salute. "Come on, let's head home. I'm starving."

Twenty-Two

Milo avoided eye contact during dinner. I kept trying to steal his attention, but Kai took over the table, ensuring each parent and grandparent did in fact love Tabitha to pieces.

Milo left the table early and I couldn't follow. Grandma Nelson asked to see vacation pictures Aunt Maddy sent me. Not only did I have to hear Kai gush about his movie make-out session, but I also got an ambush of photos. Coconut drinks, a frangipani covered bed, lagoon pools, and cutesy couple poses. At least my aunt is having fun, I guess.

I help carry plates to the kitchen and then make my way to the stairs. I walk up the steps, and then halt as Milo makes his way down. He stops midway, staring at me blankly.

"Milo," I whisper. "Can we talk?"

He leans against the banister. "Why would you want to? I'm a loser, aren't I?"

My insides crush, and I force myself up two more steps. "I didn't mean it. It just slipped out."

"Because you saw Kai and wanted to be on his side. I thought maybe you'd tell him the game wasn't so bad so he'd lay off. I saw you having fun."

"It was fun," I admit. "But the past few days, even when we're trying to make up, Kai and I end up fighting. I just wanted an easy win."

Milo hurries down the steps, slipping past me. "Well, I'm glad I made such an easy target for you."

I turn on the step, watching him descend the staircase. "Milo, don't be like this. I'm sorry. Really."

He keeps moving along the ground floor and disappears into the rear of the house. I hug the banister, getting its help to stay upright as I drag myself upstairs.

I move into the bedroom and find Alfred on the bed. He looks up at me, sprawled out, and purrs.

"Can I join you?" I ask in a wounded tone.

I pluck Mom's diary from my bag and squeeze in beside the cat. I slip my legs under the bed cover and flip over a page, hoping to be comforted by Mom's words.

Jamie.

I finally named my baby.

I don't know where the name came from, but it suits my little angel so perfectly.

Maybe I like the idea of a gender-neutral name. Baby can be anything and anyone she wants to be. The limits are her imagination, creativity, energy, and passion.

I'm so excited to see where life takes her. I'm ready to back her 100%. Call me Cheerleader Mom! OMG. I'm gonna embarrass Baby so dang much. Ha-ha. I mean, Jamie. I gotta get used to calling her by her new REAL name. Just looking at her sleeping beside me gives me chills in the best way. I can't believe I made this little girl. I'm petrified of not doing a good job. I hope I never disappoint her or let her down. I'd hate for her to ever feel or look at me the way I did with my mom. It makes me sick just thinking about the possibility.

My stomach flips. I swallow hard and rub the space on my chest over my aching heart. It's devastating to sense Mom's fear so vividly from the pages of her diary. She writes about not wanting to disappoint me, and it hurts.

Alfred rubs his head against my thigh, and I reach down to pat his head. I smile as guilt squirms inside me. Every second I waste, not working on my assignments, I'm disappointing my mom. All she wanted was for me to make something of myself. How did I not realize I'm wasting my opportunities?

Would Mom be disappointed in the fact I want a boyfriend? Would she steer me clear of Milo the moment she sensed an attraction between us. Mom's romantic endeavors didn't turn into fairytales. I remember when I was five-years-old, she'd come home from work and clean off all her makeup. She'd tell me, being home was the best part of her day. I get the feeling she didn't want a man around who could ruin the special times we had.

Mom looked so pretty when she stripped off all the makeup. There's something about plastering your face with all that junk that turns me off. A few years ago, I played around with Aunt Maddy's mascara, and poked myself in the eye. I still don't know how to use any of that stuff. Maybe Mom would've taught me.

I wonder if her protectiveness would deter me from romance all together. Is that why Aunt Maddy is only in a serious romance now at twenty-eight-years-old? Hmm. No. Probably looking after me put a hitch in her dating life.

But I'm sure Mom's track record didn't exactly help.

I nestle in closer to Alfred and run my fingers through his long ginger fur. He purrs deeper, eyeing me with a content stare. Calmness washes over me and I slip out of bed.

"Thanks, Alfie," I whisper. "I won't waste any more time. Wish me luck with my math homework."

No more excuses. It's clear I can't ask Milo for help right now. And if I want to stay at Ashworth Academy, I can't rely on him until we graduate. I need to keep this scholarship all on my own. Besides, I was smart enough to get the scholarship in the first place. It was just never explained to me it could be taken away. Not that it would've stopped me slacking off to hang with Kai.

After an hour of focusing, footsteps break my concentration. They move from Kai's bedroom, passing the bathroom, and then landing at my door.

Milo enters the doorway, his head down and his voice low. "Hey. is Alfie in here?"

"Oh, yeah," I say, turning from the desk and gesturing at the bed. "He's made himself a nest over there."

Milo scuffs his way into the room, his mood lightening as he views his cat. "Hey Alfie-kins," he says, smiling as Alfie stretches and purrs.

"He doesn't want to move from that spot."

"I don't blame him," Milo mutters, sitting on the bed and curling an arm around the cat. "I'd want to stay here too. Far away from Kai."

I suck in a bated breath. "What did he do?"

Milo's lip quirks as he pats Alfie's long fur. "Nothing, really. He's just blasting one of those conspiracy theory podcasts. I can't stand that stuff."

"Oh, right," I say, snapping two fingers. "The new A.J. Jones podcast came out today. Kai's obsessed with him."

Milo looks up. He stares into my eyes for the first time since playing Draikin Crusades. "What about you?" he asks. "Do you like him too? You could go in there and watch the stream. I'll happily take over the desk."

I reach behind me and touch the desk. "No, those podcasts go for a minimum of two hours. Then it's another two hours of listening to what Kai googles afterwards. I don't think this math homework will finish itself."

Milo looks back down, running his fingers through Alfie's fur. "Is that the extra set Mr. Pritchard gave you?"

"Yeah. I already finished the regular homework."

Milo whistles. "You did? You didn't even get my help on it."

I pick up my homework and wave it at him. "I could use some help with these questions. If you're not busy?"

He shrugs, keeping his eyes on the cat. "Sure, I got nothing better to do."

I grit my teeth, feeling a pounding in my chest. "Look, Milo, I really didn't mean what I said. You have to know I don't think you're a loser."

His gaze doesn't budge. "Why would I know that?"

The pounding gets more erratic, and I realized it's my heart trying to break free of my ribcage. "Because..." My voice warbles, causing his head to jerk in concern. "I don't know if it means anything to you, but I've never kissed anyone else." I sniff as he looks up, meeting my eyes. "It means something to me. You mean something to me."

His bottom lip moves down, and then up, as if he's figuring out what to say. I don't care that he's speechless. The way his bottom lip pouts and shines makes my heartbeat ease.

"Jamie." His voice is soft and cautious. "I've... I've liked you for so long. Like, a forever kind of long. You've never seemed to notice me before. I figured you kissed me because you were bored or something."

I laugh out of surprise. "Bored? I'd never have the guts to do something like that. How many guys do you think I've kissed?"

He shifts on the bed. "I dunno. You're really pretty. I don't get how no one's ever kissed you before."

My face flames red. "You think I'm pretty?"

He scoots to the edge of the bed. "You're beautiful."

My mind rewinds to the day he called me beautiful in the school halls. It was after he witnessed the Miss Perfects ridiculing me. I called him a brown-noser and never gave it another thought.

He meant it for real?

All this time I was fantasizing about him during our tutoring sessions, he was thinking about me too?

"I never wanted to say anything because I didn't want to push you away," Milo says. "I really like how close we've been getting. I was afraid you'd wake up and realize you were with me. A loser."

Hurt runs through me like a hot blade through cold butter. "Oh, Milo, I'm sorry. You already told me you didn't feel good enough. I didn't mean to make you feel worse." I leave the chair and sit on the floor in front of him. "I have these reactions around Kai that make me say impulsive things." I kneel and touch his thigh. "When I'm around you, my body reacts in ways it never has. I don't want to ruin what's happening between us because I like it. I'm just scared of what Kai will say or do if he finds out."

His hand brushes against mine. "Me too. He can be nasty without even trying."

I stand on my knees, pressing myself against his legs as my face nears his. "I don't want to do anything that will hurt you. Tonight sucked, knowing you were mad at me."

"I wasn't mad at—"

I place a finger over his lips, shushing him. My index finger rolls down his lips, falling to his chin. My hand cups his jawline as I edge my lips closer. His gulp pricks my ears, and my eyes close as I lightly kiss him.

He grasps my hips and kisses me back. His tongue slides between my partially open lips, and the sensation sends a thrilled shiver down my spine. My hands slide around his neck and play in the thick hair behind his head.

As our kiss increases in friction, our noses rub together. I can't help giggling the third time I knock his glasses. We pull apart and I wipe my mouth with the back of my hand as he straightens his glasses.

I'm grinning at the sparkles behind his frame. His smile is adorably crooked, and his hands pull around my back to hug me. My waist pushes between his legs, and I flop onto his chest. His soothing heartbeat plays against Alfie's purrs.

Milo chuckles. "Sounds like he approves."

I reach down and scratch behind Alfie's ear. "He's not so bad after all."

"Wow," Milo murmurs. "Will you tell Kai that?"

I nod at him. "Yep. I don't want him scaring Alfie anymore."

Milo smooths a hand over my hair and kisses the top of my head. "Thank you."

My eyes fall shut, and I let out a happy sigh.

"Kai's already snapping at me for moving clothes and books into his room. I rearranged a space for myself, and he's still whining about me touching his stuff."

"I'm sorry my moving in has caused so much friction."

"Don't be." He brushes the back of his hand against my cheek. "We wouldn't be this close if you hadn't moved in. Maybe if Kai knew about this, I could stay with you for longer."

I shake my head. "Nope. If your mom found out we weren't just studying, she'd never let you in here. Remember her 'no girls in your room' speech?"

"Well, that settles it then. I want to get away from Kai, and I want to keep kissing you. That means we're keeping this a secret."

My heart pounds. "Are you really okay with that?"

His hands press against the sides of my face and he pecks my lips. "Perfectly okay."

"I want to keep this low-key because of how important you are to me," I admit. "Do you believe me when I say you're worth it?"

He looks into my eyes, and tingles spread across my skin. "I do. No one can fake the kisses you give me."

I giggle bashfully. "You like them?"

Milo tucks a piece of hair behind my ear and whispers, "I can't get enough of them."

He pushes against my lips and I rock myself forward, fully leaning into the kiss. This time, my tongue does the exploring. When watching movies, I always wondered if, in reality, using tongue would be gross. Contrarily, it's exhilarating. It adds an extra layer of pressure and passion. I lock my arms around his neck, angling my head further. A moan tumbles out of me when his fingers run down the back of my t-shirt.

I trace a finger along the curve of his neck. His cologne wafts my way, making me dizzy in the most delicious way.

"Can I try something?" I whisper.

He nods.

My teeth graze my lip, and my stomach flips in anticipation. I wet my lips and lean in, angling my head so my mouth targets the nape of his neck. Visions of intimate moments from my favorite romantic movies flash through my mind. My lips suction to the taunt skin of his neck. I nibble and suck against the curve, making him shift his position and moan.

"Whoa," he breathes, pressing a hand against the small of my back. "Where did you learn that?"

"I told you," I whisper, breathlessly. I sneak in another kiss, just below his jawline. "I'm rom-com obsessed."

"See, I told you you were good at taking notes," he jokes mid-pant. He sits up against the wall and wiggles his eyebrows. "Can I try?"

I fan my face and then move my hair off my shoulders. "Sure."

Milo locks onto my neck, sucking and kissing, sending pulses down and past my collarbone. I grip his upper arms as he hugs me tight. My head spins, and I'm glad he's holding me. I'd surely have fallen backward and hit the floor from the waves of pleasure.

His kisses move up toward my ear. His breath is hot, and my hair buries his face. I run a hand along the back of his head, addicted to the closeness. His tongue traces my earlobe and I emit a surprised squeak. His laugh patters against my cheek, and I hurriedly turn my face to meet him in a kiss. I laugh with him as our lips brush. Tilting my head, I catch his mouth at the right moment, stealing another perfectly pressured kiss.

His hand digs into my hair, cups the back of my neck, and cradles me as he pulls away. His glasses fog up, but he smiles all the same. "I need to catch my breath."

My hands run down his t-shirt, taking in every ripple underneath. "Me too, but I don't want to stop."

He laughs. "You're a bad influence."

I peel his glasses off his face. "You want to stop?"

He clicks his tongue and then leans forward to peck my lips. "Never."

I tilt my head, and my nose crinkles, viewing his face without glasses. In my head, I know he's just as handsome as ever, but something's off. "You look strange."

Air puffs out of him. "Excuse me?'

I hold his glasses higher. "Without these. I don't like it. Are your eyes smaller?"

He smirks, taking the glasses. "There are magnifiers in my glasses."

I shudder, sliding off his lap. "Well, keep your glasses on, okay? You look cuter when wearing them."

He winces. "Do I look too much like Kai without them?"

"*Eww.* Maybe that's what I didn't like. Oh boy, please keep them on."

He laughs, nudging me. "You're the one who took them off."

"I was going for playful."

He kisses my cheek. "You're so cute."

"I mean, you don't look exactly like Kai," I say, as he slides his glasses back on. "You don't have that mystery scar."

He fixes his glasses, asking, "What do you mean by mystery?"

I shrug. "You know. The fact no one can know how he got it."

Milo scoffs. "What do you mean, no one knows?"

I deadpan him. "You know?"

He laughs. "Of course, I know. I was there."

Excitement bursts inside me. "You gotta tell me what happened. This is epic."

"Epic?" Milo furrows his brow. "What's so amazing about running into a drawer?"

"Come again?"

Milo shrugs. "That's all that happened. We were visiting our grandparents, and they had this little dog named Scruff. Kai was chasing after the dog and ran into the kitchen. Grandma left a drawer open when she went back to the counter. Because we were only six-years-old, the corner was the perfect height to smash under his eye."

"He got his scar from chasing a dog and running into a drawer?"

"It was still a big deal," Milo says. "He bled a lot and needed stitches. I just wouldn't call it an epic story."

I throw my hands up, exasperated. "He's never told me or the guys the story, saying it was too unhinged to get into."

"He's been overselling it all this time?" Milo cracks up. "Ah, that's priceless."

I grunt. "Ugh. Why would he do that? So annoying."

Milo smirks. "Isn't everything Kai does annoying?"

I smile, swallowing the instinct to laugh.

Alfie stretches and then moves onto Milo's lap. I laugh and pat his head. "Is it your turn for attention?"

Milo sniggers. "Are you jealous, Alfie?"

Alfie purrs loudly, taking away the feeling of silence in the room. "It's weird without Gandalf around, huh?"

"I know! I keep looking for him. I even thought I heard him crying earlier."

Our hands brush together as we both pat Alfie. I rest my head on Milo's shoulder and whisper, "I'm glad I got to do that assignment with you."

"Me too. But I'll be more glad to get an uninterrupted night's sleep."

I giggle. "Ditto."

Twenty-Three

The next morning, I hook my fingers inside my cleats and throw my bag over my shoulder. I descend the stairs, ready to leave for soccer practice.

"Did you have enough for breakfast, Jamie?" Mrs. Nelson calls from the kitchen.

"Yes, thanks," I call back, dumping my bag on the couch as I wait for Kai. I perch on the armrest, pulling on my cleats.

Milo buttons his blazer, moving toward me. "Are you still nervous about this morning?"

"Yeah, a bit," I say, lifting my arms to hug Milo.

He made a bogus excuse about meeting up with a teacher so he could hitch a ride to school with me and Kai. Kai took little notice, chalking it up to another of Milo's nerdy antics.

Behind Milo, Kai hurries down the stairs, causing me to step back and sacrifice the hug.

"Are you ready to go?" Kai asks, fixing the straps of his backpack.

"Mhmm."

He tilts his head, getting a good look at my less than enthused expression. "What's up, James?"

I huff, picking up my bag from the couch. "My teammates are gonna give me hell for not being at the game."

"*Pfft*. You've got nothing to worry about," Kai says, resting an elbow on my shoulder. "Your coach still wants you on the team, and your teammates are jealous of your skills."

"Jealousy or not, I still don't like the looks they give me."

Kai gives me a strange look. "What does it matter what they do? It's never affected your game, has it?"

I sink under his weight. "No, I guess not."

Kai gives a proud nod. "Right. If they're grumpy about losing the game, just remind them they have practice twice a week for a reason."

"Right." I stand tall, taking in Kai's words. "If anything, they should practice as much throughout the week as they can."

Kai pats my back. "Just like you do, superstar."

I snigger. "So cheesy."

Kai jingles his keys, moving toward the garage door. "It got the job done."

"I appreciate you saying that," I say, reaching for Kai and halting him. "Especially after what happened at your game."

Kai gives me a small smile. "It's cool. I got too in my head."

I wince. "Because Tabitha was there."

He nods. "I was trying to impress her. Epic fail, huh."

I frown as Kai turns away and disappears into the garage. My heart hurts for him. I still maintain Tabitha is a bad luck charm. That doesn't mean I want my best friend to fail.

Before joining Kai, I sneak a glance at Milo. His small smile conveys all the reassurance I need. I brush my hand by his and hook his pinky finger with mine. His pinky squeezes mine and a soft laugh puffs out of us both.

"Hey, what's the hold up?" Kai calls from the car.

I drop Milo's finger and rush toward the garage. "Nothing!"

On the drive to school, I avoid checking over my shoulder. The blush from my intimate moment with Milo still lingering on my skin. When we reach the west side parking lot, I open the car door and ask Kai if he's coming.

He shakes his head, saying, "It's early. I'm going to Tabby's house. She might want to get a smoothie or something before school."

Dang. That sounds so adorable. "Oh."

Kai blinks at me. "Did you want me to get you one? For after practice?"

"No, it's cool. Thanks for the ride."

Kai waves. "Good luck."

I close the car door and Milo steps around to my side as Kai backs out of the parking space.

"Do you want me to stick around?" Milo asks, gripping the straps of his backpack. "I don't mind."

"I can't even imagine what these girls will say to me. It makes me sick to my stomach." I step in close, clasping his wrist. "You make me calm. It'd be nice to see you on the sidelines."

An ecstatic grin springs to life on his face. "Excellent. Then I'll stay."

I leave him for the girls' locker room, and the moment of happiness is squashed by the imminent dread. Necks crack and heads whip in my direction. The tension is palpable and I hear every backpack zipper, every shoelace curl, and every stroke from hairbrushes.

I dump my belongings, grab my water bottle, shin guards, and mouth guard, and hightail it out of there.

When Coach has us run laps, angered stares point in my direction. Throughout stretches, I hear harsh whispers and notice nudges in my direction. This is torture. When they finally spit it out, it'll be as a united group and I'll be a yammering, incoherent mess.

"Coach," Hayley says with an aggravated tone. "Why is Jamie here? She missed our game. Aren't there supposed to be consequences?"

"Don't you worry about Jamie," Coach replies calmly. "She'd already organized with me to not be at the game."

Dominica huffs, slamming her hands on her hips. "Talk about preferential treatment."

"Did someone die?" Hayley asks, her short fuse about to burst. She gestures at Dominica. "Isn't that the only valid excuse?"

"Or is it more homework she slacked off on?" Dominica accuses. "We all shouldn't be punished because she let her workload pile up."

Coach gives a wry smile. "Are you saying the only way the team can win games is if Jamie shows up?"

A twinkle of pride eases the tension camping in my shoulders.

Leah snorts. "Isn't the optimal word *team*?"

Coach pans across everyone in the team. "This is exactly the problem. Everyone has sat back and let Jamie put in the effort on game days. With her absence, you fell apart. I need you girls to step it up."

Scowls and mutterings pass around the group. Contempt flashes my way, sinking me into the ground.

Coach claps at the group. "No more excuses. We're putting in five times the effort at practices this week. Now, line up for drills."

My shoulders slump and my back hunches as I drag myself into the line-up. For fear of Coach hearing them, no one is exceptionally vocal about their feelings. Although, via coughs and sneezes, I hear the words, "traitor," "favoritism," and "unfair," thrown around.

I nail the drills as I cycle through the loop, but my heart's not in it. Coach is too busy focusing on the other girls to notice my sullen mood. When I backtrack to the sidelines to grab my water bottle, Milo's concerned expression makes it easy to see he hasn't missed a beat.

"What's going on?" Milo asks.

My shoulders bunch high. "What do you mean?"

"It's like something has sucked your confidence away," Milo replies. "I don't get it. When you were hanging out with my friends, you owned the table. Heck, John and Ryan were basically scared of you."

I bat my hand. "Hanging with boys is easy."

"Why is it harder with girls?" Milo smirks and shakes his head. "I mean, I get why girls are stressful. The mean comments can fly pretty easily, especially when they're in a gang."

I scoff and motion to the field behind me. "Then why are you asking?"

"But you hold your own around boys," Milo says. "You're usually so cool and confident. I don't get why other girls shatter your persona."

I chug from my water bottle and then toss it onto the ground. "It's just the way it is."

"I'm sorry. I didn't mean to hassle you about it."

"It's fine." I take a deep breath and plant both hands on top of my chest. "It's just like everything inside constricts. I freeze and can barely speak around other girls. I'm paralyzed, waiting for them to say something mean." I drop my hands, exhaling hard. "Sometimes it's just a look. Man, they can hurt just as much."

Milo tilts his head, finding my eyes. "Why don't you give it back to them?"

I shrug, avoiding his gaze. "My mom always told me to be careful of other women. Men, she said, were easier to get along with. Women are calculating. She said she'd protect me from other women's opinions." I pause, sighing. "With her gone, it's like I don't know how to act."

"Oh." He pauses for a beat too long, causing me to look back at him. He chews his bottom lip as his eyes dart left to right.

I wave a hand, backing onto the field. "It's cool. I don't need these girls to like me. I just need to get back on the team. I have enough friends."

Milo steps forward, following me onto the field. "But you look miserable."

I purse my lips as a wave of emotions pushes through me. "No, I'm okay."

He shakes his head, sadness drooping his expression. "Tell that to your face."

I gulp, turning away from him and jogging back to the others for another round of drills. My insides slosh. I want to stand here, tall and strong, but another wave of haphazard emotion surges through me. My knees knock together and the back of my neck is slick with clamminess.

I missed whatever Coach said to the group. Leah knocks me out of my trance by tapping my arm.

"Huh?"

"You wanna pair up?" she asks with a blank stare.

"Okay, sure."

I follow her as she gets a ball and dribbles it up the field. I look around at the other pairs, trying to work out what we're supposed to be doing. Everyone is still finding a spot on the field, giving me nothing. I turn back to Coach for help, but he's chatting with Stacey.

Leah snaps her fingers. "Earth to Jamie."

I shake my head, positioning myself square to Leah. "Sorry."

Leah passes me the ball, and I stop it, dumbfounded about what to do next. I position myself to pass back, but Leah has started jogging toward me. I re-position, ready to kick as she passes me. In my haste, I fumble the ball and almost trip over my foot.

Dang it.

Knots tighten along my spine as I imagine Milo watching from behind me. I'm supposed to be the best on the team, but somehow, I'm showing off his skill level.

"What are you doing?" Leah asks, digging her cleats into the ground to stop.

"Sorry," I mumble. "Preoccupied."

"Snap out of it," she demands. "It's bad enough you've already missed a practice and a game, we don't need you snoozing while you're here."

I give her an indignant look. "Calm down. I missed a pass, not the end of the world."

Leah scowls and repositions herself to pick up the ball. I pass to her and race ahead to receive her diagonal pass. The sadness drains out of me, as annoyance flames inside me. My moves are fast, and Leah can barely keep up. Her moves are sloppy as she course corrects.

Did she really think she could dismiss my desire to be here? Milo might think I have no confidence, but my passion for soccer is one thing I won't let anyone belittle.

When we finish running the drills, Leah rests her hand on her knees, bending over as she pants for breath.

"Was I awake enough for you?" I ask, juggling the ball on my knees. I let the ball hit the ground and mutter, "You might want to work on your fitness."

I pass the ball to Stacey, who is collecting them to take back to the storeroom. I walk away, keeping my back to Leah and the other girls. As long as I keep up my skills, they can't touch me. I still have no protection in the school halls, but at least I'm a queen on the soccer field.

Milo walks along the edge of the field, and I catch up to him on my way to the locker room.

"Looks like you got some of your spark back," he says.

"Once I got out of my head and remembered how much I dominate when in control of the ball, I stood taller." I nudge him. "Thanks for helping."

Milo's hands are slung in his pockets as he walks. "I don't know if I helped that much. It felt like I only made things worse."

"You were just asking questions I didn't want to answer. I wish I had skills at school that helped with my confidence."

"What are you talking about?" Milo questions. "You've been working so hard on your assignments. You have nothing to feel inadequate about."

"I don't think becoming nerdy will help me," I joke. "Otherwise, you'd be Mr. Popular."

He smirks. "Thanks."

"You know what I mean. I'm good at video games or skating, so I'm confident with the guys. School freaks me out. It's like they've caged a bunch of wild animals together and are crossing their fingers that there's not a massacre."

Milo laughs. "Nice analogy."

I veer off toward the locker room. "Thanks for hanging around this morning. I'll see you later?"

He nods. "Absolutely."

After my streak of confidence at the end of soccer practice, I feel even more concerned about going to classes. I could get the upper hand on Leah, but what about when she teams up with Dominica and Hayley in the halls? How will I respond then? Especially without Coach keeping an eye on us.

Once Camila and the other Miss Perfects come to mind, my posture droops without hope of recovery. On my way to my locker, my head stays down. Craziness filled my weekend, draining me of energy to deal with high school drama. A smile tugs at my lips, remembering the taste of Milo's kiss.

"Yo!" a voice booms me out of my memories.

I blink hard as Kai drags me to the side.

"How was practice?" he asks.

I shrug. "Fine. Got some attitude about missing the game, as expected."

Kai scoffs. "Pathetic."

"They kept saying I got preferential treatment."

Kai slings an arm around my shoulders. "That's because you're number one."

"Hey Jamie," a perky voice pops up.

Tabitha slides around Kai, waving at me while sucking through the straw of her smoothie.

I slide out from under Kai. "Oh. Hi."

Kai smiles, hanging a thumb at Tabitha. "I was just telling Tabby about how much missing soccer has been killing you."

Tabitha plays with her curls, looking me up and down. "It's because of your grades, isn't it?"

I suck in a breath, using all my strength to stop my eyes from rolling. "Yes, Tabitha. It's my fault I'm off the team."

"Whoa," they both say at once.

"James, she was just asking a question," Kai says.

Tabitha holds a hand up. "No, it's okay. I can understand why she'd be defensive."

I groan and yank on my backpack straps. "I gotta get ready for class."

As I move away, Kai grabs my wrist. "Since when are you so eager to get to your locker?"

I flick him off me. "My bag's heavy."

Kai raises his hands in defense, wearing a mocking expression. "Geez, sor-ry."

I turn away, just in time to glimpse Tabitha's smirk as she looks at Kai.

I hurry my steps along the hall. Whatever. Kai can keep giving his attention to his girlfriend. At least he'll be distracting one Miss Perfect off my radar.

I shelter myself with my open locker door. Last Monday, Camila waved around an unsavory picture of my mother. With Tabitha bringing it up yesterday at the cafe, I can only imagine what else the Miss Perfects have up their sleeves.

The bell rings and I make my way to math class. I get in earlier than usual, allowing me to get to my desk before the Miss Perfects arrive. I settle in and open my textbook to where we last left off in class. I pull out a pen and open my notebook. My heart flutters as my eyes wander the page.

Scribbled across the page in Milo's handwriting are the words, *"You got this!"*

I cup a hand over my enlarged grin. Oh my gosh, this is so stinking cute. He must've done this last night when we were hanging in his bedroom. Sometime after that toe-curling make-out session.

The cuteness gets the better of me, and I sneak my phone out of my pocket. I snap a photo of the message and type a text to Milo. *"Found it. Thanks xoxo."*

I've never written *xoxo* in my life and am feeling sickly sweet.

"Miss West," Mr. Pritchard calls, walking up the aisle between desks. "Writing something you want to share with the class?"

I quickly click out of the message chain with Milo and slip my phone into my pocket. "No, sir."

He curls his fingers into his palm. "Hand it over, Miss West. You can pick it up at the end of class."

As laughter simmers around me, my stomach plummets as I reach into my pocket for my phone. I ensure it's locked and hand it over.

"Sorry," I mumble.

Mr. Pritchard's expression softens. "How did you do with the extra set of problems I gave you?"

I hand over my work. "It's all here. I finished them."

He smiles and nods as he takes my work. "Excellent."

As the laughter dies down, the cackling from Camila and Yvette is unmistakable. I don't give them the benefit of looking their way, but it makes no difference. They'll say whatever they want because Mr. Pritchard won't stop them. I hold the edges of my desk, bracing myself for imminent obnoxious remarks.

Camila clears her throat, and then... nothing.

"Cammy?" Yvette asks, shifting in her seat.

Still nothing,

It gets the better of me. I turn a quarter-inch to spy on the girls in my peripheral vision. Yvette stares at Camila, turning in her chair as if ready to pounce. Camila flicks her long chestnut hair over her shoulder and watches the blackboard as if her favorite movie is playing.

Yvette rears back. She flicks her eyes my way and then faces front.

What the heck? Why didn't they attack? Being singled-out by Mr. Pritchard is usually a launching pad for verbal jabs.

I scratch my head, watching Camila paying attention to Mr. Pritchard's lecture. Could it be because Tabitha's dating Kai? I was pretty sure Kai hadn't hung out with Tabitha's friends. Is it possible he said something to get them to leave me alone?

But that also doesn't make sense. Tabitha still made little digs at me when Kai was around.

I pick up a pen, rapidly clicking the top. I don't buy it. They must be lulling me into a false sense of security. Then they'll get me in the hall. They don't know me well if they think I'll relax before the bell rings.

For the entirety of class, I'm on edge. Thankfully, I have to hang back at the end of class to collect my phone. I'm stiff as a board, waiting by Mr. Pritchard's desk. Camila and Yvette walk out together, arms linked, as they giggle and flick their hair.

A small exhale of relief pours out of me, but I'm careful to stay alert.

Mr. Pritchard walks back to his desk, pulling my phone from his top drawer. "You should know better than to have this out during classes."

"Yes, sir," I respond, taking the phone.

"I'll let it slide because," he pauses to gesture to my extra-credit homework, "this is fantastic."

I step back in shock. "Fantastic?"

He grins. "You've really applied yourself, Jamie. There's still some room for improvement, but you're showing your work. You keep this up, and preserving your scholarship won't be a concern."

My insides buzz with glee. "Oh my gosh. Thank you so much."

He gestures to the door, a happy smile on his face. "Off you go. I don't want you to be late for your next class."

I nod, making my way toward the door. "Thanks again."

There's a spring in my step as I enter the hall. I sharply halt, searching up and down the crowded space. Where are the Miss Perfects? I slide along the wall and make my way toward my next class. I hug my books, keeping my shoulders high for protection, and my eyes peeled in all directions.

My heart palpitates when I spy Yvette's blonde ponytail ahead. As the crowd clears, I see her gossiping with Camila as Tabitha approaches. The two girls look Tabitha up and down. If I'm not mistaken, there's tension between them. Tabitha waves, but the other girls don't give her a warm welcome. They turn on their heels and strut through the hall, allowing Tabitha to follow behind with her tail between her legs.

Okay, that only made things a ton weirder. Did they not see me, their usual easy target?

I giggle to myself. Am I really worried about not getting bullied? I'm acting like I'm missing out on a treat. I stand taller, happy to have been a missed target for the morning.

I keep moving toward my next class, and then my breath hitches in my throat. Dominica and Hayley move down the opposite side of the hall. I skid past a group of boys, avoiding their line of sight. *Phew.* I didn't need to miss one group of girls, only to be ridiculed by another.

Something tugs on my blazer. A hand hooks around my waist, and then yanks me into the nearby alcove. I squeak, stumbling against a tall, lanky body.

"Hey," Milo whispers.

I look up, smiling in surprise. "Hey. What are you doing?"

He brushes his hand over my hair and then along my jawline. "Did you think I could let you just walk past?"

I giggle, grasping the lapels of his blazer. On tippy-toes, I reach up and peck his lips. One of his hands anchors me, sitting on my lower back. I look over my shoulder, and the traffic in the hall has minimized drastically.

"Do you think anyone saw us?"

Milo nibbles below my ear. "Who cares if they did?"

"I thought we were keeping this a secret?"

He laughs, and it tickles my neck. "We are. That's why I dragged you into this hidey-hole."

I look around the dimly lit space. "Why were you hiding here?"

His arm drops from around me and he fidgets with his stance. "I was waiting for the crowd to die out. I got shoved around."

"What?" My heart hammers. "By who?"

He shakes his head. "It's cool. I was just in the way. Besides, I got to see you." He tucks a piece of hair behind my ear. "This is exactly what I needed."

I swallow hard and clutch his hand. "I don't want anyone messing with you."

He shrugs. "It was no big deal."

"I feel bad because I was just celebrating about not getting harassed."

His head tilts, intrigued. "What do you mean?"

"Camila had an opening to bully me in class and didn't do it. It was weird. Then there was more weirdness with her and Tabitha in the hall. I think I somehow became invisible to them."

Milo squeezes my hand as his smile grows. "That's awesome. I'm so happy they didn't give you a hard time. You needed them to lay off after how your teammates treated you."

I lift his hand and give it a kiss. "I wish I didn't have to go back to class."

Milo leads me out of the alcove by the hand. "But you have to. Your grades haven't changed yet. You can't give your teachers a reason to give you detention."

"Yeah, I already dodged that today."

"When?"

I blow out a breath. "Mr. Pritchard caught me texting you."

He sucks in a breath. "Did he read it to the class?"

"No, I locked my phone right away. He just took it for the rest of the class. I have it back now."

His lip quirks. "So, you liked the note?"

"Oh my gosh, it was so cute."

He nudges me into the hall. "We'd better get going."

"It'd be worth missing class if we spend the entire time making out in the alcove."

Milo stifles a laugh, releasing my hand. "Don't give me any ideas, or I will make you miss class."

"My, my. Goody Two-shoes Milo is thinking about skipping class?"

He walks backwards, saying, "I told you, you're a bad influence on me."

I sigh, leaning on a locker as he backs away.

He points at me. "Get to class. You're a B-grade student now. Remember?"

I huff, peeling myself off the locker. "Okay. I'm only doing this for you."

He laughs, giving me a wave. "Thank you, because my willpower is fading."

Twenty-Four

The threat of detention made me walk away from Milo. But it didn't stop me thinking about him. As soon as my teacher's back was turned, I was texting. This time I was sure to be sneaky about it. I was also careful of other students around me. I didn't need a nark ruining my plans.

Milo replied to my texts during class. It was so out of character. I really am a bad influence on the guy.

He told me to meet him in Mr. Birch's classroom during our lunch break. He guaranteed we'd have it all to ourselves.

On my way toward the classroom, a chipper voice calls from behind, "Hey, wait up!"

I turn around and almost fall over when I see Tabitha Jones racing to meet up with me. "Huh?"

"I'll walk with you to our table," Tabitha says with a happy smile.

I rear back. "Excuse me?"

Tabitha gestures ahead. "You know, the lunch table. You are going to the cafeteria, aren't you?"

My eyes narrow at her. "Which table are you calling *ours*?"

She shrugs like I'm the idiot. "With Kai and the guys."

I scoff and blink hard at her audacity. I move to the side and hurry my pace. "No, I'm not going to the cafeteria. You'll have the boys all to yourself."

She reaches out to me. "Did I do something wrong?"

I turn off, toward Mr. Birch's classroom, and don't dignify her question with a response.

"The nerve of her!" I screech, entering the classroom.

"Whoa," Milo mutters, his mouth staying open in an o.

I slouch forward, frowning. "Sorry. Just had a run in with Tabitha. Apparently, my lunch table is now hers."

"You mean, like, you've swapped tables with her?"

"No. Like she's now sitting with my friends." I shake my head and walk up to him. "I don't want to think about her right now. Hi."

He chuckles, cupping his hands against my waist. "Hi."

I look back at the door. "Are you sure we have this place to ourselves?"

"Yep. I've been in here plenty of times with zero interruptions."

"What about Christie and Ash?"

"I don't think Ash is at school today. Have you seen him in the halls?"

"We don't exactly have the same schedule."

"Even if those two came in here, I doubt they'd blow our cover." He brushes a hand across my cheek and into my hair. "Last time Christie asked if we were dating, but all anyone heard about were the milkshakes. I don't even think we're part of the story."

I unbutton my blazer. "If we're truly alone, I'm getting out of this thing."

I hang it on the back of the chair, and Milo wags a finger. "You know, taking off your blazer is a detention-worthy offense."

I unravel the neckerchief from under my stiff collar. "You want me to put it back on?"

He bites his bottom lip and slowly shakes his head. I grab onto the lapels of his blazer and back onto a desk. I sit on it and Milo leans over me. His lips meet mine as if they're magnetized. I tug on his tie, ensuring he stays close to me. He mumbles a laugh in the kiss, making me want him more.

He nibbles along my jawline, and his breath tickles against my ear. I slide my hands behind his neck and close my eyes. Never has a moment felt more perfect.

"I really appreciated your support this morning during soccer practice," I say, letting my fingers play in Milo's lush mop of hair. "Sorry if I seemed snappy or ungrateful."

"No problem," he replies, his fingers wandering along my back. "I get how it feels to be on the outside."

"Will you come to the cafe with me after school?" I ask, tilting my head and attempting to appear cute. "I think dealing with these society women will be easier if you're in the same room."

His arms hug around me with avid strength. "I'll be anywhere you need me."

A Disney princess-worthy sigh escapes me. I run my hand down the side of his face and kiss him softly. "Thank you. I don't know how I've been surviving without you all this time."

Milo smirks. "You weren't. You were failing your classes."

"You're doing more than helping me with classes. I feel safe with you."

An adorable smile lights up his face. "Really?"

I nod eagerly.

"But your friends are tougher guys than me."

"Your mom always said you had emotional intelligence." I play with his hair. "I never knew what that meant before. Spending so much more time with you, I get it. The fact I can open up more about wanting to be romantic is something I could never do with my friends."

"I've never talked about this stuff either. Heck, I've never kissed anyone before. I'm so dang glad it's you I get to kiss."

I giggle and lean in close, cupping the side of his face. Our lips press together and a burst of tingles explode within. My skin vibrates and I smile against his lips. I love listening to the way his breathing changes when he kisses me. The scent of his cologne makes me melt into him, and I could scream when the bell rings overhead.

Milo pulls away. "Bummer."

I lean forward and peck his lips. "We could hide out instead of going to class."

"I'm supposed to be a good influence on you. Remember?"

I trace my fingers along his tie. "That's no fun."

"Besides, I've got French next, and I'm falling behind."

I gasp, teasingly. "Oh heavens, no. Not the great Milo Nelson behind in a class."

He laughs. "French is hard, okay."

I tug on his tie and bat my eyelashes. "Say something French to me."

"*Où se trouve la gare la plus proche?*"

My heart flutters and I shiver in front of him. "Oh my gosh. That sounded so dang sexy. What did you say?"

He struggles to hold back his laughter. "Where is the nearest train station?"

I whack his arm. "Ugh. That's the best thing you could come up with? Where's something romantic about my eyes or my smile?"

"Hey," he says defensively, backing away. "What do you want from me? We're learning travel phrases at the moment."

I groan and reach for my blazer. "Fine, have fun in class. You can make it up to me by promising to spend the evening with me, making out."

"Did you think I'd be spending my time any other way?"

It's beyond hard to pull myself away from Milo and enter the bustling hallway. At least I get to see him during last period.

Every Monday ends with English lit. Oh gosh, I can't wait to be done with King Lear. I can't stand another minute of listening to my classmates recite lines from this boring play. To make matters worse, outside the windows, a gloomy gray sky rolls in. The darkening sky makes me sleepy as I slide down my chair. Behind me, raindrops pelt against the windows.

Great.

My stamina drains until Ms. Jenkins calls on Milo. There's something about his cadence and the deliberate way he pronounces every word that keeps me hooked. My heart flutters as the sentences glide off his tongue. I feel myself wanting more every time he pauses for breath.

After Ms. Jenkins thanks him and moves onto another student, a soft sigh pours out of me.

"Huh?" Kai mutters beside me.

I jolt, clutching my pounding heart. I glance at him, and he's scribbling harsh images on his page.

"Nothing," I mumble.

I straighten in my seat and look back across the room. Unfortunately, Tabitha graces my line of sight. She smiles and waves, causing my teeth to grit under my grimace.

I shift in my seat and motion to Kai. "Your girlfriend wants your attention."

Kai drops his pen and sits up from his slouched position. His expression brightens when he locks eyes with Tabitha. He gives her a small wave, and I have to admit, the way he adores her is really cute.

But why her?

I could deal with him dating any girl other than one of the Miss Perfects.

At least the last school bell will ring soon. Although, that brings the start of a new kind of hell. The catering meeting with members of high society. Yuck.

I look across the room and watch Milo diligently taking notes. At least he'll be with me for moral support. Just having him in this classroom puts me at ease.

When the bell finally rings, I resign myself to the fact that King Lear is starting to make sense. I can always ask Milo to read a few pages to me tonight. Perhaps when we're alone in his bedroom.

I move out of the classroom ahead of Kai. With little thought, I wave goodbye.

"Just hang back," Kai says, tugging on my blazer. "Tabby's talking to Ms. Jenkins."

"I've gotta get to the cafe before this meeting starts. I'll see you tomorrow."

Kai pulls out his phone, distracted by a text. "Why are you running off? I'll drive you."

"You don't have to drive me," I say. "I was going to walk."

"Did you not look out the window? It's raining," he says, scrolling on his phone. "I'm driving Tabby over, anyway."

My fingers curl, cracking my knuckles. "Driving her where?"

He looks up from his phone. "To the cafe. Her and her mom are part of the society group organizing this event."

"You're kidding," I mutter.

He gently punches my arm. "Another opportunity for you two to get to know each other better."

I shake my head. "The thought of being around all these snooty women is already freaking me out. I can't think about talking to Tabitha."

"But she knows all these women. Wouldn't it be good to have someone in your corner?"

I scratch my head, swallowing uncomfortably. "I guess."

"Relax, James," Kai says. "Just think about it like a regular work day."

Milo exits the classroom and stops a few feet away, mouthing, "Ready to go?"

Kai notices me looking over his shoulder and turns around. "What's up, Milo? Need a ride?"

"Oh, no, umm..." Milo stammers, eyeing me for direction.

"Yeah, Kai will drive us," I pipe up.

Kai turns back to me, and I tell him, "Milo was going to walk with me to the cafe so we can study after the meeting."

Kai looks back at his brother. "What are you going to do while you wait for the meeting to be done?"

Milo shrugs. "Get a shake and a burger?"

Kai grins. "Sounds like what I need. Okay, I'll hang with you until Tabby's done."

In a flash, Milo and I share an apprehensive look. I want Milo to be there for support. I can't go up to him for a pep talk when Kai's sitting in the same booth. Kai will just tell me to suck it up, end of conversation.

Kai's jaw flexes as he watches me. "No good?"

I smooth back my hair, covering with, "I'm just still freaking out about the pack of snobs. I wish Aunt Maddy was here to deal with them."

Kai throws an arm around me. "But she'll have a video link, right? Just hook up the webcam and set it in front of whoever the head snob is, and take a step back. Maddy's dying to get in with this crowd. Surely, she'll take over."

I lean into Kai. He was right. Aunt Maddy still thinks she's done the wrong thing by leaving town when this meeting came up. I have to make sure the picture and audio are crisp, so it feels like she's in the room. Aunt Maddy is probably pacing her hotel room so much she's dug a footpath into the carpet.

I check my phone and there's still no spiraling text messages from her. I expected non-stop messages from her today. Maybe she realized I'd be freaking out too and didn't want to pile on. I quickly send her a text, saying I'm on the way to the cafe and then I'll start the video call. When I slip the phone back in my pocket, Tabitha joins us.

Her smile strains as Kai's arm slips off my shoulders. Her olive complexion gains a rosy hue when Kai kisses her cheek.

"Ready to go?" he asks her.

"Sure thing." She then asks me, "Is this your first society meeting, Jamie?"

What a dumb question. "Yep."

Kai flicks his keys between his index and middle fingers. In his other hand, he clutches Tabitha's hand and leads her toward the foyer. I follow behind, keeping a slow pace so I can walk alongside Milo.

His pinky finger brushes against mine. "You okay?"

My pinky hooks around his. "I will be when this is over."

Our fingers release as we approach the foyer. From the front steps, we view buckets of heavy rain dumping on the front lawns. With linked hands, Kai and

Tabitha run along the path toward the student parking lot. I can hear Tabitha's squeals from here.

"We should take it slow," I say to Milo.

"But you'll get all wet," he replies.

"I've seen you slip over on a dry surface. I'd rather keep you in one piece."

"I promise, I won't be that clumsy," he says, and steps down onto the first wet step. His balance wobbles, and I'm quick to plant two hands behind his back. Milo snorts. "Dang it. I immediately failed."

I giggle and move beside him. "Nice and easy."

He wipes his brow, embarrassment causing lines to dig into his face. "Okay."

With a few more near misses along the path out of school, we finally make it to Kai's car. Oh, good lord, I wish we'd taken longer. Through the front windshield, with the wiper blades moving, we get the perfect view of Kai and Tabitha making out.

Eww!

I reef the back passenger door open, blurting, "Get a room, not a car."

Kai breaks apart from Tabitha, laughing and wiping his mouth. "Sorry. I forgot we were leaving with two wet blankets."

"Speak for yourself," Milo says, getting into the car.

Kai sniggers. "Book characters or your cat don't count as love interests, Milo."

Milo rolls his eyes. I pull on my seatbelt and tell Kai to get the lead out.

Tabitha plays with her chocolate curls, turning around to view me. "Sorry. Didn't mean to make you uncomfortable."

I flash her my fakest smile. "No big deal."

Milo chokes on a laugh, his cheeks blowing out as he tries to suppress it. I flash him a look and my cheeks stretch as it becomes impossible to contain my smile.

In front of me, Kai shifts in his seat. He doesn't bite and asks what's so funny. Instead, he turns the knob on the stereo, blasting his favorite metal band.

Milo's laughter stops dead as he lowers in the seat, annoyance flaring from his nostrils.

Well played, Kai.

Twenty-Five

Besides Kai tapping along to the loud music, the car ride to Morton's Cafe was mostly quiet. Kai parked out the front, and I leaped out before the music stopped.

When I get inside, Laura greets me at the counter with the office laptop. "Are you ready?" she asks.

Dumping my heavy bag and removing my soaked blazer, I wince. "Barely."

"Geez, it's really coming down out there, huh?" Laura remarks.

I move into the office with my school stuff. "Yep. I'll change into my work gear."

I find a dish towel in a stack on a shelf, and use it to wipe my face and hair. After I change, I consider taking towels to the boys and Tabitha. I twist the towel in my hands. I'd rather just give one to Milo and let the other two suffer in wet clothes. Although, they did run. Maybe they didn't get as soaked as us.

After getting changed, I move back to the counter and open up the chat screen.

"I can't wait to see Aunt Maddy," I say with a huff.

Laura pats my back as she passes with a tray of cappuccinos. "You'll do fine. Maddy already worked everything out before she left." She gestures at the screen. "And she'll be right here with you."

"How about you do the presentation and I wait tables?" I suggest hastily. Laura sniggers. "Fat chance."

I smirk as she walks away. My eyes drift to the long table Laura set up while I was at school. It's set for ten people. Apparently the society group wants to conduct their entire meeting here after the menu tasting. I guess it's good. Even if they don't approve of us as caterers, they'll buy some coffees and sweets during their meeting.

Kai and Tabitha have grabbed a booth on the left. Milo reluctantly sits with them, craning his neck to gain my attention. Before I can say anything, Laura is at the booth to take their orders.

I can't worry about them right now. With a deep breath in, I click on Maddy's contact name in the chat screen. My elbow rests on the counter, and my cheek sits in my palm. The calling icon spins around and around. Odd. This is taking much longer than I'd expect her to answer. Honestly, I thought she'd already be on the screen when I walked into the cafe.

My hands plant on the counter, and I stand tall, stretching my back. I bounce on the balls of my feet, unable to contain my excitement at seeing Aunt Maddy's face. I've never missed her more than this exact moment. Too bad it's a public setting so I can't gush to her about my secret time with Milo.

After a few moments, the connection fails. What the heck? I check the Wi-Fi and dial again. The connection fails again. "Dang it!"

"Everything okay, Jamie?" Jake calls, popping his head out the food pass.

"Just this stupid computer," I complain. "It keeps disconnecting before Maddy can answer."

"It was giving me trouble while I was doing the meat and dairy orders," Jake says. "It's this crummy weather playing havoc with the Wi-Fi."

I groan. "Ugh. I don't need this right now."

Before I go ballistic, I turn away from the laptop and look around at the tables. My gaze moves to the door, and through the glass, I spot the unmistakable silhouette of Christie Klein.

"Hi Jamie," Christie says, entering the cafe with an older woman. They dump their umbrellas in a bucket by the door. "The rain is a total bummer. This is my mom, Mary Klein."

I meet them halfway and shake her mother's hand. "Nice to meet you, Mrs. Klein."

"You too, dear," she replies. "Christie has raved non-stop about the milkshakes here. Honestly, I don't think you need to give a presentation. I think you've already been sold on word of mouth."

"Oh my gosh, really?" I gush. "My aunt would die if she heard that."

Mrs. Klein looks over at the counter. "I heard she'll join us via video link?"

"Yep. She wouldn't miss it."

"But she'll skip time on her vacation for a business meeting," Christie teases. "Talk about a workaholic."

"I'm very jealous," Mrs. Klein says. "I've never been to Hawaii."

"Maybe you can come by when she's back and she can show you pictures," I suggest.

Mrs. Klein nods happily. "I'd love that."

More well-dressed women and their daughters enter Morton's Cafe. It's easy to tell they're part of the event committee by how they stand and talk amongst each other.

"Jamie, this is Mrs. Fisher," Mrs. Klein introduces. "She's chair of our committee."

I gulp as I take the striking woman's hand. One of her daughters is Christie's friend Meghan. A girl I remember taking part in many nasty pranks while she attended Ashworth Academy.

"Pleasure," Mrs. Fisher says. "This is quite a cute little establishment."

"Thank you, ma'am. Umm, are your daughters here?"

Mrs. Fisher hums a laugh. "Oh gosh, no. This is just a simple garden party. We don't need many numbers to get this done."

"Okay then." My knees knock together as these wealthy women give me the once over. "Umm. I'll get the video chat ready on the laptop."

I hurry toward the counter and wake the idle laptop. Christie follows, a wary look on her face.

"You look frazzled," Christie says, standing by me at the counter. "I recognize it because it's how these women make me feel too."

"Do you know the women here?" I ask, looking around at them chatting amongst themselves. "Tell me it gets easier to be around them."

"Yeah, I know them from other events. I guess, once I got a handle on Mrs. Fisher, the rest were a piece of cake." Christie fidgets as she gestures at a blonde girl and her mother. "Except, I don't know these two. They were at the last meeting, but I didn't have a chance to speak with them. As you've already experienced, I'm not the best at meeting new people."

I watch the mother and daughter. "Are they new to town?"

"Not exactly. They live in Logan's Point. Mrs. Garcia recently married a man from Victoria Falls. He encouraged them to join the events committee."

"Garcia?" I question, looking at the Caucasian pair.

Christie snaps her fingers, squinting as she recalls information. "Yeah. Mr. Garcia's daughter goes to our school. That horribly angry girl. Cammy, I think her name is?"

My jaw drops. "Camila? They're related to Camila Garcia?"

I exhale rapidly, turning to the front door and spying out the windows, dreading the moment ragey Camila enters my cafe.

Christie leans in and whispers behind a cupped hand. "I don't think they're on good terms. Camila and her mother used to attend these meetings. Since her parents divorced and Mr. Garcia remarried, they haven't been in attendance."

My jitters ease. "Whoa. Like he replaced them?"

Christie leans back with her hands raised. "I don't know. It's just what I've observed."

Tabitha leaves the booth and joins the rest of the ladies. The woman she stands next to is very clearly her mother. She's two decades older, but her beauty shines through as much as Tabitha's does.

I clear my throat and click on Maddy's name in the chat screen. "Guess we'd better get this meeting started."

After another failed attempt, I cross my fingers harder and call again. Relief floods my body as Aunt Maddy fills the screen. Her ponytail is a mess, concern is etched across her face, and her hotel room is her background.

"Finally," she cheers. "Gosh, baby, it's so good to see your face."

"You too," I reply. "The connection kept failing."

"On my end too," she replies and the picture glitches. "I've been trying to call since school finished. I wanted to ensure something like this didn't happen." Her head darts around. "Dang it. They're already here?"

I wince. "Aunt Maddy, you keep glitching. Oh man, it's the weather. We're not getting a good signal."

"I've never had such bad signals until I moved to the mountains," Christie pipes up. She moves in front of the screen. "Hi again, Maddy."

"Oh, Christie," Maddy says excitedly through the glitching. "Good to see you. Thank you again for setting all of this up."

Christie bats a hand. "Easy to do when it was so delicious."

"Everything okay?" Mrs. Fisher asks.

I turn around, allowing Maddy to glimpse the striking woman. I want to make an introduction, but my mouth opens with no sound escaping. Mrs. Fisher's hawk-like stare shreds any confidence I was grasping onto.

She views the laptop. "You must be Madeleine West."

"Just Maddy is fine," Aunt Maddy replies. "So lovely to meet you. Apologies for not being there in person."

Mrs. Fisher grimaces. "The sound and picture is terrible."

I try to respond, but I'm mute again. Christie leaps in with, "It's the weather. It's making the Wi-Fi signal weak."

Laura makes her way around the group of ladies and motions to the table. "You're all welcome to take a seat here. We'll bring out the food shortly."

The mothers and daughters take their seats, leaving the head of the table to Mrs. Fisher. The other end is supposedly for me, but right now, I'd rather run naked out in the rain.

Laura gives me a nod. I shake out my hands and turn back to the laptop. A glitching Maddy stares back at me.

"Baby, you've got this," she says in a broken tone as her image blurs on the screen. "We talked about this so much. You know our menu like you know your soccer plays."

Trying not to appear petrified, I nod at Aunt Maddy, scooping up the laptop. I place it down at the end of the table and step back, ready for Maddy to lead the meeting.

"Mom, this is Jamie," Tabitha says, elbowing her mother. "You know, Kai's friend."

Mrs. Jones nods at me. "Oh hello. Nice to meet you."

I fake a smile. "You too."

"You know, I heard the nicest reviews about the Henderson function you catered," Mrs. Jones says. "I'm very excited to try this food."

"Oh, really?" I turn to the laptop. "Maddy, did you hear that?"

An empty chat screen mocks me.

"No," I whine, tapping the keys hard. I call her again and announce to the group that I'll bring the food while I wait for Maddy to reconnect.

I plant the laptop onto the counter and scoot past, entering the kitchen where three trays of food await. I pick up one, and Jake follows with the other two. As we pass the counter, I glimpse the laptop screen. *Call Failed.*

Jake nudges me forward and whispers, "You got this, champ."

We walk back to the table and place the trays down. Jake leaves, and I clasp my hands in front, standing tall against their penetrating stares. I know I should talk. The table is awkwardly silent as they wait for me to talk. It's like my brain is on pause.

Christie's mother clears her throat. Her smile is encouraging. "So, what do we have here, dear?"

"Umm," I falter, rubbing the back of my clammy neck.

"It smells divine," Mrs. Garcia says, gazing over the eye-pleasing array of treats.

The Logan's Point local renews my confidence. I wave a hand over the display. "My aunt thought these were all cute and bite-sized, perfect for a garden party."

Mrs. Fisher picks up a finger sandwich. "I'd agree with that."

It might be a small dose, but it's optimism none-the-less. I sneak a peek over at Kai and Milo's booth. Both twins have their eyes locked on me while eating their burgers. Gosh, watching me must be the equivalent of an old-timey freakshow.

I look back at the table, and the ladies make yummy noises as they try the food. I swallow the queasiness bobbing upward, and talk them through each of the mini quiches, the tarts, and finger sandwiches available. They *ooh* and *ahh* over buzzwords like buttery, delicate, crumbly, luscious, honeyed, silky, and zesty.

Behind the counter, Laura turns on the milkshake machines. I gesture to her and say, "Seeing as it's a day event, not a cocktail event, we thought you might like some petite milkshakes for your guests."

Laura walks around the counter with a tray of mini shakes. I help her serve the chocolate and strawberry selections, and they get squeals of glee.

I backtrack to the laptop and say, "I'm just going to try my aunt again. Let me know if you have any questions about the food. Maddy's happy to change the menu. I'll let her explain it all when I get her back."

I hit call and this time it doesn't disconnect, but it seems to take a long time to get her back. I hope she's not calling at the same time and that's why she's not answering. Ugh. Why can't this be easy?

"Still having trouble?" Tabitha asks, sidling up beside me.

I disconnect and hit call again. "Yeah."

"It must be so frustrating," she replies. "I wouldn't want to do a presentation in front of these ladies."

As I cautiously watch Tabitha, Christie's comment about Camila usually being at these meetings replays in my mind. I look across at the new Mrs. Garcia. I wonder if I can get more info out of Tabitha?

"So, have you been part of this committee for very long?" I ask.

"Kind of," Tabitha says. "My family skirts the line of being in or out with this league. Mostly when numbers are down, my mother will get a call and she drags me along. Most people think high society is glamorous, but it's mostly listening to ladies who love the sound of their own voice. Afterwards, we get handed the most undesirable job for the event. We'll probably be given one of the worst tables at the garden party."

"Well, I'm just the help, so at least you're not on the bottom rung of the ladder."

Tabitha giggles. "My mom loves this stuff, so I act excited for her benefit. But it's hard when I have three brothers at home who never get dragged anywhere. Boys totally have it easier."

"I don't know about that, but they're certainly easier to deal with."

Tabitha glances over at Kai and Milo's booth, and then turns back to me with apprehension. "Sorry for acting weird after class today."

I hug my waist, feeling tension between my shoulder blades. "What do you mean?"

"You and Kai are just friends, right?"

I smirk. "Yeah?"

Tabitha presses her fingers into her forehead and huffs. "Sorry. I just see him with his arms around you and it drives me nuts."

A laugh busts out of me before I can stop it. "You're jealous of me and Kai?"

Tabitha pouts and nervously plays with her curls. "How could I not be?"

I give her a sympathetic look. "You've got nothing to worry about. Kai's my best friend, who happens to be a guy. He's like my brother. The thought of being with him makes me want to hurl."

Tabitha giggles, standing upright with her usual confidence. "Well, that's a relief. My imagination has been going wild ever since you moved in with him."

I snigger. "Kai is definitely not taking up space in my imagination."

Tabitha's eyebrows wiggle. "But someone else is?"

My breath hitches. Oh gosh, I'd better calm down, stat, or it'll be all over my face. I slightly turn toward the boys' booth but stop short. Why would I look at Milo right now? Why don't I just hold up a sign that tells everyone I enjoy making out with him?

"Dang. I'm making you uncomfortable again," Tabitha says. "Kai told me you're not into dating. I just have a habit of asking other girls about their crushes."

"It just threw me," I reply. "I hang out with boys, so no one has ever thought to ask me that."

"Yeah, I've never taken you for much of a girly-girl."

"I wouldn't exactly fit in with you and your friends." I glance at the new Mrs. Garcia, and then back at Tabitha. "I'm surprised more of your friends aren't here at this meeting."

"Yvie has been to a few meetings, but her family prefers just to show up at the main event." Tabitha sighs. "Camila and her mother used to pride themselves on coming here. It's so sad what's happened to their family."

"Sad? Maybe it's karma."

Tabitha blinks away the water pooling in her eyes. "You mean about how she's been treating you at school?"

"Doesn't exactly make me sympathetic toward her."

"I wanted to talk to you about this when I brought up your mother's picture." She shakes her head. "Oh my gosh, I had no idea how much that hurt you. I truly am sorry Camila brought it into school. She's just so broken these days. I'm never able to reason with her."

My eyes narrow at her. How could she not know that image would hurt me?

Tabitha motions at Mrs. Garcia and her daughter. "That's Cammy's new step-mom and step-sister over there. Her parents' divorce absolutely crushed Cammy. She's so angry and bitter these days. She just wants someone to lash out at."

"And I'm the easy target," I mutter.

"Mhmm." Tabitha nods. "Camila's dad is buying rundown property in Logan's Point to redevelop. He took Cammy on a tour. She said she was walking through this abandoned building and found flyers from the previous business. As you already know, it was where your mother worked."

I crack my knuckles, the heat of anger growing inside me. "She's angry at her dad for leaving her family. In retaliation, she attacks my family. My mother's not even here anymore to defend herself."

"I've asked her to stop," Tabitha says, her voice shaking. "But it just makes me a target. That's why I'm so grateful to have Kai. I can tell him what's really going on, and he protects me at school by letting me sit at your lunch table."

My skepticism meter runs high. "That was protection for you? All you did was say snooty comments to me."

Tabitha's bottom lip wobbles. "You thought I was snooty?"

"Yes. All those digs about me letting my grades slip and not putting in any effort."

"I didn't mean to sound harsh," she murmurs, clutching the space on her chest over her heart. "Sometimes things just come out of my mouth in that tone. I don't even register it anymore."

I fold my arms across my middle. "You should listen to yourself more often."

She nods. "I will. And I want you to know Cammy doesn't have your mom's picture anymore."

I stiffen, waiting for something worse to drop.

"I mean, she has the crummy picture on her phone," Tabitha says nervously. "But it didn't spread because she didn't have the original."

I frown, not following. "Where is it?"

"I took it." She sighs heavily. "I was meeting up with Kai that Sunday, and he always raves about you. I just couldn't let Camila taunt his best friend with the image. So, I took it before I left for the skatepark."

My mouth hangs open as her words cement in my brain. "You did that?"

She nods humbly. "I knew the photo on her phone wouldn't blow up because it was low quality. She expected to take another photo with better lighting. She suspects I took it, but I've played dumb."

"No wonder she was so frosty to you in the halls."

Tabitha shrugs. "She's annoyed I've been ditching them. Plus, I've stopped agreeing with the nasty things she says."

"Maybe it'll rub off on her."

"I just hope I can stop talking like her. It's automatic, and my parents always snap at me for it. They'll tell me I'm acting like a brat, and half the time, I don't even remember what I said."

I smirk. "My aunt calls me a brat too."

"It was too bad we lost the video link with her. Do you think you can get her back?"

"Hopefully. The storm is messing with their internet. But maybe I'll ask Milo to take a look in case it's something else."

"Or I could ask Kai," Tabitha suggests. "He's handy with computers."

I click my tongue and grin. "He is, but if it's too slow or doesn't do what he wants, there's a good chance his fist will hit the keys or the screen." I motion to the older ladies. "I'm guessing you don't want your mother to see that side of him."

Tabitha scoffs. "I don't think *I* want to see that side of him."

I move over to the booth and the twins both have a mouthful of burger.

"Sorry to interrupt," I say. "Milo, I keep losing the signal with Maddy. Can you take a look?"

He swallows and wipes his mouth. "Sure," he says, sliding out of the booth.

Kai drops his burger. "Why didn't you ask me?"

"Because Milo won't take it as a personal attack when it doesn't work."

Kai smirks. "You have so much more faith in my brother than me."

Milo moves over to the counter, and I stop Kai from following. I cross my arms and look him up and down. "Why didn't you tell me you're with Tabitha to protect her?"

He looks at me with confusion. "What are you talking about?"

"Tabitha said she sits at our lunch table for protection from her friends."

"Oh, yeah, that. Well, it's kinda true. Mostly, I just want her around."

"Is she with you because she's running away from her friends?"

Kai searches for Tabitha. "What did she tell you?"

"That Camila is angry and unreasonable."

Kai angles his face down and says, "Camila says messed up things to people at school, even Tabitha. But what she says to her isn't public. You think their lives are perfect because they're beautiful. You don't know the hard time Tabby's having at school. She's told me a lot of stuff in secret."

"Really?"

"I'll just say, she's trying to distance herself from Camila, but any chances she takes backfire." Kai strains against his irate frown. "I don't like seeing anyone I'm close to get upset."

Involuntarily, jealousy bubbles up inside me. "Do you say more comforting things to her than 'buck up?'"

He gives me side-eye. "Huh?"

"This whole time, you've acted like you didn't notice Tabitha was part of the clique that torments me."

"You can handle yourself. You always put Tyler and the other guys in their place. I haven't seen Tabitha handle herself the way you do. You two could actually help each other out."

I groan. "Because it's always my fault how I interact with other girls."

Kai rolls his eyes. "Why is *your* conversation with Tabitha causing *us* to argue?"

"Because she's *your* girlfriend."

"And you're supposed to be my best friend."

I stare at him hard. "I am."

"Then can you just trust I'm with a nice girl and stop bugging me about it?"

"As long as you remember, friendship is a two-way street."

"You really hate that I'm with her, don't you?" He steps away, putting distance between us. "I already told you I'm trying to balance my time between you and her."

I step forward so I don't have to yell in front of strangers. "I don't care that you spend time with your girlfriend. I get that it's important and exciting."

He nudges me toward the society ladies. "How about you put effort into this meeting? I'll show you what support looks like."

I stumble on my footing from his heavy-handed nudge. "Geez, thanks."

My eyes wander from the society ladies over to Milo at the counter. My gaze becomes laser-focused, watching Christie lean in to talk with him.

What the heck? Why are they talking? Is it about Ash? Is it about me?

I hurry toward the counter, ensuring I get there ahead of Kai.

"So, what do you think?" Christie asks, clasping her hands in front.

Milo's visibly nervous as he stammers his response. He looks over Christie's shoulder at me, and then back to her. "No, ahh. Umm. I'm not sure."

"Aww, but you'll have a great time," Christie urges. "She's not like she was in school. I promise. Meghan would love a date for this event. You'll have so much fun."

My jaw drops. Meghan? Christie's trying to get Milo to date Meghan?

I turn to Kai, and his attention is squarely on Tabitha. If I snap my fingers at him, I bet I'd be on mute.

Milo rubs behind his neck, looking down at his shoes. "Well, umm. I'm kinda... Look, I dunno. I'll think about it. Okay?"

Christie nods enthusiastically. "That's brilliant. I just think you two will look so cute together."

Ugh! How do I stop this?

Christie turns around and smiles at me. "Everyone's loving the food. It's going wonderfully."

My jaw clenches as I fake a smile. "Thanks."

Christie walks back to the table, and Milo umms and ahhs at me.

"You won't get a signal while the storm keeps up," he says, gesturing at the computer. "Maybe try your phone instead?"

With Kai beside me, I keep my cool. "Thanks for trying. I know she'd want a better view than from my phone. They're finishing eating anyway, and then they'll get to their meeting. I'll call Maddy afterwards."

Milo's smile twitches. "Sorry I couldn't help."

I nod glumly.

"Hey, how was your burger?" Tabitha asks, clutching Kai's hand.

"Awesome, as per usual." He glances at me. "Couldn't help looking over here, though."

"To watch me crash and burn," I grumble.

"Don't be so harsh on yourself," Tabitha says sweetly. "You actually did really well. And the food and shakes speak for themselves. I already told Mom we have to come next Sunday for the pancake stacks." She giggles. "My brothers are like bottomless pits, so you might want to make extra batter."

I find myself smiling. "Thanks, Tabby."

An ecstatic grin stretches on Kai's face from the use of Tabitha's nickname.

"Umm, I never actually congratulated you two," I say, awkwardly shifting my weight. "You two look like a nice couple and seem to want to spend time together. It tripped me out at first, but I wanted you to know, I'm happy for you."

Kai smiles, slinging an arm around me. "Thanks, James. And sorry for the hostility over there. Some people say I'm defensive."

I slide Kai's arm off me. "Ah, I just learned this makes Tabitha uncomfortable."

Kai looks at Tabitha in surprise while she blurts, "No, no, it's fine."

I giggle. "She thought something was going on between us."

"Jamie told me the thought of being with you makes her sick," Tabitha says bluntly.

Kai smirks. "Thanks."

"It put my mind at ease," Tabitha says, giving me a wink.

Kai scoops his arms around Tabitha's waist. "How could you think I'd have eyes for any other girl?"

"I just didn't know the history between you and Jamie. I've never seen a girl and guy, who aren't a couple, be so close."

Kai nods at the table of society ladies. "Should you be getting back to that?"

Tabitha groans, stepping back from Kai. "Yep. My mom is giving me the stink eye."

Kai moves back to the booth and Milo approaches cautiously. "You okay?"

I nod. "I'm fine."

"You just congratulated Kai and Tabitha on being a couple. You can't be feeling okay?"

"Oh, that." I move further away from the society table and lower my voice. "I saw where Kai was coming from. Tabitha has a bad habit of coming across the wrong way. From what I can tell, it's a facade. She's apparently getting bullied by Camila as much as I am."

"Really? Aren't they friends?"

"They are. Her only friends are mean girls. No wonder she wants to hang around Kai all the time."

"That'd be the only reason," Milo jokes.

"Seriously, it seems like Kai has been a confidant for her. I'm happy for them."

"They're constantly together, so I'm not surprised they've become close." His hand subtly brushes mine. "Just like us. Although, to be honest, I wouldn't mind if you and Kai weren't as close."

A surprised laugh puffs out of me. "What?"

"I get you two are best friends." His pinky hooks mine. "It's just that I want to be the one that gets to hug you and be close to you."

"Well, you do get to, just not publicly." Goosebumps sprout from my fingers up to my shoulder. "I get how that feels like not enough. But I just heard what Christie asked you? You said you'd think about it."

"Because I was put on the spot," he says in a rush. "Believe me, I have no interest in Meghan. I wanted to tell Christie I'm only interested in one girl." He gulps. "I just didn't think you'd be okay with me telling her that."

I glimpse the table, then steal my eyes back in his direction. "I don't want you dating any other girls."

His smile is small. "I don't want that either. I just want you."

The goosebumps intensify, and I muffle my giggle as a blush heats my face. "I should get back to the ladies."

He throws a thumb back at the laptop. "Do you want me to keep trying Maddy?"

"No, it's okay. She'll definitely be freaking out right now." I pull out my phone. "I'll send her a quick text that I hope gets through."

Milo gives me an adorable smile and slinks back to the booth with his brother.

I turn to the ladies, clear my throat, and slowly every eye lands on me. "I really hope you all enjoyed the food. I know I speak for my aunt when I say we'd really love to cater your event."

Mrs. Fisher clears her throat as she dabs a paper napkin against her painted lips. Everyone's focus switches to her. "Well, what can I say?" she begins, dusting off her hands. "Everything was sublime. The pastry was flaky, the fillings were light and fluffy. Don't even get me started on the sugary heaven that are those milkshakes."

I'm shaking. I grab onto the back of my empty chair, scared I'll become a wobbly mess on the floor.

"Do you have the final costings?" she asks. "I'd love to run over them during our meeting."

"Yes, ma'am," I say eagerly. "I'll get them."

I race back to the office, so excited I almost trip over my feet. I find the printed quote on Aunt Maddy's desk, and hightail it back to the table.

"Here you are, ma'am," I say, handing it to Mrs. Fisher with a shaky hand. "Again, thank you for the opportunity. Aunt Maddy will be thrilled." I pan across the table. "To all of you, truly, thank you."

I receive a mess of happy replies and leave them to conduct the rest of their meeting. I rush behind the counter and lean into the food pass.

"Jake! We got the job!"

Jake's larger-than-life grin greets me and he throws up two thumbs up. "Excellent. Never doubted you, sport."

"You got it?" Laura gasps behind me.

I turn around and pull her into a hug. "Maddy will be doing cartwheels."

Laura strokes my back. "Well done, Jamie."

I thank her and leave the counter, making my way to the twins. I scoot into the booth beside Kai and can't contain my smile. "We got the job!"

Kai crooks an arm behind my neck. "That's awesome."

"Yeah, congrats, Jamie," Milo says across the table.

I look at him while leaning into Kai and give a small smile. "Thank you."

Kai releases me, asking, "What shall we do to celebrate? Skatepark?"

"Hello?" I point to the water-streaked windows. "It's raining, you goof."

Kai laughs. "Oh, yeah. Well, video game night?"

I shrug. "I dunno. I still have to work this afternoon and there's still homework to catch up on."

"Come on." Kai huffs. "Even Milo doesn't study every night."

"Give her a break," Milo defends. "All her teachers have assigned her extra homework."

"Why don't you hang with Tabby," I suggest. "Milo is here because we are planning to study."

Kai squints at me. "I thought you were working."

"I'm doing both. This is the new me. I multi-task."

Kai throws his head back with a laugh. "*Ha.* I've only seen you care about soccer or rollerblading, and you never tried to do them simultaneously."

"Oh, gosh." I wince. "That sounds like an accident waiting to happen."

"So does Milo," Kai teases.

I whack Kai's arm. "Cool it. He's not doing anything to deserve these jabs."

"Umm, ouch," Kai says, rubbing his arm. "Doesn't mean you can jab me."

I slide out of the booth. "I gotta get back to work." I turn to Milo. "Are you still cool to stick around?"

His head tilts upward as he smiles and nods.

Kai shimmies out of the booth. "Okay, I don't need to see my brother looking at you like a trained puppy. I'm outta here."

"What about your girlfriend?" I ask.

"She told me these meetings run long. I'll tell her to text me when she's done."

Kai moves over to the table, tapping Tabitha on the shoulder. He leans down and whispers something that she nods along with. He pecks her cheek, gets a round of awes from the table, and then he leaves the cafe.

I edge my way back to Milo. "Hi," I whisper, leaning in close enough to graze his cheek with my lips.

His hand gently strokes mine. "I'm so proud of you for standing in front of those women and talking about the food. You did amazing."

I grit my teeth and my gut twists. "It was pretty rocky."

He nods. "I was worried about you. But you got it together. You're amazing, Jamie."

I stroke his cheek and sigh. "Again. How did I survive without you?"

He looks up at me with a glint in his eyes. "I'll tell Christie I can't be Meghan's date. I only have eyes for you."

"Dang. Why do people have to be here? I want to kiss you so badly."

He rubs his lips together. "You sure you still want to keep this a secret?"

I force myself away from him and slowly shake my head as I back away.

Twenty-Six

Jake and Laura let me go home before they started cleaning. Whenever I finished taking orders and there were no tables to clear, I'd sit by Milo. We'd have our books open, but I wouldn't really call what we did studying, even though our touching was at a minimum.

Milo called his mom to drive us home, and before she arrived, I finished my third phone call with Maddy. Her praise has been non-stop. She even floated the idea of me taking on more presentations with prospective catering clients. I gave her a reality check, saying I only managed to say words because the group included girls from school that made me feel at ease.

After dinner, and more praise from the Nelson family, I couldn't help wondering what Mom would think about the meeting. The good feelings swell inside me, and I excuse myself to Milo's bedroom. I grab Mom's diary and sit back on the bed to flip through the pages.

If Aunt Maddy were at the cafe this afternoon, she would've gushed about the food and told stories about the staff and prior functions. I wonder if Mom loved talking to people just as much. Skimming through these pages, it's easy to see she was popular with boys. She wasn't a girl's girl, so perhaps she would've struggled just as much as me. I've read Mom describe Maddy as a 'girl next door,' and she totally fits the bill.

The words Camila used to describe my mother filter through my mind. I hug the diary close to my heart. I hate that my mother was called those words while she was still with us. No wonder she strived to protect us. I tap the cover of the diary, thinking about Tabitha. Maybe having a girl like her on my side will save me from the harsh words thrown around at school.

I open the diary again and shiver as I read the name Trigger. Every time I find an entry with his name, Mom's words get increasingly frightened. I pick up my phone, ready to call Maddy. I need to ask her if she told the cops about Trigger. The more I read, the more suspect he appears. He might've had something to do with her disappearance.

When I flip a page, my phone slips out of my hand. On the next page, Mom's handwriting is flowy. It's full of loops whenever she's happy. And she's happy because she's talking about Buzz. I rub the space above my beating heart and can't help smiling. I haven't found where Mom identifies my dad's name, but I really hope he's Buzz. Mom seems to light up whenever she recalls her events with him.

However, the knots in my back make me hold back on my joy. Mom always said I couldn't know who my father was. It kills me that he'll most likely be Trigger.

Alfie struts into the bedroom, his tail swaying in the air. With a leap, he sits on the windowsill, meowing at the sights beyond the glass.

I get off the bed and walk over to him. Patting his head and looking out the window, I ask, "What's got your attention?"

He meows and scratches at the glass.

I giggle and scratch behind his ear. "Do you want to go outside?"

He brushes against me, purring and walking along the windowsill animatedly.

"Okay, okay." I laugh and pull the window up, letting the cool breeze in. "Here you go, boy."

He meows and leaps down onto the edge of the house. I watch him scuttle against the house and then leap onto the branch of a nearby tree. Light rain sprays into the room. I close the window and briskly rub my arms from the cold. How he'd want to be outside now is beyond me.

I move back to the bed and pick up the diary. I read over the cutesy date Buzz set up for Mom. She always calls him a friend, saying he's too good to be tied down by her. She's excited about all the great things he'll do after he graduates high school and goes off to college.

That's why I can never be with him. He can never know the truth.

If he knows he's Jamie's dad, he'll stay in this town forever.

WHAT!?

He's so smart and has so many opportunities awaiting him. It's better if everyone thinks it's a lowlife from Logan's Point. Once Brent is done with school, I'll tell him about Jamie.

Brent? WHAT!?

He's already so sweet with her. He takes any chance he can get to visit us. I'm so lucky he introduced me to Grams and helped us set up our life here in Victoria Falls. I know he'll make an excellent father one day, but that day can come later.

I want him to finish his education and not be burdened with heavy responsibility. I can do this on my own. And it's clear I'll never lose him as a friend.

I drop the diary to the ground. My mouth hangs open, stunned.

Brent.

As in Brent Anders.

The guy who knew my mom when he was in high school.

And is now my soccer coach.

He's also my dad?

My head is about to explode. I've been terrified to learn who my dad is for my whole life. And then it turns out I've always known him. And I adore him.

I care about what he thinks of me. And he cares about how I do in school, and if I'm okay when Aunt Maddy's not around.

Has he always known?

He must've had an inkling he could be my dad.

I throw my head into my hands, hunched over my knees. "I can't handle this."

"James?" Kai asks from the living room.

"Kai," I call, breathlessly. "Quick."

Kai bursts into the room. "What's happened?"

I point at the diary. "It's... It's... My dad."

Kai gulps, plonking down beside me. "It's bad?"

I suck in my bottom lip, feeling every slosh in my stomach. "Nope."

Color drains from Kai's face. "Then why do you look petrified?"

I grab onto Kai's hands and exhale hard. "Coach Anders."

Kai's eyes enlarge, highlighting his scar. "What?"

I nod, feeling woozy. "He's my dad."

"What?" Kai gasps. "And he said nothing?"

I swallow hard, bile fighting to stay in my throat. "Mom kept it from him."

Kai exhales, struggling to take in the information.

"She made up that it was a scary guy from Logan's Point, so Coach would go to college."

"I can't believe this."

I shake my head, eyeing the diary strewn on the carpet. "She planned to tell him later, but by then she..."

Kai finishes the sentence. "Was gone."

I throw my head into my hands. "Oh my gosh. This is so much heavier than I ever imagined. I've been so scared of this moment. Now, I don't know what to feel."

Kai rubs a circle on my back. "But Coach Anders is a good guy."

"The best."

"So, you can feel happy."

I lower my hands. "How can I tell him? It's been sixteen years since he ever would've suspected I was his. Now I awkwardly bring it up at practice? Ugh. This is a nightmare."

"No. A nightmare is your dad's a criminal. You'll be okay."

I throw my arms around Kai, burying my face in the nape of his neck. My body releases in convulsing shivers. "I'm so glad you're here."

Kai's arms wrap around me snuggly. "I'm not going anywhere."

"Hey, Jamie," Milo's voice calls as he steps near.

I'm wound so tightly; I don't budge an inch. I'm clasped around Kai as Milo's voice sounds from the doorway.

"Oh," he mumbles. "What... What's..."

"Scram, Milo," Kai mutters.

"Umm..." he mumbles, and soon his footsteps disappear.

I collapse ever further against Kai. I can imagine how this looks to Milo, but I have no bandwidth for it right now. This is so much bigger than finding time to kiss a boy.

This is about my dad.

Oh my gosh. My dad.

I have a dad.

Suddenly, waves of tears stream from my eyes. I muffle tears against Kai's shoulder, soaking his t-shirt.

He soothes me, rubbing my back. "I'm not going anywhere."

I hiccup and jitter against him. I hate that the past week has led to so many fights with him. At this moment, he truly is my best friend. I feel like a fool for ever doubting how much he cared about me.

He's got me. Somehow, the tears keep coming. But I feel safe, because Kai is holding me up.

Twenty-Seven

"Are you okay?" Kai asks as I lift my head off his shoulder.

I wipe my hands over my face and stand from the bed. "Oh my gosh, I can't believe I cried like that."

"I don't blame you. This is heavy stuff."

I nod. "It's a huge shock."

Kai stands and moves toward the doorway. "You wanna get a glass of water or something? Cool down a bit?"

I follow him out. "Yeah, sounds good."

He shudders jokingly. "Good, because I can't stand another minute in Milo's room."

I sniff back the last remnant of my tears, and tease, "Too clean for you?"

As we enter the living room, Milo exits Kai's bedroom. He stumbles on his footing, muttering to himself as he wavers on retreating into the bedroom.

He hangs in the doorway and clears his throat. "Are you okay, Jamie?"

I push for a smile, delaying my response until I can ensure my hoarse voice won't tremble.

Kai interprets the situation, standing in front of me. "Leave her alone. She's not interested in homework right now."

"I wasn't asking about homework." Milo cranes his neck to glimpse me, but Kai continues to block his view. "She just seems off."

"Can you just listen to me for once?" Kai complains. "Give her some space."

"Okay, I will," Milo murmurs, moving across the carpet toward his bedroom. "Let me get Alfie and then I'll go back to my book."

"He's not in there," I say, and Milo halts by his bedroom door. "He's outside."

Milo's eyes pop with horror. "What?"

My shoulders bunch high, filling with tension I don't understand. I point to the bedroom window. "He wanted to go out. What's wrong?"

Kai winces. "Oh, you didn't."

I look at him blankly. "What?"

Milo rushes to the window, pulling it open and scanning the darkened area. "Alfie? Alfie?"

Kai and I move toward the room, and I continue to question, "What's going on? Don't animals like being outside?"

Milo groans, moving away from the window. "He's an indoor cat. He can't be outside."

"Oh," is all I can manage as Milo pushes past me and hurries downstairs.

Kai sighs, running a hand over his brow. "This is bad. Last time Alfred was outside it took days to find him and Milo was a wreck."

"I didn't know." I raise my palms, dumbfounded. "I've never had a pet. He seemed eager to get outside."

Kai rubs my shoulder. "Don't beat yourself up. If you didn't know, you didn't know."

I gesture to the stairs. "Should we help look?"

Kai nods and leads the way. "Yeah. Hopefully, he hasn't gone far."

We land downstairs as all the adults are up and putting on raincoats. Mr. Nelson grabs his keys, announcing he and Grandpa will drive around the neighborhood to search for Alfred. Mrs. Nelson coaxes Grandma back to an armchair, while Milo and Kai are already out the front door.

I follow behind as Mrs. Nelson urges me to return to the house. The temperature outside has grown icy, and the rain hits my skin like needles. Foolishly, I came downstairs without a coat, but I'm not turning around now.

"He moved from the window ledge to that tree," I say, raising my voice so I'm heard over the heavy rain.

Kai moves toward the tree, grabbing onto a branch with both arms and hiking a leg up. "I'll get him down."

"Kai don't!" his mother yells from the porch. "It's a thunderstorm. I don't want you being struck by lightning."

Milo points at the tree. "But what if Alfred's up there?"

"Your cat is much too smart to be in that tree," Mrs. Nelson answers.

I look around the front yard. "Then where would he be?"

Mrs. Nelson beckons to Kai. "Come back inside. This rain is freezing and you'll catch a cold."

Milo moves down the path, calling out to his cat.

"Milo!" his mother calls through cupped hands.

Kai waves her off. "Let him go, Mom."

Kai follows his brother, ducking low and then treading on the balls of his feet, searching the surrounding area.

I move off the porch, but Mrs. Nelson grabs onto my arm. "Oh no you don't."

"I have to help," I protest.

"No, I need all you kids to come back inside." She signals to hOh,er kids. "Boys, come back in. Alfie will be hiding somewhere. He won't hear you over the rain."

Kai grabs onto Milo's shoulder, but he nudges him off. Kai gestures to the adjacent houses and Milo nods. The twins then start walking along the street path.

"Boys!" Mrs. Nelson calls, her voice giving out.

I rub the space over my heart. "Milo must be going nuts."

Mrs. Nelson frowns. "He loves that cat so darn much. I just don't want them getting hurt out in this weather."

"I feel like such an idiot." I clench my fist and hit my thigh. "I didn't ask if he could go outside."

Mrs. Nelson strokes my hair. "No one thinks you did this maliciously. Milo's not angry at you, he's just worried about his pet."

Goosebumps sprout over my arms, and when I briskly rub them away, Mrs. Nelson orders me back inside. Knowing better than to argue with her, I retreat. Grandma gives me her most heartbreakingly worried eyes from her armchair.

After what seems like an eternity, Mrs. Nelson returns with the twins. With heightened emotions bouncing off each of them, they hang up their drenched coats.

"Mom, I can't stay inside," Milo says with a hitch in his voice. "I can't leave him alone out there."

Mrs. Nelson holds the sides of Milo's face as she talks in a calm and rational tone. "Honey, there's nothing you can do about it now. Alfie's not dumb. He'll come back to the house."

Milo pulls away. "What if the storm scared him off? He could be anywhere. What if he doesn't know the way home?"

"Your dad and grandpa are out looking for him now. If they don't find him, it'll be because he's sheltering from the rain." Mrs. Nelson holds him still, looking into his eyes. "Honey, he'll be okay."

Milo chews his bottom lip and gives a slight head shake. "You don't know that."

Mrs. Nelson sighs, frowning as her eyes grow glassy. "Oh, honey."

Milo steps back, frustration breaking his posture. "How am I supposed to go upstairs when I know he's out there in the storm?"

"Maybe I should go for a drive too?" Kai says, reaching for his keys.

"No. It's too dark and you won't see anything through all this rain," Mrs. Nelson replies.

Kai throws his arms up. "So we just sit here and wait?"

"I'm sorry," I blurt, forcing everyone's head to snap in my direction. "I didn't know it'd be a big deal. I'm sorry I opened the window."

Milo looks away, giving me nothing in return. His shoulder blades flex as if ripples of pain are flowing down his back.

"Jamie, it's okay," Mrs. Nelson whispers, moving my way. She nudges me toward the stairs. "Why don't you go upstairs and get ready for bed?"

"Shouldn't I...?"

Mrs. Nelson shakes her head, ushering me away. "It's okay. There's nothing for you to do. It's not your fault."

"Umm, okay." My legs are wobbly as I take the stairs. I keep my gaze over my shoulder, waiting for Milo to look my way.

He doesn't.

It's like he's cemented in that spot.

My heart breaks in two. The reality sets in that he'll do anything to avoid me.

Kai moves up the stairs with me. "Don't take it personally," he says as we move into the upstairs living room. "He's just obsessed with that cat."

I bite my lip, willing the tears back into their ducts. "Even you knew not to let the cat out."

Kai shrugs. "Because I live here and have been through this rodeo before."

I glimpse the stairs and mutter, "You really put in the effort for Milo."

Kai snorts. "Hello? He's my brother. Of course, I care."

I plonk on the couch and throw my head into my hands. "I just feel so bad."

"I bet you ten bucks the cat will be scratching at the back door, waiting to be let in."

I look up and cross my fingers. "I hope you're right."

Kai kneels beside me. "How are you doing, anyway? You were already hit with a massive revelation tonight."

A weighted sigh exhausts out of me. "Aw, crap. I'd actually forgotten about Coach. Oh, gosh. How do I face him at school tomorrow?"

"I can be with you when you tell him."

I massage my forehead as a sting of tension fires its way into my skull. "How do I tell him?"

Kai pulls me into his arms. "You'll find a way. It's Coach."

I nod against his shoulder and then pull away. "I need a shower and then hours of sleep."

Kai stands, giving me room to move away. "I hope you can sleep. If you can't, I'll stay up with you and play video games to keep your mind off it."

I smile at him with appreciation. "Thanks for everything, Kai. You really are the greatest friend I could ever ask for. Will you apologize again to Milo for me?"

"James, you don't need to..."

"*Please.*"

He sighs and nods. "Okay. I will."

"Thanks."

After dragging myself to the shower and letting the hot water vaporize all my troubles, I found Kai was right. Sleep didn't come easy. No matter how tired I am, I toss and turn all night in bed. My head pounds with thoughts of Milo. He was so angry he couldn't look at me.

Throughout the night, I check the bedroom window, hoping Alfie's there. He wasn't, but I keep my ears pricked, regardless.

For good measure, thoughts of Coach and my mom torment me awake. I knew they were friends, but she never mentioned knowing him before the move to Victoria Falls. How could she have known the whole time that he was my dad and never say anything? She could've at least confided in Aunt Maddy.

Instead, she let us believe we should fear my dad's identity.

I grind my teeth and clench my fists. That part I can't forgive. How dare Mom make me so terrified? If she wasn't sure who my dad was, it'd be one thing. But she knew! The whole time!

When it's time to get up for school, my whole body is wrecked. I was so tightly wound last night, clenching all my muscles in rage and sadness, that getting up this morning and stretching is excruciating.

I get ready for school with less enthusiasm than a zombie. When I make it downstairs, I find out Milo already had his grandpa drive him to school. They're taking detours through the neighborhood, searching for Alfie. I suggest to Kai we do the same thing.

With no luck, we arrive at school before the first bell. Kai steers me by the shoulders to my locker and my first class because my brain is still numb. I remain glazed over during my first three classes. Milo ignoring me, and doing something that hurt him is bad enough. But I need to talk to Coach today, and it's terrifying me.

What if he doesn't believe me? He'll laugh in my face and tell me to leave his office. Or, what if he gets mad and never wants to see me again because my mom lied? He'd throw me off the team and tell the school administration to rip up my scholarship.

Or what if he already knows? What if he chose to keep it from me, just like Mom? I can't even fathom that outcome. It makes my stomach twist in on itself.

When class ends, I hold a fist over my mouth, swallowing the building sickness at the back of my mouth. I edge my way into the hall, cradling my books under one arm as I press my other arm into my gut. I edge along the wall, focusing on my shoes as my insides slosh. As I wait for the crowd to push past, I lift my gaze. Trudging close to the wall and toward me is Milo.

His glasses can't hide the bags under his eyes. He probably tossed and turned as much as me, listening to that soul-crushing storm continue throughout the night.

We could've stayed up together. Worried together. Comforted each other.

Now, in the hall, he looks up in time to lock eyes with me. His frown doesn't budge, but his eye color dulls. He pushes off the wall, diverting his path away from me.

"Milo?" I call in a pathetically soft tone.

Even if he heard me, I doubt he'd turn around. Knowing the pain he's in doesn't make the rejection any easier. A sharp pain digs into my heart. I shut my eyes and lower to the ground, pressing my back to the wall. I blow out a breath and feel bile rising from my stomach.

I hate that he's so mad at me. I hate that he can't look at me.

Gosh, I miss him so much.

I rub my thumb between my temples. I'm supposed to talk to Coach. How the heck do I do this?

"Jamie?" a voice asks with concern.

I open my eyes and look up, finding Tabitha lowering to the ground.

"Are you okay?" she asks.

With a clenched jaw, I shake my head.

She winces. "Are you sick?"

"Mhmm." I swallow roughly. "Where's Kai?"

Tabitha gestures down the hall. "I was about to meet up with him by his locker."

I stare hard at her. "I need Kai."

She rises. "I'll get him."

Another wave of sickness bubbles up and I swallow with a grunt.

"Kai!" Tabitha calls, standing on her toes and waving. "Over here."

Before I can find him in the hall, I hear him skid. He kneels by me, grabbing my shoulders and pulling my gaze toward his. "What's wrong?"

"I can't..." I shake my head and swallow again. "I can't do this."

He nods, his grip on me getting stronger. "Have you seen Coach?"

I shake my head. "I can't."

He rubs my back. "What do you want to do?"

"I want to go home," I moan. "I wanna barf."

He pulls back and I see his smile. "Not all over me, I hope."

I let out a faint laugh, and he helps me to stand. He turns to Tabitha, saying, "I'm taking Jamie to the nurse. I'll catch up with you later, okay?"

Clearly disappointed, Tabitha nods and forces a smile. "Yeah, sure."

I forget about the other students walking up and down the halls as Kai guides me to the nurses' office. Mrs. Whiteborne, the school nurse, could tell I was feeling unwell, but her thermometer detected nothing out of the ordinary. Luckily, Kai motor-mouthed our way through it. He told Mrs. Whiteborne that my aunt was away and I was staying with his family. I think he was going for sympathy, but I was barely listening. He then fibbed about something we ate for dinner, which didn't agree with us.

Visibly tired from listening to Kai, Mrs. Whiteborne agreed we should take the rest of school off. Kai fake called his mother, and soon he was driving us back to his house. We already knew his mom had taken his grandparents into the city for some appointments. Thank goodness we'll have the house to ourselves.

"I just want to nap," I grumble, trudging upstairs.

"When you get changed, come to my room."

I look back at him before disappearing into Milo's room. "Why?"

"Because I want to stay with you, and I don't want to stay in my brother's room."

I roll my eyes and step into the bedroom. "Fine, whatever."

After changing into sweatpants and a t-shirt, I make my way to Kai's bedroom while throwing on an oversized hoodie. My frown drags me down, remembering how Milo avoided me at school. I wish I were staying in his bedroom. His scent still lingers in there, and it'd be nice to curl up in his bed, thinking about nicer times.

As I step into Kai's room, I spy the trundle bed on the floor. A small smile battles my frown as I think about napping inside Milo's sheets.

Kai pats the bed as he digs his legs under his bed cover. "Get over here."

I suppose it's best I don't fantasize about Milo while alone with Kai. I move over to his bed and curl up with him. Kai's arm pulls around my middle and I rest my head against the pillow.

"Thank you for bringing me home," I whisper. "I just can't do today."

"Don't mention it. You know I'll do anything for you."

I sigh happily, closing my heavy eyes as I listen to the game sounds coming from Kai's phone.

It was almost a ninety-minute nap. Afterwards, Kai and I don't talk much. Just being around him made everything easier. I enjoy watching him play a dumb game on his phone and letting my mind stay as numb as can be.

Even though my life has been turned upside down and covered in trash, this moment feels normal. It's me and Kai, alone. No one else is getting in the way. Just like it used to be. Just like he's been asking for all week.

Once we hear movement downstairs, things get a little tense. School has technically finished, but we're still home too early. When his mother doesn't start calling him by his full name, we know we're in the clear.

I listen out for voices. Would Milo be looking for Kai to give him a ride home? Probably not, because he's avoiding me like the plague. He'd want his grandpa to pick him up, so I'm sure he's home now.

I stretch out on the bed, and Kai's fingers tap against my side. I giggle as he tries playing my ribs like a keyboard. I twist in the bed, turning to face Kai, and I squirm away from his hand.

Over the sound of my laughter, I distinctly hear footsteps.

"Oh," a startled voice says.

I shoot up in bed, Kai's arm unraveling from my middle. "Milo," I breathe.

Milo's eyes grow circular, and he's quick to readjust his glasses. He shuts his ajar mouth, moves to the closet, and snags a hoodie.

"Wait," I mumble as he stomps out of the room.

"James," Kai says gently, squeezing my shoulder as he sits up in bed. "I know you feel bad for him, but you're going through a much bigger deal."

"I have my thing, and his thing." I clutch the space on my chest over my heart. "I'm the reason for his thing. He's hurting because of me."

"You can't keep blaming yourself," Kai reassures. "You let the cat out, but you didn't want him to run away."

Should I tell him the truth? Tell him I have a crush on his twin brother? No, it's more than that. I'm falling...

My breath hitches in my throat.

My heart swells like a balloon.

Oh my gosh, it's true. I'm falling for Milo.

Kai tilts his head. "James?"

I swallow hard. The same overwhelming sickness takes over from when I thought about telling Coach the truth. I pull my legs to my chest, needing to escape this new truth bomb. I don't want to talk to Kai, but I do want to help Milo.

I scoot out of the bed, ducking Kai's attempts to pull me back. "I gotta do something."

Kai sighs. "What are you doing?"

I scoop my hair into a ponytail and make my way out of the bedroom. "Don't worry yourself."

Twenty-Eight

I move into the living room, craning my neck into Milo's bedroom to check if he's still on the second floor. I hurry downstairs and make my way to the garage for a pair of sneakers. I pull my hood over my head and make my way outside. I rub my hands together, disliking the chilly outdoor temperature. As the rain tries its best to hit my face, I move over to the tree in the front yard. From there, I look up at Milo's bedroom window.

"If I were a cat, what's my next move after going into the tree?" I look back and forth at the tree and the window. "I'd go back to the window and scratch until I was let back in. But what do I know?"

As I scan the area, my sneakers create sloshing noises against the wet grass. I move along the side of the house, certain Alfie's not in the front yard, or he'd be spotted by now. Plenty of family members have mentioned Alfie turning up at the back door. Kai said this isn't the first time the cat went missing outside. I'm guessing he turned up at the back door on previous occasions.

The sloshing continues as I make my way down the side of the house. The bottom of my pants and my shoes get soaked as I inspect the fence line and the walls of the house. The Nelsons keep a well-maintained home. It's near impossible to find a crack or hole in or under the fence.

I chew my lip, rest against the wet exterior of the house, and smack my heel against the wall. The back of my sneaker hooks to the bottom of the wall. I lower to free my heel and notice the gap below the house. The Nelsons don't have a basement, so it'd be concrete or dirt underneath there.

I lower even further to the ground, narrowing my eyes for any signs of life. A faint whimper pricks my ear, but it's similar to the howls and billows of the wind. As I push myself off the grass, the sound triggers me again. This time it's much more distinct.

"Alfie?"

The whimper replies. It's a mixture of whimpering and meowing.

"Oh my gosh, Alfie! Come here, boy!"

I squeeze myself closer to the gap, angling my head for a better look. It's pitch black. I rummage into the pocket of my sweatpants for my phone. As I fish it out, two glowing eyes get my attention.

"Alfie! Come here. Are you stuck?"

Another muffled whimper cries out, and I'm certain Alfie's stuck under something. The gap's not big enough for me to fit under. I look around the area, hoping for a long stick or gardening tool nearby. Without much more thought, I scoop mounds of dirt toward me. I dig my hands into the grass, ripping it from the earth. My sleeves turn brown within minutes. As I push my way into the gap, dirt clumps to my face. With muddy hands, I set my phone under the house, shining the flashlight toward the glowing eyes. After another meowed whimper, Alfie's silhouette moves in the light.

"Alfie! You're okay."

He still doesn't stand, but I can't tell what has him trapped. It makes sense for him to be under the house. For a cat, this probably seemed like the safest option during a thunderstorm.

With grunts that start in my abdomen, I continue to dig my way under the house. As soon as my body can squeeze through the gap, I crawl my way along the flashlight beam.

"Alfie?"

Three high-pitched meows reply.

I scuttle forward and soon the low hum of purrs vibrate toward me.

I reach out and feel his wet, muddy fur. Relieved laughter sputters out of me as my body drapes over the shivering cat. His head nuzzles against my neck and I could just lie down and sob.

Gathering my resolve, I press my hands around the area surrounding the cat. It feels like a mess of pipes and wood have entrapped him. I push them backward, careful of my pressure as Alfie whimpers underneath. I continue to whisper that he's okay, pulling pieces of pipe apart.

Alfie stands when I push the last pipe backwards. His back arches in a much needed stretch, and I scoop him into my arms. On the crawl back to the yard, he cries in my arms.

"It's okay. It's okay. We're almost out."

I snatch my phone and squirm against the gap to pull us out. I flop on the drenched grass and pant like I've run five miles. Alfie is a muddy mess, curled in my arms, but his belly expands and contracts, purring against me.

I giggle, cuddling him closer. "Oh my gosh, you little adventurer. You scared us all to death." I smile so hard my face hurts. "Milo will be so happy."

I force myself to my feet and carry Alfie into the house. "Umm, hi," I say, standing by the downstairs living room as water and mud drips off me. Now that I'm inside, I really feel the dirt caked on my face.

"Oh my gosh, you did it!" Grandma cheers, rising from her armchair.

"How in the world?" Grandpa says in awe, walking my way.

"You found him?" Mrs. Nelson says, hurrying from the kitchen. "Milo! It's Alfie!"

"What?" Milo's voice cracks as leaves the dining room. When he enters the main living space, he halts, jaw hitting the floor. "What... What did you do?"

I grin, lifting the wet and shivering cat. "I found your baby."

Milo rushes toward me, scooping Alfie into his arms. His mouth hangs open as Alfie nestles against his hoodie, purring. His gaze lifts with glassy eyes. "Where did you find him?"

I giggle, wiping mud off my face with my dirty sleeve. "Under the house. He was trapped under some stuff stored underneath there."

"What stuff?" Mrs. Nelson asks.

I shrug. "Like pipes and wood beams."

"I'll have Steven move them to the garden shed," she says. "I don't want this happening again."

"Or I could not open the window again," I joke. "Then this mess won't happen again."

Milo sighs, scratching behind Alfie's ear. "I can't believe you crawled under the house." He looks me up and down, grinning. "You're a mess, but you saved him."

"I wanted to make it right." I pat Alfie's back. "And I missed him."

"Jamie," Milo says softly. "Thank you so much."

I smile at him, feeling tingles bringing warmth back to my body. "You're very welcome."

Mrs. Nelson tugs at the bottom of my hoodie. "I want you to carefully take this off without dropping mud. Of course, I'm grateful you rescued Alfie, but I don't want you tracking more dirt into the house." She pulls the hoodie over my head and I feel like a child. "Slip out of your shoes and move it to the guest bathroom. You know where the towels are, and I'll bring you a robe."

Looking down at my mud-stained hands, I can only imagine the state of my face and hair. Before Mrs. Nelson tells me twice, I move to the back of the house. She follows me the entire way, complaining about her floor.

It all blends into white noise. Milo has his cat back. I put a smile back on his face.

Mission accomplished.

After scrubbing my hair and skin clean, I dry off and slip into the fluffiest robe ever. Seriously, I feel like a giant marshmallow in this thing. I pull it tight and open the bathroom door, entering the guest bedroom, which is filled with Grandma and Grandpa's stuff.

I move to the bedroom door, and Milo comes into view from the hall, holding a wadded-up blanket. I smile on my approach, assuming Alfie is inside.

"Is he nice and toasty now?" I ask.

Milo smiles, entering the bedroom while cuddling the blanketed cat. He's changed into a fresh sweatshirt. I guess holding a wet, muddy cat messed up his hoodie. "I gave him a bath in the laundry sink. He didn't love it, but he's clean and warm now."

"Good. I'm glad."

Milo sighs, shaking his head in awe. "I still can't believe what you went through to save him. I don't think I'll ever be able to thank you properly."

"I was already behind, considering how much you've helped me with school," I reply. "Let's call it even."

Milo's expression grows serious. "I am so sorry for ignoring you. It was really uncool."

I look away to hide the hurt. "It's fine. You were upset. I get it."

Milo hooks a finger under my chin, swinging my face back to him. "I'm really sorry. I never should've done it. I know you didn't mean to do it."

"You have him back now. That's all that matters."

Milo sets Alfie on the bed. "I was just thinking about him and took it out on you. I'm so mad at myself for putting a wedge between us. I never wanted to do that."

"Neither did I," I say, pulling the robe tighter as I shiver within. "I felt like the stupid one for letting Alfie out. I made the rift between us, and I wanted to fix it."

Milo chuckles. "Well, you sure did. You're such a fighter, Jamie. That's why I know you'll get through everything. You're really strong."

I hook my pinky around his. "I don't want to do anything that causes us to stop talking. It broke my heart to know I'd hurt you."

His hand smooths over my hair, and he tucks a loose piece behind my ear. "It was the situation, not you."

I can't help frowning. "You couldn't even look at me."

"Well, I guess..." Milo pulls away, turning a slight shade of green.

"What?"

He blows out a breath, rubbing behind his neck. "It was right after I saw you with Kai."

My stomach somersaults. After the high of finding Alfie, all the ugliness of my connection with Coach had disappeared from my mind. Now, all the hurt and confusion come tumbling back down.

"What were you two talking about?"

I look away, fighting the urge to heave. I scrunch my eyes closed, willing the icky feeling away.

"You can't tell me?" he asks.

I place a hand over my mouth, swallowing hard.

"And then you two were together this afternoon," he says cautiously. "Wrapped up in his bed."

"Milo," I say in a defeated tone. "Please don't. I can't talk about it."

I turn back around as Milo chews his lip and fidgets with his glasses.

"Is it private?" he asks, frowning.

I shrug. "I guess."

Sadness droops on his face, and he shifts his weight between his feet.

I look him up and down. "Are you jealous?"

His hands plant on his hips. "I want to be the one who's that close to you."

"Awe." I pull my arms around his middle and plant my forehead against his chest. "Don't be jealous. I was just talking with Kai."

"And I can't know what about?"

An exhausted sigh pours out of me. "It's a lot of backstory. Believe me, it's painful to get into."

"Oh. Kai's just easier to talk to?"

I lift my head and lock onto his eyes. "Don't be jealous. It's just that, if I talk about it with you, I think I'll throw up."

He grimaces. "*Eww.*"

I giggle. "See. I'm saving you from more hurt."

"Maybe you'll tell me another time?"

I nod. "I'm hoping it gets easier to deal with. Right now, I want to forget about it and just bask in the wonderful news of Alfie being home."

Milo grins and we move over to the bed to pat the sleeping cat.

"Oh my gosh," Milo whispers. "I'm so happy he's home."

I brush my fingers over Milo's hand. "Me too."

Twenty-Nine

Dinner was filled with celebratory remarks from the whole family. I even video chatted with Aunt Maddy to relay my heroics. The cherry on top was making Milo smile at me again. It was only twenty-four hours that we were on radio silence, but it hurt so much, it may as well have been twenty-four years.

I spent last night anguishing over hurting Milo and the revelations I found in Mom's diary. Thankfully, with all the talk about Alfie and my crawl through the mud, Coach is the last thought on my mind.

"Oh, thank God," Mrs. Nelson says, reading through her emails at the table. "Kai, you'd better thank your lucky stars."

Kai screws his face up. "Huh? What are you talking about?"

"After Jamie's trouble with her school grades, I suspected you were flunking some classes too," Mrs. Nelson says, turning her laptop. "I asked Ms. Thornesmith in the administration office to send over your school report. She finally got back to me and looks like you're doing very well."

Kai rolls his eyes. "Oh, is that all?"

"Wait a minute," I say, getting up to view the laptop screen. "Kai's doing well in classes?"

Mrs. Nelson nods proudly. "Seems that way."

"What the hell?" I blurt at Kai.

He shrugs, indifferently. "What?"

"What about all your speeches about not being a mindless drone and sticking it to the man? All the while, you're getting As and Bs?"

"I can't help it's easy to remember the crap they teach," Kai says, scraping a fork along his plate. "That's why I don't get why you need so much time to study. I just ask Milo what part is needed for the test, and I skim over it."

"You never told me you study before a test," I say, feeling the betrayal run deep. "I ignored everything because I thought that's what you were doing. Then I find out you're acing your tests."

"It wasn't that hard to figure out," Kai says matter-of-factly. "Ever see me in detention? No, because I have better things to do with my time."

I slam a fist on the table. "You're a fraud!"

Kai chokes on a mouthful of food.

"*Jamie,*" Mrs. Nelson scolds.

Grandma Nelson coaxes me back to my seat, but I wriggle away.

Kai swallows, coughing roughly. "Excuse me?"

"I guess I should've known," I say coldly. "Anyone who thinks running into a drawer is hardcore can't be that badass."

A mixture of confusion and realizations morphs and contorts his face.

"Forget this," I mutter, leaving the dining room and escaping upstairs.

In Milo's bedroom, I flop down on the bed, letting an angry noise sizzle out of me. Kai has been berating me about studying, and all the while, he's passing his classes. It didn't matter if his parents could pay, because he'd never have his place in school jeopardized.

Ugh! This is infuriating!

I get off the bed and pace the carpet, calming the raging blood in my veins. When my nerves settle, I sit back on the edge of the bed with a heavy exhale. Footsteps sound up the stairs, and soon, Milo is at my door.

"Just when I think everything's okay," I say dryly, "another thing sends me into hysterics."

"I don't blame you for going off," Milo says, hanging by the door. "Kai is such a butthead. Who knew he was doing well in school? He never let on."

"The night was going so well beforehand."

"Yeah. Umm, Jamie," Milo says, scratching the side of his head and digging his toes into the carpet. "Things are off between us. Don't you think so?"

I latch my hands behind my back and squirm. "What do you mean?"

"Like earlier," he says, throwing a thumb behind him at the doorway. "In my grandparents' room. We were talking, but it was a little awkward."

"Well, you had been ignoring me," I admit. "It's a little hard to get close again after that."

He nods. "That's exactly what I mean. I'm such an idiot. I never should have ignored you because Alfie was gone. There was no way I thought you did it on purpose."

I flop down to sit on the edge of the bed. "Then why did you do it?"

"Because I thought you were pulling away from me." He sits beside me, an arm's distance apart. "I thought you finally agreed I wasn't worth your time."

I frown. "Because I let the cat out?"

He shakes his head, looking at his knees. "Because you were with Kai. He told me to go away, and it seemed like that was what you wanted too."

I turn away from him, annoyed he's making me relive that moment. "Kai and I were just in the middle of talking. That's all."

"You were in his arms."

I turn back with a clenched jaw. "Because I was upset."

Milo shrinks. "I want to be the one to hold you when you're upset."

My tension dissipates as I watch his wounded form. I slide closer to him, brushing a hand over his knee. "Maybe you can hold me while I'm happy."

His lips quirk upwards, and he turns his body toward mine. "I haven't made you unhappy?"

"Only when you're not around," I whisper with a flirtatious lilt. "I don't want to do anything that'll push us apart again."

He takes both my hands. "Neither do I. Being apart from you was hell. I wish I hadn't done it. I'm sorry." His thumbs rub tight circles on my hands. "I'm crazy about you, Jamie."

My heart flutters, and tingles play under my skin. "You're... You're crazy about me?"

His adorable grin spreads, and he caresses the side of my face. "I've always been on the edge of falling for you. And now..." He pauses, running the tip of his thumb under my bottom lip. "Now, I am."

I swallow with nervous excitement, and then blink several times. "You are?"

He pushes his lips onto mine, pulling back to blurt breathlessly, "I love you, Jamie."

A soft gasp escapes me as my heart hurls into overdrive. My chest rises and falls as I work to catch a breath. "Oh my gosh," the words tremble out of me.

He kisses me again, running a hand smoothly through my hair. My pulse fires on all cylinders, surely strong enough that he feels every beat. I wrap my arms around him, kissing him back with feverish need. We slide further on the bed; careful we don't entangle ourselves while on the edge.

"Milo," I whisper, barely able to break my lips away from his.

"Yeah?" he whispers, swiftly connecting with my lips again.

"Don't ever let me go," I say, barely audible over my pounding heart. "I need you."

My words send him into a powerful lust. His hands journey from the base of my neck, down to my lower back. His nibbles and caresses across my mouth, cheek, jaw, and neck. All the sensitive areas tug moans and giggles of pleasure out of me.

Oh my gosh. This is it. My ultimate rom-com moment. We've fallen for each other. We're on the road to this thing between us becoming official.

I can't believe I almost admitted this to Kai. Right now, with how betrayed he made me feel, it makes me happy I didn't. But I wonder what he would've said. Would he have appreciated me sharing how deep my feelings are for his brother? Yes, I've kept this a secret from him, but maybe if I opened up that much, it all would've been forgiven?

Especially after I shared all that stuff with Coach. Kai was the ultimate best friend, giving up everything to hang with me while I slept the day away. Maybe revealing the truth about my crush earlier in his bedroom would've been the exact right time. Maybe he would've understood why losing Alfie hit me so dang hard.

It's such a gamble. Kai and I just got back what we'd lost over the last week and a half. If I blurted out how hard I'm crushing on Milo, it might've hurled us into an even bigger fight, and I wouldn't have left to find Alfie. But even when I'm not looking for a fight, another one happens regardless. I hate that. I don't want to keep yelling at my best friend.

I moan into my kiss, remembering the moment I pulled Alfie from under the house. The massive relief. It's a moment not worth giving up. If anything, I should be happy Kai was there for me and that I got Milo back.

Oof.

I'm flung backwards after Milo shoves me away.

I anchor my hands behind me, saving me from falling completely backwards. "What the heck?"

Milo stares at me with a horrified expression.

My face screws up in confusion. "What?"

"Do you think I'm okay with what you just said?" Milo says in a serious tone.

Lines crease in my forehead. "I didn't say anything."

He deadpans me.

I lift my palms, questioningly. "Milo, what are you talking about?"

"You said my brother's name," he says bluntly.

I jerk away, squeamish. "Huh? No, I didn't."

He grimaces. "Yes, you did."

I think hard about it. "Are you serious? I'm certain I didn't say anything."

"I know what I heard, Jamie. You were kissing me and whispered my brother's name. That's not okay."

I plant a hand on my chest, feeling the vibration of my racing heart. "I swear, I didn't mean to. Yes, I was thinking about Kai, but not like that?"

He looks ill. "Why were you thinking about him while kissing me?"

I groan, rubbing my hands over my face and into my hair. "I was just thinking about how good a friend he was to me today. Despite what just happened at the table. He dropped everything to hang with me. Weirdly, I think it gave me the strength to find Alfie."

Milo shifts, his frame becoming less tense. "So, you and Kai were together all day?"

"Pretty much after I saw you in school today."

"When I avoided you." He looks away, adjusting his glasses. "After that, you left with Kai."

"It wasn't because of you."

He turns to look at me. "Then what was it about? The thing you can't tell me?"

I gulp and nod.

"Will you ever tell me?"

I huff, looking down at the bed cover. "I don't want to talk about it. I was just happy to talk about it with Kai, that's all. Is that such a big deal?"

He chews his lip, eyes darting about our surroundings. "Maybe, because you're thinking about it while kissing me."

"It's nothing romantic," I blurt. "Far, far from it."

Tension tightens his body language, pulling him away from me.

"Milo, please," I say softly, grasping his hands. "Don't pull away. It's not like I'm keeping a secret. You know I'm talking with Kai about something. Isn't that enough?"

"Would you mind if I actively kept secrets from you?"

I frown, feeling knots intensify in my back. "This isn't about you. What is about you is the fact I'm crazy about you, and I want to kiss you."

His lip quirks, fighting the urge to smile while his frown dominates his expression.

I stroke his jawline. "If I tell you about what Kai and I were discussing, all kissing will stop."

His head tilts. "Why?"

"Because all I'd want to do is puke."

He smirks. "Well, I don't want that."

My fingers walk along his shoulders and meet behind his neck. I sit on my knees and look deeply into his hazel eyes. "Milo, you're the only person I want to think about. You're the only person who constantly makes me feel good about myself. Even when we weren't talking, all I wanted to do was make it better. I wanted to be better. When we're together, I want you to feel amazing. You're so important to me. Do you believe me?"

His eyes blink twice, and then are framed by smile lines. "Yeah, cutie. I believe you."

I peck his lips. Before I can pull away, his hands run along my sides and plant on my back. He pushes back on my lips, applying a passionate layer of pressure. His head tilts, angling his kiss and giving me plenty of reassurance he's still in this with me.

The words from Mom's diary push their way into my brain. I scrunch my eyes closed and lean against Milo as my lust amps up. Any proposed images of talking to Coach about him and my mom dissipate as Milo mimics my level of heat.

I completely understand why he wants to know what I'm hiding. It would drive me nuts too. But living inside my head with the truth is torture. Why can't I just have more time of sunshine and rainbows with Milo? Is that too much to ask?

If Milo knows, all he'll want to do is talk about it. He'll pep talk me into talking with Coach. Yes, I'll eventually need that. But right now, I'm not ready. Instead, I want things to be easy. Making out and random chats about homework are more than enough for me to handle.

I run a hand down the front of Milo's sweatshirt and trace over the embossed lettering. He mumbles a laugh, missing my lips, and tickling my cheek with small puffs of air. I lean in, angling my face toward his neck, and nibble under his jaw. His hands press into my back in approval, and another soft chuckle whispers out of him.

I'm so into him, I can't pull myself away, even though something pricks my ears. I don't want to figure out what it is, even though it comes closer. Soon there's a thud at our door.

"What in the..." It comes out of Kai with increasing volume. "James? Mi... What the... My God!"

Milo and I break apart, and I scramble to the top of the bed. "Kai, it's not..."

Kai puffs in horror. "Not what? You and my brother locking lips?"

Milo stands from the bed. "Can you calm down? Jamie and I..."

"Oh, no you don't," Kai blurts, holding up a hand like a stop sign at Milo. "Don't you dare say another word to me."

"Don't speak to him like that," I bark.

Kai gives me a crazed look. "What the hell is this? Why are you hooking up with my brother?"

"Because," I splutter. "Because..."

My eyes wander to Milo, who gives me the same bewilder expression.

Kai throws his hands up, flabbergasted. "Did you two just butt heads and not realize what you were doing? Seriously, I feel like I'm having another concussion."

"It's not that hard to work out," Milo says, taking a calmer approach. "We like each other. We're together."

Kai's face screws up. "Together? What does that mean?"

"Kai, we didn't want you freaking out," I say, edging off the bed and standing by Milo. "We kept it a secret so we could get to know each other without anyone getting in the way."

Realization intensifies the horrified look on Kai's face. "Are you telling me this has been going on for a while and neither one of you said anything?"

Milo and I awkwardly fidget in response.

Kai shoves Milo. "How many more times are you going to betray me?"

"Whoa!" As Milo stumbles backward, I step between the twins. "Kai, leave him alone!"

"Jamie, are you freaking kidding me? I can't believe this. After all the crap I got about Tabitha." Kai grunts, turning away and shaking his head. Just before he walks out, he turns back and points at Milo. "How could you not say anything?"

It takes me aback more than it does Milo. Is Kai really more mad at him than me?

Kai groans loudly and thunders his way downstairs. Before Milo and I can make it across the living room, we hear Kai shout, "I can't freaking believe this!"

"Kai? What is it?" Mrs. Nelson replies.

"Oh no," Milo mutters as we lock eyes.

With the creepiest chill running down my spine, I springboard for the stairs and race down them. My rampant heart rate keeps me lightning fast as I power my way toward the dining room where Kai and his mother stand.

"Those two!" Kai yells, pointing at me and Milo as his chest rises and falls in wild succession.

My hands raise in defense as Mrs. Nelson gives us a questioning stare. "What's this all about?" she asks.

Milo steps ahead of me, readying himself to defuse the situation, but Kai gets ahead of him.

"They were making out on Milo's bed!" Kai yells.

Gasps ricochet from the living room couches. Mr. Nelson and the grandparents' heads snap our way. Mrs. Nelson's mouth hangs wide open, processing the astonishing information.

Milo steps forward, holding an arm out in front of me. "Jamie and I..."

"Wait," Mrs. Nelson interrupts, pulling on Milo's arm. "Everyone, take a seat at the dining table and cool down. I don't want you two boys yelling at each other. Steve, get over here!"

"I'm not sitting," Kai argues.

After yanking Milo toward the table, their mother then wrangles Kai to the opposite seat. With a churning stomach, I forced myself to the table, taking the seat by Milo.

"Okay," Mrs. Nelson says, taking a steadying breath. She stands at the head of the table with her husband uncomfortably standing by. "Now, let's all take the hostility down a few pegs. Tell me what happened."

"What happened?" Kai screeches, lifting off the chair to throw a condemning hand our way. "I told you, Mom. They were in his bedroom, sucking each other's faces off."

Concern dimples Mr. and Mrs. Nelsons' faces. "Is this true?" Mrs. Nelson asks in a shaky tone.

"I wouldn't put it like that," I mutter, shrinking under her gaze.

Milo throws a pointed hand at Kai. "He's making it sound ugly. Jamie and I weren't doing anything wrong."

"Son," Mr. Nelson starts warily. "If you and Jamie were kissing in your bedroom, you know that's against house rules."

Milo rolls his eyes, groaning. "It's not like anything more was going to happen. We could've been sitting on a couch in the living room."

"My relationship with Tabby isn't a secret, but I didn't sneak her upstairs," Kai jabs.

"Would you stop," Milo snaps. "We weren't doing anything wrong. It's not like I held her any closer than you did when she was in your bed!"

Mrs. Nelson chokes on her gasp, clutching the back of the dining chair. She and her husband stare at me, disturbed and mortified.

My heart pounds like a heavy mallet, and my back aches from the tightening knots. I know exactly how they're looking at me.

I kick the seat back and stand, slamming my hands on the table. "I'm not a slut!"

Mrs. Nelson clutches her chest. "No one said you were, dear."

Mr. Nelson gently raises his hand. "Jamie, we…"

"Save it," I mutter and B-line out of the room.

I hear Milo call out to me, but I hurriedly race up the stairs. Humiliation seizes me, feeling the grandparents' eyes burning holes in my hunched back. Hating every millisecond of my weeping eyes filling with water, I run into the bedroom, slamming the door behind me. I dive onto the bed and hide under the covers, internally screaming. Every handwritten entry from my mother, cursing other women for calling her the s-word, spirals through my mind. Tears soak my pillow. She'd hate it if she knew people looked at me that way.

I collapse into a tight ball, clawing at the bedcover for protection. The voices in the dining room are so heated, I hear the agitated mumbles rise through the carpet. My knuckles crack and my palms cramp as I tug harder on the bed cover. It's now too tight, but I don't dare let go.

It's a long while until I hear other noises. Hurried footsteps bound up the stairs, and soon there's a knock at the door.

"Jamie?" Milo's voice asks with tenderness. "Are you okay?"

A soft squeak escapes me.

"I'm so sorry about what happened down there," he says through the door. "Kai can be an absolute jerk. I can't remember the last time I yelled like that."

My head sits against my knees. Can he just go away?

"I really hope you're okay," he says with concern.

"Milo," his mother's voice calls from the stairs. "You leave Jamie alone. Either study in Kai's room or come back downstairs."

Milo grumbles and moves away from my door.

I grunt and throw off the cover, breathing in the fresh air. I sit up in bed, my hands flexing in and out of fists.

Now Milo's banned from being near me? What makes them so afraid? Do they think I'll kiss him into the dark side? Does it not cross his parents' minds that we might truly be into each other on a deeper level? Kissing is just a bonus of what we share.

I stay in bed for the rest of the evening. It was already getting late before Milo and I started heating things up, so it didn't take long for the rest of the household to turn in. I'd decided before I hearing the usual cleaning up sounds of Mrs. Nelson nightly routine. I can't spend another night in this house. I'm not getting up in the morning to see their outraged faces. They might've branded me with such ugly words, but I don't have to stay here and take it. When even my best friend turns on me, I can't win.

I creep out of the bedroom and hear metal music seeping out from under Kai's closed door. Beside me, light spills out from underneath the bathroom door. While both boys are occupied, I sneak downstairs with nothing more than my cell phone. I tiptoe into the kitchen to fish Aunt Maddy's car keys from the bowl. Who cares about failing a driver's test? I know how to drive, and I know I need to be home.

Thirty

I was so enraged I didn't even care if I got pulled over by the cops. All I wanted to do was drive Aunt Maddy's car back to our house and hide for eternity. When I got home, I fled to my bedroom and was comforted by my familiar surroundings. My own bed cocooned me into dreamland.

Unfortunately, waking up in this house alone isn't such a comfort. My body aches, my mouth runs dry, and my head is a heavy mess of ugly thoughts. I drag myself out of bed, my eyes two slits as I trudge toward the kitchen. It feels like only a three-feet walk compared to spending so much time moving around the Nelson's home.

After chugging a tall glass of water, I look around for a heavy-duty aspirin. When I pinch the bridge of my nose to help my headache disappear, there's a knock at the door. My shoulders tense and a tremendous ache burrows between my eyebrows.

The jig is up.

I can only imagine an angry Mrs. Nelson on the other side of the door, ready to drag me to school. I edge my way toward the front door, too timid to ask who it is.

There's a second knock at the door.

"Jamie?" Milo's voice calls through the door. "Are you in there?"

"Milo?" I ask, reaching for the door handle. I open it up, double-taking at him not wearing school uniform. "What are you doing here?"

"Hi," he mumbles with a shy wave. "Can I come in?"

I beckon him inside, checking the street for his mom's SUV. "How did you get here?"

"The bus," he replies as I close the door.

I fold my arms and look down at the floor as I wander by the sofa. "How did you know I was here?"

"I knocked on your door last night, and found an empty bedroom," Milo replies. "I looked downstairs for you, and was at a loss, so I looked out the window. Anyway, I saw Maddy's car gone and put two and two together."

I gulp, hugging my middle. "Are your parents mad?"

"They didn't exactly catch on. I got up early and covered for you with Mom," he says, placing his backpack on the carpet. "I told her Laura needed the car to move some catering gear, and that we agreed to help before school."

"Oh. Thanks, I guess."

"Why did you leave? I was worried about you."

I frown, looking off to the side. "I just couldn't handle the way everyone was looking at me. I thought I was safe in that house, but everyone stared like I was scum."

"No, they didn't," he counters. "It was just a shock because we were throwing around words we'd never used before."

I dig my toes in and double-down. "I got the looks my mom got. The ones she promised to protect me from."

"I'm sorry for fighting with Kai in front of my family, and making things worse," Milo says, visibly angry at himself. "I shouldn't have said anything about you being in Kai's bed. I was trying to defend you, but it came out all wrong."

"Yeah, it didn't make me feel great about myself." I gesture at his bag. "Are you planning on going to school?"

Milo smiles nervously. He bends down and unzips the bag. He pulls out my rollerblades. "It's a peace offering. I know it's silly, but I wanted to prove I care."

My heart swells and I clasp my hands together. "Aw, Milo. I never thought you didn't care."

He puts the rollerblades down and moves closer. "Kai got the better of me and my mouth started running. The last thing I wanted to do was make you feel bad about yourself."

"I had to get out of there."

Milo shifts his weight, causing me to look his way. "Is it okay that I came over?"

I let my guard down and smile. "Of course, it is. You're the only person I want to see."

His grin lights up the room. He clasps my hand and tugs me toward him. Giggling, I lean into him, loosely draping my arms around his neck. His soft kiss sends my thoughts numb and I could easily float above the floor.

"I was jealous of you being so close with Kai," he whispers, stroking my cheek, "but I don't think you're a bad person. You and him have been close long before you and me."

"We have a different kind of closeness." My fingers play at his shirt collar. "I'd be hurling if I made out with Kai."

Milo chuckles. "I hope we have more than just kissing."

"We do. I feel safe with you."

He hesitates. "But only about certain things?"

I sigh and gesture to the sofa. We sit, and I plant my hands on his shoulders, steadying my nerves. "I'll tell you what I shared with Kai. You'll understand why I wanted to keep it a secret."

He gulps. "It's big?"

"It's explosive."

"You don't have to tell me."

"I want to," I reply. "It'll just take a minute."

He runs a hand along my knee. "Take all the time you need."

I stare into the frames of his glasses, noting the greens in his hazel eyes. The crinkles by his eyes make me want to smile. His full lips make me want to admit nothing and go back to kissing him.

I run my hands down his arms and clutch his hands. "Milo, I'm so glad you're here."

He smiles. "I'm not going anywhere."

I giggle. "You skipped school for me."

He squeezes my hand gently. "I told you. You're a bad influence on me."

I straighten up on the couch, fidgeting on the seat cushion. "Okay, I'll just blurt it out."

He braces himself, waiting for the news.

I grit my teeth, losing my nerve.

"It's okay," he whispers.

The calming lilt in his voice is all I need. "I found out my dad's name."

Milo sits back, floored. "Oh my..."

"I know."

"Is he...?"

"He's not a crook," I reply. "He's... Oh my gosh... He's... Nope, gonna hurl."

Milo sits closer, rubbing my back. "It's okay. Take a breath. You don't have to say it."

I rest my head on his shoulder and exhale slowly. "It's Coach Anders."

Milo jolts in his seat. "*What?*"

I latch my arms around him, pressing my face into his arm. "See? This is why I couldn't talk about it."

"Wait? This is for real? Coach Anders is your dad? Did he know?"

I shake my head against his limb. "I have no idea. I can't bring myself to talk to him."

"But you know him. It's not like he's a stranger."

I lift my head and deadpan him. "Milo, imagine you found out someone else was your dad. What if he was Mr. Birch."

Milo grimaces. "*Oof.* That's not fun to think about."

"Exactly. No matter if he's your favorite teacher, it doesn't make it easier."

"Okay," he says, his chest inflating. "Coach Anders is your dad. Good lord. No wonder the energy between you and Kai was so low."

"I'm just so angry at my mom," I admit. "I was freaking sobbing because she knew all along but made me scared of finding out who he was."

"I'm sure she had a reason."

I nod. "She wanted Coach to finish high school and go to college. I haven't read all of her diary, so maybe she did tell Coach before we lost her. But I doubt it."

"So, you found this out through her diary?"

I nod. "Kai and Aunt Maddy are the only ones who know about it."

"Does Maddy know about Coach being your dad?"

"Whenever I speak to her on the phone, she sounds like she's on cloud nine. I can't ruin her vacation with such a mind blow."

"At least she'll be home soon."

"Yeah. I want her with me when I talk to Coach."

"So, you will confront him?"

I nod, spreading my fingers between his and latching onto his hand. "I have to."

"Thank you for telling me all this. I know it was hard for you."

"I'm sorry I kept it a secret. It was just easier to keep it between one other person."

"I get it. Kai's your best friend, and I'd never stop you from talking with him."

"He was so pissed when he saw us together."

"He looked like he wanted to stab me when I went to his room last night," Milo says. "I took the safe option and slept on the couch instead. Then I looked for you."

"I don't want to think about Kai right now." I slide an arm behind his neck. "I'd much rather put my full attention on the hottie in my living room."

Milo bobs and weaves his head. "Where is he?"

I giggle and plant a hand on the side of his face. "You goof. Just kiss me already."

Milo laughs and drapes his arms around me. Our lips connect like two perfect puzzle pieces. I slide my hands down to rest on his chest. My palms massage at the fabric of his sweatshirt and he mumbles his approval.

Our kisses ramp up in speed, as we scoot to one end of the sofa. Milo lowers me against the armrest. One arm anchors behind my back, his other hand wanders against my ribs. In between kisses, I enjoy looking up at him. I smile at the way his glasses lower with his movements. His hands are gentle yet inflamed with passion as he holds me. I love that his smile is everlasting.

I pull him down further so he lies above me. He is so perfect; I never want to let him go. I could kick myself for never giving him a second look for all these years. I spent so many nights in my bedroom, dreaming of a wonderful boy coming into my life. Who knew he was here all along?

My arms wrap around Milo's middle as I kiss along his neck and explore his collarbone. I'm about to take my exploration further when a knock at the door interrupts us.

Our bodies jolt together, and we mirror alarmed expressions.

"Who's that?" I whisper in panic. "Could it be your mom?"

Milo winces. "I don't know. I don't think so."

"Hello, Miss West?" a voice calls out, followed by another knock. "It's Sheriff Lennon."

Milo and I break apart, and I jolt to standing.

Oh, crap. It's the cops. I've been picked up on surveillance cameras, driving without a licensed supervisor.

"Hello?" Sheriff Lennon's voice calls out again, followed by two more knocks. "Miss West?"

Milo steps beside me, clutching my hand. He motions to the door. "Want me to get it?"

I give him a weak smile. "I got it."

Milo releases my hand, and I move toward the door. When I open the door and find Sheriff Lennon standing before me, he double-takes.

"Ah, good morning," he says, and then clears his throat. "Is Madeleine West here?"

My head jerks back. "You want to see Aunt Maddy?"

Sheriff Lennon tilts his head and gives me a gentle smile. "Are you Jamie West?"

I nod. "Yes, sir."

This is it. I admitted to being the unlicensed driver behind the wheel. He was after Maddy because the car is registered in her name. Shall I just hold out my wrists and ask him to cuff me?

"Is your aunt home?" he asks in a soothing tone.

Okay, why isn't he laying down the law? What is this?

"Umm. What do you need to see her about?"

Sheriff Lennon looks behind me and there's a nervousness to his response. "Do you mind if I step inside?"

"Umm, no," I say in a shaky tone, stepping out of the doorway on trembling legs. "Come on in."

Sheriff Lennon steps inside and nods at Milo. "Good morning, son. Can I ask why you kids aren't in school?"

My stomach spasms and I eye Milo with a wash of guilt. "Umm."

"Jamie's not feeling well," Milo blurts. "I came over to check on her. I was going back to school, I swear."

"It's okay, kids," Sheriff Lennon says, gesturing to the sofa. "I'm not here about that. Is your aunt at work?"

"She's in Hawaii," I reply. "Why do you need to see her? Is it about her car?"

"No." Sheriff Lennon's eyes narrow. "Why? Did something happen to it?"

I edge toward Milo and link hands with him. "No. Just wondering?"

"Look, Miss West." He sighs. "Jamie. Can I call you Jamie?"

"Yes, sir."

"I came here because I have news for you and your aunt." He motions to the sofa. "Jamie, can I have a word with you in private?"

As if he's a life raft, I cling to Milo. "Can Milo please stay?"

Sheriff Lennon holds a poker face. "I've brought some heavy news with me. It's up to you if you want to share it."

I squeeze Milo's hand tight. "Milo's my boyfriend. I want him with me."

Sheriff Lennon nods. "That's fine. Take a seat, kids."

We do as instructed, and Sheriff Lennon takes a chair from the dining table. He places it in front of the sofa and sits. His posture is friendly and welcoming. With Milo's arm around me, I ease into the tense situation.

"Sheriff," I stammer. "What's this about?"

"There's no easy way to say this," he admits. "A prisoner in custody started feeling remorse and has admitted to further crimes." He pauses before revealing more. "Jamie, this man is in prison for violence against women. His worst offense was manslaughter."

I clutch the space over my heart and gasp. I shiver by Milo and instinctively he briskly rubs my arm.

"With the information this man detailed, we've found the unmarked graves of three missing women." Sheriff Lennon's face drops, unable to hold his steady expression. "Jamie, I'm so deeply sorry to tell you this. One of the women has been identified as your mother."

I gasp harder, shooting my hands over my face. I breathe in, sucking my fingers over my nostrils. My heart sledgehammers against my ribs, and my head is ready to cave in.

Milo's arms wrap around me, and he rests my head under his chin. "Oh, Jamie," he whispers. "I'm so sorry."

Tears form in my eyes. Part of me was prepared for this. We've said for years that Mom passed away. But this clear, concise ending still riddles me with despair.

Sheriff Lennon leans forward, touching my knee. "My deepest condolences. I'm sure this isn't the news you were hoping for. I hope, in some way, it gives you closure." He slips a card out of his pocket. "This is the number of a crisis care hotline. You can call anytime and have a confidential conversation with a trained counselor."

Milo takes the card for me, thanking Sheriff Lennon.

My mouth hangs ajar as I struggle to process everything I've heard. "She was buried?"

"We don't need to get into specifics," Sheriff Lennon says gently.

I fling my head back against the sofa. "How do I tell Aunt Maddy about this?"

"How long has your aunt been in Hawaii?" Sheriff Lennon asks. "Are you staying here alone?"

Milo cups my shoulder, keeping me close to him. "She's staying at my house. She only came here today."

"Do you want me to drive you over there?" Sheriff Lennon asked. "Do you have any parents at home?"

"My mom and my grandparents will be there."

"No," I cry out, covering my face with a hovering hand. "I don't want to leave. I want to stay here."

I collapse my head against Milo's chest, closing my eyes. Finding out this news in this house makes me feel closer to Mom. Her presence lingers, helping me process the devastating information.

"You need someone here," Milo says softly. "I can call Mom to come here."

I nod against him, hesitant to move a muscle.

"That's a good idea," Sheriff Lennon says. "I don't like the idea of you kids being alone. Not after hearing about this."

"Sheriff." I gulp before asking. "Was this man in prison named Trigger?"

The sheriff gives a knowing look. "No. I remember that name from your mother's missing person file. We investigated that individual at the time. He had nothing to do with your mother's disappearance. Plus, he's been living across the country for the past eight years."

It's a small win to know the person who took Mom away wasn't known to us.

Sheriff Lennon excuses himself to take a call, and I agree Milo should call his mom. Mrs. Nelson is organized and practical, and I need her presence around.

Milo kisses the top of my head, and I peel myself off him. He pushes off the couch and pulls his phone from his pocket. I notice the tremor in his hand as he lifts the phone to his ear.

I hug my knees and fight to keep the contents of my stomach down.

"Mom, don't get mad," Milo says warily. "I'm at Jamie's house. Just hear me out. Sheriff Lennon's here... It's Jamie's mom... They found her."

I shudder as Milo courageously relays everything to his mother.

After a weighted pause, Milo says, "Yeah. She's gone."

"Milo," I whisper weakly.

He looks at me with heightened concern.

"Can you ask her to call my aunt?"

He gives me a sympathetic smile. "Mom?" He rubs a hand behind his neck. "Can you call Maddy and let her know? Jamie can't." Milo nods along, finally saying, "Okay, thank you. See you soon."

He turns back to me with an exhausted sigh. "Mom's calling Maddy now."

I drop my face into my hands. "Oh my gosh. She's going to hate not being here. This will send her into a meltdown."

Sheriff Lennon lowers his phone, becoming alarmed. "She's unstable?"

I lift a hand to slow his reaction. "No, she was just already feeling guilty for leaving me. She'll hate the idea of me hearing this news without her."

He nods. "I don't like it either. I had to notify next of kin. It's a bad situation, however it needs to be handled."

Sheriff Lennon's phone call was about an urgent situation downtown. With knowledge of Mrs. Nelson on her way, and Milo and I insisting we were fine waiting alone, Sheriff Lennon left. Not before ensuring I remembered about the crisis care hotline he mentioned earlier.

"Oh my gosh," I mumble, pressing my hands over my face.

Milo sits back down, sweeping his arms around me. "I'm so sorry, Jamie."

I lower my hands as tears pool in my eyes. "I never did anything."

Milo tilts his head, getting a better view of my face. "What was that?"

"I didn't do anything to find her," I whimper, tears rolling down my face. "She's been gone all this time, and I never looked." I swipe my hands over my cheeks, smearing the tears dry before new ones appear. "What if we could've done something? Milo, I crawled under a house for a cat, but I never did anything to find my own mother."

"Jamie, you were a kid," Milo says rationally. "No one expected you to do anything."

"I grew up. I could've gotten off my butt and done something."

He cups my face, staring into my eyes until my breathing decelerates.

"Jamie," he says in a low, calm voice. "The sheriff said this guy hid several bodies. If the police couldn't find them, a sixteen-year-old high schooler wasn't going to."

I collapse against him, hugging him with all my might. "Oh, Milo. I'm so glad you were here. How could I have heard this news without you?"

"You'd be okay. But I'm always here to stop you from spiraling."

I giggle against his shoulder. "I'm never letting you go."

I lift my head and smile at his beautiful face.

"About that." He tucks a piece of hair behind my ear. "When the sheriff arrived, you called me your boyfriend."

I look into his eyes, forming a small smile. "Is that okay?"

He grins, a nervous laugh breezing out of him. "Yeah."

I touch the sides of his face and sigh. "No one makes me feel the way you do. My body's never erupted in so many tingles, my hearts never fluttered, I've never been more calm, or felt so protected. Milo, I love you with all my heart. I want to be your girlfriend."

Milo can't contain his contagious smile. "As in, official? Like, no more secrets?"

I nod. "No more secrets. I don't want to hide my feelings for you."

We stay wrapped in each other's arms until Mrs. Nelson bustles into the house. I get off the couch, and she embraces me with a bear hug.

"Oh, Jamie," she whimpers. "You poor thing. I'm so sorry about this horrible news."

"Thank you. I'm okay, though."

"Grandma and Grandpa want to know if they can get you anything?" Mrs. Nelson says, rubbing a circle on my back.

I give her a grateful smile. "No, I'm fine. I just want to stay here. I wish Aunt Maddy was home."

"She's on her way, sweetheart," she says, nuzzling her head against mine. "She's arranging a flight back ASAP."

I sigh in relief. "Thank goodness."

"She'll call as soon as she has a flight plan. She wanted to call you first, but I told her I was on my way. It's better she has a way to get home first."

"Yeah, I agree."

Milo fidgets beside us. "Does Kai know?"

His mother releases me and turns to him. "No. I didn't want to call him while he's in class."

"Should you call the administration to pull him out of class?" Milo asks. He gestures at me. "He'd want to be here for her."

Mrs. Nelson nods. "He definitely would." She turns to me. "Do you want me to call him?"

I swallow roughly, feeling every piece of my wounded heart. "Yes, please."

While Mrs. Nelson calls the school administration, she simultaneously makes sandwiches in the kitchen. She's truly amazing in a crisis. She gets a message to Kai to leave class and call her right away. Hearing her tell Kai what has happened is like hearing it from Sheriff Lennon all over again.

She offers to pick Kai up from school, but he tells her he's on his way to the parking lot and will be here soon. Waiting for him to arrive feels like I'm living in slow motion. Thankfully, I have Milo to lean against, so I don't turn into a sad puddle of goo on the kitchen floor.

"James!" Kai's panicked tone echoes through the house before I see him.

As I turn, Milo steps away from me. Kai jogs toward me, and in an instant, his arms are curled around me. His embrace is filled with life-recharging energy.

"I can't believe this," he says in astonishment, holding me against him. "I'm so sorry about your mom. And I'm even more sorry about being a massive jerk."

"It's okay," I whisper, patting his back.

Kai moves back slightly so he can see my face without lowering his arms. "No, it's not. I feel sick about how I treated you."

"It was a shock. I get it."

"I don't even want to talk about that right now." Kai shakes his head, shock contorting his expression. "I just want to make sure you're okay. I don't know how you handle news like this."

I hold on to his forearms as his grip on me loosens. "I've been prepared," I admit. "Aunt Maddy always said Mom was gone."

Kai's frown twitches as he holds back his emotions. My heart swells. I've never seen Kai on the verge of tears before.

"How do I stop being stupid?" he whispers. "I don't want to do another thing that jeopardizes being best friends with you."

"It's both of us, Kai," I reply. "We were both keeping secrets. We gotta stop doing that."

Kai releases me and his eyes wander across to Milo. He gives his brother a half smile and then releases a forlorn huff.

I beckon him to follow. "Come with me. I need to show you something."

Kai follows me to my bedroom. I take the TV remote and click around until the menu shows all the movies I've streamed in the past month.

"I don't get it," Kai says. "What are you showing me?"

"This is what I'm into," I say, gesturing at the screen. "I'm a desperately hopeless romantic."

Kai smirks, surprised at the random comment. "Okay? Since when?"

"Since always," I say, plonking down on the edge of the bed. "I didn't tell you because I knew you wouldn't approve."

Kai's forehead creases as he looks at the TV and then back at me. "What gave you that idea? Yeah, this stuff is super cringe, but I wouldn't tell you not to like it."

"You would've made fun of me."

Kai shrugs. "That's what we do. We all make fun of each other."

I shake my head. "We wouldn't have stayed friends."

Kai sits beside me. "You think some movies would've stopped me from hanging out with you?"

"I couldn't make friends with girls. I didn't want to do anything to ruin my friendship with the boys. So, I hid the girly stuff I liked."

"James." Kai sighs. "I said I like that you're not into girly stuff, because you told me you didn't. I believe what you tell me."

"So, you don't care if I talk about rom-coms and what kind of dates I want to go on?"

"Boy, what's wrong with us?" Kai asks, wincing as he rests his head in his hand. "Why do we keep hiding things from each other?" He huffs and looks up at me. "You're my best friend. Literally the person I trust most, and I hide the fact I'm good at school. Like, what is that? And you can't even tell me you're into ultra-girly movies. Why do we do this to each other?"

I smile and brush my hand over his. "Maybe because we want to be perfect for each other."

Kai laughs, smiling as he shakes his head.

"And maybe that's why we both found people we can be honest with," I suggest. "That's how Tabby makes you feel, isn't it?"

"Yeah. And Milo does that for you?"

"Kai, I really like him."

"It still weirds me out."

"Do you want me to stop seeing him?"

He clutches my hand. "No way. I saw how you two look at each other. It reminds me of being around Tabby. I couldn't break that up."

"Whoa. You like Tabby as much as I like Milo. You've got it bad."

"At least I've been more out in the open about it."

I laugh, nudging him. "Yeah, right. I found out about you two by witnessing your make-out session."

"It wasn't as hardcore as you and my brother."

"Our first kiss was much more timid." I snort. "Milo ran away afterwards."

Kai throws his head back in laughter. "Lame!"

I slam my hand over his mouth. "*Shush.*"

He chills out, smiling. "So, are we good?"

"Yeah, I think so. You cool with the real me?"

"I can deal. Maybe you can even talk with Tabby about this stuff."

A tired chuckle seeps out of me.

"So, these dates you want to go on," he says, hesitantly looking out the door. "They're with Milo?"

I swallow hard. "We're official."

Kai's eyes grow glassy. "Why didn't you tell me?"

"I was fighting my feelings for so long; I didn't think there'd be anything to tell." I kick my feet against the bed frame. "Then we started up, and I didn't want anything to ruin it."

Kai nudges me. "You didn't want me to ruin it."

"You kept Tabby a secret from me until you got serious about her."

He gestures at the TV. "Because the version of yourself you shared with me wouldn't have approved."

I rest my head on his shoulder. "This is why we can't have any more secrets."

He pats my knee. "Totally agree."

Thirty-One

"Oh my gosh, Jamie!" Eight hours later, when I hear Aunt Maddy's voice, it's like sweet relief.

"Aunty!" I cry out, racing to meet her by the sofa.

We hug, and she pants her breaths. "Oh, Jamie. I can't believe this. I'm so sorry I wasn't here."

"Don't be. It wouldn't have changed the outcome. We already knew Mom was gone."

She nods. "Now we have closure."

I look over her shoulder. "Where's David?"

"He'll be back in the morning," Aunty Maddy replies. "He raced to the airport with me, but there was only one seat left on the plane. Nothing was stopping me from getting back here, and he supported that."

"I'm sorry you had to cut your trip short."

"Are you kidding me?" Aunt Maddy cups my face as her eyes become glassy. "Nothing's more important than being with you right now. Gosh, I missed you. Are you okay, baby?"

I nod, smiling. "I'm okay. I'm so freaking thankful you're home."

Aunt Maddy sighs with relief, enveloping me in the warmest hug. When we part, Mrs. Nelson embraces my aunt while I wander toward Milo. An adorable smile brightens his face, and I can't help melting.

"We should get going," Mrs. Nelson says. "Leave you guys to process everything."

"Can Milo stay?" I ask, interlacing my fingers with his as I clamp down on his hand.

Aunt Maddy double-takes at us, gesturing at our linked hands. "What's this?"

"Umm, we..." Milo trails off nervously.

"Milo and I are dating," I blurt. "We've been getting close for a while, but everyone has only recently found out."

Aunt Maddy's hands make an explosion sign off her head. "What? Last I checked you were making any excuse to *not* be around Milo." Aunt Maddy gives Milo a sympathetic look. "No offense, Milo."

Milo shrugs, embarrassed.

"At least you're only seeing them holding hands." Kai smirks, folding his arms. "I caught them in full make out mode."

"All right, Malakai," his mother blurts, shoving him away. "Time for us to go home. Milo, you should probably come with us too."

Aunt Maddy shakes her head, still figuring out what's between me and Milo. "It's okay, he can stay. I'll drive him back later. Oh, thanks for bringing my car back, by the way."

"Oh, Laura did that," Mrs. Nelson replies.

Aunt Maddy looks at me questioningly, and I quickly say, "I'll explain later."

When Kai and his mother leave, Maddy enjoys asking Milo and I about our new connection. We enjoy telling her our ups and downs, for a moment leaving the sadness bubble. I even ask her about how her trip with David was to avoid these tough topics. Of course, David comes off as a pure gentleman in all her tales.

Unable to put it off any longer, I ask Milo to heat the tea kettle in the kitchen. I didn't want him to disappear too far away, but I thought I should tell Maddy this in somewhat private.

"There's something else you need to know." I exhale and drag a hand through my hair. "I found out something and didn't want to lay it on you while you were enjoying your vacation."

"Baby, you didn't need to hide anything from me," Aunt Maddy says, her eyes shining with tears. "You always come first."

"I know, but this was your time. You needed to come first."

Aunt Maddy clutches my hand. "I appreciate that. Tell me what's happened."

I steady myself. "Remember how I found Mom's diary?"

Aunt Maddy braces herself. "Did you find out who...?"

I nod slowly. "Mom lied."

Aunt Maddy's head jerks. "What was that?"

"My dad's not dangerous," I whisper harshly. "We've known him all along."

"Jamie, you're freaking me out. Who are you talking about?"

Tear pool in my eyes. The happy kind. "It's Coach."

It's still not sinking in. "Coach?"

I tap the space over my heart. "My coach."

Aunt Maddy shakes her head, unable to compute. "Brent? Are you talking about Brent Anders?"

I laugh with a mixture of nerves and joy. "Yes! Coach is my dad!"

Aunt Maddy's jaw drops. "What?" She gasps. "Brent is your dad? And Lily hid it? Why would she do that? He was the nicest guy she knew. Maybe she didn't know who your dad was at first?"

I shake my head unequivocally. "She knew. She didn't want to tie him down."

"Good lord!" She gasps again. "How could she keep such a big secret? He'll be devastated to find out she kept this from him."

I cling to Maddy. "Will you be there when I tell him?"

She sucks in her bottom lip and locks onto my eyes as she nods. "Absolutely. Are you okay about this?"

I grin as my heart swells in size. "I'm beyond happy. I already love Coach."

"Oh my gosh, baby." Maddy giggles, letting her tears stream. "He's your dad."

I wipe her tears, smiling. "I know. Crazy."

"When do you want to speak to him?" Aunt Maddy asks. "We could call him in the morning. Maybe arrange for him to stop by the cafe?"

I wince. "I don't want it to be a public scene. Plus, I don't know if I can take another night of feeling sick over this."

Maddy rubs my back tenderly. "Then what do you want to do, baby?"

"Can we call him tonight?" I ask. "We need to tell him about Mom anyway."

Maddy eyes fill with concern. "You want to do this now?"

I hold on to her forearms. "All I've needed is to have you back. I can't face him without you."

Aunty Maddy rests her head by mine. "I'm here for you. Want me to call?"

I gulp. "Absolutely."

Aunt Maddy calls Coach. I sit close to her and hear his part of the conversation. When she asks him to come over, his concern is over her cutting her trip short. She tells him she'll explain everything, it just needs to be in person.

Even though Coach wastes no time in driving over, I need Milo to hold me upright while we wait. I'm sick with dread when Coach knocks on the door. Aunt Maddy answers the door, and I quickly peck Milo on the lips for good luck. We break apart as Coach enters the house.

"Oh, Milo," Coach says with surprise. "It's late for a tutoring session, isn't it?"

"Ahh..." Milo stammers, looking at me for help.

"That's not the reason he's here," Maddy answers for us.

"You told me you had some big news," Coach says. "But it didn't exactly sound like a happy tone."

"You might want to sit for this," Aunt Maddy says, gesturing at the sofa.

Coach doesn't budge. "Maybe you should just tell me what this is about."

"There's no easy way to say this." Aunt Maddy wrings her hands together, growing pale. "They found Lily's body."

Coach collapses on the sofa, resting his hand over his mouth. "Oh, no." He sighs heavily. "I mean, I knew this day was coming, but..."

"Doesn't make it any easier," Maddy and I say at once.

Coach nods in solemn agreement.

Maddy sits down by Coach. "We were wondering if you wanted to be a part of the memorial. I know we already had one, years ago, but she'll have an actual burial plot now."

Coach smiles. "I'll do anything to help celebrate Lily's life."

"Umm, Coach," I say with a shaky voice. My hands fidget nervously, and Milo is quick to give me a comforting smile.

Coach looks at me with kind eyes. "Yeah, kid?"

"I know this is heavy stuff, but I have something else to lay on you."

He looks at Maddy and then back at me. "What is it? You can tell me anything."

I nod at Maddy. "Aunty, I got this."

Aunt Maddy gets up, giving me a pat on the shoulder for good luck. She motions at Milo and they move into the kitchen. They're still within earshot, and that's a good thing. The whole reason they're here is for moral support.

I sit by Coach and curl my hair behind my ears. "Did you have any idea my mom kept a diary?"

Coach grins. "No, I didn't."

"Well, I recently found it, and you're in it. A lot."

Nervousness ripples through his expression and posture. "Oh. You didn't read anything you didn't want to know, did you?"

"Mom didn't go into excessive details," I say, skirting their love life. "But she did drop a bomb."

Coach straightens up. "What is it?"

"Did you ever suspect you were…"

He leans in closer with a serious expression. "Suspect what?"

I blow out a breath and whisper, "You're my dad."

His hand cups his mouth, and his eyes widen. When he slowly lowers his hand, he murmurs the words, "I knew it."

My heart pounds with bated excitement. "You did?"

His hands land on my shoulders and run down my arms. "Oh, Jamie. I wish she'd told me."

"She planned to," I reply. "It was all in her diary. She knew you'd want to stick by her, but she wanted you to finish college."

"There was just something in her eyes every time she let me hold you." His gaze drifts into memories. "I always expected her to tell me. When she denied it, I believed her."

"Wait. She told you I wasn't your kid?"

He nods. "I half believed her."

I frown. "I'm so sorry she lied. You must be so angry. You said you knew her as someone who didn't lie."

"What she said was one thing. How she acted was another. I couldn't deny how much she loved you. Whenever I came home on breaks, she always encouraged me to visit you." Coach smiles. "When she kept your dad's identity a secret, I still didn't lose hope he was me."

I grin. "You wanted to be my dad?"

"I loved Lily so much," Coach admits. "I felt it in every fiber of my being that we had made something special. I looked at you and it was undeniable."

"You never said anything. Even when she was gone."

"I couldn't be sure. But with her gone, I looked out for you even more. I've always cared about you like you were my own." His posture tenses. "How are you feeling about this?"

"It's a crazy mix of emotions," I admit. "But I'm so relieved that it's you. I was so scared to find out who my dad was. I never imagined you were him. It was a total mind blow, but not in the least bit scary."

Coach smiles. "That's good to know. What happens now? Do you call me dad?"

I wince. "That feels super weird. Can we stick to Coach?"

Coach chuckles. "That feels right. I like that."

I lean forward, roping him into a loving hug. "Good. I love you, Coach."

He rubs a circle on my back, exhaling deeply. "I love you too, kiddo."

Milo edges away from the kitchen counter, subtly looking our way.

A wry smile creeps across Coach's face. "So, you and Milo?"

I jerk away. "What?"

"What's happening between you two?" Coach can barely contain his chuckle. "You two have been sticking together like glue. On the soccer field, praising each other at the cafe, and now he's here. You're constantly looking at each other with moony eyes."

I sigh. "Is it that obvious?"

Coach pats my back. "Only because you two barely shared the same space before he started tutoring you."

"Well, if you must know, we're dating now."

"Really? And it's all going well? I don't need to give him the stern parental figure lecture?"

I laugh. "Okay, now you're weirding me out."

"In all seriousness, though, I don't think you could've picked a better guy. Milo's intelligent and loyal. I'm happy for you, too."

I lean forward and hug him. "Thank you, Coach."

When Coach and I stand from the sofa, Aunt Maddy is quick to give Coach a hug. As they embrace, I move toward Milo.

Milo takes my hand and lets out a ragged breath. "How'd it go?"

I nod ecstatically. "Good. He always had his suspicions, so it wasn't a monster shock."

"I'm glad he took it well."

I giggle. "He asked me about you."

"What? Why?"

"Because he suspected something was going down between us." I click my tongue. "We spent all that time in your house, and no one noticed anything. Coach, however, saw right through us."

Milo chews his lip. "And he approves?"

I grin wholeheartedly. "He agrees with me. You're my perfect guy."

Milo pecks my lips and nuzzles his nose against mine. "Good, because I'm never letting you go."

Epilogue

Three Weeks Later...

The end of the match is nearing. The whistle blows, giving the other team's forwards opportunities to attack. Leah blocks a pass and kicks the ball toward me. Weaving up the field, I do the rainbow kick over a defender, hamming it up for Kai on the sidelines.

"Nice work, West!" Coach calls from the sidelines. "Girls, remember your formations!"

I pass the ball to Hayley, and she runs the field toward the goal circle. She beats a defender and then passes to Dominica. I grit my teeth hard when Dominica loses control of the ball. I dodge and weave the other teams' players and run at an angle toward the player in possession of the ball. With some fancy footwork, I regain the ball.

Now, without looking for help from my teammates, I enter the goal circle. I size up the keeper, swing my leg back, and shoot. The ball soars under the top bar, the referee's whistle blows, and the crowd cheers.

It takes a few moments to register. When it does, I jump in joy.

The buzzer sounds for the end of the game, and my team rallies around me. I smile up at the sky and hang my arms over Leah and Hayley's shoulders. We won, four to nil.

"Good job, Jamie," Dominica says. "Great to have you back on the team."

"Thanks," I reply. "It feels good to be back."

"It's good to see you've still got your A-game," Leah says. "All the focus on schoolwork didn't kill your skills."

"We're sorry for giving you such a hard time," Hayley says, frowning. "We just didn't want to lose our games. We didn't want to lose *you*."

"It's completely selfish. We know," Dominica adds. "But it really feels like a huge piece of the puzzle is missing when you're not on the field with us."

My heart bounces in my chest. Not that long ago I couldn't string two sentences together in front of these girls. Now, this feels genuinely amicable.

"Maybe we can hang out outside of practices and games?" I suggest. "There's a sequel to Katarina and Jeremy's movie now streaming."

Leah smirks. "You watch those movies?"

"I can't get enough," I gush.

Dominica nods. "I'm down."

As we move off the field, Coach gathers us for a celebratory pep talk. I hang in the back so no one sees how Coach looks at me. We still haven't announced our newly found connection to everyone. First, we had some tests done to confirm what Mom wrote. Thankfully, she was right.

I still haven't called him dad, but I love spending extra time with Coach. He has come over to our house for dinner a few times. The next step will be for me to spend time at his house. I just haven't been ready yet.

After the paternity test confirmed everything, we had a meeting with Principal Harvey to disclose our relationship. Even if the rest of the school is in the dark, Coach's boss needed to know in case something slipped and went into scandal territory. The principal was weirdly sympathetic to everything. He even reminded Coach of the privileges given to children of alumni and faculty.

Coach wants to pay for my tuition. Aunt Maddy and I feel weird about it. Mom kept the fact he's my dad a secret because she didn't want to seem like she wanted his family money. I don't want to hurt his feelings. Coach insists he can help because he *is* my family.

It's moot at the moment, because my scholarship is intact. Oh my gosh, am I relieved! I've never felt more pride than reading that letter to Aunt Maddy, discovering all my hard work studying is paying off.

When the team disperses after Coach's talk, he steps up to me as casually as possible. "Hey, kiddo. Good game."

I grin. "Thanks, Coach."

"Do you need a ride to the cafe?"

I shake my head and nudge my shoulder to the right. "No, I'm good. Kai's here to drive us over."

"Okay, I'll leave you to it," he replies. "Good luck with the catering job today. Is Maddy still stressed?"

I roll my eyes. "Oh my gosh, yes! I refused to let her come to the game because she's been such a basket case. David's at the cafe to keep her calm during food prep."

Coach chuckles. "At least she's got a good man by her side. Speaking of which, your boyfriend looks eager to see you. Everything's still going well with you two."

My smile grows tenfold. "Never better. Milo is amazing."

"You've really evolved as a person since spending more time with him," Coach says. "Milo too. You've really helped him come out of his shell."

I lean in and hug Coach in the most subtle way possible. "Thanks, Coach."

Coach wishes me luck for the rest of the day, and I make my way over to Milo, Kai, and Tabitha.

"Good game, James!" Kai cheers, greeting me with a fist bump.

I thank him and move on to Milo, whose hug I've been dying for.

He kisses the top of my head. "You were amazing."

"Did you keep up?" I joke.

Kai laughs. "Barely. I had to keep him focused on the game rather than his essay outline on his phone."

"I can't blame him," Tabitha butts in. "Sitting through an entire game is tough."

"You said you loved watching my games," Kai says, hugging Tabitha close.

"And now you've rewarded me by letting me miss a game." Tabitha's eyes fill with bewilderment as she turns to us. "Can you believe he's giving up a soccer game to be my date? I must be special or something."

Kai smirks and kisses Tabitha's cheek. "Special doesn't cut it."

"How in the heck did Coach Lyle agree to let you skip the game?" I ask skeptically.

Kai sighs. "He's got a brutal training regime for me this week."

"I'm so excited about the garden party," Tabitha asks, eagerly bouncing in place. "Jamie, do you get to sit with us?"

"I'll be breezing past your table with canapes," I say light-heartedly.

"Surely you'll get to join us," she replies. "Then it can be like a double date for the four of us."

The twins share perfect 'yikes' expressions.

Tabitha nudges Kai. "Come on. Don't be a party pooper. You know I want a double date."

"Milo and I are still getting used to the whole going on dates thing," I say. "Hanging out at the cafe is more our speed."

"You'll get there," Tabitha says. "I'm changing at Kai's house, too. Do you want me to do your makeup?"

I giggle at the happiness radiating off her. "You'd do that? I've never worn makeup."

Her nose crinkles. "Like, ever?"

"Yeah." I look at Milo and he gives me a coy smile. "Thanks for the offer, but I like how I look. I don't need makeup."

Tabitha shrugs. "Suit yourself. I just like to play. And now that Cammy's gone and Yvette's giving me the silent treatment, it feels weird getting ready alone."

I shake my head. "What do you mean, Cammy's gone?"

She deadpans me. "You didn't hear? She and her mom are leaving town."

"Whoa." It comes out of me in a low hum.

Milo rubs my back, and just audibly, he mutters, "Thank go"dness."

I watch the sadness on Tabitha's face. "I do feel bad for Camila. It'd be hard dealing with your family breaking up. But she was mean to me long before her parents' break up."

Tabitha nods. "I wouldn't blame you for celebrating that she's gone."

I grin and look at Kai, mouthing, "Yay."

Kai smirks, jingling his keys. "Ready to go?"

Milo slings my bag over his shoulder, and we walk hand in hand to Kai's car.

"Were you totally bored today?" I ask him.

He chews his lip, suppressing his grin. "Not totally."

"Well, get ready to be on edge," I say, swinging his hand in mine. "My aunt will give us fifty tasks as soon as we walk into the cafe."

"I'm sure it won't be that bad," Milo says with hope.

"Don't bet on it. I was just telling Coach how panicked she's been over this event."

"Speaking of him, he looks like he's about to burst when he watches you play. I can tell he can't wait until everyone knows you're his kid."

"I wish people already knew," I admit. "It'll be so awkward. Oh, hi, everyone. By the way, Coach was my mom's boyfriend, and turns out he's my dad. Any questions? Uh, yeah, like a million."

Milo laughs, pulling me in for a side hug as we approach the parking lot. "At least your friends, the guys at the cafe, and my family know. It'll help soften the blow and diffuse the situation. Showing everyone it's not a big deal."

"Once everyone knows, it'll blow over. I just don't want to rip off the band-aid and have everyone know my secret."

"It was okay when we stopped being a secret, right?"

My heart flutters. "More than okay. It's like a dream."

Milo's eyes sparkle behind his glasses. "So, this will all work out, too."

I nod, awestruck by this beautiful boy.

"Do you think you'd change your last name?" Milo asks. "You know, once everyone knows Coach Anders is your dad?"

I chew on my fingernail and smirk. "No way. Then I'd lose my moment of everyone cheering from the sidelines, 'West is the best,' when I'm a professional soccer player."

"Is that your big career goal?"

I cup a hand around my hip, smiling with stars in my eyes. "Yes. It's the only thing that gives me a thrill. The cafe will be my retirement plan after I win the world cup."

"Ah, makes total sense," Milo replies with a hint of laughter.

"Besides, my mom and aunt have their mom's last name."

"Lovebirds!" Kai calls from the car. "You coming or what?"

"Coming!" I call, tugging on Milo's hand.

I run up to the car and Kai chucks me his keys. "You want to drive?" he asks.

"Absolutely!" I cheer. After successfully driving home and coming clean to Aunt Maddy about it, I realized something. I could try for my license again. If I can comprehend King Lear, algebra, and memorize the ten amendments, anything is a piece of cake.

I drive us to the boys' house. It's easier for me to shower and change here than my house because I need to get to the cafe ASAP. Tabitha and I share the guest bedroom, and I'm dressed and brush my hair, while she's still in a towel, blow drying her hair.

I'll never understand why other girls need to do all that primping. I've learned the easy way that boys don't really care about all that stuff.

Milo also changed into all black clothing, ready to help out at the cafe. Mr. Nelson drives us over, and I feel the chaotic energy as soon as I enter. Kylie and Laura are in charge of tables, while Aunt Maddy and Jake get the trays of food prepared. We are to load them into the van and take them over to the garden party.

Before entering the kitchen, I see Parker and Lewis at a table and give them a happy wave. When I get to the kitchen, I almost collapse. Mr. Stuffy is wearing an apron and haphazardly dusted with flour.

"Oh my gosh, David," I say with a giggle. "You're helping?"

"I'm trying," he jokes.

Aunt Maddy hugs him from behind. "Honey, you're doing a fantastic job. I'd be lost without you."

With a goofy grin, David picks up a tray and moves to the rear kitchen doors.

"Aunt Maddy, you look in better shape than this morning," I say, linking an arm with me.

She blushes. "David talked me down. He reminded me I run a business every day, and that this should be no different just because the clientele has a larger net worth."

"He looks so different out of a suit," I say, smiling as David walks back into the kitchen.

"He's really lightened up," Maddy agrees.

"So, I should retire the nickname?" I tease.

Aunt Maddy's eyes widen. "Immediately."

I giggle and nod.

Milo asks Maddy how he can help, and she teams him up with Jake. My heart balloons, seeing him help in the kitchen. Mom did a good job of scaring us out of romanticizing bad boys. She wanted us to both find gentlemen, and oh my gosh, did we ever.

I didn't give David credit when he started helping out at the cafe, even though Milo pointed it out. Now I see it's undeniable how much he loves and cares for Maddy. I'm coming around on his personality and I'm trying to stop my eyes from rolling when he's near. My aunt is completely swooning over him, and that's all that really matters.

With Aunt Maddy rallying the boys in the kitchen, I move to the counter to check on Laura and Kylie.

"Everything okay?" I ask, sidling up to Kylie.

She jolts, a guilty look crossing her face. "Huh?"

"What's wrong?"

She looks back at the tables. "Nothing."

I spy where she's looking, and it's at the section that includes Parker and Lewis.

"Are they giving you a problem?" I ask. "Did they say something?"

Kylie cups a hand over her face, shying away. "What? No. Why would they? I mean, what would he even say to me?"

"He? Which he?" I look at the boys and then back to bashful Kylie. "Oh my gosh! You like one of them. Which one?"

Kylie squeals in embarrassment. She hides her face, leaving the counter. "What? Nothing. I gotta clear the tables."

My mouth hangs ajar, and I shake my head with a giggle. She's crushing so hard on one of my friends. This will be fun to watch.

After helping clear tables and taking payments, we're ready to leave for the event. When we arrive, we unload the food into our serving station. Trestles of flowers frame the round tables, which are covered with pale pink cloths, and surrounded by white, cushioned chairs.

Mrs. Fisher stands with the best posture I've ever seen, liaising with Aunt Maddy. I link arms with Milo as we ogle the crowd. I spy Christie and Ash and can't help remembering when Christie propositioned Milo to be her friend's date.

"Do you regret not agreeing to be out there and mingling?" I ask.

Milo scoffs. "And give up the chance to be a kitchen hand? Never."

I giggle, leaning into him. "You goof."

"Oh lord. Look at Kai," Milo says, pointing out his brother, who escorts his gorgeous girlfriend. "Who knew he could play a doting boyfriend so well?"

"Oh my gosh," I murmur. "He totally looks like rom-com material."

Milo smirks. "I've now watched enough of them to know exactly what you mean."

I elbow him playfully. "Admit it. You love them."

He kisses my cheek. "Sure, sure."

Before the teasing can continue, Aunt Maddy breaks us up to start serving. Jake pulls the tray of mini milkshakes out of the van. I pick up a serving tray and fill it with as many as I can carry. As Aunt Maddy and I begin with serving drinks, Milo and David ready the food trays to follow.

It doesn't take long for the serving to run its course. Once we've made our rounds with the food, it's time to hang back and wait until it's time to clear. Aunt Maddy stays wandering around tables, soaking up the compliments on the food and handing out business cards where appropriate.

I can't help watching people from school. Christie and Ash are so loved up, they've barely noticed my existence. Kai and Tabitha continue to be cute, but take any chance they get to wave at me and ask me to join their table. Instead, I introduce them to Christie and Ash. It simultaneously makes both of their days.

Then there's Yvette. She sits at the table with the new Mrs. Garcia and their families. Yvette looks beyond bored. My mind flicks back to all the times she encouraged Camila to harass me or anyone else in their line of sight. She fed off a tarnished memory of my mother. I want the news about my dad to come out, but I want some control over it. I'm not ashamed or scared of everyone knowing. If someone like Yvette knows, surely it'll run like wildfire.

With a gulp, I make my approach. I stand before her, and she looks at me up and down in my server uniform.

"Umm, hi," I say with a mediocre wave.

Her brows lift. "Hi?"

"I thought you might want to know, Coach Anders is my dad."

Yvette spit takes. She hunches over, coughing and spluttering, trying to catch her breath. "What?" She finally gasps.

I nod happily. "Yep, it's true. Would you like to spread it around?"

She blinks wildly. "You want me to tell people?"

"Yeah. I know Camila's gone, but you are the next best person."

Yvette frowns. "You think I'm mean like her?"

I shrug. "You agreed with everything she said."

Her eyes water. "Yeah, that's true."

My eyes narrow. "I'm sorry. Are you upset? I thought you'd already be at the next table, gossiping about me."

Yvette stands. "Look, I'll definitely let this slip. It is totally juicy. But I don't want to do it to be mean. With Cammy gone, I feel so alone. I'm scared that I'm now a target."

"You're not alone. You have Tabitha."

"We had a fight when she didn't want to go along with Cammy anymore."

I snap my fingers at her. "Cammy's gone. Go make up with your friend."

"Do you think she'll want to?"

"One-hundred percent." I point out where Tabitha sits with Kai. "She's over there. Tell her I asked you to spread the news about Coach Anders being my dad. I want her to help you tell everyone."

She eyes me dubiously. "Why would you want that?"

"Because I want people to know, and I don't want to tell every single person."

Yvette shakes her head, grinning. "I knew you were a weirdo."

I laugh. "Yeah, maybe I am. I'm so happy to know he's my dad. I'm not ashamed of what he and my mom did, but I have no energy to tell everyone about my family connection."

"I can't control how much this spins out of control."

"In the grand scheme of things, it's not that interesting," I reply. "That picture of my mom was old news pretty quickly. I'm just looking forward to that part."

Yvette nods, excusing herself and moving over to Tabitha's table. Maybe gossiping will help them mend fences. What do I know? I'm new to talking to other girls.

"Hey, are you okay?" Milo asks, rushing over to me. "I saw you talking with Yvette."

I grin nervously. "I told her Coach is my dad."

Milo's eyes widen. "What? Why? That's crazy."

"I know she's a gossip," I reply, taking his hand. "I want people at school to find out. Plus, Coach wants people to know. By Monday morning, everyone at school will know."

"Oh my gosh." He sighs and pulls me in for a hug. "Well, you know I'll be with you through this."

I kiss his lips, soft and sweet. "I wouldn't want anyone else."

"Looks like it's time to clean up soon," Milo says, looking at discarded plates scattered around the tables. "What do you want to do after this? Movie night?"

"Absolutely," I cheer. "And I know this is completely nerdy, but can you help me with my essay at the same time?"

Milo laughs. "Yeah, of course. You're the cutest nerd of all time."

"Well, I gotta get my nerd on for our next game of Draikin Crusades."

"You know, John is still gunning for you."

"They need to learn there's no game I can't master."

Milo leans in with a kiss. "As long as I'm always your teammate."

I kiss him back. "I don't win if I don't have you."

Thank You

Thank you for reading. Scan the QR code and get a FREE prologue from Milo's perspective, showing his long-standing crush on Jamie. Plus, stay subscribed to the newsletter and get an extended epilogue, plus over 20 bonus scenes from other books in the series.

About The Author

Milly Rose is an animal-loving romance enthusiast with a swoon-inducing book formula. Shy girl + hot guy + first kisses. Her YA sweet romance books will have you falling in love every instalment. Milly Rose is the quintessential shy girl, who you can contact via her mailing list and reply to her monthly email blasts! Milly spends her days vying for her cat's affection, dreaming up her next book boyfriend, and writing a fun meet-cute under candlelight with a lovely brewed cup of tea.

Join Milly Rose's Mailing List
millyrosebooks.com
Follow on Instagram @shy.author.milly.rose
Follow on Tiktok @shy.author.milly.rose

Also By

ALL BOOKS SET IN ASHWORTH ACADEMY

Shy Girls Can't Date Billionaires (Christie & Ash)
Shy Girls Can't Date Bullies (Ava & Beau)
Shy Girls Can't Date Frenemies (Jamie & Milo)
Shy Girls Can't Date Bad Boys (Vanessa & Dax)
Shy Girls Can't Fake Date (Kylie & Parker)
Shy Girls Can't Date Celebrities (Josie & Wyatt)
We Shouldn't Be Together (Tabitha & Kai)

www.ingramcontent.com/pod-product-compliance
Lightning Source LLC
Chambersburg PA
CBHW050614170726
48283CB00001B/247